By Christopher Dow

Fiction
Effigy
    Book I: Stroud
    Book II: Oakdale
The Books of Bob
    Devil of a Time
    Jumping Jehovah
The Clay Guthrie Mysteries
    The Dead Detective
    Landscape with Beast
    The Texas Troll Unlimited
    Darkness Insatiable
Roadkill
The Werewolf and Tide, and other Compulsions

Nonfiction
Lord of the Loincloth (nonfiction novel)
Book of Curiosities: Adventures in the Paranormal
Occasional Pilgrimage: Essays on Film, Literature, and Other Matters
Living the Story: The Meandering, True, and Sometimes Strange
    Adventures of an Unknown Writer
    Vol.I: Growing Up Takes a Long Time
    Vol. II: Growing Old Takes Longer

Martial Arts
The Wellspring: An Inquiry into the Nature of Chi
Circling the Square: Observations on the Dynamics of Tai Chi Chuan
Elements of Power: Essays on the Art and Practice of Tai Chi Chuan
Alchemy of Breath: An Introduction to Chi Kung
Leaves on the Wind: A Survey of Martial Arts Literature (Vol. I–VI)

Poetry
City of Dreams
The Trip Out
Texas White Line Fever
Networks
A Dilapidation of Machinery
Puzzle Pieces: Selected Poems

Editor
The Abby Stone: The Poetry of Bartholo Dias
The Best of Phosphene
The Best of Dialog

Devil of a Time

Devil of a Time

Christopher Dow

Phosphene Publishing Company
Temple, Texas

Devil of a Time
© 2009 by Christopher Dow
ISBN: 0-9796968-2-8
ISBN 13: 978-9796968-2-4

Published by:
Phosphene Publishing Company Temple, Texas, USA
phosphenepublishing.com

2.1

For Dad

Thanks to DeliriumRealm.com, whose excellent ency-
clopedia of demons allowed me to name and describe
many of the characters in this book.

Therefore, since the world has still
Much good, but much less good than ill,
And while the sun and moon endure
Luck's a chance, but trouble's sure,
I'd face it as a wise man would,
And train for ill and not for good.

Alfred Edward Houseman
From *Terence, This Is Stupid Stuff*

Devil of a Time

❧ 1 ☙

BOB'S DEAL HAD GONE WRONG. Terribly wrong. Everything he'd worked for was going down the toilet.

He didn't care that half the stock option plans of the entire company he worked for would have collapsed had his plan succeeded. ENDRUN Corporation was a house of cards, anyway, and its sole purpose was to bilk investors so the corporate officers could line their pockets just as Bob was about to line his. The results for Bob's fellow employees would have been the same, and that was their problem, not his. He'd be sitting on some sunny beach somewhere with a piña colada in one hand and an exotic young woman in the other.

Nor was Bob bothered by the effects his lack of moral scruples might have had on his soul. Throughout his life, he hadn't failed to notice that the most zealous religious people were the ones who did the most wrong to their fellow human beings. Look at the Crusades and Jihad and Aztec priests ripping living hearts from the chests of their brothers and sisters. And the smaller stuff was just as bad—from Southern Baptist bigotry, Catholic pederasty, and Islamic misogyny to Jim Jones poisoning his own followers and AUM's moronic gassing of commuters in Tokyo subway stations. There was no end, Bob thought, to the evil people commit against one another in the name of holy righteousness. What did it matter what he did? It wouldn't even begin to approach the examples laid down by the world's paragons of piety.

But none of that solved the dilemma he now found himself in. And it had started off so beautifully. Bob had joined EN-DRUN because it seemed that the wages of sin in the corporate world were pretty good. ENDRUN billed itself an energy exploration company, but it obviously was an exploitation company that profited by being a middleman without the encumbrances of fiscal or social responsibility. Nothing really productive went on there, making it the perfect place for Bob.

He'd been at ENDRUN, toiling as a mid-level legal flack for about three years, when he was assigned to oversee the reorganization of a bankrupt fiber optic cable operation recently acquired by ENDRUN. His job was to convince corporate partners to invest in a broadband cable that would be laid across the Atlantic Ocean. It was a hell of a deal.

And sheer baloney. After some research, Bob understood that the project, while technically feasible, was beyond EN-DRUN's ability to realize. But he also realized that he still could raise tremendous amounts of capital and sell lots of shares before anyone else found out that the project was destined to go nowhere except to the bottom of the Atlantic. By then, he'd have skimmed off enough of the investors' money and sold his own worthless stocks to retire in luxury.

But what Bob hadn't taken into account was that if it was a hell of a deal, then vultures other than himself probably were involved. In fact, ENDRUN's CEO, CFO, and other officers, who were doing their damnedest to grab as much loot as they could from as many people as possible, had been keeping tabs on Bob's deal and weren't about to let a measly underling like Bob get away with one red cent. Just before Bob signed the papers on the final deal that would have stuffed his Swiss bank account with stolen funds, someone found out about Co-Ed Head.

Bob had financed his legal education by running a porno website named Co-Ed Head, featuring college girls he met and finagled into giving him and his friends blowjobs under the scrutiny of a video camera. The business not only was fun but had its practical aspects, too—persuading the young women to submit to him and his camera was good experience in constructing convincing arguments, which he knew would come in handy later in his legal career. He didn't figure anyone would ever find out about the website because he kept all the porno files for Co-Ed Head on his grandmother's computer. He'd so very kindly set up the old dame with an Internet connection, but she only used it for basic email and a bit of surfing, mostly to AARP's homepage, and she had no inkling just how hardcore her hard drive was.

At Bob's corporate hearing, all of the board of directors looked down scornfully on the accused—not because of the porno site, which several of them recalled fondly, but because he'd let himself get caught trying to get away with *their* money. For added measure, ENDRUN's VP of IT had his staff downloaded a cache of images from a child porno site into Bob's home computer and anonymously tipped off the federal authorities, who promptly charged Bob with violation of a large number of statutes.

And so, at age forty-six, Bob found himself facing not simply an uncertain future but the fact that the house of cards that had came fluttering down was not ENDRUN's but his own. It was the ultimate in public humiliation—the whole world was about to learn that he was a thief, a scalawag, a pornographer, and a pedophile. Even if the last was untrue, would anybody believe it?

"God damn it!" Bob, completely enraged, bellowed at the uncaring walls of his expensive high-rise apartment, from which he was being evicted the following week. "I'll get whoever is responsible for this if it's the last thing I do! Curse 'em! Curse 'em 'til the day they die!"

As soon as he'd uttered the last word, he felt a great painful pressure clamp down inside his chest. Bob knew he had a bad heart, he just didn't know it was *that* kind of bad heart. It wasn't surprising, really. Bob ate poorly, smoked, drank too much, and never exercised. His corporate machinations had left him neither the time nor the inclination.

At that very instant, a huge earthquake—eight point nine on the Richter Scale—rocked the Challenger Deep in the depths of the Mariana Trench in the Pacific Ocean. Despite its strength, the quake did surprisingly little damage to any Pacific island, and it didn't even generate much of a tsunami, to the curiosity of geologists and oceanographers everywhere.

Bob didn't know about the earthquake, nor would he have cared. He had other things to worry about. All his life, he had prided himself on keeping his eyes wide open, but now he found everything going dark.

♋ 2 ♋

"THE BOARD MEMBERS ARE HERE, sir."

The Devil looked up from his PDA, into which he was entering notes, using the talon on his forefinger in lieu of a stylus.

"Tell them to come on in."

"Yes, sir."

Behemoth left the door open, and the six Archons entered and went to their places at the huge obsidian table that dominated the board room. Not all of the places had chairs. Belphegor was cone-shaped, with a wide, fleshy mouth arced across it just above the mid-point, and it didn't need one. Leviathan settled her big, whale-like body into a large tub filled with brine, which promptly began to boil. Beelzebub, today in his guise as a man covered with shaggy black fur, sported two horns on his head, bat-like wings, duck feet, and a lion's tail. Flies flitted in and out of his large nostrils. He had a special chair with a hole in the seat for the tail. Asmodeus—mostly human except for the serpent's tail and webbed feet—sat in a chair with an especially broad upper back to accommodate his three heads: bull, ram, and human male. Both Mammon and Lucifer were human-shaped but couldn't have been more different in appearance. Lucifer looked like a beautiful but petulant boy with gray skin, except for his arms, which were blue. He was dressed, as usual, in red culottes decorated with ribbons. Mammon, on the other hand, looked like a beefy, hawk-nosed, middle-aged man, graying at the temples. His expensive three-piece suit would have been at home on a chief executive of some mega corporation back on Earth, and Mammon often played that part with no other disguise.

But of course, this was Hell, and Mammon wasn't CEO here. The Devil called the meeting to order.

"All right," he said. "This better be bad."

It was—for humans on Earth.

"I'm happy to report, sir," said Beelzebub, "that Operation Feed 'Em and Bleed 'Em is proceeding ahead of schedule." The rest of the Archons always let Beelzebub go first. It wasn't so much a matter of propriety, although Beelzebub was foremost in power and crime right after the Devil himself. It was more a matter of practical concern. If they didn't let him go first, he'd get upset and, in retaliation, would constantly interrupt with procedural questions that could bog down the meeting for hours. Gluttony, after all, comes from glut, and that can work both ways.

"We now have complete cooperation from all of the major fast-food chains," Beelzebub went on. "They will increase the sugar and fat content of all their food as agreed, and our chemists have come up with a new addictive additive to replace the one currently in use. Mammon can give you more information on the business end, but we're expanding our operations into every corner of Earth. We project that we'll have at least 70 percent of the world's population eating at our trough within a decade. And, as an interesting sidelight, we've had a dramatic expansion of all-you-can-eat buffets throughout most of the United States. It's an irresistible lure that's produced a 30 percent growth in gluttony—not to mention waistlines—since we started pushing the program."

Lucifer went next, relating that vanity and pride had become major influences not simply in America and Europe, but throughout much of the rest of the world. Everything from consumer purchasing choices to nationalism and religious fervor were involved, with everyone vying to seem to be better off than their neighbors and trying to tear their neighbors down if they couldn't top them.

"Keep an eye on the war of pride we've got going between the Christian and the Islamic fundamentalists," Lucifer finished. "It's sure to wreak worldwide havoc soon."

"It had better," the Devil commented dryly. "You've been working on it for two millennia."

"This sort of thing takes time, Boss. Remember, they started as neighboring tribes that both worshipped your brother, and it took hundreds of years of hard work to separate them and get them squabbling over the name they give their deity. Once they did that, they were doomed since neither had it right. That might have been the end of it, but we managed to keep the dispute in high gear, and now we've magnified their petty regional dispute into a worldwide crisis that endangers the entire planet."

"I thought you fast-tracked the Christians," the Devil said.

"Oh, we gave them help, all right. If they're to be encouraged to self-fulfill their prophecy of Armageddon, they had to be given the chance to develop the kinds of weapons of war that can do the trick. We've come a long way in the last millennium considering we started out only with swords and spears and the like. We're ready, now, at least logistically. We just have to convince enough of humanity that war is in their best interests. As it stands, though, only a few fanatics seem willing to slaughter enough people to qualify as a real apocalypse—the rest of them remain unconvinced or are too apathetic to get aroused for very long about anything. Belphegor, maybe you should let up on the sloth a little. We're not after Armageddon lite, and I'd like to wind up this business in another decade or two."

"I suppose I could give it a rest," Belphegor said. "I'll start tomorrow. Right now, as you can see, I'm busy sitting on my fat ass."

Everybody laughed except Leviathan, who was jealous of Belphegor's comedic ability, but being the demon of envy, she was jealous of just about everybody and everything.

"Seriously, though," Belphegor continued, "I've been working closely with Beelzebub on Operation Feed 'Em and Bleed 'Em. It's not enough to stuff them with food if they just turn around and exercise it all away. We have major investments in television production, pro sports, and furniture companies that manufacture sofas and easy chairs, and our best investments yet have been the Internet and video games. All are doing boom business. Or should I call it *doom* business?"

Everybody chuckled again.

"Our disinformation campaign against outdoors activities is doing well among the youth," Belphegor went on, "but we're not up to capacity, yet. It seems that a percentage of the human population persists in going out and living a healthy lifestyle. I don't think any amount of persuasion will change that."

"Brand them as liberals, progressives, communists, apostates, and sexual deviants," the Devil suggested. "Put out the word that they're riddled with social diseases."

"Thanks, Boss. We'll get right on it. I've been working with Leviathan on another possible solution, but I'll let her tell you about it."

The Devil turned his attention her way.

"It is a rather ingenious plan, if I do say so myself," Leviathan said, preening, as she wallowed in her tub. "As we all know, nobody is more prone to envy than Christian fundamentalists. When they actually do foment Armageddon, it won't be hard to make them perceive all the health nuts as threats and take them out even before they go after the Islamic nations. In fact, we've already laid the groundwork, and envy, in general, is on the upswing. We've had surprisingly good results with all those television programs that tour the homes of the wealthy and famous or where people do expensive remodels that cost more than most people's homes. Automobile commercials based on jealousy also are instilling a lot of resentment, especially since almost no one can afford even the cheaper models."

"Unfortunately, lust isn't going so well," Asmodeus said, using his human head to speak. The problem, he went on, wasn't so much religious dictates prohibiting sex—or at least, relegating sex to narrowly specific situations. Even mass spam attacks by XXX-rated porno websites wasn't having the desired effect. Most people were too busy or tired or worried or unhealthy or unhappy to do more than get a little titillated. And it seemed that even sex scenes in movies were down to discreetly glimpsed nipples. Worse, too many movies were being released based on love stories or reconciliation dramas.

"What can you do," Asmodeus complained, "when a movie about a male hooker turns into a feel-good comedy that plays up love, compassion, and tolerance?"

"I guess it can't be helped," the Devil said. "Unfortunately, my brother is going to win some of the time. It's a statistical certainty. We'll probably have to buy our own movie studio to make sure we get the kinds of product we want."

"That'll cost us," Asmodeus pointed out.

"You have to spend money to make money," the Devil shrugged. "And speaking of money." He turned to Mammon, who always gave his report on greed last.

"We've been having astounding success in using corporations to perpetrate evil," Mammon said. "Not only do they squander valuable resources, but they pollute the world with toxic chemicals, non-biodegradable packaging, and useless consumer goods that clutter people's lives, distract them from more important matters, and then go into landfills to further pollute, waste space, and lock away resources. The corporations also do a great job of brainwashing the consumers into engaging in and accepting corruption as the price of doing business, and they subvert their stockholders into happily accepting profits at the expense of the environment and general human welfare. Not to mention that it's really gratifying to see the high level of complicity we get from the employees. You remember that especially sweet fiber optic deal recently set up by a minor corporate climber in Houston?"

"The one I ordered you to co-opt?" the Devil asked.

"The very one," Mammon said. "We took it over just a couple of days ago, and it promises to help ENDRUN go into a downward spiral that will financially ruin nearly every employee and stockholder and damage the national economy."

"Excellent," the Devil said. "And the money?"

"The CEO and other officers have most of it in overseas accounts, but I, of course, have their PIN numbers. We'll leave them enough to mount inadequate defenses, but most of the funds will be transferred to our accounts."

"You bastard," the Devil praised.

"Thank you, Boss." Mammon didn't smile, but then he never did. When Lucifer once asked him why, Mammon replied, "We're in the business of taking in, not giving out."

"What happened to the corporate climber?"

The Devil didn't really care about the fellow's feelings, but anyone who set up that kind of deal might be worth using to organize future scams.

"Get this," Mammon answered. "He got so pissed that he croaked from a heart attack."

They all had a good laugh at Bob's expense.

"I assume he's here."

"Right, Boss. I think he's going through processing as we speak."

"Thank you for your reports," the Devil said, and he paused for a few moments to enter some information into his PDA. There wasn't an Archon among them who wouldn't have given an arm or a leg—except Belphegor and Leviathan, of course, who had neither—to get a look at what was on that PDA. Each of them had a guess or two about the contents of that little device, and they even speculated among themselves. Whatever it was, it had to be something momentous—maybe even a plan for the Big Crunch or a universal wipeout by dark energy. But none of them had ever had the slightest glimpse since the Devil never let it out of his sight.

"As for myself," the Devil said when he finished entering his notes, "I'm happy to tell you that everyone is angry at something or someone or something. Tempers are flaring everywhere, and it shouldn't be long before full-fledged wrath breaks out." His eyes lit enough to give off a definite glow, and the Archons all winced and flinched, dreading that the Devil would find this an apt moment to demonstrate his wrathful power. He'd done it a few times in the past, and it hadn't been pleasant for anyone. But the Devil just chuckled, and his eyes dimmed to their usual piercing gaze.

"All right," he said. "Go forth and do evil."

The Archons left to do just that.

❧ 3 ☙

BOB'S VISION RETURNED, AND HE found himself on the way to Hell. There was no intermediary meeting with St. Peter and subsequent rejection, with the angel at Heaven's gate driving him off by brandishing a flaming sword—or at least a few harsh words of rebuff. Bob wasn't especially surprised since he didn't expect that to happen, though he really didn't know what to expect. When he died, there was a swirling feeling of dislocation, and suddenly, he found himself floating in a vertically oriented tunnel. He was naked.

The tunnel was a freakish place, its wall composed of writhing human forms, all apparently interacting and completely oblivious to the void inside the tunnel. At the top end of the tunnel was a blinding but cool and fragrant glow that seemed to promise every sort of relief from every sort of sorrow. The lower end of the tunnel was a black pit that reeked of the a familiar stench and gave off waves of radiant heat.

Bob barely had time to wonder at a light that was cool and a blackness that was hot before he was sucked downward, ass first, away from the light. It was all so abrupt that he barely had a chance to gasp, much less scream. It was like falling down an incredibly deep well. The writhing human forms making up the inside wall of the well blurred as Bob's speed increased, finally becoming just a gray smear. All the while, the glowing circle above diminished in circumference until it was a mere point, like a single star in a black sky. At the same time, the heat and stench grew.

After a couple of minutes, Bob realized what it was about the stench that seemed familiar. During his college days, Bob had the unfortunate experience of living near a large slaughterhouse, which he had to walk by on his way to the university. Apparently, most of the slaughter went on at night—he guessed that was because they probably loaded the processed meat into trucks in the morning for delivery to grocery stores during the day. Or maybe the smell was just worse in the early morning because the heavy night atmosphere laid the stench over the landscape like a damp blanket of death.

Whatever the reason, the odor was overpoweringly oppressive and the worst that Bob ever smelled before or after, including the chokingly bitter redolence of petrochemical processing. He could imagine the accumulated blood, urine, feces, and digestive-tract secretions running in rivulets across the cement floors of the slaughterhouse, merging into streams that ran.... Where? They had to collect it somehow. Were there huge vats or tanks of the filthy stuff? And what did they do with it afterwards? Jeez, he'd thought at the time. They probably cooked it down and made sausage or dog food or something out of it.

Bob never ate sausage after that—or owned a dog, for that matter—but now he wasn't so sure he'd deprived himself of sausage and a pet for no reason. Apparently the slaughterhouse—and all of the other slaughterhouses everywhere on Earth—poured all their waste down this hole.

"I'll probably get used to it," he thought, remembering that every time he returned to Houston from a vacation in the country, the city smelled bad, but after a few hours, he no longer noticed.

He'd just finished thinking this, when he landed on his ass in Hell. He didn't stay in that position for long since the surface beneath was really hot and nearly fried his naked buttocks. Springing to his feet, he looked around, hopping from foot to foot, trying to keep his soles from getting burned.

He was in a dimly lit circular room that was the dead-bottom end of the well down which he'd fallen. The gray wall now resembled smooth iron and was featureless except for a single open doorway. Thankfully, there was no pool of slaughterhouse sludge, though the odor remained oppressively heavy, but beside the door lay a large, nasty-looking pile of rubbish. At least Bob thought it was a pile of rubbish until it raised its head.

It's heads.

Three of them. They were attached to the shoulders of a huge dog, but despite its tremendous size, it was the mangiest, scrawniest-looking mutt Bob had ever seen in his life. If its flesh had been any more threadbare, its bones would have poked through. In fact, several were.

"What the fuck you staring at?" asked the mouth in the head on Bob's right. One of the canines was broken off at the root, and Bob didn't need to see to know that black rot had spread across the few other teeth that remained in place—the breath that carried the words held that news as well.

"You can't be Cerberus...."

"You know of another three-headed dog guarding the gates of Hades?" asked the left head.

"No," Bob admitted. "But you're not quite what I expected. What happened to you?"

The creature rose to its feet, and Bob could see that, while its forequarters and heads were doglike, the hindquarters and thick, lengthy tail were quite reptilian. He also noted nervously that it was not chained or restrained in any way.

"What do you mean what happened?" the left head asked belligerently. "This is Hell. You think the employees get perks the inmates don't?"

The other two heads gave barking laughs in unison.

"We were young once," said the center head. "Young and powerful. We ate raw flesh and howled with voices of brass. It took Hercules to bring us to our knees."

"Yeah," said the right head, "but at least that was an honest fight. Not like that damn Orpheus or that bitch the Sibyl."

"What happened?" asked Bob. "They double-team you?"

"Naw," the right head replied. "They didn't even know each other. Orpheus came down first. He was after his wife. What was her name...?"

"Eurydice," the center head reminded the right head.

"Yeah. Anyway, people later said he had an enchanted lyre, but the truth is, his playing was so damn boring it put everyone right to sleep."

"Including us," the left head supplied.

"Then the Sibyl brought Aeneas down to talk to his father, and she tossed us a honey cake drugged with sleep," the center head said.

"You were the one who ate the damn thing," said the left head.

"Don't listen to him," said the center head. "He wants to blame me for everything. Besides, it was a tasty morsel."

"And it's the last thing we've eaten since," said the left head. "The Boss might have allowed us to let one un-damned human slip by but not two. Especially after Hercules whipped us. He used to feed us lots of raw flesh. We could eat a whole bull in half an hour."

"I could eat a whole bull right now," said the right head, gray drool from its mouth dripping onto the floor, where the drops sizzled and steamed. It stared meaningfully at Bob.

"Now look at us," said the center head. "There's practically nothing left."

Indeed, the heads were right. Cerberus was a wasted mess. Bob wondered if he might be able to get out of this after all.

"Forget it," said the right head. "You're here to stay."

"Did you just read my mind?" Bob asked, amazed.

"Mind!" the right head sneered, and it and the other two heads laughed some more, their combined halitosis adding a nasty tang to the already reeking air.

"We've been seeing chumps like you for millennia," the right head continued. "You think you're all that original?"

"Besides," the left head asked in a sarcastic tone, jerking its wrinkled, mucusy snout upward. "What you gonna do, climb out?"

Bob looked up. Above him was pitch blackness punctuated by the single star of Heaven, which now looked impossibly far away.

"Go on," said the center head. "We'll let you have a go at it. Climb if you can."

Bob went over to the iron-gray wall. It was as smooth as glass. There was no way he or anyone or anything could climb it.

"There's only one way out of here," said the center head, "and there it is." It nodded toward the doorway.

"What if I don't go in?"

"Oh, you'll go in," said the left head. "What're you gonna do, hang around here with us for eternity?"

"Not that we'd mind," said the right head. "The Boss said we could eat anyone who remains in this chamber for more than ten minutes."

"You've been here for six," said the left head.

"Damn, but I'm hungry," said the center head, licking its chops and drooling. More steam hissed.

Bob headed for the doorway as fast as he could. It took him a while to get through it, though. The closer he got, the smaller it shrank until, at last, it was barely large enough for him to slither through like a snake on its belly. Before he'd reached the other side, the hot floor had burned his front side to a raw red. It was all he could do to cup his genitals while he crawled to keep them from getting scalded, too.

On the other side of the door, he stood up and found himself in another room where a hideous scaled demon with huge flaring nostrils that oozed gobs of green snot stood behind a counter.

The air was filled not only with the horrible stench but an equally terrible cacophony of screams, shouts, moans, babbling, and all sorts of other cries of pain, frustration, and madness. Bob instinctively put his hands to his ears, but the din didn't diminish one bit. It was, he realized, all in his own head. He knew this was the case because the demon's mouth was moving, and Bob could only hear the muffled rumble of its words. He dropped his hands.

"That's better," the demon said, it's voice quite clear through the tumult in Bob's head. "Welcome to Hell. I'm Remoron, and I'll be your admission officer today."

"Why am I here?" Bob asked.

"Because you were a shitty asshole who let greed and lack of compassion rule your life, and because you smugly crapped all over everyone you met in your attempt to gratify your worse impulses."

"I object to that categorization," Bob began, but the demon interrupted him.

"I know you're a lawyer, Bob, but don't try to get technical with me. The judgment's come and gone. I'm just a jailer."

"But I didn't get a chance to defend myself."

"You had a lifetime to do that," Remoron pointed out. "Now, if you'll just admit to your various crimes...."

"But I'm innocent."

"They never admit to anything," the demon said to the air above its head. "Especially the lawyers." It looked back at Bob with a judicious eye. "Okay, since you won't repent, it's time for your orientation. You are, as you've undoubtedly realized, in Hell."

"Are we under the Earth?"

"What an antiquated notion," Remoron snorted, blowing green globs. "No. Hell isn't under anything. It's beside everything."

"So Heaven isn't above?"

"No, it's on the other side of everything."

"But Heaven looked like it was up, and I fell a long way to get here."

"You fell long, all right," the demon pointed out. "But it was all before you died. When you were coming here, it was just your limited human perceptions that made it look like it was an up-or-down proposition. But enough of that. Here, take this."

Remoron pulled a large leather-bound book from beneath the counter and handed it to Bob. The leather was extremely fine grained, and it looked suspiciously human to Bob. Worse, it squirmed slightly beneath his fingers.

"What's this?"

"*The Rule Book.* It's got all the rules written down just so there's no misunderstanding."

"Rules?"

"Yes," Remoron said. "Heaven is about freedom. In Heaven, you can do anything you want. The problem is, no one there wants to do anything fun. A bunch of sticks in the mud, if you ask me. Believe me, I've been both places, and personally, I think it's a hell of a lot more fun here."

"So if Heaven is about freedom," Bob said, hefting heavy book in his hands, "then...."

"You got it. Hell is about rules."

❧ 4 ☙

"WHO THE HELL ARE YOU?" the Devil demanded. He had been about his daily round, inspecting his kingdom, and was perfectly content at its hellish productivity. After all, it was a manifestation of his potency, wasn't it? And he was plenty potent and righteously proud of it.

He was, at that moment, checking up on Alrinach, a relatively minor worker demon whose task was supervising the labors of a mutant rat. The subjects of the mutant rat's labors were two men chained to either side of the filthy hold of a decrepit thirteenth-century sailing ship. Twice a day every day, the rat would attack one of them and spend six hours totally consuming every morsel of flesh but the still-living brain. Then the rat would slosh fatly through the bloody bilge to busily devour the other. And while that was going on, the first man would regenerate—a process nearly as painful as the consumption.

The "who" the Devil referred to was a lovely maiden with long, wavy blond hair and large, liquid blue eyes. He knew she was a maiden because he had a sixth sense about that sort of thing— much like a predator knows vulnerable prey the instant it sees it. For the same reason, he knew that she was a natural blond.

She stared back at the Devil rather vacantly. Or so he thought. Unlike every other human in Hell, who was naked, she was dressed in a simple one-piece muslin shift, pure white in color, that covered everything but her graceful hands and pretty bare feet and was one disappointing shade shy of translucent.

"What's that you're doing?" she asked, ignoring his question.

"Having a bit of fun," the Devil replied. "Want to help?"

"No," said the young woman, shaking her blond tresses. "What did they do that you're torturing them so?"

"Me and Hugh had some fun and profit with many the likes of you, lassie," one of the men supplied. The other man—Hugh, apparently—made no response, the rat having just got his tongue.

The maiden peered more closely at the first man in the dim light. "You have no skin," she said.

"It'll be back soon enough," he said with a shrug.

"And gone soon after," laughed Alrinach.

"Why does that rat have the face of a child?" the young woman asked.

"It's the nature of the punishment to be meted out to these two," the Devil replied.

"To be eaten by a child-faced rat?"

"Ever hear of the Children's Crusade?" asked Alrinach.

When the young woman shook her head, Alrinach looked askance of the Devil.

"Can I tell her, Boss?"

"You're doing all the work. Why should you have any fun?" The Devil snorted, and his elegantly arched nostrils issued a little drift of smoke. Then he looked at the girl. "That's the nature of Hell," he said, and he laughed.

"Aw, cummon, Boss."

"Okay," the Devil said with a shrug that made the large horny spines on his shoulders even more prominent. "Have it your own way."

"This here is Hugh Ferreus," Alrinach indicated the one who was now little more than a skeleton with lidless, staring eyes, "and this one's William of Posquères. These two gentlemen lived around the beginning of the thirteenth century, and they participated in, or should I say profited from, an event called the Children's Crusade. During that most interesting incident, tens of thousands of European children were struck with a religious mania. The rulers of Europe, seeing a first-rate opportunity to rid themselves of an entire poverty-stricken generation that would eventually become a burden to the state—or worse, cause trouble when they grew up and demanded decent lives—sent the children off to the Holy Land to liberate the Holy Sepulcher of Christ from the Muslim infidels." Alrinach laughed, and an ugly, raspy sound it was. Slobber dangled from his pallid, blubbery lips. "As if they could succeed where their elders had failed. Many of them died like the innocent fools they were, and the few who returned were starving and in disgrace. The world is full of idiots, thank goodness...." He flinched and looked quickly at the Devil's cloven hoofs then away again. "Er, thank His Dark Highness," he amended, rather too loudly.

"Did these two men convince the children to go?" the young woman asked.

"No," the Devil said, turning his baleful, yellow, slitted eyes from Alrinach to her. "But they did promise to ferry seven shiploads of them overseas from Marseilles to the Holy Land in ships such as this. All in the cause of God, of course, and at no cost."

"Everything has its price," the young woman said. "My daddy taught me that."

The Devil's elegant lips, which had been twisting sardonically, halted in mid-sneer. He studied the girl again. She reminded him all too much of his brother's angelic, kiss-ass spawn, and though her big, weepy blue eyes still looked vacant, her words hinted at some sharpness beneath her rather sickeningly golden and white exterior.

"Quite right," he replied. "This time, it was the children who paid, most with their freedom and some with their lives. The ones on the two ships that sank were probably the luckiest of the lot since Hugh and William sold the rest into slavery in Bougie and Alexandria."

"That's terrible," the maiden said, nose wrinkling. She turned her large, liquid, blue, and slightly vacant eyes on the two men, one now a still-living skeleton, the other once again whole.

"Oh, look!" she exclaimed in an almost delighted tone. "The rat changed its face!"

Indeed it had. It had just gobbled Hugh's second eye and was turning to waddle toward the bilge and William on the far side. William's flesh crawled visibly as the rat made its way toward him, and he writhed in his chains.

"Each time the rat eats them," the Devil said, "it wears the face of a different one of their victims."

"How horrible," the young woman said, "to make the children who suffered at their hands suffer even more by eating them."

"It's not really the children," the Devil told her. "It's just a little conceit of mine to make things a little more interesting. The children all became martyrs, of course—at least the ones who died young. A few turned into bad apples later and wound up here, but most of them went to the other place."

"Oh, God!" William screamed as the rat began to eat his toes.

"Too late to ask *him* for anything," the Devil chuckled.

"I hate this!" William moaned. "I can't stand any more! Please make it stop!"

"What'll you give me?" the Devil asked.

"Anything!" William gasped as the last of his toes disappeared.

"Give me your sole," the Devil said.

William just looked dumbfounded and screamed anew as the rat went for the bottom of his foot.

"Not ticklish?" the Devil asked.

Just then, he felt a gentle touch on his arm, and he flinched.

He turned as the maiden retracted her hand.

"You dared touch me?" he blazed, huffing himself up so that all his spines stood erect and the red veins striating his pitch-black flesh stood out with pulsing prominence.

Actually, he was a little surprised. No one besides his brother had ever touched him without his permission, and even with his permission, he knew, it was difficult because he radiated a potently repellent aura that everyone found impossible to tolerate at close range.

"I couldn't help myself," she said lightly. "You have such lovely skin."

"Lovely?" Alrinach started to laugh then withered beneath the Devil's glance.

"All those little red vein thingies," the maiden went on. "They look like they're running through beautiful obsidian."

The Devil's body wasn't black, exactly, but more as if his flesh was a denseness that precluded light, though like obsidian, it was somewhat translucent near the surface. The effect gave the Devil a certain haziness, making it difficult for most people, and even demons, to focus on him for any length of time. Their eyes kept trying to work their sight into and beneath his surface where, at any depth, entrapment lay.

Putting aside the momentary but curious and alien feeling of perplexity that tickled the back of his mind, the Devil loomed over her.

"All right," he boomed threateningly. "Who are you, and why are you wandering around loose in my domain? You should be someplace."

Privately, he doubted that she belonged any place in Hell. She just didn't have the right feeling of wrongness.

"I am someplace," she said with a confidence that sounded a trifle smug but that matched her obvious lack of intimidation at the Devil's imposing bulk and repellent aura. "I belong by your side."

ᚱ 5 ᚱ

"Okay, Bob," Remoron said. "I'm going to read your sentence."

"I thought St. Peter was supposed to do that," Bob said.

"You'd better learn something quick around here," the demon told him.

"What?"

"To shut the fuck up and listen."

"Is that in *The Rule Book*?"

"Rule #1."

Bob looked, and sure enough, there it was, written in what looked like dried blood: "Rule #1: Shut the fuck and listen."

"I don't especially like rules," Bob began. "They exist only to maintain the status...."

"Shut the fuck up," Remoron said, and suddenly Bob couldn't speak. His throat just clamped down and wouldn't let any words pass his lips.

"It's pretty obvious you don't like rules," Remoron said. "Otherwise, you wouldn't be here. Here's the short and sweet of it, the real skinny, the down-low lowdown: Hell isn't about pain, though there's plenty of that. It's about rules. Nothing but rules. People are sent to Hell because they broke the rules when they were alive, so what better punishment than being forced to obey every rule, no matter how complex, painful, and degrading it might be? You're not here because you 'did bad things,'" Remoron scratched quote marks in the air with its talons. "You're here because you didn't, or wouldn't, obey the rules. The pain and degradation and all the other stuff is just a way to enforce the rules and, at the same time, make them unbearably difficult to obey. But let me be perfectly clear: You *will* obey."

Remoron noticed that Bob was struggling to say something. "Okay," it said. "You can speak now."

"Whew," Bob gasped. "How did you do that?"

"You mean prevent you from speaking?" The demon shrugged. "Wasn't me, Bob, it was the rules. Call it some kind of esoteric force. Way I understand it, it comes with the territory. It just operates. Don't ask me how. I don't think even the Boss or you-know-who know." The demon rolled its eyes toward the right, and Bob followed the gesture with his own gaze. All he saw was a wall, but he understood that Heaven must be over that way, somewhere.

"But what you're saying is crazy," Bob said. "It should be the other way around. Heaven is the place of rules—you can't do this because God won't like it, or you can't do that because it'll tarnish your wings."

"Not so," Remoron explained. "Heaven is the place of perfect freedom because everyone there has self-control. And just for your information, only the angels have wings. From what I hear, the humans are just balls of light. The demon leaned close enough to shroud Bob in its halitosis, and a big blob of green snot dripped off its nose and plopped onto the counter between them, where it began to eat a hole in the surface. "Frankly, though, almost everybody who isn't down here is in purgatory. Self control is a trait not possessed by many humans."

"Whose rules are they?" Bob asked. "The ones I broke?"

"Whose?" The demon laughed. "Why, *your* rules. People's rules. The codes by which people profess goodness and to which they hold others with harsh constraint but which they always seem to break with such ease when it suits their whim."

"I never saw them," Bob pouted. "Nobody ever explained...."

"Oh, come on, Bob. They're part of the fabric of human cultures worldwide, and the ones that really count are the same no matter where you go."

"But what about sin?" Bob asked. "You know, gluttony and greed and lust and all that?"

"The seven deadly sins play a large part," Remoron acknowledged. "Important enough that they're each ruled over by one of the Archons."

"What are Archons?"

"Who, not what. The embodiments of six of the seven deadly sins. There's Lucifer, the demon of pride; Mammon, greed; Asmodeus, lust; Beelzebub, gluttony; Leviathan, envy; and Belphegor, sloth. Wrath, of course, is the Boss's personal stomping ground, so to speak."

"I never heard of Asmodeus or Belphegor," Bob admitted. "And I thought Lucifer was, you know, the Boss."

"That immature little pipsqueak?" Remoron snorted, and more green snot splattered onto the counter. "Not likely. Anyway, if you really think about the seven deadly sins, you'll quickly see that each one is simply a way to break the rules through loss of self-control."

"Does that mean I could have done all sorts of bad things while I was alive and still gone to Heaven as long as I did it all with self control?"

"It's not that simple, Bob. Doing bad things is really just a euphemism for breaking the rules. Most evil arises from actions based on a desire to further oneself at the expense of others. In other words, you try to get others to do your living for you. That not only wastes other people's time—and time is all anybody really has—it exhibits a definite lack of self-control."

"The meek shall inherit the Earth, is that it?"

"I wouldn't go that far," Remoron chuckled, sounding a little like a huge chicken cackling. "Meekness often is a disguise for weakness, which also is a lack of self-control. And sometimes it's a sneaky way to manipulate others. We have lots of meek people down here. You should see the Debating Society in action. That's where a bunch of meek people spend all the time yelling at each other. Watch that for a few minutes, and you'll see that meekness isn't all it's cracked up to be."

Suddenly a musical chime sounded from somewhere.

"Well, Bob, I'm afraid we're going to have to wind it up. Several people just dropped into Cerberus's pit, and I have to admit them as soon as they get through the door, so we'd better finish the technical stuff. For laying a deathbed curse, you are hereby sentenced...."

"Wait a minute!" Bob interrupted, dumbfounded. "What curse?"

"'I'll get whoever is responsible for this if it's the last thing I do!'" Remoron quoted, reading from a document. "'Curse 'em! Curse 'em 'til the day they die!'" It looked up from the document. "Recognize that, Bob?"

"Yeah," Bob said. "You mean I'm here because I cursed somebody and not because of all the bad stuff I did—all the rules I broke?"

"Ah," Remoron waved dismissively. "All that petty crime you did when you were an adolescent doesn't count. Even Co-Ed Head only would have landed you in Purgatory since you never really forced anyone to do anything—being able to construct convincing arguments, even to obtain blowjobs on camera, doesn't necessarily break the rules. And the more sordid moments of your corporate rise simply twisted the rules in an environment where that was de rigueur. They might have lengthened your stay in Purgatory, but that's all. You were pretty slick, in fact, until you laid the curse. Face it Bob, except for that, you were just a venal little fellow with aspirations to immorality. Curses, on the other hand, are more sinful than just about anything because they're an attempt to call on a higher power to break the rules for you."

"But I didn't really mean it," Bob whined. "I was just mad."

"What a pity you died right then and couldn't take it back. You'd be in Purgatory now instead of here. But since you died with the curse on your lips, well, here you are."

"I don't understand how a curse can be so bad."

"It's quite simple, really," Remoron explained. "A curse is bad because it actually does have consequences for the one cursed. Usually, those consequences aren't nearly as bad as the curser intends since most curses are, as you pointed out, passing whims and don't have a lot of directed purpose behind them. Humans are, after all, a lazy, complacent lot. But that's not the case with a deathbed curse. They're the worst of all because they carry the entire weight of curser's life behind it."

"Can't I take it back now?" Bob asked.

"Sure."

"And what happens then?"

"Purgatory."

"You mean I can get out of Hell and have a second chance?"

"And a third. As many chances as you need. You don't think measly humans can perfect themselves in one lifetime, do you?"

Bob felt a sudden surge of hope.

"What do I have to do to rescind the curse?"

"Find the person you cursed and tell them you forgive them while, at the same time, admitting your own error. And say it with real feeling."

Bob's surge of hope popped.

"But I don't know who it was I cursed. And he's probably not here, anyway. Yet."

"Well, then, I guess you're shit out of luck," the demon said, then it chuckled. "Or, should I say, you're luck's about to be in more shit than you ever imagined, because you are hereby sentenced to an eternity in the lake of boiling shit."

"The lake of boiling shit?" Bob sounded surprised.

"You want worse, maybe?" Remoron asked hopefully.

"No, no. I'm sure it's bad enough. I just thought…."

"You just thought you were hotter shit than boiling?" Remoron scorned. "Lava, maybe? We have that here, too. Or how about something completely different like the glacier. Hah! Let's get one thing clear, Bob. You're small change around here. Ponder that, then read Rule #2,795."

Remoron paused, and Bob realized that he was being given a moment to look up the rule. Hell revolves around you, it read. You are the focus of its attention.

"If you think that fact, combined with your pitiful insignificance, doesn't chap my butt, then you'd better think again," Remoron continued. "If it wasn't for cheap, lazy-ass sinners like you, me and all the rest of us demons would have an eternity to fuck around on Earth and have fun. But no, we gotta spend it in Hell with crapulent little turds like you. And that's why you're going to the lake of boiling shit, Bob. Because you're an insignificant, crapulent little turd."

The demon stated all this in such a matter-of-fact voice that Bob was tempted to think it was joking, but something in the murky depths of the creature's watchful gaze made him realize that nothing was funny about his situation.

At that moment, the door behind Bob began to shrink.

"Here they come," Remoron pointed. "We're out of time. So, if you have no further questions, I'll send you on to your punishment."

"Do I get to keep this?" Bob asked, nervously hefting *The Rule Book*.

"By all means. We give a copy to all our inmates."

"Thanks."

"Don't thank me. Giving you a copy is one of the rules. And I'm sure you'll read it."

"Another rule?"

"You're a bright boy, Bob. Now, off you go."

Remoron gave Bob a somewhat perfunctory wave, and suddenly Bob was somewhere else.

Miasma, smoke, and fetor lay over the land in a low mass of clouds, heat convections like the breaths of a blast furnace causing the clouds' churnings and roilings to create phantasmagoric but hideous faces and images of fiendish torment and sadistic torture. Half the cacophonous din that hammered inside Bob's head seemed to emanate from these clouds.

But that wasn't the worst of it. The worst was that, as Remoron promised, there was a lake of shit, and Bob was in it about half way up his thighs. And it was boiling.

Bob screamed.

↝ 6 ↜

THE DEVIL LAUGHED.

"Belong by my side?" he asked, voice heavy with sarcasm. "You mean this side?" He spread his huge, left, bat-like wing, raised his left arm, and flexed his intercostal muscles. Sharp points with barbs sprang up like ranked rows of tank traps along his ribs. The tip of each metallic-looking curved thorn glistened with a drop of purple venom.

"Or this side?" he showed her the same along his right rib cage.

"What a lovely color," she said bending close. "I just adore lavender. Though rose is nice, too."

The Devil laughed again, retracted his rib spines, and switched his long tail. The spade-shaped, blade-like tip brushed against William of Posquères's shoulder, opening a substantial gash, and the child-faced rat lunged at the wound and began lapping at the blood.

"You're such a peculiar one, aren't you?" he asked. "Come with me; we'll see where you belong."

"I belong...."

"I heard you the first time," the Devil said. "Come with me, anyway."

"I belong by your side," she said as the Devil levitated out of the ship's hold. "How can I do anything else?"

He waited a bit impatiently while the young woman climbed gingerly up the ladder to the deck, then he led the way off the ship, whose yardarms were thick with the hanged—though perpetually living—bodies of pirates swaying in the wind of a hot blast from a nearby foundry manned by nineteenth-century American industrialists. She didn't seem to mind the effort it took. Too bad, he thought, and he decided to push her a little. Flapping steadily, but at a regally sedate pace, he headed off across broken ground toward the northwest. She followed, climbing daintily over heaps of rubble and rubbish when she couldn't find a clear path around or between them.

Soon, they were circumnavigating Corporate Stadium, where former corporate executives in gladiator garb fought to the death for the right to name the stadium after themselves. Since all wounds eventually were healed and there was no such thing as mortality this side of Earth—or the other side, for that matter—the stadium remained perpetually unnamed, but that only inflamed the combatants' enthusiasm for vicarious glory.

Just beyond Corporate Stadium lay a square mile of barren ground strewn with the ruins of temples of all faiths. The landscape, at least in this vicinity, looked a lot like Hieronymus Bosch's *The Garden of Earthly Delights*. All around, minor demons were performing hideous, painful, and degrading acts on all manner of humans. At least, that's how it appeared at first glance, but as the young woman followed the Devil through the middle of the area, her eyes widened.

"It looks like a lot of the people here are tormenting the other people more than any of the demons are," she observed.

"It's more cost-effective to let people punish themselves or each other whenever possible," the Devil explained. "All these people here were priests or nuns or such from all the world's religious orders, present and past, and they're all too happy to oblige in the name of their faith."

"I'd have thought that they'd get some sort of special dispensation, being religious and all."

"They do have special dispensation," the Devil chuckled. "Evil done in the name of any deity increases the punishment. Sort of like traffic fines doubling for infractions committed in work zones."

They passed on, and just over a high berm formed of pulchritudinous sinners stacked like cordwood, all writhing and suffocating and trying to stay on top of their fellows, they came to another open field with a round stone tower crowned with a crenellated battlement. Soldiers circled its base, hacking each other to pieces with medieval weaponry, reforming, and hacking again.

"Who's that?" she asked, pointing to a monstrous and hideously ugly crow perched on the tower, cawing down on the soldiers with a raucous voice and showering the combatants with gallons of slimy yellow droppings.

"That's Malphas. He's one of the grand presidents of Hell. I've given him command of forty legions."

"Is that who's fighting below?"

"Only the privates," the Devil said. "Of course, they all were generals once."

By and by, they came to a simple iron door set in a rock wall, and the Devil ushered her through. Inside was a room with black walls, a counter, and a huge scaly demon with wide nostrils that dripped gobs of green snot.

"Okay, Remoron," the Devil said caustically. "Look what I found untended and unemployed." He indicated the girl. "Get her placed, and be quick about it. I can't have people wandering about unless wandering is their punishment."

The demon behind the counter peered at the girl, a puzzled frown creasing his scaly brow.

"I don't recognize her, Boss."

"Don't be ridiculous," snorted the Devil. "She just came through. Look, her gown is still white, and you know nothing stays white here for long." He turned to the girl. "How long have you been here?"

"I woke up just before you met me," she said.

"Exactly fifty-two minutes ago," the Devil said to Remoron. "Come on, look in the book, fool! I haven't got all night."

The demon hastened to obey, flipping through the Book of Admissions and peering at the entries. At last it looked up at the Devil without quite meeting his eyes.

"Sorry, Boss. The only person who came in fifty-two minutes ago was some guy named Bob. He came in alone, and no one came after for about ten minutes. I remember thinking it was kinda odd since they normally come in droves, all piled on each other. I usually have to give group orientation sessions, but because I had just him for a while, I chatted him up and gave him a more thorough orientation than usual."

"You're certain about that?"

"Sure, Boss. Maybe she's lying about the time. If I knew her name...."

"What's your name, girl?" the Devil said with obvious impatience. Damn, did he have to do everything himself? He'd spotted half a dozen torments he'd wanted to dabble in on his way here, and he was anxious to get back and have some fun.

"I'm not sure I should tell you," she replied.

"Out with it," the Devil demanded in a thick, threatening voice, suddenly growing three feet taller. Remoron cringed behind the counter, but the girl just stared blandly back at the Devil.

"I think not," she said, pursing her lips and giving a quick shake of her golden hair. "After all, names are power, aren't they? I think you're a nasty fellow, and I certainly don't want you to have any power over me."

"Foolish mortal bitch!" the Devil bellowed in a voice of thunder, inflating himself like a puffer fish, all bulk and sharp, venomous spines. His thick, leathern wings blocked out the light, and Remoron threw itself to the floor behind the counter, which was a good thing, since the razor-edged, spade-shaped barb on the tip of the Devil's lashing tail struck sparks off the rock wall where it's head had just been. In a trice, the girl was backed into a corner, dozens of venom-dripping spines hovering within an inch of her tender flesh.

"Tell me your name, or you shall suffer the gravest punishments I can mete!"

"No." Her voice wasn't defiant, only resolute.

The Devil thrust his venomed spines forward, piercing her frail little body.

Only they didn't pierce. In fact, they didn't even scratch her. It was like her skin was surrounded by the minutest but most adamant of invisible barriers that caused his erect spines to flex like limp rubber.

The Devil, suddenly driven to pique, reared back, opened his mouth, and blew out a billow of fire—he was, after all, the inspiration for the wyrm.

The flames danced around her, but not a thread of her gown or a hair of her head shriveled, and her flesh remained un-blackened.

But her nose wrinkled.

"Don't you ever brush your teeth?" she asked. "Your breath is terrible. I'll have to get you some Listerine the next time I'm at the drug store."

The Devil grabbed her, intending to rend her, or at least dash out her brains against the wall. But he couldn't grip her, and the slippery bitch was heavy enough to seem rooted like a tree.

"Remoron," he ordered. "Rip her apart!"

Remoron, seeing an opportunity for rapid advancement if he succeeded, snatched at her but failed miserably, only gouging himself with his own claws. She just stood there and watched them like they were antic but boring clowns.

"I don't think you can do anything to me," she said.

"And why is that?" the Devil demanded, put out but, by now, a little curious. And a little tired of holding himself all puffed up. He allowed himself to deflate to his normal size.

"Because I'm pure as the driven snow," she said. "I'm unsullied as the morning dew, spotless, inviolate, and blue-eyed and blameless. I'm...."

"I get the picture," the Devil interrupted. And he did. If she was all she said she was, he couldn't do a thing to her, and if he couldn't do a thing to her, she must be all she said she was.

"If what you say is true," he said, "you're in the wrong place."

"When I look around this awful land, I think you must be right," she said. "But when I look at you, I know I'm right where I'm supposed to be."

"And why is that?"

"I'm not entirely sure," she said. "I am pure innocence, and you're an ugly, nasty, and cruel thing. I mean, look at this hideous place you created."

"I didn't create it, and it's not a place, it's a state of being, just as Heaven is a state of being. They created themselves. And if there is a state of being, there must be a being to inhabit that state. Old gods and daimons simply represent forces of nature at play on the human mind, body, emotions, and spirit. In any case, somebody has to be the best at what they do—or in my case, the worst. God and I are simply logical extensions of the equally powerful and necessary states of good and evil."

"Okay, maybe. But I think you enjoy all this horror just a bit too much."

"Oh, I don't know about that. That might be excessive. I like to think I enjoy it perfectly."

"See what I mean?" she asked with a helpless shrug.

Remoron sniggered under his breath.

๑⇥ 7 ⇤๑

BOB DIDN'T HAVE A CHANCE to study *The Rule Book* for some time after he arrived at his place of punishment. In fact, he nearly dropped it into the shit as the boiling feces turned his legs into pillars of scorching pain and a horrible and suffocatingly heated stench assailed his nostrils. But somehow he managed to retain his grip—he later learned that it was Rule #734, which came some six hundred rules after the rule that stated that every inmate was to be given a copy of *The Rule Book*. Rule #734 stipulated that inmates must retain their copy at all times and that it must be maintained in pristine condition. Thus, Bob kept the book out of the shit even though he paid for it by scalding his balls.

He'd barely recovered when he heard a loud and harsh voice demand, "What's the difference between a lawyer and a terrorist?"

"What?" Bob asked looking around, blinking back tears that had come unbidden because of his searing legs. Through his watery gaze, he saw a large, dark figure hulking on a ledge or embankment just above him, silhouetted against the dense, roiling, and glowing red atmosphere that billowed all over Hell. It carried a large bullwhip coiled in its right hand.

"What's the difference between a lawyer and a terrorist?" the figure asked again.

Bob rubbed the moisture from his eyes, trying to focus, and the figure resolved into the person of a demon. He was pretty hideous—thick, flabby body covered with coarse but sparse clots of stiff black fur. The skin that was visible between the clumps of fur was a mottled, diseased pink and green. His shoulders and arms were simian, but his feet looked like they were grafted on from some primeval reptilian raptor, and a ridiculously stubby pair of wings sprouted from his shoulders. Bob thought of the thing as a he because of the tremendously large set of male genitals that pended from his groin.

The lumpy head that sat directly on the demon's hunched, simian shoulders like a large, warty growth, was completely devoid of hair, and from it, piggish, bloodshot eyes stared at Bob without the slightest hint of humanity. Below the eyes projected a yellow beak lined with sharp little teeth. The thing couldn't have smiled if he wanted to, despite the teeth. His voice was not birdlike, however. It sounded exactly like one of Bob's professors back in law school—the one who'd taught legal ethics and hated Bob's guts.

"Uh, I don't know. What is the difference?"

"Terrorists have sympathizers," the hideous figure said.

"That's not very funny," said Bob.

"It wasn't intended to be. I was just informing you of the a priori modus operandi of our relationship."

"No sympathy?" Bob asked.

"That's right. Now, let's get down to brass tacks...." The thing consulted a PDA. "Bob."

"Is this the circle of hell reserved for lawyers?" Bob asked.

"Yeah, I can see it now," the demon sneered. "Some giant courtroom full of lawyers all suing each other and perpetually objecting to objections and constantly being overruled. Or maybe," he laughed nastily, "a huge bar where drunk lawyers slug it out." He peered at Bob. "You know what really would be hell for your kind? A courtroom where lawyers, instead of the witnesses, had to swear to tell the truth."

"But I wasn't a trial lawyer. I was a corporate lawyer...."

"Shut the fuck up," the demon said. "That's even worse."

Bob shut the fuck up. He couldn't help himself.

"Don't get some antiquated notion that Hell is made up of concentric circles, with the inner circle the place where supreme evil resides," the demon went on. "What makes you think that supreme evil is confined only to one localized area?"

"I don't know," Bob said as the paralysis left his throat. "I guess I never thought about it."

"And you call yourself a servant of the law." The demon said derisively. "Well, Hell doesn't have circles. It's got angles. Heaven's got circles. Hell's not that organized—it wouldn't be Hell if it wasn't chaotic. And we don't reserve any specific place for lawyers. But with all the angles here, lawyers usually manage to find their way into the darkest corners. Okay...." He consulted his PDA again, hummed a bit, then snorted shrilly and gave Bob a contemptuous look.

"Such penny-ante corruption, Bob. With a mind and drive like yours, I would have expected far more or far less. No wonder you're only thigh deep. I mean, look at them." He waved to Bob's left. "Some folks out there are in some deep shit."

Indeed they were. Bob saw that the lake of boiling shit he was in was maybe half a mile or so in diameter, and all around, people were standing in it at varying depths, some ankle deep and some with only their noses lifted into the air. He couldn't actually see any of the latter, of course, but each held his or her copy of *The Rule Book* as high as possible above the plooping surface like a sort of marker buoy.

"I was only forty-six. I didn't have a chance to completely fulfill myself." Bob said it a trifle defensively, but looking at *The Rule Books* waving in the air over the submerged inmates made him really glad he hadn't.

"Every one of our inmates has excuses," the thing said. "My name is Sapason. I'm a minor demon of Hell, but don't let the minor part fool you. I might not have the Boss's power, but I'm dedicated, and what I've got's plenty to keep you in line."

Sure, you big, ugly asshole, Bob thought. Until you turn your back. Then I'm outta here.

He scanned the bank on which the demon stood, which also was the shore of the lake of boiling shit, looking for an easy way out. The demon showed a lot of teeth, and Bob realized he'd been wrong—the thing could smile, but the smile was completely without humor.

"You have your copy of *The Rule Book*, I see," Sapason said. Bob nodded.

"Better start reading, then. You wouldn't be here if you weren't already familiar with Rule #1, so I suggest you begin with Rule #11,793."

"What about Rule #2?"

"I'm sure you'll get around to it, but #11,793 is more to the point."

Bob opened the book and quickly found Rule #11,793: Inmates are not allowed to escape from their punishment.

"In case you don't believe it," Sapason said, "why don't you give it a try?" He stared at Bob then jerked his thumb like a baseball umpire signaling an out. "Go on, Bob. Get yer ass outta there. I know you want to. It's hot as boiling shit in there. I know that for a fact. Every once in a while, one of you dorks splashes some of it on me, and it burns like hell. So go on. Climb out, and walk away."

Now or never, thought Bob. He started his legs moving toward the shore, though the act of movement itself made the sewage seem hotter and rawer than before and caused some of it to slop higher on his thighs. Gritting his teeth, Bob forged ahead. He was willing to put up with a little extra pain if the result got him out of this seething ordure. But the more he waded toward the shore, the farther the embankment seemed to be. Or rather, it just never got any closer.

"You see," Sapason said. "Maybe you want to escape, and who wouldn't? I certainly would. You want to—you really want to—but it's pretty obvious that you can't make any headway no matter how fast or far you go. And the real pisser is that your inability to escape doesn't remove your desire to escape or your amazed and angry perception that you can't."

After several minutes, Bob, worn out from wading through the viscous, boiling muck, stopped. Sapason was still where he was, and so was Bob.

"No fair," said Bob. "You made that happen."

"How many lawyers does it take to screw in a light bulb?"

"Are you trying to be evasive?" asked Bob.

"Come on," the demon said. "I'm your jailer, not a witness on the stand. Why the hell would I have to be evasive? Besides, I'm a straightforward kind of guy, really. How many lawyers does it take to screw in a light bulb?"

"I don't know," Bob admitted.

"One. The lawyer holds it while the world revolves around him."

"Very funny," Bob said. "Haw, haw."

"Not really," Sapason said. "Consider this: The world may not revolve around you, Bob, but Hell sure does. Rule #2,795."

"And you are the focus of its attentions," Bob recited. "I already know that one. What's your point?"

He was feeling pretty nervous. He didn't like being the focus of that much attention—at least not that much negative attention. Plus, the way Sapason's voice sounded like that legal ethics professor reminded Bob of the call-and-response methodology the professor used that seemed geared specifically toward public humiliation. He probably thought it was good training for the courtroom, but Bob never gave him the chance to embarrass him, though he'd certainly tried. If anything at all good had come of that situation, it was that it forced Bob to learn to really apply himself to his studies to avoid the professor's contempt. If there was anything Bob really hated, it was contempt aimed in his direction.

On the other hand, he thought, looking down, maybe boiling shit ranked right up there with contempt.

"You said it was unfair that you couldn't wade to the shore and said that I made it happen." Sapason shook its head. "Not me, Bob."

"Well, who, then?"

"Not who," Sapason corrected. "What." He waved around. "All this is like that. Like *that*." He pointed at *The Rule Book* in Bob's hand. "It's the rule of rules. It's like one of those Russian dolls that opens up and there's a smaller doll inside, and inside that a smaller one. Only here, there's never a smallest doll. Rules within rules within rules, and there is no escape from them any more than there is from your punishment."

Fuck that, Bob thought, staring at *The Rule Book*. One way or another, rules or no rules, I'm getting my ass out of here.

"Any questions?" Sapason asked.

"You mean I can ask questions?"

"No rule against it. We can talk as much as you like. You can talk to any of them, too." He waved out toward the other people trapped in the lake.

"I only have one question, right now. Am I going to have to listen to you tell bad lawyer jokes all the time?"

"Mai, oui. It's part of your punishment. But I will admit that there is something wrong with lawyer jokes."

"What's that?" Bob asked.

"Lawyers don't think they're funny, and other people don't think they're jokes."

"So," Bob said, ignoring the jibe, "it's all down here in *The Rule Book*? All the rules and regulations."

"It's all there," Sapason affirmed. "Except one thing. It isn't a rule, exactly, but it's highly encouraged since it adds immeasurably to the ambience of this wonderful realm in which we find ourselves as well as increases the personal torment of those nearby."

"What's that?" Bob asked.

"You can scream."

Bob complied.

☍ 8 ☌

THE DEVIL HAD TO ADMIT he was intrigued with Angel. That's what he'd taken to calling her since she wouldn't tell him her real name. He knew she wasn't actually an angel. He was personally acquainted with every angel, just as his brother knew all the demons, and he frequently interacted with quite a few of them as he and they went about their mutual collaborations on Earth. And because he knew them all too well, he just couldn't equate those sanctimonious pricks and their unrealistic logic with this young woman's innocent yet oddly perceptive behavior.

But he had to call her something. Naming her Angel allowed him to use one of the half dozen words he almost never used in a way that didn't insult his ethical sense, and it also gave him a private way to sneer at her and keep her at a psychological disadvantage.

The Devil wondered if his better half had sent her down here to spy or on some sort of obscure errand, and he asked her just that.

"Not that I know of," she answered, a forthright look in her eyes. He was tempted to believe her. So far, she'd been in Hell about twenty-four hours, and she seemed totally guileless. Even her refusal to tell him her name spoke of her inner veracity. Had she been a liar, she would have given him a pseudonym and been done with it. But he had learned something important from her refusal—or rather, from his enraged reaction to her refusal when he'd tried to skewer her with his venomous spines and rip her to shreds with his talons. She was invulnerable to his torments—at least physically. He could not rend her, burn her, poison her, crush her, bruise her, or even remove the tiniest golden hair from her head. In fact, he couldn't touch her at all. At least, not with evil intentions or without her permission.

Nor did the flames and acids and caustics and filth of his domain sully her one bit. Her bare, pink feet—immaculately manicured and quite dainty—didn't show the least bit of grime, though he'd made her walk quite a long way. She didn't even seem to sweat, and around her hovered a perpetual floral aura that was impervious to any fetor she encountered. And after an entire day, when anything else would have long since blackened and singed and become bespattered, her chemise remained the purest white.

Secretly he thought the color contrasted nicely with the ebon of his flesh.

What intrigued him most about Angel was that she was here in Hell when she obviously shouldn't be. Not that she was squeamish about any of it, though she occasionally wrinkled her nose in distaste at an especially noisome stench or averted her eyes demurely from particularly violent acts or scenes of outrageous sexual misconduct.

She was, in short, the greatest puzzle Hell had ever seen—a pure innocent wandering its precincts with an open but aloof curiosity that permitted none of the personal involvement that might have doomed her to become one of its inmates. But if his brother over on the other side hadn't sent her, who had? And why?

When he put these questions to her, she didn't resort to the same bald denial she'd used in refusing to divulge her name, but that didn't mean she was entirely forthcoming.

"I'm not sure why I'm here," she said. "I can't imagine why anyone would have sent me to such a horrible place. Thank goodness I don't have to suffer the torments you put all those poor people through. I still can't believe you enjoy it as much as you say you do."

"Oh, I do," he said, noting that she didn't volunteer her origin or anything else and that she'd neatly turned his question into a counter attack. He went along only for the fun of it. "You think that I—or my minions, for that matter—treat the inmates badly because we're stuck in these hellish conditions, too, and hate the circumstances of necessity that force us to remain so much that we take out our frustrations on the prisoners?"

"It had crossed my mind."

"Forget it," the Devil said. "My demons are here because it is their proper realm. Their intellect knows only the truth of darkness, not light. They have a deep knowledge of nature, which is expressed in intellect, but not much knowledge of grace or love."

"You'd think after all these millennia of participating in what goes on down here, they'd have some sort of feelings for those they make suffer."

"They're an obstinate bunch," the Devil admitted with a touch of pride. "Besides, they can't learn from experience. And anyway, you've got their nature wrong. They're not like people. They don't experience emotions like you or I—no fear or sorrow or joy, and especially not grief at the commission of sin and evil."

"How nice for them, considering all the sin and evil they perpetrate around here."

The Devil laughed.

"Let me explain something about what you see going on around here. None of what you see—none of the punishments and torments—is sin or evil."

"I find that hard to believe."

"Well, it's true. All this is simply justice. Now what we do on Earth is another matter, and I'll make no bones about it. My business on Earth is to perpetrate evil with a capital E, and those of my minions who work there pursue their calling with outstanding energy and enterprise. It's the same with my brother...."

"You have a brother?"

"Sure. You know, the one over there." The Devil jerked a thumb toward the right.

"Over where?"

"Over on the other side."

"You mean God?"

"Call him what you like."

"But he's not your brother. He created you."

"I don't know why he always gets the credit," the Devil said a trifle hotly. "Sometimes I think he's a glory hog. For your information, he did not make me. Nature made me, though I suppose if nature hadn't, humans would have invented me. They need something to focus their fear and excuse their own evil impulses."

The Devil paused, thoughtfully perusing her. She calmly perused him back.

"Look," he said at last. "In a binary universe, thesis and antithesis mutually create each other, so don't go giving him any false preeminence. My demons are no less spiritual beings than his angels, they just have the opposite polarities. The angels have no emotions and can't learn from experience, either. It's just that they know only the truth of light and not darkness, and they might have a lot of knowledge of grace but none whatsoever of the necessities of nature. Hence, the angels love beatitude but are totally impractical, while my demons love common sense, which is why they're so good at torment."

"You're pretty good at it too, from what I've seen."

"Of course. In fact, only one thing gives me greater pleasure."

"What's that?"

"Seduction."

"Well," she said, drawing herself up a little. "I certainly hope you're not going to try to seduce me."

"And why shouldn't I?"

"It won't work," she said. "I'm pure as the driven snow. I'm the unsullied dream. I'm...."

"Yes, yes, you told me."

"Anyway, how could you seduce me, now that you've told me that's what you're going to do?"

"It increases the challenge," he replied with a smile.

"Don't smirk," she said. "It's not polite. And don't think you'll get anywhere, either. I may have to be with you, but that doesn't mean I like it. Or you. So don't try anything, buster."

"Okay, I won't."

Like hell, he thought. I'm going to get into this bitch's psyche and then into her white gown, and then she'll be mine. No one comes into my realm over whom I cannot hold sway. I am the Devil, after all.

Recognition of his special and vaunted identity made him feel pretty damn good, and he began to plot how he could use his irresistible wiles to swing this lovely creature to his side. He envisioned special things for her. Though she looked human—and a knock-out at that—she couldn't be since she was impervious to the heat, poisons, acid, filth, and squalor all around her. Maybe he could twist her to his purposes and, in the twisting, evade the rules that would demand she become an inmate or transmogrify into another grotesque servant of the dark dimensions. Hell, he could figure out ways to manipulate her innocence, even if he couldn't twist her to the evil side. Someone with her looks and invulnerability could come in quite handy in a number of situations. Already he was envisioning whole scenarios built around her that would bring empires tumbling.

With a shock, he caught himself imagining something more intimate. Not the crude, rough, frigid, and, frankly, boring intercourse he performed with those ignorant sacrificial sluts they offered him at Black Sabbaths, but something gentler and more touching. If she would give herself to him, he would treat her properly as only the master of the profane and fleshly could. He could see them now, enjoying a nice meal and fine wine, nestled in front of a cozy fire of sinners burning in the large fireplace of his palace bedroom.

But no, he thought, shaking his head. It wouldn't work. Love is for those who see themselves as equals, and he had no equals—over here on this side, at least—and he wasn't about to propose to his brother that they get it on. Not that the homosexual aspect put him off any more than it would bother his brother. But the Devil just couldn't imagine fucking anything that was that good. It would positively make his cock shrivel. Hell, it might even hurt!

Anyway, he didn't want a relationship with Angel; he just wanted to sully her. She was so pretty, so innocent, so pure as the driven snow that it was an affront to his aesthetic and a gauntlet thrown in the face of his powers. If only she weren't as invulnerable as she was innocent.

The Devil knew the two conditions were intertwined, so he reasoned that if he destroyed her innocence, she would become his physically as well. He began to ponder how he could turn her.

⅋ 9 ⅋

BOB HAD STOPPED SCREAMING. HE felt like it, sure. The pain in his legs was unbearable. But after screaming continuously for hours, so was the rawness in his throat, and he figured that, while he probably had to suffer the pain in his legs, anything else was self-inflicted and could be foregone.

At least for now. Who knew—maybe he'd scream again when his vocal cords felt okay. Right now, he was looking around, taking in his surroundings. Even if he couldn't wade out of the lake of boiling shit, he wasn't prevented from turning around, though he couldn't see much aside from the lake itself. The dense, smoky, red-tinged atmosphere and the surrounding six-foot embankment hid just about everything else except Sapason and assorted other demons and sprites who would walk, fly, or slither by, smirking at the people in the shit. Occasionally, one would squat at the lake's edge to add its own contribution.

Most of the lake's inhabitants either were screaming or looking around like Bob, but not far away, a knot of people clustered in what appeared to be a group activity of some kind. Bob noticed that quite a few people were reading *The Rule Book.* He wondered why anyone would bother even opening the covers, when suddenly he found himself opening the book and flipping the pages until his eyes lit on Rule #6,935: Inmates must completely memorize all the rules.

Rule #6,935, he thought against his will. Inmates must completely memorize all the rules. He even said it aloud.

"Rule #6,935: Inmates must completely memorize all the rules." At last, after a few more repetitions, he had that rule memorized. "This shouldn't be too hard," he said to himself, hefting the tome. "It'll be like memorizing all those law books back in school."

To get back in practice, he memorized another rule. Two down and...how many to go?

He flipped to the end of the book, and his heart sank as he saw the sheer number of rules. There were 17,653 of them.

"This could take forever," he thought, then his dismay turned to horror when he realized he did, indeed, have forever. And more.

Well, he thought. A few a day should do the trick. He shut the book with a snap.

And just as quickly opened it again at random. On page 327, he read Rule #8,042: No caressing except where caressing is an element of the punishment.

With that memorized, his eyes moved to the next rule, and when that was etched into his synapses, he moved on. And on, and on.

Apparently, he was going to have to memorize all the rules before he'd be allowed to just look around.

He'd forgotten the people screaming, but remembered quickly enough when he broke off memorizing to exercise his tenor. Raw hours later, he gratefully returned to the rules, wondering if there was any way he could indefinitely prolong the memorization process, especially by extending the intervals between the screaming binges.

Bob was a smart fellow with a ready memory that could not be thwarted no matter what he did. After a period of intense concentration from which he could not sway himself and that, he judged, lasted several solid days, he knew the rules by heart.

His mind reeling with the 17,653 rules, which danced through his head like the refrain of a hated song that just wouldn't leave him in peace, he closed the book and rubbed his eyes. They were burning from all the reading as much as from the caustic air.

When he could see properly again, he surveyed his surroundings with more attention than he'd been allowed before he'd committed the rules to memory. Off in the distance, beyond the embankment closest to him, jutted the top of a smoking volcano with several visible rivers of lava flowing down its flanks, and the towers of a freakish city crumbled in the near distance of the opposite direction. Far beyond that stood another mountain as tall as the volcano, this one crowned with some sort of castle that was pitch black and appointed with numerous spiky spires.

Flames occasionally flared here and there, billowing smoke, but since his head was well below the edge of the embankment, Bob couldn't see the source of the fires or what they were burning. Some of it was flesh—he couldn't mistake that odor—but some of it smelled like petrochemical plant reek and burning rubber. Not all the smells were from burning, though. Aside from the steady stench coming from his own brine, the fetors of overripe wharf, drained lake, and rotting bodies, among others, assailed his nose. And the air was made incredibly dense by the perpetual shrieking, moaning, and wailing that came from the clouds.

"Hey, Bob!" Sapason was grinning down at him from the bank. "Guess what? I just learned what they engraved on your tombstone."

"You did?" Bob had been wondering about that. "What is it?"

"Here lies another lawyer."

With a cackle, the demon sauntered off down the bank.

"Pay no attention to him," said a voice. Bob turned and saw a man who appeared to be Middle Eastern standing about ten feet away, the shit lapping around his waist. He wore a goatee and wavy, shoulder-length hair.

"I'm Ahmed," the man said. "What's your name?"

"Bob. Sapason said it's permitted to talk."

"No rules against it," Ahmed said, "and the jailers don't seem to mind. Say, you sure memorized the rules fast."

"I had a lot of practice," Bob replied. "I was a lawyer."

"That would explain it," Ahmed nodded. "What you in for?"

"It's a long story," Bob said.

"Aren't they all?" Ahmed asked.

"Pardon me," Bob said, "But you look Arabic."

"I am," Ahmed said.

"So you're a Christian Arab?"

"Christian?" Ahmed laughed. "No. I was Islamic."

"I don't understand. Isn't it strange that you're in Hell?"

"I thought it was pretty strange, too, when I first got here," Ahmed said. "But after I'd been here for awhile, I realized that Heaven and Hell know no religious or denominational boundaries. They don't even care if you were religious at all. I hear there are atheists and pagans and apostates in Heaven. As for Hell, it's a state of evil, not of manmade belief systems."

"Yeah, I guess the Greeks had Hades, and such.

"That's right. The first thing people did when they gained sentience was start mistreating each other, so there had to be an appropriate destination when they died. Wrong is wrong, no matter what language you do it in or what customs or beliefs you use to justify it, and the corollary to that is punishment, no matter what you call the place or how you envision it."

"Makes me wonder if our different cultural outlooks give us different perceptions."

"Maybe different prejudices," Ahmed said, "but I don't know about perceptions. I'm standing in a lake of boiling shit. How about you?"

Bob took the question to be rhetorical, so instead of answering, he asked one of his own.

"But what about all these demons? They seem to me to be from Judeo-Christian beliefs."

"That's your prejudice speaking, not your perceptions. And I could say it was because Christians invented more demons than anyone else, but that would be *my* prejudices. The truth, as far as I understand it, is that they are all primal beings, and most have been recognized by many cultures throughout history. Belphegor, the demon of sloth, was Baal-Peor to the Moabites, and Asmodeus, the one governing lust, was Aeshma-deva to the Persians. And so on. We have them from every culture, probably because every culture has been had by them."

"I guess there must be a head demon. Satan?"

"Satan is what the Christians call him, but he calls himself the Devil. And he's not really a demon. He's a primal force, and all the demons are simply aspects of him, just like the angels are aspects of God. Parts of both are spread throughout reality, intertwining like the arms of two octopuses clenched in mortal combat. Or sex." Ahmed chuckled. "Probably a little bit of both. Anyway, the bodies of the octopuses are their separate realms that contain their full essences, while the clenching arms are the interplay whose energetic interaction creates reality and manifests as the forms and creatures that inhabit it."

"You sound like you've been here a long time," Bob said.

"I've been here for five hundred seventy-eight years, eight months, one week, three days, sixteen hours, forty-eight minutes, and eleven seconds."

"Wow," Bob said. "I'm impressed. How'd you do that? You're not even wearing a watch."

"It's in the book," Ahmed said. "Rule #2,944."

"'All inmates shall keep an accurate accounting of the time they've spent in Hell,'" Bob recited from memory. "Whew," he said. "I only just arrived, and I'm not sure I can remember how long I've been here."

"Sure you can. Try it."

"Okay. Let's see, going backward, I was memorizing the rules for a long time. Several days. And I was screaming for maybe eight or ten hours before that, but it's a little hard to remember. And before that, I talked to Sapason...."

"Forget it," Ahmed said, waving dismissively. "You'll never do it like that. I've been here for five hundred seventy-eight years, eight months, one week, three days, sixteen hours, forty-nine minutes, and thirty-six seconds, and do you think I can remember the exact duration of every event? Not likely."

"How then?"

"It's a lot simpler. That's what the rules do—they make things simpler. You just say, 'I've been here for five hundred seventy-eight years, eight months, one week, three days, sixteen hours, forty-nine minutes, and fifty-seven seconds.' Of course, your number will be different. Try it."

"I've been here for seven days, twenty-two hours, sixteen minutes, and thirty-nine seconds." Bob blinked and brightened. "Say," he said. "That's pretty easy." Then his face fell as he contemplated how long Ahmed had been here. "Sounds pretty wimpy," he said. "Compared to you."

"Oh, I'm nothing. We've got cavemen from before the Ice Age. Now that's tenure." He didn't sound particularly envious. "Not that any of it really matters. It's all a drop in the bucket when you consider we'll be here an eternity."

"I can't even contemplate it," Bob admitted.

"Excuse me," Ahmed said. "I think I'm going to scream now." And he did, most unnervingly.

Bob was so unnerved, in fact, that he felt compelled to join in. They harmonized nicely.

⟫ 10 ⟪

"IF I DO SAY SO myself, Your Highness, you look stunning."

The tailor stepped back, squinted an eye, and ran his gaze down the Devil's form. As his gaze ran back up, though, he noticed that the Devil was frowning at him.

"*Absolutely* stunning," the tailor amended with a quaver in his voice, quickly stepping forward to adjust a cuff.

"What about you, Deumus?" The Devil turned to the room's other occupant. "Do you think I look absolutely stunning?"

Deumus had four horns on her head, and beneath her sharp, hooked nose, four fangs curved like little sabers out of her mouth—two from the top, two from the bottom—making her head resemble a huge, animate staple remover. Her feet would have been at home on a vulture, but her hands were human-shaped, though clawed with phosphorescent green talons. In the left one, she held a squirming soul from which she occasionally took bites. But it wasn't Deumus's occupation as an instiller of fear that brought her here—it was her gender. The Devil needed a feminine eye to help appraise his new outfit.

"You always look absolutely stunning, sire," she replied. Her voice sounded sincere, but the Devil knew she had a thing for bulky, hairy demons, and the Devil preferred the sleek and natty look, himself.

"Come on," the Devil insisted. "Does it make me look...I don't know...?"

"Sexy?" she supplied.

"Not necessarily," he said, a trifle disappointed in her. "Call it sophisticated."

"Desirable, you mean?"

"No, no!" He gestured impatiently, nearly impaling the tailor with his knuckle spikes. The man did a quick two-step that took him out of the line of fire. A good thing, too, since the Devil'd had to pull a few strings to get the fellow off his punishment long enough to measure and sew this suit. "No," he repeated, absently waving the little man back to work. "I'm after a certain look."

"You can't fool me," Deumus said, the edges of a smile bravely drawing back her lips, making her fangs stand out in her blood-red gums. "It's that Angel bimbo who's been following you all over Hell all the time. Tell me, how did you manage to shake her long enough to let this cut-thread do his work.

The tailor shot her a dirty look but prudently said nothing.

"I led her to the top of Mount Etna," the Devil said, referring to Hell's volcano and dominant power source. "Then I flew back here as quickly as I could. She has to walk, you know, so I don't expect her to arrive for quite some time."

"I don't understand what you see in her," Deumus said, wrinkling her pointed nose. "She's just not our kind."

"She's interesting."

"She's a freak. She waltzes all over Hell looking and acting angelic and asking questions that would make Socrates envious, all with equal nonchalance and innocence."

"She's pure as the driven snow," the Devil said.

"So I've heard, but if that's so, what's she doing down here?"

"Hell if I know," the Devil said. "And that's what makes her so interesting. I'm going to get to the bottom of it if it's the last thing I do."

"Famous last words," she pointed out.

"I know," he smiled. "I coined them."

"What we don't understand...."

"We?"

His voice had turned a trifle scary, and Deumus couldn't help but blanch.

"Yes," she said, trying to act as if nothing was wrong. "The gang. You know."

"By that, do you mean you and your friends, or do you mean my entire domain?"

"Well I don't know," she temporized. "I haven't been *everywhere* lately."

"Exactly what is it *they* are saying?"

"It's not that they're saying anything, sire. More like observations, that's all."

"And what are they observing?"

"That you give her special privileges and let her go anywhere she pleases." There, it was out. "Everyone else has to follow the rules, except for her. I know you made the rules...."

"I didn't *make* the rules," the Devil said in a hissing tone that cut her to the quick and made the tailor faint. "I *am* the rules!"

The Devil nudged the tailor's unconscious body out of the way, into a corner, and paced the length of the room, at last stopping in front of Deumus, who cringed and looked at his hooves. Even in her fear, she couldn't help but think that the way he'd had those diamonds inset into them was really classy. But damn if she didn't hate it when he used that tone of voice. At least, when she was the recipient. It was pretty fun, though, watching it directed at someone else.

"Yes, sire. I understand they're simply a manifestation of your nature."

"Even I find it almost impossible to break them, since it goes against the grain," the Devil said. "Do you realize how hard it was to get *him* out of that roomful of needles so he could make this?" The Devil gestured at the supine tailor then at the resplendent black suit he'd had the tailor cut from the cloth of nightmares. The fabric shimmered and roiled with foreboding, lurking danger. "I had to have Melchom use accounting procedures that would make the slickest Mafia money launderer envious. In fact, he was envious."

Melchom was Hell's chief accountant and paymaster.

"Then *do* something about her."

"What do you suggest?"

"Squash her. That disgusting white gown would look great with her blood and guts oozing out or her head pinched right off the top."

"Tried it. And burning. And rending. I even tricked her into swimming in that lake of sulfuric acid where the usurers dive for glass pearls. It didn't even singe her hem."

"Did she find any of the pearls?"

"Of course. The usurers were positively apoplectic until she gave one to each of them."

Deumus shook her head and absently took a bite of the sinner clutched in her claws. "You can't keep letting her run free."

"I know. It's bad for morale. Besides, she's always around pestering and asking questions in that insipidly musical voice. But since she doesn't really belong here, I seem to have no control over her."

"You should let me and some of my gang loose on her."

"You think you can do something I can't?" the Devil demanded, and Deumus cringed.

"No, sire. But it would be fun trying."

"And a complete waste of time," the Devil said, shaking his head. "You know the only demon I allow to do that is Belphegor. But don't worry. I have a plan, and this new suit is part of it."

"Ah." Understanding lit her eyes. "Seduction."

"If you can't get 'em from the outside, work from the inside."

"In that case," she said, eyeing his suit. "I think you're on the right track. Sophisticated without being snobbish, casual enough to match her light evening wear, and expensive enough to remain in good taste. Plus, it's sure to upset the faint of heart."

"So you approve?" He pirouetted to give her a full view, extending his wings only modestly.

"Yes, sire. And your wings make a marvelous cloak. But the finest touch is that glorious codpiece."

"I think so, too. Velcro fasteners for quick release." The Devil demonstrated, the Velcro fly opening with a ripping sound.

"Ah," Deumus sighed and nodded approvingly. "No hands." She sidled a little closer.

"By the way, sire. I've been meaning to congratulate you on that coup with the president of the United States."

"What coup? Did someone finally take it over and rid us of that ridiculous notion of an egalitarian government?"

"They're working on it, sire. But I was referring to you getting him and his war-profiteering cronies to convince the entire country to wage an illegal war that killed tens of thousands of innocent men, women, and children among his own people."

"Thanks," the Devil said, "but it wasn't my work. Some people are evil without my influence."

"Maybe, sire, but he certainly doesn't have your flare."

"Obviously, since he got caught. Did something stupid, which figures."

"It seems he couldn't approach your lowness or craftiness, either, sire," Deumus fawned.

"Oh, shut up and quit trying to suck up to me!" the Devil snapped. "You're almost as bad as the Archons."

"I'm sorry, sire," Deumus said contritely. "I'll try to do worse."

"In the meantime, do something useful," the Devil said. "Wake him up." He jerked his chiseled chin at the still-unconscious tailor while using his hands to stuff himself back into the codpiece. "Can't have him slacking on the job. He's only on parole for two more days, and I want him to finish this."

❧ 11 ☙

BOB WAS PERUSING *THE RULE Book* since there wasn't much else to do besides feel pain and scream, and he didn't feel the urge to scream right at the moment. He didn't really need to look at the rules to know them—not since his marathon memorizing session. But it helped for him to see them as he contemplated them because his thoughts were as jumbled as the order of the rules—or rather, their disorder. None of them were in any kind of logical sequence, and he'd memorized them almost at random, so all 17,653 were milling around in his head like an agitated mob in which it was difficult to separate individuals.

Take Rule #14,342, for instance: Each inmate is to be punished in a manner equitable with his or her crime(s). It seemed to work in conjunction with the rule that stated: Jailers are charged with meting out the exact punishment required, but that second rule was #719, separated from the first by about five hundred pages.

"Say, fella," he called out to his Middle Eastern neighbor. The man ignored him. "Hey, fella!" he said more loudly. Ahmed was turned away from him and screaming, so maybe he didn't hear Bob call. When Ahmed still didn't respond, Bob bellowed, "Hey, Ahmed!"

This time, Ahmed turned, blinking.

"Were you talking to me?"

"Who else?"

"I don't know. I thought you were talking to some peasant."

"Peasant? What gave you that idea?"

"You called, 'Hey, fellah.'"

"And?"

"And what?"

"So what's me calling, 'Hey, fella,' have to do with peasants?" Ahmed looked confused, then he brightened.

"Ah, I understand."

"Well, I'm glad somebody does."

"No, it's really quite simple. You don't speak Arabic."

"So?"

"You said, 'fella,' which I mistook for 'fellah.'" Ahmed spelled it. "That's short for 'fellahin,' which means peasant. As I am not a peasant, I naturally thought you must be addressing someone else."

"What are you? Or were you? In life?"

"I was a—how do you say?—procurer."

"You mean women?"

"Please don't equate me with those gaudy, cheap, and violent men you Americans call pimps," Ahmed protested. "Women—and men—were part of my trade, but that was a different time and a different culture. Those who worked for me did so voluntarily and were well rewarded. I also supplied excellent food, libation, and other pleasures of life. Actually, I was quite well known along the caravan routes. Caliphs and princes numbered among my clientele. It was an honorable profession."

"If you were so honest, how'd you end up here?"

"Dishonesty had nothing to do with my fall," Ahmed answered a bit haughtily.

"You must have done *something*."

"I broke my own cardinal rule. I fell in love."

"You're in Hell because you fell in love?"

"I'd prefer not to talk about it," Ahmed said.

"Come on," Bob urged. "I'm a lawyer. I've heard lots of strange stories." He almost said, "excuses."

"Oh, all right. I don't have any choice, anyway." When Bob looked puzzled, Ahmed reminded him of Rule #409.

"If someone asks, you must admit your crimes," Bob recited. As he did, he realized for the first time that knowing the rules and applying them to real situations were two different things. It was kind of shocking that he'd never quite seen that before.

"It was foolish of me—of a man in my position," Ahmed went on. "I had all the pleasures of life I could want, but after a time, I began to tire of them. I finally understood that it was because I had no one to share them with. And then Bahira came along. She was a houri, but still young and fresh and so lovely. And quite nimble in bed. I fell for her immediately. I admit it was probably little more than infatuation, but you know how these things can get out of hand. I tried to possess her, and for a time, she was pliable. But she had ambition beyond even a successful businessman like me. She had her eyes set on the Caliph of Jashyari. He was reputed to be the wealthiest in all of Persia."

"And you didn't let her go."

"How could I? I had a reputation to consider."

"The bigger they are, the harder they fall."

"So very true."

"How did you keep her? Did you lock her up or something?"

"Worse. I addicted her to the poppy."

"You turned her into a junkie?"

"Alas, yes, and in doing so, I destroyed everything about her that I had found attractive. In the end, I foisted her off on a second-rate prince out of Baghdad and was glad to be rid of her."

"So you turned her into a junkie and destroyed her life, and that's why you're here."

"You mistake matters, my friend. Those actions would merely have assigned me to Purgatory. What sent me here was the fact that I broke the cardinal rule of my profession—don't get personally involved. I did, with dire results, and that's what damned me."

"Man, that doesn't seem like much."

"Praise Allah! If it had been more, I might be up to my neck in this boiling shit. Or worse."

"You have a point."

"And you, my friend. What brings you here?"

"I guess it was that I connived my way toward the top of the corporate heap," Bob said, unable to prevaricate thanks to

Rule #409. "I was a lawyer, and I manipulated the company rules and the law for my own purposes, stepping on everybody I could. Actually, thinking back on it, I often acted as I did not because it might actually help me attain a goal but because it was fun to fuck people over and watch them squirm."

"Ah," Ahmed said. "You broke the rules of your profession to take pleasure in the pain of others."

"I didn't actually break any rules," Bob protested. "I bent them. Twisted is the word, Remoron used. If you twist the rules and get caught, you get slapped on the wrist instead of with a legal action. I admit that I was on the verge of breaking the law, but I hadn't actually done it yet."

"Bent and twisted instead of broken," Ahmed chuckled. "If I didn't already know you were a lawyer, I would be able to guess it from that. Ah, well," he shrugged. "Even so, it's an old story down here."

"And yours isn't?" Bob snapped, a bit disgruntled to have his sins so casually dismissed.

"It's quite common," Ahmed admitted. "But what else did you do?"

"Nothing."

"You must have done something a little more aggressive than what you've told me. There are plenty like you in Purgatory."

"There's nothing, I told you."

"Come on," Ahmed said. "You know the rules."

"Okay," Bob admitted, unable to help himself, and thinking that this really was hell for lawyers. And probably for politicians, too. "I guess there was one thing."

"Which was...?" Ahmed prompted.

"I died with a curse on my lips."

"Ah. That would do it. And who, if I may ask, was the un-lucky recipient of your curse?"

"I'm not really sure," Bob said.

"You cursed somebody, and you don't even know who it was?"

"I had this scheme going," Bob explained. "It was develop-ing quite nicely, too, and I was on the verge of cashing in. Then suddenly something went wrong. I realized that someone higher up was manipulating my own manipulations and leaving me to take the fall, but I never found out who. I was ranting about it in my apartment and cursing him, whoever he was, when bam! It felt like a ton of bricks was pushing an ice pick right into my chest. Then I fell down a long tube and ended up here."

"If you'd only known about curses and their consequences." Ahmed shook his head sadly.

"If I'd known it would send me here, I might have been more judicious with my phrasing."

"You couldn't have disguised the intent," Ahmed said. "That's what counts. It's the intent. But from what I've heard, curses are not irreversible. If you'd lived longer and forgiven the one you cursed, you probably wouldn't be here right now."

"That's what Remoron told me. He said that if I had, I'd have gone to Purgatory."

"Ah, Purgatory" Ahmed sighed, a distant and wistful look on his face. "What I wouldn't give to go home."

"Purgatory? But you told me you lived in Arabia."

"I did. Purgatory is Earth. Didn't Remoron tell you?"

"He must have forgotten. But I guess it makes sense."

"That's what reincarnation is all about. You don't cut the mustard the first time—and who does?—they send you back until you're good enough to go one place or bad enough to go to the other."

"Yeah, well, here I am. If only I knew who it was I cursed. You really think I'd be able to forgive him and get out?"

"Who knows? But don't get your hopes up. From what I can tell, death is some kind of impermeable dividing line. Before you died, you could just have forgiven in the abstract and gone on with your life, but now, the only way you can used the forgiveness clause is to forgive the one you cursed face-to-face."

"That's what Remoron said."

"But that means he—or maybe it was a she—would have to be down here."

"Oh, I'm sure whoever it was will be down here eventually," Bob said. "He was even better at manipulating the rules than I was, and I was pretty good. If he took over my operation and completed what I started, he'd have broken a lot of rules."

"Even if he was so good at it—or bad, actually—that he'd end up here, you'd still have to know who he was."

"Yeah, that's true." Bob shrugged. "Well, that shoots that way out all to hell."

"Just try not to think about it," Ahmed advised. "It's hard enough getting by here without letting self-recrimination eat you up."

"Listen," Bob said. "I've been meaning to ask you. Why are the rules so messed up? I mean, there's no order to them. Sure makes it hard to make sense of them."

"Maybe that's the point," Ahmed said. "Keeps you on your toes and thinking about them all the time. Or maybe it's just because this is Hell. Everything else here is in chaos, why not the rules?"

"How is it you know all this stuff?" Bob asked Ahmed. "Being stuck down here in this pit of shit, and all."

"When you've been here as long as I have, you can get a lot of information from Sapason."

"I thought he was here to punish us. Why would he give us information?"

"He'll often offer some tidbit of valid information even if it's just because he's trying to prove how superior he is to us," Ahmed replied. "He can't help himself."

"Can I ask you something else?"

"Make it quick. I'm feeling the urge to scream."

"Okay. Where does all the shit in this lake come from?"

"You're one curious guy," Ahmed chuckled. "Does it really matter?"

Bob started to answer that it might, but Ahmed's smile already was contorting as his mouth opened to vent his scream.

"I'll check with you later," Bob told the Arab, and Ahmed nodded in response without breaking the note of his shriek.

Turning his back to blunt the sound of Ahmed's outcry, Bob again opened *The Rule Book* and read some more, trying to organize his thoughts.

᷑ 12 ᷐

"I SEE YOU'RE UP EARLY," the Devil said as he came over to Angel. She was standing on a high parapet that afforded one of the palace's best views of Hell. Certainly it was the most expansive, overlooking all the region between the palace and Mount Etna. The River Acheron, which snaked its gangrenous way across the hellscape, curved broadly just below them, catching the reflected glare from the volcano in gorgeous reds and oranges.

"Did you sleep well?"

"Not too well," she said. "The bed was too hard."

"Really?" The Devil acted surprised, though actually he'd ordered Behemoth to give her the densest pallet in the palace. "I'll have Behemoth take care of that."

"Behemoth?"

"Yes, my personal servant. You've met him—the fellow with the trunk and tusks and body of an allosaurus."

"I thought Behemoth would be, well, bigger than he is."

"Size is all relative," the Devil said. "It wouldn't do to have some monstrously large butler, would it, if he couldn't get through doorways and such."

"I suppose not."

"Well, anyway, you look lovely, this morning."

"I look terrible," she said. "Isn't there any running water in this place? I need to freshen up."

"I'm afraid that all we have at the moment is either boiling or frozen solid," he admitted. "But I'll have Behemoth take care of that, too."

"No wonder everyone here smells so bad. Including you."

"I'm sorry," the Devil said. "Force of habit. What is it you need? I'll send someone for it."

She shot him a jaundiced look.

"Don't trust me, is that it?" The Devil gave her a wry smile.

"Never trust a man to shop for a woman," she said dryly.

"But I'm not a man."

"You're masculine enough," she said.

"Okay," he said, feeling pretty good that she'd noticed. "How about if I assign one of my female demons to shop for you? Would that be satisfactory."

"We'll see."

"Okay," he said. "Excuse me for a moment."

He left her and went over to his butler, who was standing a discreet distance off, near the doorway back into the palace.

"Call in a female demon to serve our guest," the Devil ordered. "Give her anything she asks for. Then I want you to send someone to Walgreens for mouthwash."

"Should I have it delivered to her apartment, Boss?"

"No, to mine. And while you're at it, pick up some soap and deodorant."

"You want I should get a comb, too, Boss?" Behemoth asked.

"You idiot! Look closely at me!"

The demon butler did, although the Devil was difficult to focus on as well as hideously fearsome in his evil magnificence.

"Does it look like there is any hair on my head? Or anywhere else on me, for that matter?"

"No, Boss." Behemoth shook his head, and his trunk waggled limply back and forth.

"Then what possible use would I have for a comb?"

"I don't know, Boss, but you never needed any of this other stuff before, either."

"Just go out and do my bidding," the Devil snapped. "Have the items delivered to my apartment within the hour."

"Yes, Boss." The butler scurried away, his trunk wagging back and forth, and the Devil returned to the parapet.

"Quite an impressive sight, isn't it?" he said, holding out his arms and wings as if embracing his domain.

"Lovely," she responded in a tone that implied the opposite.

"I'm sorry you don't like it."

"It's awful," she said. "Not to mention a sickening waste of space and resources."

"I'm inclined to agree with you."

"You are?"

"Certainly. You don't think I really approve of all this, do you?"

"But you made it."

"I?" He chuckled lightly. "I may be guilty of many things, but making all this isn't one of them. Nor did God make Heaven. They're both just natural constructs. Think of it like the Chinese concept of yin and yang. First there was an undifferentiated void, which the Chinese call the Tao. This void separated into two equally powerful halves that, through their interplay, created the dynamic that manifests everything we know as reality. My brother over there, who we affectionately refer to as the Big Cheese, is the yang, and I'm the yin."

"I thought the yin was the feminine half. You're pretty masculine to be feminine."

"Being contrary is part of my nature," the Devil replied.

"So God is a creative force, and you're an uncreative force?"

"Something like that," he said, looking a bit chagrined. "Though I like to think I have my own share of the creative impulse. But you must remember that neither of us is really the force itself—we're just manifestations of our respective forces."

"Something like personifications?"

"Exactly. And all this," he waved across the hellish landscape, "is simply a further manifestation of the essence of which I am the supreme personification. It's the same with the Big Cheese and Heaven, only in the opposite way, of course."

She was quiet for a few moments as she stared out over Hell. The hot breeze stirred her golden hair, exposing a lovely bit of neck. The Devil suddenly was tempted to bite it right then and there, but he controlled himself. All good things in their time, he thought, then he smiled innocently at her as she turned to face him.

"I just don't understand how you can do these terrible things to all these people," she said.

"Me?" He put a hand tenderly over his own chest where his heart would be if he had a heart. He blinked demurely. "I assure you that I am not doing anything to anyone."

"But I've seen you torturing people," she said.

"I'm sure it looks that way," he said. "But really, it is they who are torturing themselves. I'm just the instrument."

"Come on," she said. "A hammer doesn't look happy when it's pounding a nail, but you sure looked like it was fun when you were disemboweling that man or watching those rats eat those two men in the ship."

"You ever read books or go to the movies?"

"Yes. What's that got to do with it?"

"You ever feel glad when the villain gets his comeuppance? Even if he's blown up or crushed or falls onto a jagged piece of metal and dies painfully?"

"I guess so," she admitted.

"Sometimes the more painful the better, right?" She didn't answer, so he shrugged and went on. "Well, I guess it's the same with me. And believe me, I've seen a lot of villains in my time. I suppose I've become completely irritated—not to mention disgusted—with those who care so little about the true quality of their own actions or the results of those actions to themselves or others that they live their lives with such willful ignorance and stupidity. It's hard not to smile a little and even feel good about dishing out punishment."

"It's still horrible."

"Look, Marcus Aurelius once said...."

"Marcus who?"

"Marcus Aurelius. He was a ruler of Rome, in the late second century. He said that all the natural dichotomies, such as living and dying, reputation and disgrace, pain and pleasure, wealth and destitution, are neither good nor evil but are simply part of nature's work. It's how we respond to those dichotomies that counts. Humans can follow the course of love, which subjectifies and respects other people, or hate, which objectifies others and doesn't give a damn about them. That's why Hell is governed by rules. Subjectifiers have their own built-in sets of rules, but objectifiers don't. They have to be told what to do. So we give them rules and try to instill those rules through negative reinforcement."

"Why don't you use positive reinforcement?" Angel asked. "All the psychiatrists say that works better."

"Perhaps," the Devil said. "But the inmates had that chance back on Earth, didn't they? Besides, do you know how many psychiatrists are in Hell?"

"You don't have to enumerate," she said with a sigh and resigned expression.

"Anyway, Marcus goes on to say that the only thing that makes the good man unique is that he loves and welcomes whatever happens and, by harmoniously following God, does not pollute the divine daemon within himself. Except for the part about following God, which is a logical inconsistency, Marcus was right. Nature has made me evil, and I love and welcome it."

"I guess everyone should do his work well," Angel said, though she didn't sound completely convinced.

"Indeed," the Devil said. "Perhaps you will permit me to show you around. Maybe you will learn to accept the truth of what I'm saying."

"All right," Angel said. "I don't suppose I can stay cooped up here all the time. Besides, since I'm compelled to be by your side, I can't help following if you leave."

"Fine," the Devil said. "Just let me check my calendar to make sure I don't have any important appointments."

He produced his PDA, consulted it, tapped on the keys, then made a notation, using the talon of his left forefinger in lieu of a stylus.

"I'm surprised you have that," Angel said, pointing to the PDA just before in the Devil put it away.

"I have a busy schedule," the Devil said. "Not even I can remember everything."

"That's not what I meant. I guess I didn't expect computers down here."

"Computers are of my realm," the Devil chuckled. "After all, they're nothing but rules—millions and billions of them. Whole networks of rules. Nets, just like those woven by my lovelies, the spiders."

"It's just that everything else down here seems so primitive."

"Actually, we are very sophisticated," the Devil said. "Only the inmates are primitive. The rest of us have all the amenities. My demons, in fact, live in excellent hotels that would rate five stars back on Earth and are staffed by experienced hotel and restaurant professionals. Come, let me show you."

He gently draped his arm around her shoulders. He'd discovered that he could actually touch her if the act wasn't intended as a threat. She was quite soft, making her imperviousness all the more remarkable. Cloaking her with his wing, as if to protect her, and being careful to keep the venomous inner layer away from her skin, he escorted her into the palace.

๑ 13 ๑

"HEY, BOB!"

Bob looked up from *The Rule Book* to see Ahmed wading toward him with a man who looked East Asian and a Caucasian woman. Both, of course, were naked, but Bob didn't even look at the woman's breasts and pubis, even though she was an attractive brunette. He knew why: Rule #9,237, which read, No ogling except where ogling is an element of the punishment.

"Want you to meet a couple of folks," Ahmed said. "This is Margaretha and Yung-tzu. This is Bob."

"Always nice to meet new people," Margaretha said. Her accent sounded European.

"Margaretha was a famous double agent during World War I before the French executed her," Ahmed explained. "And Yung-tzu served as a tax collector for the emperor of China until the emperor caught him stealing and promptly collected his head."

"I didn't realize we could move around so much," Bob said. "Sure," Ahmed replied, "as long as you stay at your prescribed depth and don't try to get out."

"Of course you can go deeper," Margaretha chuckled, "but not many people want to do that. We usually just associate with folks at about our own level."

"I see you're still reading *The Rule Book*," Yung-tzu said.

"He's always reading the rules," Ahmed said. "Bob was a lawyer."

"I should have guessed," Margaretha laughed. "The lawyers always examine the rules, trying to find some hidden clause they can exploit."

Bob searched her tone for either sarcasm or a come-on but found neither.

"I take it that none of them have," he said, keeping the disappointment he felt out of his voice.

"Not yet, though some of the best are down here," Yung-tzu said.

"Really?" Bob said. "I'd like to meet them."

"That's probably not likely," Ahmed said. "Most of them are in worse places than this. At least the corporate lawyers are. Almost all the defense attorneys go upstairs."

"I don't know why," Bob said a bit petulantly. "They aren't any better than the rest of us."

"Apparently somebody else thinks differently."

"But what about those guys who defend mobsters and known killers and try to get them off even when they know they're guilty."

"It's their job, isn't it?" Yung-tzu said. "If they do what they're supposed to do to the best of their abilities, that makes them *good* lawyers, doesn't it?"

"But it doesn't make them good."

"Be that as it may," Ahmed said, "they stuck to the rules. I've heard that the lawyers for the really big mobsters are sitting right up there with the Big Cheese. Of course, they're all at his left hand, but they're up there, anyway. I guess he appreciates their expertise and advice."

"I think he just keeps them in reserve in case somebody raises a big fuss about some religious war that kills a lot of innocent people," Margaretha said. "If it comes to a class-action suit, who better to have on your team than a whole mob of mob lawyers?"

"All right, all right," Bob said. "I get the picture. I'm nothing special. I'm just a low-level corporate law geek who's probably lucky I kicked off when I did, or I'd be in one of those worse places you mentioned. But that doesn't mean I might not learn something useful from this." He tapped *The Rule Book*.

"You already have," Margaretha said.

"What?" Bob was genuinely curious.

"You've learned how powerful the rules are." As if to demonstrate, she shook her tits at him and writhed her hips seductively. The movements were very professional, but Bob couldn't help but not stare. "See?"

"Pay no attention," Ahmed said pointlessly. "She always does that to the new guys."

"It's not a taunt," she said with a shrug. "Just a demonstration. You don't think I don't want to eye a dick now and then? Or more. After all, look at me, I'm in the prime of my life. You don't think I'm horny as hell?"

They couldn't look at her prime of life, of course, but they all knew what she meant.

"No sex, I guess," Bob said.

"Rule #13,049," Yung-tzu intoned sadly. "No sex except where sex is part of the punishment."

"But there is *some* sex?" Bob asked hopefully.

"Of the authorized sort," Yung-tzu said. "From what I hear, it's not especially pleasant."

"Well, we're going over to see Pedro, now," Ahmed said. "He and Mwendi managed to get a deck of cards from one of the sprites a few years ago, and we're going to play poker."

"That's allowed?" Bob asked.

"No rule against it," Margaretha said.

"What do you play for?" Bob was curious since none of them had anything but their skin and their pain, and of course, their copies of *The Rule Book*, and he didn't think any of those could be gambled away. Not down here, at least.

"It's just for fun," she answered. "Sometimes we play rummy or spades or whatever. Today it's poker. Want to join us?"

"Later, maybe," Bob said. "I want to look at the rules some more."

"Suit yourself," Ahmed said. "But feel free to come on over when you get bored."

Bob watched the trio wade off toward a couple of other people sloshing around about a hundred feet down from where he was, then he turned back to *The Rule Book*. But after a while, he grew frustrated.

"Hey, Sapason," he yelled up at his demon jailer, who was busy pissing copiously onto of the inmates who was up to her waist in the lake's bubbling slop. The demon squeezed the last acidic drops from his huge hairy cock before ambling over to the bank nearest Bob.

"What do you get when you cross a lawyer with a horrible demon from Hell?" Sapason asked.

"I don't know," Bob sighed. "What?"

"Another lawyer."

"Very funny."

"I knew you'd like it, Daddy. Now, did you have something to say?"

"Yeah, why aren't these rules in any kind of logical order?" Bob complained, shaking *The Rule Book* at the demon. "You've got 'No ogling,' and 'No sex,' hundreds of pages apart. And they're not the only ones. It's practically impossible to make sense of it all."

"You're a lawyer," Sapason said. "You should be used to jumbled rules that don't make any sense."

"But that was on Earth," Bob pointed out. "If we have to live strictly by the rules here in Hell, they should be more clearly delineated."

"The rules were clearly delineated back on Earth, and you fucked up," his jailer replied. "As you so astutely pointed out, this is Hell. Why should we make it easy for you?"

"It just seems that they'd be simpler to learn if they were in some sort of order," Bob said. "Or at least in basic categories."

"Maybe we make it hard so you'll keep going over them until they're really well set in your mind. Besides, Bob, look around you. Do you see any kind of order, logical or otherwise?"

Bob had to admit he didn't. Hell—at least the limited areas he'd seen—was pretty disorganized.

"But things here seem very rigid," he pressed. "We really have to toe the line."

"Yes, rigidly chaotic does define this realm rather well. Or would you call it chaotically rigid?"

"But why?" Bob persisted. "If Hell *is* rules, then how do you explain the disparity between the rules, which dictate order, and the great disorder all around us and the disorder of the rules themselves?"

"Perhaps you simply do not comprehend the underlying order implicit in chaos and the rules," Sapason replied. "Anyway, I don't have the answers. I'm just an enforcer of the rules, not the one who generated them."

"But as a representative of the legal system, you have an obligation...."

"You're a fine one to preach obligation to law, order, and rules," Sapason snorted. "I have only one obligation, and that's to stand here and enjoy watching you suffer. And I do, Bob. Believe me, I do. What I don't have is the inclination or patience to debate with you. Besides, I see that Pedro has a card game going. I think I'll go piss on it."

"I thought there wasn't any rule against playing cards."

"There isn't," the demon said. "But there isn't any rule against pissing on a card game, either."

Sapason strode off down the bank, leaving Bob thoughtfully staring after him. But Bob wasn't really seeing the demon's gnarly, clumpily furred back. Instead, a couple of wheels were clicking into place in Bob's mind.

What was it the demon had said? There wasn't a rule against pissing on the card game. Did that imply that there were rules for the demon jailers as well as for the inmates?

Bob thumbed through *The Rule Book*. It took a while, but yes, right there was Rule #14,342: Each inmate is to be punished in a manner equitable with his or her crime(s). And Rule #719: Jailers are charged with meting out the exact punishment required.

That essentially stated that the jailers had rules—in this case, to punish not only exactly but equitably. But if playing cards wasn't against the rules, and not everyone played cards, then punishing card players for playing was neither exact nor equitable. Everyone would have to play cards and be pissed on for Sapason's actions to follow the rules, even if there were no rules against pissing on card games.

Bob glanced down the lake, and sure enough, Sapason was shooting a tremendous yellow arc across the bubbling fecal surface. The card players scattered in haste.

Yes, Bob smiled. There are rules for the jailers as well as for the inmates, but it seemed that there was some discrepancy in enforcement. Maybe there was some rule that governed that.

Bob couldn't remember one right off the top of his head, so he began looking, pausing now and again to scream when bursting boils of blistering shit spattered on his balls. But now that he knew what he was looking for, he was persistent. And at last, he found what he sought.

It was Rule #666: It cuts both ways.

↣ 14 ↢

"YOU POOR WOMAN," ANGEL SAID. She was bent over the woman, who was prostrate on a bed of red-hot nails. There was a faint sound of sizzling and the odor of cooking flesh, and the woman was moaning.

"What did she do?"

"She used sex and false appearances of love to manipulate others for her own ends."

"Sometimes women have to do that to men just to get by," Angel said a bit defensively.

"Who said she did it to men?"

"Give me some water," Angel said, unfazed.

"All right," the Devil said good-naturedly. He created a pitcher of water and handed it to her.

Angel attempted to pour the water onto the woman, but the liquid couldn't quite seem to touch her, and it ran off onto the parched, sandy soil, where it instantly soaked in.

The Devil wasn't going to tell her how futile her effort was because then she might stop, and he didn't want her to stop. When she bent over like that, her ass was outlined nicely against the soft, loose material of her gown. It appeared that she didn't have on any underwear, which the Devil found quite titillating.

"Do something," Angel said, straightening and staring at the Devil.

"What would you have me do?"

"Let her loose, of course."

"Sorry. I can't do that."

"You beast."

"Yes, certainly. But...." He waved her over to him. "Come closer. I want to tell you something."

She reluctantly obeyed, though she didn't seem any too happy with him.

"I admire your effort," he said when they were out of earshot of any of the inmates. "I really do. And believe me, I'd do something if I could. I don't *like* to see these people suffer, but I can't release them."

"You could if you wanted. You're the big shot down here."

"Yes, I am, but that doesn't mean I have any more control over reality than you do. In fact, I may have less."

"Sophistry."

"I'm simply trying to get you to see that, as the embodiment of a pure force, I am bound by nature in ways that people aren't. People might have their natures, too, but they also have a choice to act in ways contrary to both their hot animal impulses and their cold reason. How they deal with that balancing act is what determines their destination after they die. Some go to my counterpart on the other side, some come here, but most are somewhere in the middle, and they remain in Purgatory to work on things some more."

"But people have such a short time to live and learn," Angel complained. "How can they learn to do your balancing act properly in just one lifetime?"

"Only one lifetime?" the Devil answered with his own question. "Do you think Purgatory is some kind of gray land full of grey people who couldn't be black or white?" He shook his head. "Nope. Earth is Purgatory, and you keep getting reborn until you get it right enough—or wrong enough—to drift one way or the other."

"It's still horrible," she said. "What you do to them."

"I don't know," he shrugged. "It's kind of satisfying sometimes to see people get their proper due."

"I thought you said you didn't like tormenting them?"

"I don't *like* it," the Devil said, then he grinned a bit fiendishly. "But I do *love* it."

"That's even worse."

"Not really. There's a difference. You don't necessarily like what you love, or vice versa." He peered intently at her. "Wouldn't you agree?"

"I think you're trying to trap me with words."

"Not at all. Look at it like this: To help balance out creation, those of us who work here must turn our worst faces to the world. Angels are, perhaps, lucky in having a unified spirit motivated in a single direction by a single force. Those who must pose as demons indeed do the Devil's work—remember, we're forced to live in and endure Hell, too, except on the rare occasions that we visit Earth and experience relative, if transient, peace. Actually, we're simply divided—created that way for some reason. And not by God, if that's what you're still thinking. He's simply the one forced to do good. Don't you think he'd like to get drunk and punch somebody in the snoot then go get laid once in a while, just as I'd like a change of pace from all this pain, nastiness, and extremes of temperature? But the poor sod is bound to his cold, windy aerie as surely as I am to the dark, noisome furnace. And our bonds are much more powerful than those that hold that woman to her bed of nails. I'll let you in on a little secret if you promise not to tell anyone."

"I don't think I want to know any of your secrets," Angel said, but the Devil could see the glint of curiosity in her eyes. He cocked his head at her, raised an eyebrow, and gave an inviting little smile. "Oh, all right," she said. "I promise."

He bent and leaned so close to her that the spines on his bicep brushed her shoulder, but he noticed that she didn't flinch, and it sent a shiver up his dorsal ridge. "These people down here," he waved around. "All of them. They can leave any time they want."

"I don't understand."

"Look at her," he said, pointing to the woman prostrate on the bed of nails. "You see any ropes or chains? Is anyone holding her down?"

"Not that I can see," Angel said. "But just because I can't see it, doesn't mean that some force isn't keeping her there."

"You're right," the Devil said. "There *is* an invisible force holding her there. It's her own guilt."

"I don't buy that," she said. "You can't tell me that all the bad people feel guilty about what they've done."

"Maybe not consciously," he said, "but only true psychopaths can't tell the difference between right and wrong, and even we don't let those sorts out of high-security detention. For the rest of humanity, bad deeds have a way of depleting one's soul, and it's a full soul that allows you to drift in my brother's direction. Sort of like a balloon. Fill it with helium and it goes up. Half filled, it finds a median level, but empty, it falls to the floor."

"So you're saying that guilt is like an absence of helium in the balloon?"

"No. The human spirit is naturally buoyant, making its helium all the time. Guilt is like a leak that prevents the balloon from filling."

"And if these people patched their leaks, they'd float?"

"Exactly. But the trick is admitting that they have a leak, finding it, and figuring out how to patch it. If that woman would only realize that fact, she'd be off that bed of nails in a second."

"But I thought people were here for eternity."

"We tell them that to help keep them under control, but eternity's a long time," the Devil said. "Hell may be a pretty large place, but it would fill up eventually if we didn't find some way to let people go." He smiled. "We have to have our own leak, I guess."

Angel looked at the woman, her eyes thoughtful, then she turned back to the Devil.

"But what about the bed of nails?" she asked. "And the rats and the boiling lakes and all the other tortures and torments? Do all those just magically appear?"

"Of course not. My demons make them. We have quite a workshop. Naturally, there are a lot of old tried and true methods—many of them, incidentally, invented by humans, such as that bed of nails. But I have an ongoing contest to award new design concepts. Often, frankly, no special device is necessary, but when one is, the person just gravitates to it. Sure, we pretend that we assign particular torments, but really the torments just happen spontaneously. Remoron, our admissions officer, is quite adept at predicting the place each person will go."

"I don't know whether to believe that or not," Angel said. "I'll have to see more."

"Right this way," the Devil grinned, gesturing toward a path that led around a huge boulder. "You may get the idea from what you've seen that Hell is all hot and smoky and stinky, but there are other aspects. Let me show you."

He led her toward the path, and as they walked, he offered her his arm. After a moment's hesitation, she took it with a light hand, which thrilled him to no end.

After a few moments, the path took them through a gap in a stone wall. A group of brick masons was demolishing the wall on one side of the gap to lengthen the wall on the other side, so of course, the width of the gap remained consistent. Beyond the wall lay a plain mounded with piles of rubble and dominated by a large, flat-topped pyramid. Surrounding the pyramid were several thousand short men with brown skin, black hair, and hooked noses. They all wore ceremonial robes and headdresses made from fine cloth decorated with gold and brightly colored bird feathers.

As the Devil escorted Angel around the pyramid, she realized that all the men were not simply standing there—they were in a long line that began at the back side of the structure then circled the base to a winding queue that snaked in and out of the rubbled landscape. Finally, the queue went up the steep steps on the front face of the pyramid. At the top squatted a huge serpent with wings of brilliant plumage. It was quite as beautiful as it was fearsome.

"Is that a dragon?"

"Quetzalcoatl," the Devil replied. "The Toltecs and Aztecs thought it their god, and they sacrificed mightily to it. But like most religions, it all was really a power play used to control the masses."

"Those must be the priests."

"Yes. They had the joyous habit of cutting the living heart from their sacrificial victims. Now, it's their turn. See?"

The Devil pointed as Quetzalcoatl used it talons to snatch up the next priest in line. The man screamed and struggled until, with a quick jab of its beak, the feathered serpent bit out his heart then casually tossed the still-writhing body off the back side of the pyramid. Almost as an afterthought, the dragon spit the heart after the vanished body before reaching for the next priest in line.

"I suppose each one is resurrected," Angel said.

"Yep. They collect their hearts at the bottom, stuff them back into their chests, and get back in line. They're all healed up by the time they start back up the stairs."

"Is this what you wanted to show me?"

"Oh, no. We're headed to our glacier. Alpine ski runs complete with avalanches. Snowed-in passes. Matches that won't light. Ravenous sled dogs, wolves, and polar bears. There's all sorts of winter sports and cold-weather fun." He eyed her with some amusement. "I hope your dress will be warm enough."

He was really hoping it would be cold enough to make her nipples pop up.

↬ 15 ↫

"YOU ARE ONE CRAZY SON of a bitch," Ahmed said, sadly shaking his head. "If you're looking for either sympathy or brownie points from Sapason, forget it. And if you think you can somehow cut time off your sentence by increasing the pain, you can forget that, too. It doesn't work that way. Rule #9,169."

Rule #9,169 was, Bob remembered, No time off for good behavior.

"We're here for eternity," Ahmed said. "Might as well accept it." Ahmed wasn't just talking to Bob; he was talking down to Bob because Bob was sitting so that only his head remained above the surface of the boiling lake. His left hand was out, too, holding *The Rule Book* above the plooping splatters. Bob was listening to Ahmed, but he couldn't talk much because he was too busy screaming. If the boiling shit had hurt when it was only up to his thighs, it *really* hurt when it covered almost his entire body. Even so, Bob tried to make the best of it by thinking back to when he'd been about fifteen and had passed a couple of lazy, blissful summer hours lounging on a vine-covered boulder in a small copse of trees. The copse was on the edge of a field of knee-high grass, and all around, the sound of birds and insects wafted on a warm breeze that rustled the leaves above him, covering him with ripples of light.

Bob wasn't remembering the sunlight through the leaves or the birds and insect sounds, though, but the aftermath of the experience. The vines covering the boulder had been poison ivy, and he'd spent the next few weeks in raw paroxysms. But he learned that if he got into the shower and ran hot water on the rash, it would itch so badly that the sensation suddenly transformed into a pleasure that washed through him like a drug. It wasn't until later that he learned about endorphins and realized that he probably *had* been making himself high. At the time, he only knew that the sensation was the most intense pleasure he'd ever felt.

Bob wasn't sure that this particular effort was producing endorphins. In a way, he hoped it wasn't. If it was and he still felt this much suffering, then God help him if his body stopped producing the endorphins.

"Come on, Bob," Ahmed urged. "Get up. You're making a spectacle of yourself."

Ahmed seemed concerned, but curiosity was in his eyes, too. He thought he heard in Bob's scream a note of joy that he'd never heard in all his time in Hell. But it was as downright unsettling as it was odd, so Ahmed left Bob and headed toward the card game that was going on before Sapason, who was presently occupied on the far shore, noticed and returned to piss on it.

Bob wasn't sorry to see Ahmed go, though he liked the Arab. But right now, Ahmed was distracting him from his work, which was to become the model inmate of Hell, to really appreciate the nuances of his punishment, and above all, to take pride in a job well done.

That last was the key, he thought, and it all hinged on an obscure rule that wasn't a rule. Not exactly. Instead of being an admonition or command, it was a simple statement sandwiched between two lengthy and rather technical rules that were somewhat boggling with their strings of counter negatives and reversals that made them seem to say the opposite of what they stated. Or, maybe even what they meant.

This one little statement—#3,387, to be exact—said, "You are in Hell because you didn't follow the rules on Earth."

Well, hell, Bob thought when he'd first read it. No shit. Hadn't the demon jailers said that from the outset? So he'd passed over it, looking for more fertile ground. But it was while he was pondering the ramifications of Rule #14,342: Each inmate is to be punished in a manner equitable with his or her crime(s), and Rule #719: Jailers are charged with meting out the exact punishment required, that he came across it again, and this time, something about it seemed odd.

On its surface, it was, of course, a simple statement of obvious fact. But after he thought about it, was that fact really so obvious? Or was it simply apparent? He remembered a line from the Lord's Prayer that went, "on Earth as it is in Heaven." That seemed to imply that Heavenly behavior was possible on Earth. Combined with Rule #3,387—bolstered, in fact, by Rule #666: It cuts both ways—did that mean, by extension, that Earthly—and, by extrapolation, intentionally Heavenly—behavior was possible in Hell? And what would be the consequence of that? If you behaved in a good and admirable way, did it somehow make your spirit less corrupt? And if it was less corrupt, shouldn't your punishment then be less, according to Rule #14,342, to make it equitable with your crime?

But Bob had to admit that there were a couple of sticking points. First were the facts that time seemed to flow forward in Hell, just as it did on Earth, and that his crimes already had been committed. That would seem to make alternate readings of Rule #14,342 moot unless he somehow could make his diligence to the rules retroactive in a way that negated his past behavior. He pondered that idea hopefully before realizing it just wasn't going to happen. Also there was that rule Ahmed just had mentioned about no time off for good behavior.

But deep down, Bob couldn't believe that behaving—dare he say it?—angelically wouldn't have some positive effect on his circumstances. If he behaved well, then certainly he would suffer less. Rule #4,206—Punishment does not preclude pleasure, as long as the pleasure isn't in the punishment—did not prohibit it.

The only way that Bob could see to behave in a good and admirable way in this place was to accept his punishment as just and not fight against it. That was not something that anyone else he'd met here seemed to do. Instead, they all complained and tried to avoid Sapason's urine and whip and other random acts of cruelty. Rule #4,206 seemed to mean a couple of things.

First, that he couldn't take pleasure if pleasure was part of the punishment he was receiving, and second, that he could not masochistically enjoy the pain he was feeling. But neither implied that he couldn't take a moral satisfaction in the rightness of his situation. After all, he *had* been a bad boy in life. He could admit that. But he had been somewhat industrious, too. Back in law school, he'd often hit the books when he could have partied—thanks in large part to that asshole legal ethics professor. So he knew how to discipline himself and immerse himself in something unpleasant with the prospect of better things to come. And wasn't discipline the first step on the road to living properly?

That left only one question: If he suffered less because he was a better person, could his jailers do worse to him to help maintain the status quo of his punishment? He wasn't sure, but if they heaped a greater punishment on him, then that would seem to be inequitable and certainly in contradiction to Rule #14,342.

Despite the potential pitfalls, Bob thought his plan was worth a try. He'd squatted into the boiling shit and felt the pain, and with each bubble of fetid air that rolled up his body and burst beneath his nose, he more fully understood the rightness of what was happening.

About an hour after Ahmed had gone to join the card game, Sapason came over and sent a golden, gleaming shower of piss onto Bob's head.

"You fucking freak," the demon sneered. "You think you're something special, dunking yourself like that? Well, let me remind you that you're nothing but a pipsqueak in Hell. We've got people here who flay and devour themselves alive. We've got suicide bombers who blow up their own families every day. We've even got one asshole named Hitler who has to sit in front of a mirror and constantly stare into his own eyes while he counts to eleven million over and over. You're just bad enough to be thigh-deep in shit, so don't inflate your own importance."

Sapason quit pissing on Bob—not because he was drained, since he seemed to have an unending supply, but because he'd finally caught sight of the card players huddled up the lake.

"Be seein' ya, Bob," the demon said as he padded off on his well-worn path along the bank.

Bob barely noticed him leaving. He was too taken aback by the demon's words. Was he really as arrogant as the demon said? By so fully immersing himself, was he taking punishment that was, perhaps, undeserved? That would be prideful. Gracious, he thought. What an error!

Bob stood up, absently watching Sapason break up the card game. He kind of wished that the demon would come back and piss on him again to rinse some of the shit off his body, but no matter. He'd sweat it off soon enough.

And, yes, this really was much better—not because he was suffering less, but because he was suffering properly. The thought brought a small flush of pleasure that wanted to be pride, but Bob stopped that quickly enough, and that felt good, too. Yet he could, he discovered, take a sort of abstract pride in a job well done and pleasure in the fact of his own proper punishment.

He screamed for a while, hearing just the right note of righteous joy mingle with the pain, but a couple of hours later, he saw Ahmed approaching, and he stopped. It wouldn't be polite to ignore the man who had become his best friend here.

"I see you've quit acting foolishly," Ahmed said as he came up.

"I had to try it," Bob said. "Besides, what does it matter? This is Hell. What worse can happen?"

"You're not thinking clearly," Ahmed said, shaking his head. "You just spent the last thirty-six hours up to your neck in boiling shit instead of just up to your thighs, so I'd say it is possible for worse to happen if you choose."

"I guess so," Bob admitted, chagrined.

"Come on over and play cards," Ahmed urged. "Sapason went off around the lake, so we're getting together again. Today's gin rummy day."

"All right."

Bob sloshed after Ahmed to the small group.

In addition to Margaretha and Yung-tzu, who he'd already met, there was a strapping African named Mwendi, and the laconic but sharp-eyed Pedro, who hailed from Mexico. The two men had something in common, which was why both were exactly groin-deep in the lake: They'd fucked over their own kind. Mwendi had been a warlord back in the eighteenth century who'd sold several villages of his tribe to Arab slavers, and Pedro had been a nineteenth-century bandito who'd betrayed his own gang for part ownership in a tequila distillery.

"I liked running the distillery and drinking shots better than running around in the desert and getting shot at," Pedro shrugged.

Mwendi was less circumspect. "I got to shag all the women before the Arabs took them," he confessed.

"He went to Hell because he had hot balls," Margaretha said with a trace of sarcasm. "And now they're hotter than ever."

"Yeah," Mwendi winced. "Man, I wish I could air them out now and then."

"Not much chance of that," Pedro said, gritting his teeth. "Come on. Let's get on with the game before one of us starts screaming or Sapason comes back."

"Bob has to be the table," Yung-tzu said.

"The table?" Bob asked.

"One of us has to hold out *The Rule Book* for the others to play on. Since this is your first time, you get the honors."

"Sounds fair," Bob said, holding out his copy of *The Rule Book*.

"You might not think so after an hour," Ahmed chuckled. "That book can get mighty heavy."

Bob held out his book about sternum height.

"Lower it down some, Bob," Margaretha said.

As Bob did, Ahmed stared at him, puzzled. "I didn't remember you being quite so tall."

Bob didn't either. Until now, he'd always thought that Ahmed was about his own height, but now the Arab seemed shorter.

"Shit, Bob!" Ahmed gasped, pointing at Bob's legs.

Bob looked down and saw the tops of his knees, then he stared back at Ahmed. Bob wasn't taller—he was simply in shallower shit. Several inches shallower.

"How did you do that?" Ahmed asked, awe tingeing his voice.

"I'm not sure," Bob admitted. "Maybe it was faith in the rules."

❧ 16 ☙

"MORE WINE, MY DEAR?" THE Devil held out a crystal decanter filled with a blood-red cabernet.

Angel shook her head. "One glass of red is enough for me," she said. "I prefer a white, like chardonnay."

"Of course," he said, pouring another glass for himself before setting the decanter down and stoppering it. "Unfortunately, the term white is somewhat of an anathema down here, and items referred to that way are rather difficult to come by. Your own attire excluded, of course. Would you settle for a blush? That would be perfectly acceptable. I can have Behemoth order a case."

"You needn't bother."

"But I want to bother." He peered at her. "Did you enjoy your meal?"

"It was all right," she said, delicately patting her lips with her napkin.

"You didn't like it," he said. "I can tell. What was wrong? Was it too spicy?"

"No, really, it was fine."

"Oh, I know," he said, shrugging helplessly, waving at the food. "All this stuff looks really good, and it should be the best Hell has to offer, but there's always something wrong with it—a little too much pepper here, too much salt there, or not enough of something where it's needed."

"Perhaps you should get a new cook. Not that I want you to punish the old one," she added hastily.

"It's not the cook," the Devil admitted. "It's just that this is Hell, and even I can't get a really good meal. The chef is—was—world-class, and his assistants are all five-star chefs themselves. They're the best we have, and we provide them with the finest ingredients we can, but their punishment is to cook great meals that always taste off-color. Frankly, I'm sick of eating their lousy cooking, but what can I do?"

He tossed his own napkin onto his half-eaten plate of food with a gesture of frustration.

"Maybe...," she began tentatively, then stopped.

"What?" he prompted.

"Oh, nothing," she said, waving airily. "Just a fleeting thought. Can we go outside for a while?"

"Onto the battlements?" he suggested, rising and coming around the table to pull out her chair.

"Yes," she said.

She took his arm, and they went outside. The battlements on this side of the Devil's palace overlooked a broad but shallow plain, here and there pitted with noxious swamps and lakes filled with various sorts of vile substances and dangerous creatures. All of them were fed by the diseased River Acheron after it wound its way around the base of the palace's mountain. Just beyond the plain snaked a long, narrow, and very ragged ridge that resembled the spine of some titanic and horrific creature embedded in the earth. The ridge masked the ground between itself and an even-more distant range of forbidding mountains whose jagged peaks were lost in a dark-gray smoky haze slashed with pitchfork-shaped bolts of lighting.

The two of them leaned on the parapet in silence for a few moments, Angel staring out over the hellscape, the Devil watching her. He was trying to trace the line of her breasts, but though Angel's gown was just diaphanous enough to let through a glimpse of the dark buds of her nipples when they pressed against it, it was a trifle too loose to show much else. But it was pulled a bit more tightly over her back and ass, so he turned his attention there.

"I just don't understand it," she murmured after a pause.

"Don't understand what, my dear? All that?" He gestured with his chin outward, over the battlements.

"No, not that. Your explanations have been most informative about all that." She straightened and turned to face him, her eyes on his and as frank as his own. "You."

"Me?" He chuckled. "I'm not all that difficult to understand. As I said, I'm simply the embodiment...."

"Oh, I heard what you said." She turned her eyes from him, but she didn't look out over the hellscape. Instead, she stared at the sooty flagstones.

"Are you unhappy?" he asked.

"Unhappy?" It was her turn to chuckle. "Yes, I guess I am."

"What can I do?"

"Do? I don't suppose *you* can *do* anything," she said. "Or maybe you've already done too much."

"It's not like you to talk in riddles," he said.

"You already know me so well?" she asked, a bit sharply.

"No," he said truthfully. "I'm not sure I'll ever know you well, though I admit I'd like to know you better."

"And I you," she said, looking at him again, this time with a strange light in her eyes that he found perplexing. Only one being had ever looked at him that way before, and that was his direct counterpart on the rare occasions they had face-to-face interactions. But while he always despised it in his counterpart, in Angel's eyes, it held a certain allure.

She reached out and took his powerful ebony hand in her soft white fingers and absently stroked the talons. It was quite nice, he thought. Soothing.

"Don't get the idea that I like this place," she said abruptly. "I don't. I hate it. I hate almost everything about it." She looked to be on the verge of tears.

"No, you don't," he said, gripping her hand. "You don't have hate within you. You pity. What you see disturbs you, and you wish things were different."

"Call it what you like," she said. "But there is one thing I don't hate."

"What's that?"

"You," she said. "You seem so unlike what's going on here."

"You do not think I am demonic?" he asked, pulling his talons away from her hand, stepping back, and spreading his arms and wings majestically, revealing every bristling spine dripping poison, every glistening inch of toxic skin. He flexed his talons, and the air sparked where they tore it, leaving little puffs of smoke.

"You are perfectly demonic," she said without dropping her eyes. Nor did they fill with fear as anybody else's would have but, instead, glistened even more with that mysterious look he'd noted earlier. "Maybe that's why it's happened."

"Why *what* has happened?" he asked, lowering his wings.

"Me."

"I don't understand."

"Of course you don't." She raised her eyes, and he was shocked to see they were brimming with tears.

"Has something hurt you," he asked, voice filled with concern. "If one of my minions has so much as touched a hair on your head...."

"It's not them," she said. "It's you."

"Me? I didn't hurt...."

"It's not hurt."

"But you're crying."

"I'm crying from joy."

"Joy?" The Devil had heard of such a thing, but he'd never witnessed it this close. "I don't understand."

"Of course you don't, but you see, it's really very simple. I've fallen in love with you."

"With me?" The Devil said it demurely, but he could feel a stirring in his loins. He stepped up to her and put gentle talons on her shoulders. "That's crazy."

"I know," she said, sliding her arms around his waist and moving into his embrace. "But they say opposites attract."

"Is that what they say?" he asked, folding his arms and wings around her. The stirring in his loins stirred a little more.

"I love you," she said, "And I don't know why. Do you love me?"

"I?" The Devil was suddenly nonplussed. There was something stirring in his chest, too, but it was so alien to him that he couldn't identify it. "I?"

"Say it, my love," she urged, her breath hot on his chest. "Say it. I know you feel it, too."

"I...I," he stammered. "I...." He was stuck between the words that wouldn't come and the sudden stiffening of his member, which was beginning to lift the hem of Angel's diaphanous gown.

Suddenly, her eyes hardened, and she jerked out of his embrace and slapped the head of his cock, which abruptly deflated.

"Uh-uh, buster," she snapped. "None of that, now!"

"But isn't that what people in love do?"

"I'm pure as the driven snow," she reminded him. "We can do that all you want after we're married."

"Married?"

"Yes, isn't that what people in love do?"

"But if we know we're going to...."

"Uh, uh, buster. "You may be a big, handsome brute, and maybe I'm in love with you, but don't get the idea that I can change my nature any more than you can yours."

"So no whoopee until we hear the chapel bells?"

"That's right."

"But there are no chapels down here, and no bells."

"We can go somewhere else."

"But isn't there a residence requirement? I can't leave here on some extended jaunt. Who'd run things while I was gone?"

"I prefer not to know anything about your work," she said. "You know I don't approve."

"What about Las Vegas or Reno?" he said. "We can get hitched in just a few hours."

She shook her head.

"I'm sure you'd feel very at home there," she said. "But I had a real church wedding in mind. Back home in Kansas."

"I'm not sure I'd be welcome in a church," the Devil said morosely. "Or in Kansas. Even for that."

"No matter, my dear," she said giving him a hug that was too quick to encourage another display of his devilhood. "Love will find a way."

♋ 17 ♋

"WHAT THE FUCK IS GOING on around here, Bob?"

Bob looked up at Sapason and shrugged.

"Why ask me? You're the one in charge."

"You're the only one acting normally," Sapason snapped. "Besides, I know you must have something to do with it. You sank yourself neck deep, and now everybody is doing it. I want to know why."

Indeed, it was true. Bob was standing at his new, slightly elevated height, but everyone else in the lake was neck deep. Of course, some of them—those farther out in the lake—always were neck deep or worse, but now, even that fat old Russian woman, who normally was only up to her ankles, was flat on her back like a beached whale. Every once in a while, she'd flop over to baste her other side, sending out miniature tsunamis that engulfed the heads of those closest to her.

Everybody was submersed because they'd all heard that Bob had somehow raised himself out of shit, even if only a little way, by first sinking himself deeper, and they all were emulating him in hopes that they, too, would ultimately find less suffering. But Bob wasn't about to tell Sapason that. So far, the demon hadn't noticed that Bob was only knee-deep instead of thigh-deep, and Bob didn't want to draw undue attention to that fact.

"I'd've thought you'd get a kick out of it," Bob said. "They're all suffering more than they have to. And listen to the nice chorus they make."

Everyone was screaming, and they did, indeed, make fine, if somewhat incoherent, harmony.

"It is kinda nice," Sapason admitted. "Sounds like a banshee's wail." He shook his shaggy head. "I still don't like it. Something's going on, and I know it has something to do with you."

"Why me? I'm just reading *The Rule Book* like always. I'm not even close to any of them." Bob waved across the lake, and as he did, he laughed.

"What's so funny?" demanded the demon.

"It's just that they remind me of a bunch of apples floating around in a barrel, waiting for someone to come along bobbing for them."

"Yeah. Too bad I can't call in some ogres to do just that. But I can go piss on those suckers until they have to stand up for air." Without another word, Sapason stomped off down the bank.

That was fine with Bob. He didn't care what the demon did, as long as he left him alone because Bob had some thinking to do. He opened *The Rule Book* and began studying it.

His new line of reasoning followed logically from the old, though he now suspected that immersing himself neck-deep in the boiling shit hadn't been what had elevated him. He was sure that many before him had tried the tactic of increased suffering, despite Rule #9,169: No time off for good behavior. If it worked, it would have attracted notice and been common knowledge long before now.

But Bob's elevation did seem to be related somehow. Wasn't self-discipline the first step on the road to living properly? True, the self-disciplined could wander astray as easily as the undisciplined—a disciplined murderer is still a murderer. But that did not negate the fact that discipline was the foundation of any higher aspiration. He'd learned that back in law school, where hard work had put him near the top of the class, and more recently, when he'd found himself in shallower shit after forcing himself to suffer for the rightness of it rather than for a desired result.

At a gut level, he knew that it hadn't been the extra suffering that had raised his level, but something else, and he had an inkling

108

of what it was. Interestingly enough, the key lay in the rules. Or rather, the dichotomy between the rules and his surroundings.

Until now, rules had simply seemed to be what they purported to be: a pattern to follow for proper behavior. Live by the rules, and you didn't get in trouble. But simple adherence to the rules, per se, or even behaving properly, didn't ensure that you would advance—they only maintained some sort of status quo. How had Remoron put it? Only the people who had internalized rules went to Heaven. That meant that the rules in *The Rule Book* were enforced by external obligations and compulsions. And probably most of the rules back on Earth were the same. For the first time in all his legal career, Bob felt that he truly understood the term law enforcement.

The confusing thing was something Bob had complained about before, though the true implications hadn't fully struck him until now. And this is where the dichotomy came in. If, to be true and real, rules are a pattern for behavior, then they had to adhere to their own internal definitions to have genuine meaning. And the operative word was pattern. Rules, themselves, have to follow a pattern. But as Bob had noted, those in *The Rule Book* were a jumbled mess, with rules that should logically follow one another often separated by hundreds of pages.

On it's face, that seemed perfectly reasonable. This was Hell, after all, as Ahmed and Sapason had pointed out. A near-chaos of the irrational. Why should *The Rule Book* be any different? But if the rules were so jumbled that it was impossible to get a glimpse of the overall pattern the rules made, how could it be possible to really and truly follow the rules in spirit as well as in individual instances? There was, in short, no order to the rules of Hell even thought their purported purpose was to maintain order.

And it went even deeper. Hell was disordered, and it also was rule driven, but how can something that is rule-driven be disordered if rules are those things that make patterns and order? It just didn't make sense. Not that it had to, Bob realized, but if it didn't, then the rules would have no force, and Bob knew quite well that those in *The Rule Book* did. He'd been made to shut the fuck up, and he'd tried to walk out of the boiling shit but couldn't. But if the rules were real and made actual patterns that enforced themselves on this reality, why was this rule-driven place so chaotic? Order had to breed order, or intrinsic disorder had to negate any rules.

After all, according to Rule #666, it cuts both ways.

Bob wasn't entirely sure what was going on, but he thought he had a way to cut through this procedural Gordian knot, and he bent over his copy of *The Rule Book*, reading rapidly and flipping the pages.

He was so engrossed in his work that he didn't see Sapason piss on everybody who was trying to make things worse for themselves—all those he could reach, that is. Finally, one by one, they all stood up, gasping and sputtering, still at their same old level but secretly glad that the demon had forced them to abandon their extra, self-imposed torment. None of them really believed it would work, anyway.

After they'd dried off sufficiently, Bob's friends gathered once more to play cards, taking the opportunity while Sapason was on the far bank. Ahmed went over to Bob to see if he wanted to play.

"No, thanks," Bob said. "But stay for a minute. I've been meaning to ask you about Rule #14,342."

"You're not going to try to argue that you aren't being punished in a manner equitable with your crime, are you?" Ahmed asked.

"No. Remoron made it perfectly clear that a little turd like me belongs in a cesspool. I was just thinking about how Sapason goes around whipping everybody and pissing on them."

"Yeah. So?"

"Is that part of their punishment? Rule #719 says that jailers are charged with meting out the exact punishment required."

Bob distinctly remembered Remoron sentencing him to an eternity in the lake of boiling shit, but he didn't remember any mention of whipping or getting pissed on.

"I don't know," Ahmed said. "You'd have to ask them."

"How about you? Is that part of your punishment?"

"I'm not sure," Ahmed admitted. "I was sentenced so long ago, I don't remember. What are you getting at?"

"It just seems that the whipping and pissing puts the people nearest the shore at greater risk."

"I guess it does. I never thought about it like that."

"Hmm," Bob said, pondering this bit of information.

"He can piss a really long way," Ahmed mentioned helpfully.

Indeed, Sapason's penis practically looked and functioned like the nozzle of a fire hose. Even so, Bob suspected that the inmates inhabiting the more central regions of the lake would be out of the demon's range, and he'd never seen Sapason drench anybody farther out than about sixty feet.

"Sure you don't want to play cards?"

"Maybe later. I want to think some more about this." Bob indicated *The Rule Book*.

Shrugging, Ahmed returned to the game.

"He's busy studying *The Rule Book*," the Arab explained to the others.

"All work and no play makes Bob a dull boy," Mwendi commented, and they all laughed, but not very hard. They all liked Bob, and they admired what he'd accomplished, but they also pitied the way he seemed to be so desperate to find a way out of the lake that he forsook the few small pleasures that could be had in this place.

Bob remained completely oblivious, even when Sapason returned and pissed on him for good measure. He simply held *The Rule Book* out of the shower and stood resigned but un-reacting until Sapason got bored and wandered off.

Bob could afford to be patient because something had finally clicked in his head. It wasn't the extra suffering that had elevated him but the way he'd put several of the rules together into a logical sequence that had done it. It was order, not suffering. If Heaven was peopled with those who adhered to internal rules and Hell peopled with those who ignored those rules, then the only way out of this place was to internalize the rules. But by definition, the inmates did not know how to internalize the rules, so Bob had to approach his escape in another way. He had to reach an intermediary between internal adherence and external enforcement, which seemed to indicate that he needed to do more ordering of the rules—something far more extensive than simply memorizing them.

With a start, Bob realized just how insidious Rule #6,935 was. Inmates must completely memorize all the rules, it read, and it was insidious precisely because the inmates invariably memorized the rules in a haphazard order that was further compounded by the already disordered sequence displayed in *The Rule Book*. In effect, it led the inmates to a chasm that separated the only apparently true from that which really was true, leaving them with no way to cross and no clear picture of what lay on the other side.

But Bob thought he knew what lay on the other side. It was a way out. All he had to do was to build a bridge across the chasm using the only tools at his command—the rules.

The next time Sapason passed close, Bob flagged him down.

"Say, Sapason, you got a pen or a pencil on you?"

"What the hell do you need one for?"

"It's these rules. I'm having a little trouble remembering some of them, and I just wanted to make a few notes."

"Tough shit."

"I really think you should give me something to write with. You might be in violation of the rules if you don't."

"Where's the rule that says I have to give you a pencil?"

"Rule #6,935." Bob thumbed to the appropriate page. "'Inmates must completely memorize all the rules.'"

"So?"

"So, I'm having trouble and need to make some notes, and if you don't help, that means you're willfully obstructing me from my sincere and honest attempt to abide by the rules. That means *you're* the one breaking the rule."

"Sounds like a lot of legal double-speak to me," Sapason said, but he produced a pencil and tossed it to Bob. "Now I suppose you want a note pad."

"That's okay. *The Rule Book* has wide margins. I'll just use those."

"I'm not sure you should do that."

"There isn't a rule against marginalia," Bob pointed out.

"You're right there. By the way, Bob, what's the difference between an onion and a lawyer?"

"I don't know," Bob replied dutifully.

"You cry when you cut up an onion."

"What a card," Bob said. "You should go on stage."

"I consider this bank my stage. Theater in the round, so to speak, although the audience is full of crap. But speaking of cards...." He lumbered off toward Ahmed and his friends.

That was fine with Bob, because he had work to do. He set to it, and at last, after exactly fifteen days, eight hours, thirty-seven minutes, and eighteen seconds, Bob made his last notation and closed the book. It had been a hell of a job, but he'd put all the rules in a logical order, complete with cross-references. And he didn't even have to open the book now to know what rule was where and which other rules it was related to. Even better, he'd ordered them in his head, and they formed neatly ranked rows indelibly fixed in his memory.

He smiled to himself, realizing that he had become, in a sense, an embodiment of the rules in their true order—perhaps the first in the history of Hell to accomplish that task. It may not have been truly internalizing the rules, but it was the next best thing. It was a beginning.

He glanced up and around. The card players were playing cards, Sapason was a quarter of a mile away, cracking his whip over one of his favorite inmates, and the rest of the people in the boiling shit were doing whatever it was they'd chosen to do to pass their incredibly boring and painful existences. Bob smiled again and tucked the pencil behind his ear and *The Rule Book* beneath his arm.

Then, feeling absolutely no trepidation, he turned toward the bank and started walking.

❧ 18 ❧

"WHAT'S THIS?" THE DEVIL WAVED over the several dishes of food that Behemoth set on the table.

"Your dinner, sire."

"It can't be. It smells too good."

"I believe that madam prepared it herself."

"Madam?"

"Your consort, sire. Angel."

"There's been no consorting, you lummox. At least not yet. By the way, where is she?"

The Devil was suspicious. Angel insisted on being by his side as much as possible, but he hadn't seen her for several hours. Not that he wasn't glad for the respite. It could be taxing as hell to have someone watching you all the time and making inane, counterproductive comments about your work, especially when you took your work as seriously as the Devil did.

"She is in the kitchen. She says she'll be out shortly."

Angel emerged moments later, wearing a flowery apron over her white shift, but she took off the apron before she reached the table and handed it to Behemoth, who held it between his thumb and forefinger as if it were a soiled diaper.

"Please bring in the wine, Behemoth," she told the demon, who used his other hand to hold her chair.

"Yes, madam." Behemoth scooted the chair beneath her then headed for the door.

"Don't tell me you prepared all this," the Devil said to her as Behemoth left the room.

"I did, and I hope you like it since it was hot as...well, you know. It was very hot in the kitchen."

"You shouldn't be doing things like that," the Devil said. "That's what I have servants for."

"Try it," she said, lifting the lid of one of the serving platters and handing him a carving knife and fork. "Will you do the honors?"

"I suppose I'll have to," he replied as a delicious smell wafted up from the meat on the platter. It not only smelled good, it looked that way, too, like a carcass that had been exploded from the inside, leaving all the rib bones pointing outward. "Is this a rack of lamb?"

"I hope you like it. I had trouble ordering lamb down here. Your supply department told me that lambs weren't allowed in Hell. But I told them it was a baby goat, and that worked."

"You're quite ingenious, my dear." The Devil forked some meat onto her plate and then piled his own high.

"Vegetables?" she asked, lifting a couple of other lids.

"You know I have trouble digesting anything but meat," he said.

"You might reconsider," she said. "Here are Brussels sprouts. Some people think they're bitter, but they might be to your taste. And there are artichoke hearts."

"I like that name," the Devil said. "I'll try one, and one of those Brussels sprouts." He put one of each onto his plate beside the huge pile of steaming meat. "All this smells delicious. I hope you didn't let my usual chefs interfere."

"They helped, but I insisted on doing the seasoning and final cooking."

At that moment, Behemoth reappeared, bearing two bottles, both labeled pinot noir. He deftly opened one and poured some into Angel's glass, but instead of being deep red, the wine that came out was white. Then he opened the second bottle and poured a glass for the Devil, and this one was red.

"I can't believe it," the Devil said, raising his glass in a toast. "How did you get a white wine down here?"

"It took some doing," she admitted, clinking her glass against his. "First, I had Behemoth instruct one of the demons who was going to Earth to engage in a bit of deviltry at the printing plant where they print the labels for a certain small vineyard in southern France known for its excellent stock. Instead of having some labels for the chardonnay and some for the pinot noir, they all read pinot noir. Then the demon went to the vineyard and caused the bottling crew not to notice that they were mislabeling all their chardonnay as pinot noir. After that, I simply had the supply department purchase their entire stock of pinot noir and ship it down here. Because the bottles were labeled as red, they didn't know the difference."

The Devil gave a hearty laugh.

"If I didn't know better, I'd say you have a bit of devil in you, after all."

"Oh, no. The demon that Behemoth sent was happy to wreak a little havoc on both the printer and the vineyard. But the printer got paid, and the vineyard didn't have to deal with any mislabeled bottles since we bought them all, which made their fiscal year. And we're both happy with the kinds of wine we like. Everybody is happy and satisfied at the same time."

"You don't think you were dishonest with the supply department in deceiving them about the contents of the mislabeled bottles?"

"Not really. But if I was, they're demons and probably would appreciate the gesture."

"I suppose you're right."

"Be sure to eat your vegetables," she said.

Looking dubious, the Devil speared the Brussels sprout and held it up for examination.

"It bears some resemblance to a small, green brain," he commented, wrinkling his nose. She gave him a severe look, and he said, "Oh, all right," and popped the sphere into his mouth. "Yes," he said after a few chews. "It is wonderfully bitter. Perhaps I'll have another."

"Don't talk with food in your mouth," she said.

He acquiesced, not because she commanded him to but because he hadn't had such a good meal in a millennium.

When dinner, which included a dessert of chocolate mousse, was over, Angel hurried back to the kitchen.

"Let the servants clean up," the Devil told her.

"I can't leave them unsupervised," she said. "They don't do a proper job. Why go to all the trouble of fixing a good meal like this if the pots and pans are dirty and the plates and glasses smudged?"

"I hadn't really noticed," the Devil said, though he had. He couldn't remember the last time his wine glass actually had sparkled like it did tonight.

After she left, he took the opportunity to go to his office to take care of a few administrative matters. Thanks to the time he was spending with Angel, he was falling behind on routine paperwork, and lately, he found himself having to work more and more during the evenings.

On the way to his office, he was distracted by small changes here and minor alterations there. Carpet runners had appeared in the hallways, curtains were on windows that formerly were starkly and pleasingly barren, and there were even vases of—well, not flowers, exactly, but dried weeds. But they were arranged very artfully. And everything seemed to have a sheen that was unfamiliar until he realized that someone had been cleaning the accumulated grime of millennia from the floors, walls, and sparse furniture, some of which had been freshly upholstered.

What he noticed most were the splashes of color lent by the fabrics and dried plants. The black obsidian from which the palace was carved seemed to have been transformed from an overwhelmingly grim construct into an elegant background for Angel's colorful palette.

Too damn colorful, the Devil thought, his upper lip drawing back in a sarcastic leer. He had to admit that Angel was an intriguing bit of work, but her tastes really were a bit sickening, mixing various styles indiscriminately and gluing the whole together with liberal dollops of kitsch.

And speaking of bad taste, he now noticed one cloying the inside of his mouth. He worked his tongue and lips, stirring his taste buds, and immediately regretted it. The food Angel had prepared had smelled and tasted wonderful, but it left an aftertaste that wasn't so pleasant. Maybe it was that chocolate mousse. It *had* tasted a bit chalky.

He found himself longing for a good hunk of slightly tainted beef or pork—anything that would assuage the unsavoriness coating his tongue. He hoped Angel would soon tire of cooking and leave the chefs alone.

He felt a hot sensation bubble in his chest, and perplexed, he stopped until a large belch worked its way up his throat.

Heartburn!

He almost laughed at the irony, but then he realized that antacids were an anathema in Hell. Resigning himself to an uncomfortable night, and feeling a bit of ire rising with the next belch, he stalked off to his office.

↬ 19 ↫

ALL BOB'S COMPANIONS IN THE lake of boiling shit were standing around at their relative depths, watching in amazement as Bob slowly slogged up and out of the mire.

"Get back in there, you little turd!" Sapason bellowed, and he deployed his lash to make Bob heed his order. But though the whip snaked and snarled all around Bob, it never actually touched him. At last, Bob was on the edge of the muck, with only one foot separating him from dry land, but for some reason, he couldn't seem to take that final step.

Bob flipped through his annotated copy of *The Rule Book*, seeking the answer. It was a little difficult to concentrate with Sapason's whip hissing around his ears, but he forced himself to ignore the sound, and finally, he saw his mistake.

It was a simple rule—so deceptively simple he'd considered it more a clause than a dictum. In fact, it really hadn't made much sense until now, so he'd appended it to a rule that dealt with time management. First, the misplaced rule read, decide what you can do without, then find other things to get rid of.

"I've decided I can do without the confusion in the rules," Bob muttered. "Now, I'd like to get rid of this damn shit burning my feet." He looked down at the boiling shit lapping around his ankles.

121

Unfortunately, the thought didn't do much good since he still couldn't take that last step onto the shore.

So, what could he get rid of? He looked down at himself and saw only his naked body, coated from the knees down in drying, scaling shit. All he had was himself and *The Rule Book*. The rules precluded divesting himself of *The Rule Book*, and he couldn't very well get rid of himself.

He pondered for many long minutes, anxious to get moving but knowing he had to make the right decision, which seemed completely impossible under the circumstances. While he pondered, he took the pencil from behind his ear and moved the misplaced rule to what seemed like its logical location at the end of *The Rule Book*. After all, it was part of what prevented him from taking that last step.

When he finished writing, he was tucking the pencil behind his ear again when he stopped and stared at it.

It was nothing more than a common, yellow #2 pencil, but as he looked at it, noting the blunted lead and worn nubbin of an eraser, he realized that he'd completely and thoroughly ordered the rules, and he didn't need it anymore.

With a smile, Bob tossed the pencil to Sapason, who caught it without breaking the heated rhythm of his furious, if ineffectual, whipping. And with the pencil went the last vestiges of leadenness keeping Bob mired. His heart lifted, his feet moved, and in two seconds, he was out of the lake.

A sudden noise from behind Bob caught his attention, more by the very alienness of its nature in this place than by anything else. His former comrades were cheering and clapping. It made Bob feel pretty good, but Sapason didn't like it at all.

"Stop that, you crapulent bastards!" the demon shouted, and he whipped a few of them, but the rest kept on cheering, and there were too many to whip all at the same time.

"Come in and make us!" one of them yelled, and everyone laughed. They knew that Sapason hated the boiling shit as much as they did, and that if some of the stuff got into his fur, it would take days to wear out since demons didn't sweat. At least not at Hell's normal temperatures.

"Hey, Bob!" Ahmed called. "How did you do it?"

"What people want is hope that tomorrow will be better than today," Bob pronounced, holding up his hand. "It's only when they abandon hope and realize that nothing will ever be better that things actually do improve."

That should keep them busy, he thought.

"What are you going to do now?" Pedro asked.

"I think I'll have a look around," Bob said. "Hang tight, and I'll come back and let you know what's happening."

Bob glanced around. Now that he was up on the bank, he could get a general idea of the lay of the land in the immediate vicinity, but in most directions, anything farther than the near distance was blocked by walls or boulders or barren hills or crumbled buildings or some other sort of obstruction. None of the obstructions were trees, and there wasn't a green plant in sight, though some huge, deformed toadstools stood here and there.

In the one direction that Bob could see any sort of distance, there was a vista of lakes similar to the one he'd just emerged from, all spread across a broad depression.

"Hey, Sapason, why so many lakes?"

"I don't think I ought to be talking to you," the demon said, a sour note in his voice. He'd stopped trying to whip Bob and was standing dejectedly, his shoulders slumped.

"Oh, don't be so upset. It's not your fault I found a way out."

"Maybe not, but I'll be a laughing stock, and I'm probably gonna catch hell for it, anyway."

"Just tell them it was out of your hands," Bob soothed. "You have plenty of witnesses—everyone saw you trying to keep me in there."

"Yeah, I suppose you're right," Sapason said, though he still didn't sound to happy. But then he was a demon, and Bob didn't suppose demons were ever really happy.

"Why so many lakes?"

"Boiling shit, boiling oil, boiling water, boiling mud, acid, molten lava." Sapason shrugged. "Just different degrees of punishment.

"Is that all there is? Just lakes?" If it was, Bob was going to be depressed that Hell was such a measly, monotonous place.

"Naw. These are just the lowlands. There's all sorts of stuff going on elsewhere. Sisyphus Hill is over there." Sapason gestured one way then another and another. "Over there is the grandfathered petrochemical plant, and that way is Developers' Swamp. It goes on and on. I couldn't begin to tell you about everything, but you name it, we've got it."

"What's that?" Bob pointed to a gray stone wall about fifteen feet high with an open archway in it showing a cross section of narrow corridor.

"That's the Maze of Science," Sapason said. "Buncha fuckin' geeks in there. Scientists who deliberately used their knowledge without regard for the human consequences."

"You mean like scientists who made atomic bombs and killer viruses and stuff like that?"

"Some of them, but a lot worked for pharmaceutical and cosmetics companies. They wander around trying to find a way out of the maze, but they keep getting distracted. Look, there's one now."

Bob saw a hunched-over man stumble up to the door. But instead of seeing the archway leading out of the maze, he suddenly crouched against the section of wall visible through the opening and stared at something lying in the dirt. He picked it up, dusted it off, and turned it over in his hands a few times, then he stumbled on, oblivious to the exit he'd just passed.

"Why isn't there a gate?" Bob asked. "Seems like it would be safer just to have them all locked in."

"Every one of them was led into the maze through that door and turned loose, so they know it's there if they can only find it. Knowing there's an exit that they can't find is what really makes it hell for them. Otherwise, there'd be just despair, not punishment. Real punishment always holds out a means of escape, even if the means always escapes the one being punished."

"But what if one of them finds the exit and does escape?"

"Hell if I know," Sapason said. "You're the first one I ever saw actually get out of their punishment." The demon gave him a humorous look. "But you're still in Hell."

"You have a point," Bob said. He could order the rules and memorize them, but he still had a lot of work to do before they were truly internalized and he could completely get out of this land of the damned. "Which way do you suggest I go?"

"Sorry, Bob, can't help you there. There are no roadmaps in Hell. But I'll tell you this: Even if you go into the Maze of Science, you wouldn't get lost because that's not your punishment. But it would be futile since that's the only entrance. You'd just end up back here."

"Okay," Bob said, looking around and seeing a path threading its way between the lakes of various flesh-rending substances. "I guess I'll just go this way. Be seeing you."

"Most likely," Sapason said.

"Hey," Bob nudged the demon. "Look."

A number of the crowd that had gathered to see Bob leave the lake had gotten bored watching him converse with Sapason and had wandered off, and several of them were congregating for a card game.

"Better get your whizzer ready," Bob said.

"Hey," Sapason said with a trace of excitement. "Thanks."

As the demon hurried off toward the card players, Bob turned to the path and began walking.

♄ 20 ♄

"MAMMON IS HERE TO SEE you, sire."

The Devil had been sitting quietly, staring out a wide window that overlooked one of his favorite parts of his domain, the Slough of Despond, when Behemoth's voice came over the intercom. The Devil lifted one side of his face in a disgruntled frown. The morning—a relative term in Hell, of course, where there is no day or night, but things have to start sometime—already had been less than satisfactory. Normally, he'd have taken care of a few administrative matters by now, then flown off to make the rounds of his domain, stopping here and there to help exact torment from some doomed soul. That would have worked up a nice appetite by dinner time, but today, it was only ten-thirty, and instead of an appetite, he had acid indigestion.

Angel had cooked up a dish of kung-pao beef, and like everything else she cooked, it started out tasting great, with a robust load of pepper, but it soon cooled to a tepid impuissance that left a glutinous residue on his tongue. Frankly, though, it had been the devil's food cake that had done him in. It had been entirely too rich. He frowned. Every night it was some sort of chocolate thing. He didn't understand how she managed to stay trim much less keep that shift so spotlessly white.

Unfortunately, for some reason, he couldn't bring himself to ask her to let the chefs resume their duties, though he knew they didn't mind her help despite their well-known arrogance and propensity to excoriate anybody they considered inferior in the culinary arts. The thing was, Angel helped make the food taste right to them, though none of them seemed to care what it was doing to *his* palate or *his* stomach.

"Does he have an appointment?"

"No, sire, but he says it's important."

"Very well. Send him in. And have someone go to a pharmacy and get me a bottle of antacids."

"Antacids, sire?" Behemoth sounded a bit dumbfounded.

"Are you questioning me?"

"No, sire. Right away, sire."

Behemoth cut the connection and turned to the Archon of greed. "Go on in," he said. "But be careful. He's been kind of touchy the last couple of days."

Mammon nodded as he went through the door. As usual, he was dressed in the best three-piece suit money could buy, an immaculately folded handkerchief in the breast pocket and a pair of specially cobbled heavy wingtips on his clawed feet. His sharp eyes stared out of a leathery and saturnine face, a gold band set with a huge diamond sparkled on his left ring finger, and his talons were manicured to perfection.

"Something eating at you?" Mammon dryly asked the Devil.

"Very funny. What's so important that you can't let me have a bit of peace?"

"Peace? You want peace?"

"Relative peace, okay? Spare me your witticisms. It's been a rough morning."

"What's going on?"

"A lot of crap," the Devil said. "Or rather, not enough crap. Adramelech told me that the sewage inlet pipe is clogged and we're not getting enough fresh shit." Adramelech was the head of public works.

"That should be easy enough to fix," Mammon said. "I'm sure we've got plenty of dishonest plumbers down here."

"Adramelech says its old infrastructure. He's got a team working on it right now."

"Well," Mammon said, "If that's all...."

"It's not," the Devil growled, and a bit of St. Elmo's fire shimmered around his spines. Mammon looked at his boss with some amazement—he hadn't seen him this agitated in quite awhile—not since Hitler had failed to live up to expectations. He wasn't sure if he dared speak or dared not to. If the Boss was upset, either could be the wrong move, and Behemoth's warning was echoing in Mammon's head.

"Do you want to share?" Mammon asked tentatively.

"Of course not," the Devil snapped. "You know I never share. But I will unload on you, whether you like it or not."

"I'm all ears," Mammon said.

"You know that hole we opened to the South Pole so we'd have adequate freezing capabilities to feed the glacier?"

"How can I forget? The damn thing cost a fortune to excavate and twice as much for the disinformation campaign once the Hollow Earthers got wind of it."

"Well, you'd better get ready for additional expenses," the Devil said. "The glacier is receding so much, Paimon says we won't be able to use it much longer."

Paimon was the chief glacial engineer.

"How could that be happening?"

"Paimon says he it might be due to global warming."

"That happened after you ordered that we increase the temperature out there...."

"I don't need you to remind me what I did or did not do," the Devil said dangerously.

"Do you want us to make the hole bigger?" Mammon asked contritely.

"If it was any bigger, we'd have the inmates near it trying to escape that way," the Devil snorted snidely. "Or we'd have some polar explorers vanishing unexpectedly. Besides, I suggested that already, and he said that there might be some other unknown factor involved, so let's hold off until he's sure of the cause."

"But what'll we do until then?"

"We'll just have to install some refrigeration units. Let global warming try to fuck with those."

"Well, sir, I'm afraid we might have a problem there," Mammon said, ready to bolt if his boss exploded.

But instead of exploding, the Devil just sat there quietly behind his big obsidian desk. Mammon thought he did detect a slight stiffening of the Boss's shoulders, and a few lines of tension wrinkled the corners of his eyes.

"All right," the Devil said. "Tell me."

"It's Mount Etna." Mammon was referring to the huge, constantly erupting volcano that was Hell's most dominant feature, dwarfing even the Devil's palace—not to be confused with the volcano of the same name in Sicily though it was named for similar reasons. He paused, unsure of how to continue since he well understood just what the volcano represented to his boss.

"What about it?" the Devil prompted.

"Maybe you should see for yourself, sir."

Mammon opened the plate glass doors and waited for the Devil to rise from behind his desk and go through them onto the balcony. The volcano was clearly visible in the distance.

"Look at it, sir. Do you notice anything?"

The Devil stared, his brow darkening—if that was possible. "Where is the ejecta?" he asked, referring to the burning rocks, clots of lava, and searing ash and cinder that usually threw a crown of fire around Etna's head.

"You'll also notice," Mammon said, "that the river of magma flowing down the western flank is somewhat narrower than usual."

"Damn it!" the Devil snarled, turning back to Mammon. "What's wrong with it?"

"Xaphan tells me that the lava dome that feeds the volcano is retracting." Xaphan was the chief volcanologist.

"Retracting? How can that be? There's no place for it to retract to!"

"I don't know, sir. Xaphan has put some seismic engineers and volcanologists on the problem, but even if they determine what's causing the retreat, there's no guarantee that they'll be able to do anything about it."

Mammon watched while his boss fell into a black study.

"You know what this means, sir?" he asked at last.

"Spell it out for me."

"Mount Etna is our power source. We depend on it for heat, smoke, and much of our light, and we use it to generate electricity for the palace and the staff's quarters. We even rely on the convection currents over the peak to produce those perpetual lightning storms you like so much. The heat's fallen off enough in the last few weeks that electrical output is down nearly 20 percent and falling. That being the case, I don't see how we can manage to power refrigeration units sufficiently large enough to replace the receding glacier."

"What the hell is going on here?" the Devil muttered.

"Sir?"

The Devil stared at Mammon, who prepared to cringe but was amazed to see a touch of despair lurking behind the anger in his boss's eyes. That made Mammon quail. He'd seen the Devil like this only twice before, and those had been enough for his taste. The despair had quickly been replaced by a rage that had spared no one, not even Mammon and the other demons of the first order. When it was all over, Hell had been laid to waste and had to be rebuilt, and everyone was so terrified that it took even longer for them to recuperate and return to optimal operation. But even that hadn't been as bad as the time the Boss got really mad and chose to reverse everyone's sensations for a whole millennium, causing everything to become as frigidly cold as it now was blisteringly hot. It was the only time in Mammon's entire existence that he'd had to wear an overcoat, but those mukluks had been downright humiliating.

Besides, Mammon liked things to run smoothly, like clockwork, with every little cog whirling in its place. That's what made money and showed a profit. Problems always caused setbacks and cut profits as well as caused headaches, not to mention additional expenses. Rebuilding Hell after it was laid to waste had been fantastically expensive, and that really went against Mammon's grain. As he was fond of saying, "We're in the business of taking in money, not giving it out."

"Listen to me, Mammon," the Devil said. "I want Mount Etna back on line and fully powered up immediately."

"I understand."

"You'd better. Now get out."

"Uh, sir, if I might have one more moment."

"What?"

Mammon blanched, which wasn't easy, but he held his ground. He had to. If he didn't get this out now and the Boss found out about it later, his ass would be grass.

"I believe I've discovered a small accounting irregularity, sir."

"Accounting irregularity? You mean someone's had the temerity to embezzle funds from my coffers?"

"I'm afraid it appears to be true, sir."

"Who is it?" the Devil demanded. "I'll have him for lunch."

"It may not be quite that simple," Mammon said. "You see, it's Adramelech."

"You mean I've been talking to that little bastard all morning about the sewage inlet, and he faced me like nothing was going on, and all the time, he's been ripping me off?"

"Apparently so, sir. Him and maybe the rest of the administration over there."

"Crap! If I eat them all, who'll be left to fix the problems?"

"Precisely."

"All right. Arrange a meeting with Adramelech, but don't tell him I know about the embezzlement. Say it's about the sewage problem. Have all the administrators there. I want the rest of those bums watch me eat the bastard alive, just in case they think they might be able to pull the wool over my eyes."

"Yes, sir."

"Anything else?"

"No, sir."

"There's the door." The Devil waved in the appropriate direction, and Mammon hurried off the balcony, through the Devil's office, and out into the antechamber.

As the door shut behind him, Mammon took the immaculately folded handkerchief from his breast pocket and mopped his leathery face. It came away grimy with soot and oil, but that didn't matter—a fresh one was automatically in its place in his pocket. He dropped the old one to the floor, where it began to yellow and dry from the heat. In the past, he reflected, it would have crisped almost instantly.

Sighing, he went out, thinking that he'd have to visit his tailor for a new overcoat right after he set up the meeting with Adramelech and reamed the ass of the chief volcanologist.

ᕈ 21 ᕫ

BOB WAS FINDING HELL AN endlessly fascinating place. Sure it was stinky and ugly and horrible, and hideously revolting things constantly were going on all around him, but the more he wandered and the more he saw, the more he appreciated the appropriateness of the punishments Hell inflicted on the wicked. It reminded him of law school, where justice always prevailed appropriately. It had been an idealistic time—except Bob had never been all that idealistic. He'd entered law school not to improve the system but to learn to manipulate it. But even that had its points of excellence since Bob had become very good at manipulation. He felt a small surge of pleasure at a job well done and, thus, rules scrupulously followed. He was careful to keep pride out of it, and suddenly the ground beneath his feet felt a few degrees cooler.

Bob had long since wound his way through the lakes and headed across higher ground. He wasn't sure where he was going, but it didn't seem to matter. He had no job, no appointments to keep, no physical needs. So he just kept walking, thinking, this is like the weirdest vacation I ever had, and it's free.

For the most part, he tried to avoid the many demons and even more numerous inmates. He'd never get anywhere if he had to stop to explain why he was simply wandering around every time he came close to anybody. But sometimes, a direct encounter was unavoidable, and that was okay, too. Bob wasn't the hermetic sort, and he had to have occasional bits of human contact. Or demonic, as the case may be.

The first person he actually spoke to was a woman sitting in front of a typewriter on a small table right next to a narrow place in the path.

Bob looked her over. The rules forbade ogling, but Bob had discovered that he could stare all he wanted if he kept the idea of ogling out of his mind. He didn't stare at this woman for long since she was dumpy and middle-aged, and her unlovely features were partially obscured by heavy, black-framed glasses with thick lenses.

She was typing furiously on a typewriter—so furiously, in fact, that her fingers were nothing but bloody stumps. Curiously, there was no paper in the typewriter.

Bob stopped in front of her. "What are you typing?" he asked.

"Can't you see I'm busy?" she snapped, peering at him through her thick lenses without dropping one beat of her pounding stubs.

"It looks like you could use a break," Bob said.

"I don't have time," she replied. "This is the story of my life, and it's so endlessly fascinating that it will probably take an eternity for me to finish it."

"But there's no paper in the typewriter," Bob pointed out.

"There isn't?" Her eyes dropped to the machine and widened. "Why, that little fucking shit!" she snarled.

"Who?"

"Billy. My son. He must have taken it all."

"Is he writing something, too?"

"Him?" She snorted. "The little bastard isn't smart enough. All he does is draw pictures."

"Is he here, too?"

"Here?" She seemed somewhat befuddled. "I don't know. I don't think I've seen him for a while."

"Maybe he isn't the one who took your paper."

"Who else would it have been?"

"Your husband?"

"Him? *That* bastard ran out on me a long time ago."

I wonder why, Bob thought.

"Well," he said, "I can see why there's a reason your typewriter is empty."

"What are you implying?" Her voice filled with cold hostility. "You some kind of hack literary critic?"

"No," he replied. "You could say I'm a sort of a writer, too." He opened *The Rule Book* and showed her a couple of pages of his closely scribbled marginalia.

"Amateur," she sneered. "Plagiarist. Copying the work of others. I, on the other hand, am a complete original."

"So I see," Bob said, closing the book.

"Just get away from me," the woman shrilled.

"Or what?"

"Or I'll make you a villain in the next chapter, and everyone will know what a cretin you are."

"Can't have that," Bob chuckled, and he went on down the path, leaving the woman with her truncated fingers still rampaging over the bloody keys.

Before long, the path opened onto a wide field that seemed to be completely empty. That was unusual. So far, most of the areas Bob had been through were fairly crowded, implying that Hell might be slightly overpopulated. But this field was barren of people. Indeed, it was devoid of any sort of structure or life, though a few wisps of sere brown weeds poked through the lumpy, churned earth along with strands of something that looked a little more substantial and ragged.

Bob eyed the field with suspicion, but the way to the left was blocked by a sheer cliff of dark-gray granite, where people were climbing and falling, and the way to the right quickly dipped into a fetid swamp overhung with a greasy miasma. A closer inspection of the swamp revealed that the evil-smelling water crawled with huge serpents and crocodiles, and the miasmic brume concealed clouds of flying insects. One of the insects, adrift from its fellows, chanced to land on Bob's arm, where it bit the crap out of him. It felt like he'd been jabbed with a red-hot needle, and the bite left a painful welt.

"Tsetse fly," Bob thought as he pinched the offending insect into a red and black pulp, though he had never seen a tsetse fly in his life.

As he wiped the insect remains onto his thigh, he realized that, while he wasn't in the lake of boiling shit anymore, he remained subject to physical discomforts. As Sapason had noted, this was still Hell. He wondered absently if he now was going to contract sleeping sickness, but he thought that would be unlikely. Rule #7,684—18.31.7 in Bob's new nomenclature—forbade unconsciousness except where unconsciousness is an integral part of the punishment, and so far, it seemed that Bob was doomed to remain fully awake at all times.

As his eyes adjusted to the gloom beneath the miasmic clouds, Bob noticed that the swamp was punctuated by numerous small hummocks covered with stiff, saw-blade grass, and on most of them, people crouched. As he watched, he saw clouds of tsetse flies here and there descend on the inhabitants of the hummocks, completely enveloping them. The people would break out in a great flurry of waving and slapping, trying to fend off the flies. That would prove impossible to do, and invariably, the people would leap into the water to seek protection from the biting hordes. But as soon as they did that, they'd be attacked by snakes and crocs, and screaming and leaving bloody trails, they'd thrash toward the nearest hummock. If they were lucky, the new hummock would be vacant and thus provide the illusion of haven, but often as not, the hummock would be occupied, and a battle would ensue between the current owner and the usurper, with the loser going into the water to thrash through snakes and crocs to the next hummock.

Bob wondered if this was Developers' Swamp, but he wasn't about to brave the crocs, snakes, and flies to ask one of the inmates. He turned back to the field. It looked like the only way to go, so he tentatively set out across it.

The more-ragged strands poking through the clay along with the shreds of dead grass were, he quickly discovered, rusty lengths of barbed wire. Some of it looped from clod to clod as well as stuck out like twisted, thorny sticks, so he had to pay a lot of attention to keep from stepping or tripping on it. It wasn't easy. Clods of the smashed earth kept crumbling beneath his bare feet, causing him to stumble, and it was impossible to maintain a straight course.

He hadn't gone twenty yards when he noticed a particularly ugly clod with something white showing through its shreds. Bending close, his nostrils were assailed with the stench of decay, and he realized that the clod wasn't a clod at all but a hunk of rotting flesh showing a few inches of exposed bone. He straightened and moved on, but the farther he went, the thicker the barbed wire became and the more he saw—and smelled— the clumps of death intermixed with the earth. He thought about going back, but he realized that he was nearing the center of the field, so he reasoned that as soon as he passed the middle, things would start getting better—or at least he'd be closer to the other side—and he pushed on. There was nothing behind him, anyway, that he wanted to see again.

Suddenly a harsh voice yelled, "Stand right there, soldier! Give me the password, or I'll blow your heathen ass to smithereens!"

Bob froze, then slowly, he looked around. About fifteen feet to his right was a small pit in the ground with a low berm of earth all around it. It was a foxhole, and standing in the foxhole was a middle-aged man wearing an army helmet with four stars emblazoned on it. In his hands was one of the most formidable machine guns Bob had ever seen outside of a Rambo movie, and the gun was pointed right at his chest.

Password?

Bob wondered if he should try to duck and run, but the general looked itchy and a little crazed, and Bob didn't think he could run across the broken field fast enough to escape the spray the machine gun looked capable of delivering. But he certainly couldn't admit he didn't know the password, at least not right at first.

"I'm a civilian," Bob said as meekly as he could.

"Ain't no civvies in this war, boy!" the general barked. "Goddamn enemy all around. Where's your uniform?"

"I'm with the Congressional military budget committee," Bob said. "We were flying in to assess the situation and see what you need to fight the evil empire. But we got shot down over there." He pointed back the way he'd come. A plume of smoke was rising a couple of miles away, and though Bob knew it was from a huge barbecue pit where sinners were charred to a cinder only to be resurrected and charred again, it could as easily have been from a plane crash. He'd seen a couple of those, too.

"Senator Hawkes," Bob choked, allowing his shoulders to slump. "And Senator Wright. They were both killed. Then a bunch of Arabs started attacking the plane...."

"Arabs?" The general, looking alarmed, dropped the aim of his machine gun an inch or two. "They in this thing, too? I thought it was just the gooks. You sure you aren't shell-shocked, boy?"

"I don't think so."

"You know what shell-shocked is? I'll tell ya. It's being thumped so hard your spirit is jolted out of sync with your body. 'Bout like a coma, only more drastic 'cause you stay awake. I ought to know—happened to me often enough. Sometimes you can get back in sync, or partially, and sometimes you can't."

"I'm not shell-shocked," Bob said, wondering how to get away from here. "I think they're after me."

"You better duck down in this foxhole, then, boy, and get outta the line of fire. Sorry I don't have another weapon for you, but I got enough ammo for the both of us."

Bob saw that the general was right. Boxes and boxes of the stuff lay in the bottom of the hole. The general had even stacked a couple of crates to make himself a seat.

"Sorry, sir," Bob said. "I can't. I have to complete my mission, get back to Washington, and tell them what I've seen. You need more weapons and ammo, more men. Maybe even some tanks."

"Don't forget the air support," the general said.

"I think they'll want to nuke 'em after I tell 'em the kind of hell you're going through."

"You tell 'em, boy. And tell 'em General Means won't let 'em down."

"I will," Bob said, then he glanced quickly over his shoulder. "Is that them?"

"Where?" General Means straightened and stared over the mound of dirt ringing his foxhole.

"Over there." Bob waved vaguely back the way he'd come. "I think they're after me. I'd better go."

"You keep safe, boy, and have 'em air drop me more troops. I could use a battalion, but I can hold the heathen off until then." He cocked the huge machine gun and propped the barrel on the berm.

"Good bye, General," Bob said. "And good luck."

"You hurry up, boy!" the general called after him. "I'm sick of being in this hole!"

Bob did hurry, leaving the foxhole behind. After he'd gone a couple of hundred feet, he heard repeated machine gun bursts blasting behind him. He ducked, hoping that the general wasn't shooting his way. Glancing back, he saw gun smoke billowing out of the foxhole and drifting across the field, and beyond that.... He rubbed his eyes. It almost looked like clumps of earth had risen from the field and were staggering disjointedly toward the foxhole before being blasted to bits by the machine gun.

Turning, Bob made for the edge of the field, the general's hoots of triumph fading from his hearing.

❧ 22 ☙

"HAVE YOU SEEN NICK?"

"Nick?" The demon asked, giving Angel a puzzled look. "I don't think I have any Nicks here right now."

The demon was Mara, head of the electrical power-generating plant. She looked a lot like a giant vulture except her feathers were iridescent, and she had arms as well as wings.

"No, no," Angel said. "Not one of the inmates. You...." She caught herself before she said, "people," but she wasn't sure if the thing before her would take offense. "You call him the Boss."

"Oh, the Boss. Yeah, he was by a few hours ago. Routine inspection, he said, but he stayed for an hour or so to lend me a hand with them."

Mara gestured toward the row of electrical generators, where a number of men and women held large, bare electrical cables together with their bare hands, their bodies rigid with the current arcing through them.

"What have *they* done?" Angel asked, unable to keep the exasperation out of her voice.

"They're electric company executives."

"That doesn't sound so bad," Angel said.

"Oh, no?" The demon chuckled. "Well, most of them were responsible for running old power plants with obsolete coal-burning generators or defective nuclear piles that helped poison the Earth. Then they gouged their customers, who had no choice but to pay out the ass or live in the cold and dark. Or the hot and dark as the case may be. And a lot of them colluded to eliminate cheaper and more environmentally safe power sources just so they could maintain their obscenely large profit margins and live high on the hog."

"Well," Angel said. "When you put it like that, I can see that they deserve some sort of punishment."

"Yeah, but I bet they never expected such a shocking outcome."

"Very funny."

"You take what you can get," Mara replied. "Say, you must be that angel who's been hanging around with the Boss."

"I'm not an angel."

"Well, that's what they call you."

"Nicky started calling me that when I wouldn't tell him my real name."

"What is your real name?"

"If I wouldn't tell Nicky, why should I tell you?"

"Us girls have to stick together. Besides, I'm curious."

Angel hadn't realized that the demon was female. How could you tell a female vulture from a male, she wondered, without being indiscreet. Unless you saw it lay an egg, maybe.

"Curiosity killed the cat," she said, a little flustered.

"Do I look like a cat?" The demon asked. "Say, are you and the Boss...you know...." She wagged her bald, raw-looking head back and forth.

"We're in love, if that's what you mean."

"In love?" The demon gave a series of short squawks that Angel took for laughter.

"What's so funny about that?"

"No offense to you. I can tell you might be capable of an emotion like love, but it's hard to imagine the Boss reciprocating."

"He's shy about it," Angel admitted. "But I can tell."

"I guess." The demon cocked her head. "But if you're in love with him, why won't you tell him your name?"

"Names are power," she said, "and he's got enough power down here. No sense in making it absolute."

Mara chuckled.

"I like that. A bit of poetic justice."

"You like poetry?"

"Poetry and justice both. Reading is a great pastime. Much better than the vapid crap on television. Besides, the reception here isn't all that great."

"I bet you like Dante."

Mara gave her squawking laugh again. "Not really. I've read him, of course, but I prefer Blake—he's as involved but much more intriguing and less hung up on temporal constructs based on religious prejudice and superstition. He was after the primordial guts of reality."

"Blake is too confusing for me," Angel confessed. "You have to carry around a Blake dictionary if you want to understand him."

"Only at first," Mara said. "You know, I believe you could call Blake the great grandfather of comic books. He had all these super characters, some good and some bad, using their powers to battle it out, with the fate of the world—of reality—hanging in the balance. And he not only wrote it all in an arcane language recognized only by fans who immersed themselves in the realms he created, but the illustrations were as important as the text. All that was left to invent was the word balloon."

"Yes," Angel agreed. "I think you're on to something."

"Who's *your* favorite poet," the demon asked.

"I'm partial to Emily Dickinson."

"A deceptively simple poet," Mara nodded. "Even more obscure in her lifetime than Blake was in his. She was great and original, though."

"I like her best because she was intensely loyal to those she loved, and she deeply appreciated their love and loyalty in return."

"Yes, I can see that you'd find that admirable. And if I recall my poetic history correctly, you seem to share with her a similar taste in clothing."

"How nice of you to notice," Angel said, laying a hand on Mara's arm. As soon as she did, the demon smiled. The smile looked pretty hideous on a vulture's beak, but Angel could tell it was genuine and not of nasty intent.

"Well," Angel said. "This has been a very nice conversation, but I really must find Nicky. Could you tell me which way he went?"

"I can, but I won't," the demon said, still smiling.

"Why not? I thought were getting along nicely. Almost like friends."

"Oh, we are," Mara assured her. "And I *will* tell you which way he went, but you'll have to trade for it."

"Trade? Do friends barter for favors?"

"No, but they share."

"But I have nothing to share."

"Sure you do," the demon said. "You can tell me your real name."

"Not a chance."

"Come on," Mara pleaded. "I'm your friend."

"You promise not to tell anyone?" Angel asked, giving Mara a level stare. "Not even Nicky?"

"I don't know," Mara admitted, considering the possibility of having to lie to the Devil.

"I won't tell unless you promise."

"But I'm a demon," Mara said. "What makes you think I'll keep a promise?"

"I'll just have to take your word," Angel replied.

The demon blinked at her, then flushed slightly, which turned her bald red head a dark shade of purple.

"You'd take *my* word?"

"If you gave it as a friend."

"Nobody's ever said that to me since I was assigned to work here." Mara sounded a little choked up. After a thoughtful pause, she said, "Okay, I give my word. I won't tell anyone, not even the Boss."

She looked sincere, even though she shuddered a bit as she finished the pledge.

"Okay," Angel said. "But first tell me *your* name."

"Mara," the demon said.

"Beatrice," Angel replied sticking out her hand. "My name is Beatrice. Pleased to meet you, Mara."

"Beatrice?" The demon chuckled, gently shaking Angel's hand with her clawed foot. "No kidding?"

Angel nodded, smiling.

"That's rich," Mara said. "Thanks for sharing. I wish I *could* tell somebody now."

Angel shot her a severe look.

"Don't worry, don't worry," the demon said quickly, holding up her wings in protest. The feathers shimmered and shone. "I gave you my word, and it may be the first and last time I do something as foolish as that, but I'll keep it. We're friends, aren't we? Besides, like you said, why should the males have all the power down here?"

"So, which way did he go?"

"He flew off toward the glacier. I heard there was some kind of thawing problem over there." Mara gestured toward the south. "That way, about two day's walk."

"Two days?" Angel said, looking distressed.

"It's a long way," Mara said in a concerned voice. "It might be dangerous for you."

"I'm not worried about that," Angel told her. "Nothing harms me, here. It's just that I haven't seen him all day, and two more days without him.... Just the thought is unbearable."

"Too bad you don't have wings," Mara said in a commiserating tone. "Maybe you should make him to give you a chauffeur who can fly you around. It's the least he could do for his girlfriend."

"Yes," Angel said. "I'll do that. It would be most helpful. Well, I'd better hurry if I'm going to catch up with him. Thanks for your help."

"You too, Beat...I mean, Angel."

"Come on up to the palace sometime," Angel said. "We can discuss poetry some more. Maybe start a reading group if we can get enough of the girls together."

"How lovely," Mara said. "I know a few who'd be interested."

"Great! Why don't we say next Wednesday afternoon?"

"I'll be there," Mara promised.

"I'm looking forward to it. See you later." Angel turned and hurried out of the door.

"Bye," Mara called after her. Then chuckling to herself as she repeated Angel's real name, she turned her attention back to her charges.

ᗣ 23 ᗧ

SOMEHOW, BOB HAD LOST HIMSELF in a labyrinth. It wasn't lying on the ground, surrounded by a wall, as the Maze of Science had been. Instead, it was three-dimensional, like a huge, freakish metropolitan downtown spawned from the mind of a madman. He'd first glimpsed it in the distance when he'd been incarcerated in the lake of boiling shit, but as he approached it during his perambulations around Hell, he was amazed by just how bizarre it actually was.

"Excuse me," he'd said to a demon supervising a group of people at a well-appointed dining table set with fine china and golden tableware. Right in the middle of the table was a huge roasted pig. "What's that?" He pointed to the city.

"Caligari City," the demon said. "Where all the architects go."

"All of them?"

"Yeah. Can't have them running about willy-nilly. If we don't confine them, they try to build weird shit everywhere."

"Thanks," Bob said, then he looked at the diners. "What are they doing? Doesn't look like much of a punishment to me."

"Move a little closer."

Bob did, caught a whiff, and felt his stomach grow a little queasy when he realized that that the roasted pig in the middle of the table wasn't a roasted pig at all, but a bloated, rotting human corpse.

"What did they do?" Bob asked, backing away from the necrophagous feast.

"They're gourmands who put their gustatory pleasures over their humanity. Say," the demon peered at Bob. "Why are *you* here? What are you doing running around free?"

Bob found that he could lie since the demon hadn't asked what his crime had been or what his punishment was.

"I'm not running around free," he said quickly. "I'm an eternal messenger. I have to keep looking for someone to give my message to, but I don't think I'll ever find him."

"You're probably right," the demon said. "Well, you'd better run along, then, and keep looking."

"Yes," Bob said as he hurried off. He intended to skirt the immense structure of Caligari City, but it seemed to spread everywhere, and every path he could find led to one of its many entrances.

I'll never get anywhere trying to go around, Bob thought. He remembered Sapason saying that other punishments, such as the Maze of Science, had no power to trap him since they weren't his punishment, so he decided that he probably could go right through the conglomerate structure quickly enough. Faster, at least, than going around.

He went in one of the doors and promptly got lost.

The problem was that no corridor or passage ran very straight for very far. Everything inside was a jumble of architectural styles from every period and civilization, all coexisting unhappily together, and nothing made any sense, not even the street signs. It was worse than trying to find one's way around Pasadena, the small city that adjoined Houston, or navigate the Dallas freeway system. After about an hour, he stopped to ask directions of a man who was busily sketching a modernistic rendition of the Italianate facade in front of him.

"I'm trying to get to the other side of the city," Bob explained. "Can you point me in the right direction?"

"A city has many aspects," the man said. "Many sides. The relationships of these sides is in direct proportion to the uses to which spaces, both public and private are utilized by the multivariate constituencies inherent in the urban ethotic at all levels. We cannot speak, thus, about what is the meaning of side until we explore the indigenous economic substrate that gives rise to the ways and means of recall in coordination with perception and utility."

The man returned to his drawing.

"Thanks," Bob said, though the man seemed oblivious.

The next person Bob asked was a woman. She was pacing up and down in front of a building that looked like a huge glass cube.

"Green space is gray space in obverse," was all she said in reply to his query.

Bob moved on, realizing that, unless he was willing to spend years learning architecturese, he'd have to find his own way out of this urban mess. He'd just have to trust his instincts. After all, if this wasn't his punishment, he should be able to just blindly walk right on through. So, he ignored logic and just let his feet control his direction when he came to an intersection or alternate hallway or door. Sometimes his feet led him into places he'd never have rationally thought would lead anywhere. Once he even found himself going through a door in an office building only to find a chintzy bridal suite, complete with a heart-shaped bed. The closet door took him into an alley, which opened onto a street that led him onward.

He saw lots of people everywhere. Some, he supposed, were architects. They all were drawing or arguing or directing demolition and construction. The ones doing the actual work probably were corrupt contractors or the like. Bob didn't stop long enough to ask, for he wanted to get out of this place as soon as he could. All the clashing styles and colors were beginning to wear on his nerves, and he found himself longing for some sort of natural vista or, at least, an open space where he could breathe.

The odd thing was that he didn't see a single demon. Apparently, this place was so self-contained and self-regulating that supervision wasn't necessary. So, when he rounded a corner while wending his way through a building that fused Greco-Roman sensibilities with the lines of Frank Lloyd Wright and came face-to-face with a demon, he halted in his tracks.

And a good thing, too. If he'd taken another step, he'd have fallen through a round hole in the floor.

The demon was crouched on the edge of the hole, which was about four feet in diameter. Except for his lion's head, he looked like a human dressed in medieval armor. Clutched in one hand was a half-eaten chili dog with cheese and onions, and sitting on the floor beside him was a soda.

"Whoa, there, fella," the demon said around a mouthful of chili dog. "Wouldn't want to mess up all his fine work."

As he pointed down into the hole, a blob of chili dripped off his gauntlet finger and disappeared through the opening.

Bob stared over the edge. About twenty feet down was a man building something just below the hole.

"Is that a house of cards?" Bob asked.

"Yep."

The blob of chili sat right in the middle of the top tier of cards.

"And he's an architect?"

"Yep."

"What's he doing that for?"

"You can't see from here, but that's an oubliette down there."

"An oubliette?"

"Yeah. A kind of prison cell. It's a room whose only entrance is a hole in the ceiling."

"But what's he building a house of cards for?"

"He thinks that if he builds one high and strong enough, he can climb onto it and get out of the oubliette."

By now, the demon had finished his chili dog and was licking the remains of the chili off his gauntlet with a fat, red, slightly furry tongue.

Even as they watched, the man had completed the house of cards as high as his own head, and he attempted to climb up onto it to construct yet another tier, but the whole thing gave way, and he fell onto his ass on the stone floor.

"Don't tell me," Bob said. "He built rickety buildings."

"Yep," the demon said. "One of his schools collapsed, killing a bunch of children."

"What a shit," Bob said, but the demon just shrugged.

"No worse than a lot of people down here. Say, what about you? What are you doing running around free?"

Bob gave him the song and dance about being an eternal messenger who can't deliver his message.

"Haw, haw," the demon chuckled. "You need to team up with that guy over there." He pointed to a slight, balding, middle aged man with a beak nose who was hurrying down the corridor. "He's got the key to eternal knowledge, but he can't find the lock even though he's been here a really long time."

"Yeah, thanks." Bob hurried after the little man. As he caught up, he saw that an antiquated looking padlock was floating along in the air behind the man.

"Say," Bob said. "I hear you have the key."

The little man turned, and as he did, the lock moved, too, staying behind his back. The man did, indeed, have a key, and it looked old enough to fit in the lock, though he quickly and suspiciously secreted it behind back, and Bob got only a glimpse of it.

"What do you want my key for?"

"I'm trying to find my way out of this city," Bob explained. "I thought you might be able to help."

"This is not the key to anything so prosaic as a door," the little man said, and he hurried on.

Bob, not to be put off, followed.

"What, then?"

"I'm not going to tell you."

"Why not?"

"It's a secret. If I told you, you'd steal the key."

"I'll bet you've been looking for the secret this key unlocks for a long time," Bob said.

"Two hundred eighteen years, seven months, two weeks, six days, nine hours, fifty-three minutes, and eleven seconds."

"I imagine you've been through this place a lot."

"Every square inch of it."

"But you haven't found the lock yet?"

"I'll find it," the man said defensively.

"I already know where it is," Bob said.

"You lie!" the man shouted, clutching the key tightly, as if Bob's words were a threat to wrest it from him.

"Not at all," Bob said. "In fact, I saw it not long ago. I don't know how you missed it if you've been everywhere."

"Keep away from me," the man shrilled, stepping back.

"Take it easy," Bob soothed. "I don't want your key or your secret. But I do want to make a deal. I'll tell you where the lock is if you do something for me."

"What" the man demanded suspiciously.

"Lead me to a door that'll take me out of this city. You can do that, can't you?"

"Yes. If I do, you'll tell me the location of the lock?"

"I will."

"All right, but keep back. If you try to get close and take the key, I'll run away, and you'll get lost, and you'll never find me again."

"Just don't panic and run away unnecessarily," Bob said, "or I won't be able to tell you where the key goes."

"All right," the little man said. "Follow me."

Bob did, carefully maintaining at least twenty feet between himself and the little man. Once, he dared sneak a little closer, and he reached out to touch the lock floating along behind the man. It was cold metal—seemingly just another ordinary padlock, even if it was antiquated. Bob considered grabbing it, but the way it stayed right behind the key holder would probably preclude Bob's keeping hold of it, so he just backed off and followed sedately, keeping his hands to themselves.

At last, they reached a door labeled, "Custodian."

"I'd never have thought of that," Bob admitted. "You sure this is the way out?"

"See for yourself." The man pulled it open, and sure enough, a barren landscape lay beyond it. "Now tell me like you promised."

"Turn around," Bob said. "It's right behind you."

The man spun, and Bob quickly moved to the door.

"Liar!" the man yelled.

"No," Bob said. "It's right behind you."

The man turned, but the lock maintained its relative position, and he couldn't see it.

"Maybe if you find a mirror and look at yourself, you'll see the truth," Bob said.

"I'll kill you!" the man yelled, and he leapt at Bob.

Bob didn't think that would be possible, but he hopped through the door anyway and slammed it in the man's face.

Outside at last, Bob took a deep breath, only now realizing how claustrophobic he'd felt in the city. He sat down to contemplate his next move.

I'm wandering aimlessly, he thought. I have eternity before me, and I'm bartering purpose for movement.

That thought brought the realization that his whole existence has been aimless except at some half-imagined "high position." But he knew he couldn't continue to wander haphazardly around Hell because it was too lonely and arduous and frightening and hideous and disgusting. Some of the torments were pretty damn funny, but a lot of them pulled at his heartstrings, though he hated to admit it. Or made him want to puke, which he couldn't do, not having had a meal in two months, three weeks, five days, seventeen hours, nine minutes, and twenty-seven seconds.

Anyway, Hell was as boring as hell. In some ways, he'd been better off back in the lake of shit because there, at least, he had friends. True, they were all suffering, him included, but at least they suffered together and, through that suffering, experienced a camaraderie despite their varied backgrounds.

"I need a goal," he said as he pulled himself from the reverie and glanced around the landscape. "I need to direct my energy toward a higher level. But what?"

At that moment, his eyes lit on a distant object that stood above everything else in this awful place. It was a black castle on the peak of a high, black, craggy mountain.

Bob got up and hurried away from the margins of the crazed city from which he'd just emerged. At the first demon he encountered, he pointed to the castle and asked what it was.

"The palace," the demon said.

"You mean that's where the Devil lives?"

"That's right." The demon peered at Bob. "Say, what are you doing running around free?"

"I'm a messenger," Bob said, "and I have a message for the Devil."

☊ 24 ☋

"WHAT THE HELL IS GOING on around here?" the Devil demanded, pounding his fist on his obsidian desk.

All the Archons were present in his office except Mammon, who was off to Earth, tracking down Adramelech, the former head of public works. Apparently the renegade demon had been tipped off that the Devil planned to feast on his flesh, and he'd absconded with his embezzled funds and was gallivanting around the human sphere, living high and wild, as if there was no tomorrow. He was right about that, once Mammon caught up with him and brought him back to Hell.

"The power plant is on the fritz," the Devil went on angrily, "the glacier is melting, and Mount Etna is cooling. I want some answers!"

The Archons hemmed and hawed and shuffled their cloven hoofs, clawed feet, or splayed pads—except for Leviathan and Belphegor, who didn't have any—but none of them would look at him. And no wonder. He was so mad that his eyes were glowing like hot coals, and smoke was rising off his shoulders. With every angry breath, little squirts of toxin jetted from his spines.

"Um, sir," ventured Asmodeus, the demon of lust. "It's not cooling off. It's just that the lava dome is shifting...."

"Shut the fuck up," the Devil snapped, invoking Rule #1, which, for him, worked even on the Archons. "I don't want lame excuses based on natural laws. This is Hell. There's nothing natural about this place. What I say goes, and we do what we do because I am one of the two supreme expressions of reality. If we need a glacier, I say we have a glacier, and there it is. If we need a volcano, I say we have a volcano, and there it is. And if I say we need both side by side and fornicating until the cows come home, well...?"

"We've got them," came the dutifully intoned chorus from the assembled advisors.

"I want you to go out and find out why Hell is falling apart, and I want answers and solutions, not a bunch of whiney excuses. Is that understood?"

"Yes, sir."

"Sir?" Leviathan raised a flipper from her tub of brine. "May I make a suggestion?"

"If you think it will take us closer to restoring the status quo around here."

"I don't mean to contradict you, sir, but instead of trying to fix the problems, maybe we should try to find out what's causing them."

"Brilliant, Leviathan," the Devil sneered. "Absolutely brilliant."

"I think she's got a point," Lucifer ventured, his childish voice resolute. Lucifer may have looked like a boy, but he was the Devil's left hand and often the only one brave enough to confront the Devil with hard truths. "We can work to fix the glacier, the volcano, and the power plant, but those are just symptoms. We have to eradicate the central cause of the problem. The disease, if you will."

"Disease is of my domain," the Devil said. "This place is nothing but spiritual disease. How can there be a diseased disease?"

"Okay," Lucifer said. "Call it easedis, if you want."

Belphegor chuckled, but a glare from the Devil made his conical top wilt, and he fell silent. Actually, he fell asleep.

"You mean a sort of reverse disease?" The Devil seemed interested.

"Exactly. If you send disease to help destroy happiness, then isn't it possible that someone," Lucifer didn't say the name, but he rolled his eyes toward the right, "might have sent easedis to destroy unhappiness?"

The Devil leaned back in his stainless steel chair, tenting his fingers in front of his face and looking thoughtful. After a few silent moments, he nodded.

"You might have something, but how can we locate the point of disinfection?"

"I don't think that will be too difficult," Leviathan said in a slightly sarcastic tone.

"What do you mean by that?" the Devil asked shortly, glaring at her.

"Think about it," Lucifer cut in, earning a grateful look from the whale in the tub. "When did all this begin? A little more than three months ago. And what else happened at that time?"

Thinking he'd said enough, he quit talking, and the rest of the demons shut the fuck up, too. None of them wanted the Devil's wrath falling on their heads. Best to let him work it out himself. It didn't take long.

"That fucking bitch!" the Devil snapped. "She's been here about three months."

"Exactly," Lucifer said, relieved the Devil hadn't seen fit to blast him with his Godzilla breath. Of course, Lucifer would have regenerated his flesh, skin, and curly mop, but it would have been a painful and wasteful interim. Besides, it wasn't his fault that Angel was here, so why should *he* suffer? His job was to make *others* suffer.

"I knew there was something wrong about her," the Devil muttered. "Ever since she showed up, my whole rhythm has been screwed up."

"We all know what a trial she's been," Belphegor commiserated.

"Trial isn't the word for it," the Devil said morosely. "I can't get rid of the bitch. She follows me around everywhere like my shadow."

To a one, the Archons refrained from commenting that a white shadow might be appropriate for the Devil.

"It's hell trying to shake her," the Devil went on. "Do you know what I had to go through just to have enough free time for this meeting? I've had to inspect the power plant, the glacier, and the volcano. She has to travel on foot, so she'll have to go to all three in a row before she discovers I've come back here, but damn it, she always seems to find short cuts even I don't know about. And she's a damn fast walker, too. I have to fly at top speed everywhere I go. If I don't, she catches up and starts bugging me with all that lovey-dovey crap, wanting me to polish my spines and use deodorant and mouthwash and disrupting everything. I can't get any serious work done when she's around, and when she's not, I'm too exhausted to concentrate because I have to flap like a madman all the time to get away from her. It's insane."

He looked up at his executive staff, and those who were brave enough to look back were shocked to see a touch of resignation in his eyes.

"We have to do something about her," Beelzebub said bluntly.

"You know I've tried," the Devil said. "I can't touch her. Nothing here can touch her. She's pure as the driven snow." His voice dripped with bitterness. "She's unsullied flesh. Hell, her feet don't even get burned or dirty or cut after two days of walking barefoot."

"Well, something's got to give," Lucifer said, "and it can't be you, so it has to be her."

"If we can't destroy her, maybe we can send her back where she came from," Mammon suggested.

"That's an idea. You know it has to be him," Lucifer said, rolling his eyes rightward, "who sent her. She doesn't belong here, so that would seem to be a violation of the strict separation of powers. Make him take her back."

"But she swears he didn't send her," the Devil said.

"And you believe her?" Asmodeus asked.

"You've met her," the Devil said. "Don't you?"

"She seems pretty straightforward," Asmodeus admitted. "Maybe she just doesn't realize it."

"An unwitting dupe?" The Devil mulled it over.

"Call him," Lucifer urged. "He'll have to tell you the truth. That's *his* nature."

There were three telephones on the Devil's desk. The black one was a line to Earth, the red one to the president of the United States, and the white one.... As the Devil picked up that one, Lucifer couldn't help but roll his eyes to the right.

"Hey, Yah," the Devil said after a moment. "Yeah, it's Nick. Who the hell else would it be? How's everything?" Pause. "Yeah, I'm sure things are going fine over there." Pause. "It's been pure

Hell. Listen, I want to talk to you about this woman you sent over here to pester me." Pause. "She's about five-six, wavy golden-blond hair, wears a white chemise." Pause. "Yeah, she's beautiful. Musical voice, too." Pause. "No, no wings." Pause. "Yes, I know all your people wear wings." Pause. "Look, bro, did you send this woman over here or not? If you did, you need to take her back before something drastic happens to her or she somehow upsets the balance of nature. This is no place for an innocent babe, no matter how sexy...." Pause. "You swear?" Pause. "Yeah, I know you don't swear." Pause. "All right, I guess I have no choice but to believe you, but if you're prevaricating, then whatever happens to her—or to the universe—is on your head." Pause. "Okay, okay. I said I believe you." Pause. "Yeah, we'll do lunch. Take care." Pause. "Okay."

The Devil hung up the white phone.

"Like hell we'll do lunch, you sanctimonious bastard," he snarled as he looked up at his Archons. "He says he doesn't know who she is or where she came from."

"You think he's telling the truth?" Lucifer asked.

"He's done some shitty things in his time," the Devil said, "but lying isn't one of them."

At that moment, there was an urgent knock on the door. "What is it?" the Devil barked impatiently.

Behemoth stuck his head in and said, "She's back."

"Damn! How long do we have?"

"About thirty seconds."

That wasn't enough time for the Devil and his executive staff to do more than arrange themselves before Angel traipsed through the door.

"Oh, Nicky, you wouldn't believe what trials I've gone through these last two days." As she ran over and gave the Devil a kiss on the cheek and a big hug, the Archons couldn't help but notice the Boss's spines wilt like soft rubber beneath her touch, though they sprang back as sharp as ever when she released him and stepped back. She turned and surveyed the demons. "I see the gang's all here. I suppose you're going to watch football all afternoon. Anybody want a snack or a beer?"

"Yeah, Angel," the Devil said. "Get us some beers, won't you? And some nachos. Heavy on the jalapeños."

"I'll be right back."

"I'll bet you will," the Devil muttered as she exited the room. Then he turned back to Archons. "Listen, we don't have much time. I've got to get rid of this bitch, and quick. She had to come from somewhere, and if it wasn't from over there, it must be from over here. Assign someone to it. Assign the hounds of Hell if you have to, but I want results, and I want them *now*. Understood?"

They all understood.

"Okay, get the hell out of here before she comes back, or she'll trap you here and delay things."

They hurried out and were all gone by the time Angel returned with a tray full of beers and nachos.

"Where did everyone go?" She looked a little disappointed.

"The game was cancelled," the Devil said. "Bring those over here." He gestured to the beers. "I'll drink them."

"But there are seven," she said. "That's too much. You'll be sloppy drunk by dinner."

"I don't get drunk," he snapped.

"So *you* say." She set two beers and the plate of nachos on his desk. "Here, you can have two. I'm taking the rest back to the kitchen. But I'll be right back." She winked. "We can cuddle and watch *Wings of Desire*. You did have Behemoth get a copy, didn't you."

"I still have some work...," he began, but she gave him a nagging stare.

"You promised, remember? Besides, you've had two days solid of work, and you know what they say about Jack and no play."

"Yeah," he said, thinking, *I'd have played plenty if you weren't around wasting all my time.* "I've heard."

"I'll take these back to the kitchen and meet you in the den."

The den used to be the Devil's private torture chamber, all blackened iron and blood-varnished wood, but Angel had it completely redecorated a few weeks ago in neo-Georgian style. Instead of the rack, there was a soft couch, and in the place where the iron maiden once stood now sat an entertainment system in a big oaken cabinet.

"Of course," he said as he watched her take the beers away, a disgruntled frown clouding his brow. As soon as she was gone, he ate the jalapeños and guzzled the two beers before emptying the nachos into the trash can where they instantly incinerated.

Cuddle, he thought disgustedly. He was horny as hell, but all she ever wanted to do was cuddle. He'd have to fly off again and find some whore somewhere to wax his prong—if he wasn't too tired to get it up, that is.

Sighing, he rose and went to the den, where she already had the movie in the DVD player. As the opening credits rolled, he wished it was something a little more exciting like *Deep Throat* or *Babes in Boyland*. Hell, he'd have settled for *Rosemary's Baby*. That was a chick flick, wasn't it? Even if it came out fine in the end.

⇥ 25 ⇤

BOB FINALLY FOUND A BOULDER that wasn't too hot or cold or lumpy or sharp to sit on. He was tired. He didn't know how far he'd traveled, but he'd been moving for about ninety-six hours straight since leaving Caligari City. Lifting his right foot onto his left thigh, he massaged the sole. It had toughened up and gotten pretty leathery since he'd begun his jaunt across Hell. He put the foot back onto the ground and stared around.

This particular precinct of Hell looked a lot like the main quadrangle of a university campus. Imposing buildings stood on all four sides, but on closer inspection, they all seemed to have false fronts, like a cheap movie set. Standing on soapboxes here and there around the quadrangle, which was about the size of a football field, were men and women wearing academic gowns—the first clothing Bob had seen in Hell. In the extremely hot ambient temperature, however, the heavy gowns seemed more detriment than benefit, and the three professors who were near enough for Bob to see clearly were sweating profusely.

All the professors were delivering lectures to crowds of students who milled around, paying the lectures little attention. Actually, all the students seemed to be redneck hillbillies who were scratching their heads in dumb amazement or gathering together in angry groups, glaring and pointing at one or another of the lecturers. Bob heard some of the closer ones talking angrily about "know-it-all perfessers" who "was subvertin' tha will 'a God," "exhaltin' tha evil 'a purmissiveness," and "preachin' everlushun."

Suddenly, one of the student groups rushed en masse toward one of the professors like a squad of linemen attacking a quarterback caught in the open. They piled onto her, fists flailing and feet kicking in such a vicious melee that they must have done as much damage to themselves as they did to her. After a few minutes, a handful of demon keepers ambled up and drove off the attackers with whips and cattle prods. The attackers dispersed to begin milling around with the other students. One of the demons hauled the mauled professor to her feet, dusted off her robe, and set her back onto her soapbox, where she resumed her lecture. Bob wasn't close enough to see if she was bruised or battered, but if she was, it didn't seem to deter her.

"Hey, you!" a harsh voice barked behind Bob. "Back in class!"

"I'm not a student," Bob said, turning to see a demon approach. Its apelike body was covered with blue fur, and its head resembled that of a camel with ram's horns. A foot-long, well-chewed cigar jutted from its jaws, and a cattle prod swung casually from one simian arm.

"Sure," the demon said around his cigar. It raised the cattle prod. "That's what they all say. Now get out there."

"That's not my punishment," Bob said. "Rule #13,013 states that punishments can be meted out only by the demon officially assigned to a particular punishment or by the Devil, who can do whatever he pleases, and since I'm not assigned here, and you aren't the Devil, you have no jurisdiction over me."

"Oh," the demon grinned. "A jailhouse lawyer. I didn't think we had any of those in this sector."

"I just got here," Bob explained.

"Well, Mr. Jailhouse Lawyer, let me explain to you how things are. You go to class. If you don't, you have to face a truant officer. That's me. And this is what happens if you don't do what a truant officer says."

Before Bob could speak or react, the demon jabbed him in the stomach with the cattle prod. Electricity jolted from the tip, but other than a slight tickling, Bob felt nothing. It was the demon who looked shocked.

"What the fuck?" the truant officer asked, taking out its cigar.

"I told you I'm not part of this punishment," Bob said blandly. "I'm just passing through."

"Nobody just passes through," the demon said. "What's your name, and where are you going?"

"Bob, and up there." Bob pointed to the obsidian castle in the distance.

"To the palace, huh?" The truant officer stared thoughtfully at Bob for a moment. "You gotta lotta chutzpah, going up to see the Boss."

"Not really," Bob said. "I just wanted to meet him."

"Shit, you coulda stayed where you were," the demon said. "He gets around to everyone here eventually. Likes to add his personal touch." The demon chortled some very foul breath.

"That could take an eternity," Bob said. "I can't wait that long."

"Like you got something else to do?"

"Anything's better than standing around in a lake of boiling shit," Bob said.

"I can thinka worse," the demon said. "In fact, I have." It paused. "Is that where you were?"

"Yep. Up to my thighs."

"You had it easy," the demon said. "But howja get out?"

"I'm an organized fellow," Bob said.

"Yeah," the demon snorted dismissively. "Tell me another."

"Say, isn't that student over there supposed to be listening to the professors?" Bob pointed to a man who was snoozing underneath a bush. "Go get him."

"You telling me what to do?" the demon asked belligerently. "You aren't my boss."

"Obviously you aren't either," Bob retorted without heat. "Rule #7,684 states that inmates may not sleep, faint, pass out, or in any other way become unconscious except where unconsciousness is an integral part of the punishment. That inmate is clearly and inappropriately asleep. Do your duty."

"I'll deal with you later, Bob," the demon said as it stalked off toward the sleeping man.

"No you won't," Bob said, following. "Hey, you ignorant peckerwood, wake up!" he bellowed into the man's face before the demon could jab him with the cattle prod. The man, startled from his sleep, crawled hurriedly from his hidey-hole, rubbing his ears.

"That was pretty good," the demon said to Bob.

"You ain't no demon," the man said, looking at Bob. Anger began to cloud his eyes. "Whyja have ta interfere?"

"Shut the fuck up," Bob said experimentally. To his surprise, the man's mouth suddenly clamped shut.

"Wow," the demon said, obviously impressed, then suddenly suspicious. "Say, who are you?"

"Bob."

"Yeah." The truant officer inspected him closely. "You sure you aren't the Boss in disguise?"

"No, I'm just another inmate."

"You're not *just* another inmate," the demon said.

"I'm afraid I am," Bob shrugged.

"No inmate runs free around Hell, impervious to torment and giving orders."

"I just haven't found where I'm supposed to be," Bob said.

"Is that why you're going to see the Boss?"

"Hey, when you need to find your place, go to the top, is what I always say."

"I like that," the demon said, noticing that the student Bob had chastised was still standing there. "You get on over where you belong, and don't let me catch you playin' hooky again." It turned back to Bob as the man petulantly stalked off. "These ignoramuses think I'm their redneck peckerwood father who drives them off to school saying it'll be good for them but who is a stupid, slovenly, drunken abuser at home."

"I can see how this might be hell for the professors," Bob said. "What did they do?"

"Oh, most of them were intellectually arrogant pricks who were more interested in cowing their students and making them sweat than really teaching them anything."

"But how is it punishment for the students? Seems to me that beating up intellectuals is something these kind of people would like."

"They gotta spend eternity not only knowing they're dumb-asses but having it constantly rubbed in their faces every time one of the professors speaks. And every day, they have to take a test, which makes their ignorance utterly obvious. And no matter how hard or often they beat up the faculty, the lectures never stop."

"An eternity of knowing you're a complete idiot. I like that. But what if they're too dumb to realize they're dumb?"

"We get a few of those," the truant officer admitted. "It's the Dunning-Kruger Effect. But we don't keep that sort here. They're in the kindergarten class taught by Catholic nuns. You think the demons here are bad, wait till you meet one of those nuns. They'll shrivel your peter for sure."

Just then, the demon noticed that about twenty students had grouped around the one Bob had awakened. The man was talking angrily and pointing at Bob and the demon.

"What the fuck?" the demon said.

"They look plenty pissed," Bob commented.

"I think you're disruptive influence on the other inmates."

"Maybe it's not me," Bob said, "but the way you handle them. Surely there is a better way to organize things here. It's not their fault they're ignorant redneck peckerwoods any more than it's your fault you're a demon."

"Yeah, right."

"No, really. Don't you ever get tired of running all over, enforcing a bunch of pointless rules on people who don't understand them and wouldn't give a damn if they do? What a waste of time. Get these students in line, and you'll have it easy. Maybe even have enough free time to audit some courses and improve yourself. Some of these professors must have something worthwhile to say."

By now, the knot of angry students had grown into a small mob. "They're getting ready to attack," Bob warned.

"No shit. Look, Bob, you mind getting out of here?"

"Sure," Bob said. "Which way to the castle?"

"Take that path there, between the Inhumanities Building and the Hall of Antisocial Sciences."

"Thanks," Bob said, and he set off in that direction. The demon truant officer thoughtfully watched him for another moment, then it lifted the whistle hanging around its neck and blew a sharp blast.

"Campus riot in progress!" it bellowed to its compatriot truant officers, pointing to the gathering rabble. "Go get 'em!"

Lifting its cattle prod and grinning ferociously, it charged the mob of angry students.

❧ 26 ❧

"TELL HER I'VE GONE TO the lowlands to inspect the pits," the Devil snapped, slumping lower in his seat and glowering.

"Are you sure you want me to do that?" Behemoth asked.

"If she thinks I've gone to the pits, she'll follow me there, and you know how long it will take her to walk around and between all them. Even she won't be able to find a shortcut, and it might give me a few extra hours of free time."

"It wasn't that...," Behemoth began, but he stopped, discretely averting his eyes.

"All right," the Devil said. "Out with it."

"I'd hate to incur your wrath, sire."

"You'll certainly incur it if you don't tell me what's on your mind."

"Very well, sire. It's this Angel person. Everywhere she goes, trouble follows."

"What's the matter with a little trouble?" the Devil asked.

"Not trouble, then, sire. Call it counter-trouble. She's like a little dove of peace that leaves a feather of remembrance behind everywhere she lands. If you ask me, she's the source of all the disruptions that have plagued you of late."

"So tell me something new," the Devil groused. "I already know she's winning hearts all over Hell."

"It's not just what they say about her that disturbs me, sire. It's what they're saying about you."

"About me?" The Devil jerked up in his seat. "Who the fuck is saying what?"

"I hesitate...."

"Let me ask you, Behemoth: Do you like it here?"

"Like it in Hell, sire?"

"Not Hell, you moron. The palace."

"Why, yes, sire."

"Pretty cushy. Good food, a nice mountain breeze, a comfortable bed, not too hot or cold."

"Yes, sire."

"So you wouldn't like me to assign you to, say, oversee the lava gleaners?"

The lava gleaners stood waist deep in a flood of live magma from Mount Etna—just before it poured into the highest lake to make it boil—and picked out any chunks of rock that weren't completely molten. Many of them had been quality control staff on assembly lines who hadn't done their job properly. The demon who watched over them stood on a solid block of adamant set in the middle of the flood. It was unbearably hot, and the unfortunate keeper invariably came away from his shift dehydrated and with singed fur or a baked hide. The duty was generally reserved as a punishment for recalcitrant demons.

"No, sire."

"Then talk."

"Yes, sire. They say...they say you're going soft."

"Soft?" The Devil laughed. "Is that all?"

"No, sire," Behemoth replied, wondering if that had been a note of nervousness he'd heard in the Devil's laugh. "They say you're in love."

"In love! That's revolting." The Devil peered at his servant. "You've seen it all. You know I'm not even infatuated with that slinky bitch, much less in love."

"I do, sire, but most of your subjects haven't seen what this Angel person has done to you. Besides, you certainly gave that impression when she first showed up."

"I suppose I did," the Devil admitted. "She is a rather fetching piece, don't you think? But surely everybody realizes I was simply using my wiles to corrupt her."

"No, sire. What they saw is that you courted her, and there were declarations of love—albeit only from her. And that minor demon I sent up to Earth to purchase those hygiene products...."

"He *bought* them?"

"Well, no, sire. I believe he coerced somebody to shoplift them for him. But if he has that point in his favor, he turned right around and shot off his big mouth to all his buddies about how the Boss, himself, had him running errands to Earth to procure deodorant and mouthwash so he could impress that white-robed twit."

"That little bastard."

"Perhaps you should send *him* to supervise the lava gleaners," Behemoth said hopefully.

"You're right," the Devil said, brightening slightly. He snapped his fingers, which rasped out a little shower of sparks and left a puff of smoke. "Done. But so is the damage." His brow darkened again. "What else are they saying?"

"That's really the worst of it, sire, except they say she's making you slack off, and that's giving them the excuse to slack, too."

"Damn it," the Devil said. "If there is anything I hate, it's a slacker. But I suppose it could look that way. What with all those trips to the volcano, the glacier, and the power plant, not to mention all the extra flying around I've had to do to avoid Angel, I haven't had the time to make my usual rounds."

He swiveled in his chair and stared thoughtfully out of his window at the barely smoking volcano. As if on cue, the lights in the office flickered then came back on. "No wonder things are going to shit around here." The Devil turned back to his servant. "From now on, I want a complete report every day regarding any negative rumors being spread about me. I also want the names of those responsible. And get me a list of the fifty most degrading and uncomfortable positions we have. I'll teach those measly rumormongers to trifle with me."

"Yes, sire."

"Well, get to it!"

"Yes, sire." Behemoth hurried out but almost immediately stuck his head back inside. "Beelzebub is here to see you, sire."

"What does he want?"

"I believe you sent him to investigate the origins of the Angel person."

"That's right. Send him in."

"Hi, Boss," Beelzebub said as he entered, surrounded by a swarm of flies.

"Don't 'hi' me. I'm not in the mood. And get those damn flies out of my office."

Beelzebub's dark and bloated but imposingly wise face fell a bit, and he brushed the flies out of his shaggy fur and shooed them out the door with his bat-like wings. He quickly shut the door, but a few of the flies managed to dart back inside, and they began lazily buzzing in and out of his ears and arched nostrils.

"Did you find out anything?" the Devil demanded.

"Maybe. No one seems to have any knowledge of Angel, but there is one peculiarity, albeit tentative, connection. She appeared at the exact moment that one of our inmates was assigned here."

"What's so peculiar about that? We have multiple admissions all the time. Just last week that flood in the American Mid-West sent half a dozen down here at once, and there was that terrorist cell that blew themselves up. We had to chain Cerberus to keep him from eating one of them."

"Well, yes, sir, that's true. But I checked with Cerberus and Remoron, and both of them say that this particular inmate was the only person to come through at that exact time."

"Yes, yes," the Devil mused. "I seem to remember now when I asked Remoron about Angel after she appeared. Rob, wasn't it?"

"Bob, Boss."

"Right. So you think that there is some kind of link between Angel and this inmate?" the Devil asked, eyes narrowing. "It seems pretty circumstantial."

"If that's all there was, I might not even have mentioned it," Beelzebub said. "But there's one more interesting bit of information. Bob was originally assigned to the pit of boiling shit...."

"What do you mean 'originally?'" the Devil interrupted angrily.

"That's just the point—he's not there now."

"What? How can that be?"

"I don't know, Boss."

"Well, where is he?"

"I know it's mighty peculiar, but apparently he's out and wandering around."

"What the hell is going on around here?" the Devil shouted. "First that bitch, and now an inmate who's escaped his punishment!"

"Oh, he's still in torment, Boss," Beelzebub temporized quickly. "Just not as bad."

"I don't give a damn if it's still bad or not. I want that bastard back in the shit right now! And while you're at it, find out if he knows anything about Angel."

"You want me to find out how he got out of the lake of boiling shit, too?"

"Yes. You're authorized to use any and all means necessary, including force and torture."

"You'd better make that official, or I can't act. Remember Rule #13,013."

"Right." The Devil whipped out his PDA, made a notation, then looked at the gravely grotesque figure in front of him. "What are you waiting for?"

"Okay, Boss. I'll get right on it."

"You damn well better," the Devil shot at Beelzebub's retreating back.

The door closed, leaving the Devil alone.

Damn it, he thought. It was getting so it was all he could do just to keep things running on an administrative level. Hell just wasn't fun anymore.

⚬⟶ 27 ⟵⚬

"MAYBE I SHOULD HAVE BROUGHT a pitchfork," Beelzebub muttered to himself as he flapped toward the lake of boiling shit. "Or a whip. Anything."

He knew that his personal physical appearance would be terribly fear-inspiring to the average human, but this Bob character probably had seen a lot of Hell by now and might be inured to the appearance of demons. A weapon would help impress on him not only Beelzebub's personal power but the seriousness of the situation. Unfortunately, Beelzebub had left the palace in such a hurry that he hadn't thought of it, and now it was too late. There, below him, was the lake of boiling shit.

Beelzebub descended until his feet touched down not twenty yards from the lake's keeper. What was his name? It was so difficult to keep track of everyone down here, especially the lower echelon demons who watched over the more visceral punishments. He consulted his PDA. Ah, his name was Sapason.

Sapason saw Beelzebub land, and he hurried over.

"Something I can help you with, sir?" Sapason asked. He, of course, knew who Beelzebub was. All the Archons were known by sight to every demon in Hell.

"The Boss sent me to check on one of your inmates. Fellow by the name of Bob."

Fear flickered through Sapason's eyes.

"He's not here," the demon said. "I put it in my report," he went on nervously. "There wasn't anything I could do about it. He just got up and walked out. Once he was on the bank, there wasn't anything I could do to him. You know, Rule #13,013...."

"Don't worry, Sapason. I'm not here to chastise you. Management realizes special circumstances are operating in this case."

"I never heard of anything like it," Sapason said, obviously relieved. "And none of my buddies have, either."

"How have the other inmates reacted?"

Sapason chuckled. "Look at them." He waved toward the pit. Out in the roiling, bubbling effluence, the inmates stood quietly at their appropriate depths, each alone, head bowed over *The Rule Book*. "All Bob did was diligently read the rules—at least that's what it looked like—and suddenly he's out. Now they're all reading. Like it'll do them any good."

"You say it looked like all he did was read the rules. That must mean something else was going on."

"Well...."

"Spit it out," Beelzebub snapped, swallowing a handful of flies, which promptly flew out of his nose. "I don't have time for prevarication."

"He did make a lot of notes while he was reading."

"Notes? How did he make notes, and where?" "With a pencil. In the margins of *The Rule Book*."

"You gave him a pencil?"

"Yes," Sapason admitted, then hurriedly said, "There wasn't a rule against it, and Bob had a good argument."

"Lawyers always do, even if it's wrong. What was it?"

"He said he was having trouble memorizing all the rules correctly and wanted to make notes in *The Rule Book* to help him. He cited Rule #6,935 and said I would be in violation if I didn't give him the pencil to help him comply. I didn't think it would do any harm."

"Apparently, it got Bob out."

"Yes, sir, Bob is a clever sort. Most of those idiots out there wouldn't know a clause from a phrase."

"Well, just in case, don't hand out any more pencils." Suddenly, a frown crossed Beelzebub's face.

"What is it, sir?"

"Rule #734 says that *The Rule Book* must be kept in pristine condition. How was Bob able to write in it?"

"I don't know, sir. I never saw what he wrote."

"It certainly is a puzzle. But whatever happened, we can't afford to let it happen again. Bob has caused a disruption, but it's up to you to keep the rest of the inmates here in line. It might be best to distract them a little here and there."

"They don't give me much chance these days. They used to play cards and such, which gave me the opportunity, but I can't punish them extra for reading the rules."

"I know: Rule #6,935."

"I wouldn't worry, sir," Sapason said confidently. "They'll get bored soon enough. But it might help if you get some hot young couple in here to help stir things up."

"But Rule #9,237 says no ogling."

"So it does, but there's no rule against peeking."

"Is that so?" Beelzebub eyed Sapason with a bit of respect.

"Yeah. They," Sapason waved toward the inmates, "do it as much as they can. I think that's why they play cards so much— not to pass the time but to given themselves a chance to peek at each other over their hands."

"Maybe we should amend the rules," Beelzebub suggested.

"I wouldn't recommend it, sir," Sapason said. "Peeking may not be breaking the rules in and of itself, but it gets them in a position where they can be punished for other infractions."

"I see. Give them an inch so you can take a foot."

"A foot to their asses," Sapason laughed, and Beelzebub joined in.

"I like your spirit," the Archon told Sapason. "But to get back to Bob. As I said, the Boss isn't holding you responsible, so you don't need to worry. But I need to find him. Did you see which way he went?"

"Sure," Sapason said, pointing. "That way."

Beelzebub looked and saw that the path between the various pits of sundry boiling substances was lined with some unsightly, hairy, green substance. An offensive odor wafted from it each time the hot breeze blew.

"Is that grass?" he asked in amazement.

"I think so," Sapason said. "It wasn't there before. Came up right after Bob left. Ugly as hell. Do you think you could send a maintenance crew down to dig it up or poison it or something?"

"I'll do my best, but it may take a few days. Public Works has its hands full right now."

"I heard there was some problem up at the power plant."

"We are having some difficulties," Beelzebub admitted, then before Sapason could ask more questions or get too buddy-buddy, he said, "I guess this Bob won't be too hard to track. I'll report your helpfulness to the Boss."

"Thanks," Sapason called out as Beelzebub launched himself over the lake of boiling shit, caught a thermal, and rode it up a couple of hundred feet. Staring down at the grass-lined path, he saw it winding between the seething pools until it was lost amid a jumble of boulders. Twisting in that direction, he flapped along, following Bob's trail.

Pursuing Bob wasn't all that difficult, and it wasn't just because of the grassy path. A swath of order followed wherever Bob had gone. Beelzebub passed over a woman who had been writing the memoirs of an empty life, only to see that she had fashioned a golem child out of mud and her own blood, and the two of them were laughing and drawing pictures in the dirt next to her abandoned typewriter. Dipping lower, he saw that the pictures were somewhat crude but amusingly sarcastic caricatures of the demons in their vicinity.

Soon after, Beelzebub saw that the inmates of Developers' Swamp had banded together to weave the saw-toothed grass from their hummocks into fences to keep the crocodiles and serpents at bay. Even more amazing, they'd also worked together to weave huts to keep out the tsetse flies. When he got to General Means, he found the old soldier playing poker with the reformed clots of bloody clay who had been his erstwhile enemies. They were using rounds from his machine gun for chips. Means was on a winning streak.

Later, as Beelzebub passed over Caligari City, he noticed that whole groups of the architects were working together to build a huge, gleaming, and rather beautiful spire constructed from the demolished derangement around it. And at the university, he was so amazed to see the campus quadrangle in such order that he descended to find out what was going on.

Whatever it was, things certainly were not as they should be. Instead of watching milling students gather in small mobs to attack a faculty member, all he saw were organized groups sitting quietly around the various professors on their soapboxes. And as he landed, he got an even greater shock. None of the regular students were there. All the groups listening attentively to the professors consisted solely of demons. One of the demons saw him land and hurried over.

"Hello, sir. Welcome to the campus."

"You're one of the truant officers?" Beelzebub asked.

"Well, yes, sir, that's what we used to call ourselves. But these days we prefer the term proctor."

"Where is your cattle prod?"

"We don't use those any more, sir."

"And where are all the students?"

"We sent them to the dorms."

"And why did you do that?" Beelzebub's sneering tone held a note of curiosity.

"They're on the day shift," the demon replied, but seeing Beelzebub's curiosity turning to irritation, it quickly amplified, "There are only so many professors to go around, sir, and we were suddenly flooded with requests from the demon ranks for continuing education courses."

"Continuing education? What kind of continuing education?"

"Oh, all sorts, sir. Foreign languages, computer technology, sociology, ethnography. But our biggest draws are the business fundamentals, accounting, and MBA courses. Perhaps you'd like to register for...?"

"I suppose a human named Bob came through here," Beelzebub interrupted.

"Why, yes, sir. He did. He said he was looking for the palace. He went off that way."

The proctor pointed toward the grassy path as it lead off between two buildings. Beelzebub noticed that the grass border was liberally spattered with delicate blobs of color. Flowers, he realized, feeling gorge rise in the back of his throat. About sixty yards along the path, an inmate maintenance worker was using a hose to water the plants.

Shaking his head, Beelzebub rose into the air again. As he pursued Bob's wake, he was all the more convinced that Bob must be the cause of the disruptions that Hell was going through and very likely the reason that Angel had appeared. He began to build up an image of what Bob must be like, and it was an impressive picture. He couldn't help but feel let down, then, when he finally spotted the tiny figure below him, strolling along at the apex of the swath of order, and descended to see Bob in the flesh.

It was pretty average flesh, Beelzebub mused to himself as he settled onto the path in front of Bob and waited for the man to get to him. When Bob did, he glanced at Beelzebub but didn't seem to really see him. Instead, he started to walk around him.

"Bob," Beelzebub said in his most commanding voice, blowing clouds of flies from his nose and ears.

"You know me?" Bob stopped, looking surprised.

"His Malignant Majesty, the Supreme Power of Evil and Absolute Master of Hell and all its Dominions orders you to return to the pit of boiling shit! At once!"

❧ 28 ❧

"ARE YOU THE DEVIL?" BOB ASKED. The demon before him looked pretty ugly, fearsome, and powerful, but if he was the Devil, Bob had to admit to being less than overwhelmed.

"I am Beelzebub, first of the Archons."

"That's one of the highest in the hierarchy of demons, isn't it?"

"The highest."

"Wow," Bob said. "That makes you something like a vice president or something."

Beelzebub felt an irate flush fill his head, and he snorted derisively, blowing out another swarm of flies, which Bob batted at ineffectually.

"No, I am not a vice president or something. For your information, I am the Devil's right hand."

"So, if the Devil is the CEO, that makes you the president."

"Turn around, now," Beelzebub ordered, tired of the chitchat, "and return to the place of your appointed punishment."

"Well," Bob said unperturbed. "There's the rub, isn't it? If the lake of boiling shit is my proper punishment, that's where I'd be, isn't it?"

"Go!" Beelzebub augmented his fearsomeness by turning his eyes into pits of eternity, and he grew a large pair of horns that writhed like python tails. To top it off, he discharged a bolt of fire from his fingertips.

The bolt was aimed at Bob, but it didn't connect, rebounding instead and scorching Beelzebub, leaving his three-piece suit smoking. Several thousand immolated flies fell to the ground like tiny World War I dogfighters aflame and trailing smoke.

"Nope," Bob said, folding his arms. "Rule #14,342: Inmates are to be punished in a manner equitable with their crimes, and Rule #11,793: Inmates are not allowed to escape their punishment."

"You dare quote the rules to me?"

"Why not? Isn't that what Hell is all about? Rules? Carrying around and memorizing this?" Bob brandished his copy of *The Rule Book*. "I think even you have to obey them."

"Your point?" Beelzebub asked, composing himself and waving the smoke away from his face. He really was curious. After all, this fellow seemed to be far more than met the eye.

"Since I cannot escape my punishment and I am no longer in the pit of boiling shit, then obviously that was not my proper punishment. Maybe my crime on Earth was so brief that my punishment was equally short. Who knows? In any case, I'm not going back."

"The Boss insists," the demon said.

"I don't care what the Boss insists. I only seek my true place in Hell in accordance with the rules. If you demons were worth a damn, you'd have put me in the right place to begin with. But no; someone had to screw things up. Just a little clerical error, and it resulted in an injustice: me in the lake of boiling shit when obviously I wasn't supposed to be there. Some petty-ante bureaucratic error, and it could potentially disrupt all of reality. I'm just doing my best to rectify things."

"Shut the fuck up!" Beelzebub snapped, insulted at Bob's highhanded attitude. He figured that once Bob was speechless, he'd just grab him by the foot and fly back to the lake of boiling shit and drop him into it from the highest altitude of which Beelzebub was capable.

"Shut the fuck up, yourself," Bob replied without rancor.

For a second, Beelzebub was speechless, surprised that Rule #1 had no effect on Bob. But he wasn't totally shocked. Nothing about this guy was normal.

"Until I find my proper place," Bob went on, "all bets are off. I know the rules—probably better than anyone else—and because there's been a mistake, none of them apply to me. So you can go back and tell the Boss I don't give a damn what he says."

"Are you kidding? I don't dare do that."

"Well, tell him anything you like. I don't care. But right now, please move aside so I can pass."

"You don't seem to understand," Beelzebub said, a little taken aback by the word "please." No one had ever dared use such a pejorative term to him in all the millennia he'd been in Hell. "The Boss is, well, the Boss. You don't tell him anything—he tells you. And if he tells you to go somewhere, that's where you go."

"If the Boss wants me to go somewhere, then he can come and tell me himself."

"He has far more important things to attend to than one miserable, low-level sinner."

"I should think he does," Bob said. "But obviously I'm not just some low-level sinner. He'd never send his second in command to take care of a routine matter."

Beelzebub had to acknowledge the truth of that. He'd never seen any inmate running around loose in Hell—or any demon, either, for that matter. Not until Bob and Angel. But the Archon wasn't going to go back to the Devil and admit that he'd failed to make a mere mortal do his bidding.

"Hey," he yelled at a three nearby demons who were wearing filthy hospital scrubs and standing around an operating table. A quack surgeon who had successfully evaded a dozen malpractice lawsuits for wrongful death was strapped to the table, his torso laid raggedly open. One of the demons was poking at various organs with a scalpel while the other two laughed and smoked cigarettes, dropping the ashes into the gaping wound. There was, of course, no anesthetic.

All three demons and their patient had been watching the exchange between the Archon and the mutinous human.

"I need some help over here," the Archon called, and the three demons left the table and waddled over.

"What's the trouble, sir?" one of them asked.

"I have an escaped prisoner here who refuses to return to his punishment."

"What?" the same demon asked. "How can that be?"

"Yeah," said the second. "I never heard of such a thing."

"How did it happen?" asked the third.

"It doesn't matter how it happened," Beelzebub snarled. "I simply want you to take him back where he belongs. Use force if you like."

"I don't think we can do that, sir," said the first demon surgeon. "Rule #13,013 says punishments can be meted out only by the demon officially assigned to a particular punishment. We're assigned to Dr. Applewhite, here."

"Damn it!" Beelzebub barked. "Don't *you* start quoting the rules to me, too!" The three demon surgeons flinched a little as the Archon's eyes blazed, but Bob simply looked on, a bored but tolerant expression on his face. "Besides, I have the Devil's imprimatur on this." A piece of parchment appeared in his hand, and he gave it to the first surgeon, who read it and passed it to the others.

"All right," the first surgeon said. "Rule #13,013 also says that the Devil can do whatever the hell he pleases. We'll help. What do you want us to do?"

"Remove this prisoner and take him immediately to the lake of boiling shit."

"What about the doctor? We can't just leave him, or he won't suffer sufficiently. You know Rule #14,342 says...."

"Two of you should be enough to handle one human," Beelzebub interrupted impatiently. "One of you can stay behind to attend to the doctor until they get back."

The three surgeons dickered about who was going to keep the operation going, but it seemed that none of them wanted the job. All three were weary of the protracted operation and vied for the change of scenery and the chance to create a little impromptu mayhem along the way. At last, according to some demon etiquette that was obscure to Bob, the matter was settled, and two of the demons descended on him.

It struck him that their attack wasn't all that inspired, as if they not only thought him easy prey but also really didn't care much about giving their all to their work. At about three paces, they suddenly stopped and dropped their arms.

"Well, go on!" Beelzebub urged. "Get him!"

"Can't, sir," shrugged the first surgeon.

"What do you mean you can't?"

"I don't know, sir. It just doesn't feel right."

"Doesn't what?" Beelzebub was dumbfounded, but he managed to keep it hidden. He puffed himself up again, blew more flies from his ears and nose and rumbled, "Do you know who I am?"

"Yes, sir. You're Beelzebub."

"You don't want me to go back and tell the Boss you refused a direct order, do you? *His* direct order?"

Both the demons blanched, and the one who had been forced to stay behind gave a contemptuous guffaw at their expense.

"No, sir," said the first surgeon.

"Well, then, get to it, and show a little spunk."

"Yes, sir." The first surgeon elbowed his companion. "Come on." Muscles flexing, claws grasping, and big, snaggled-toothed grins splitting their ugly faces, they rushed Bob.

To no avail. Both just bounced off and landed on their duffs.

"It's no use, sir," the first surgeon said, getting up and dusting himself off. "We can't get near him."

"It's the rules," Bob told Beelzebub. "I'm not supposed to be in the lake of shit, and that's that."

"Well, would you kindly tell me where you *are* supposed to be?"

"I'm not sure," Bob said truthfully. "But I'm looking for it."

"Maybe you should just let him go, sir," said the second surgeon. "He can't get around the rules. He'll eventually wind up where he's supposed to be."

"Don't presume to give me advice, you fucking quack," Beelzebub growled, and the surgeon shriveled beneath his gaze. "Go on back to your duty, and be glad the Boss doesn't send you to supervise the lava gleaners like he did another miserable upstart today."

The surgeons hurried to rejoin their companion at the table, and all three paid assiduous attention to their patient. His screams would have been most gratifying to Beelzebub if he wasn't so concerned about this situation with Bob.

"What the hell am I going to do with you?" the Archon asked reflectively.

"Nothing, obviously," Bob said.

"Nothing for the moment. But this isn't over."

With an angry thrust of his legs, Beelzebub launched himself into the air and flew off toward the palace.

Bob watched him go, a thoughtful look on his face, then he turned to skirt the three surgeons and continue along the path.

29

As Bob passed the surgical table, he noticed that one of the smoking demons lit a cigarette and stuck it between the lips of the eviscerated patient.

"Thanks," the man said, taking a big puff. Bob could see his lungs inflate, and here and there, tiny jets of smoke squirted out of holes the surgeons previously had poked in them.

Averting his gaze, Bob hurried on. The sight wasn't any worse than many of the other grotesqueries milling all around the plains and hills and valleys and labyrinths of Hell, but Bob found he couldn't steel himself to some of the more graphic elements of his environment. Moving out of view of the surgeons and their patient, he forgot about them as he pondered the new turn of events presaged by Beelzebub's visit.

Now that had been something, hadn't it? Number two in Hell's hierarchy had come to put him, Bob, one minor sinner, in his place, and he hadn't succeeded.

But the Archon couldn't have known ahead of time that he would fail, and anyway, that wasn't the point. What was important was that he'd come at all. It certainly seemed like overkill—akin to sending an elephant to stamp out an ant. Bob suddenly realized that, while he was only a minor sinner, something about him was important, and it had to be more than the fact that he was walking around when he shouldn't be. That was easily explained by his discovery that order was the key.

He thought back over the miles that he'd come, and he couldn't help but reflect on certain words of dissension he'd heard. How had General Means put it? "I'm sick of being in this hole." But inmates could be expected to complain, and that was, it seemed to Bob, not only an element of their punishment but a way of keeping them in their places. If the inmates concentrated exclusively on the smaller things, such as their physical discomfort or boredom or the like, they wouldn't have time to look at the bigger picture.

As Bob had.

And Bob had gotten out. Obviously, it wouldn't benefit the jailer demons if other inmates replicated Bob's feat. After all, from what Bob could tell, there were a whole lot more inmates than jailers—most likely millions of times more. He chuckled at what Hell would look like if all the humans threw off their bondage and started running around loose. Now, *that* would be chaos!

But the next moment, he sobered. Yes, it was natural for the inmates to complain, but Bob also recalled the grumbling he'd heard from the jailers. In this, the surgeons had not been exceptions. There was Sapason, the truant officer, and others.

Something was going on, but what?

If you need answers, one of his better law school professors once advised, ask questions.

All around him were demons torturing and tormenting inmates— as well as inmates torturing and tormenting each other and themselves. Bob went up to the nearest demon, who was wearing the uniform of the Selma, Alabama, Police Department and holding a slavering, horned German shepherd on a loose leash. The shepherd had a mouthful of really big, sharp teeth and was using them to chew the hell out of a fat, middle-aged white man with a buzz haircut.

"Hey," Bob said to the demon.

The demon eyed Bob suspiciously. "I don't believe I ever seed you round here, afore," he said in a Southern accent as thick as molasses. "Why ain't you in eternal torment, boy?"

"Let's just say I'm on parole," Bob said.

"Ain't never heard a such a thang." Curiosity began to edge out the suspicion.

"It's a quirk in the rules," Bob said, holding up *The Rule Book*.

"Always did admar a man who cud twist tha rules ta his advantage," the demon said.

"Got a few minutes to chat?"

"Sure," the demon replied, jerking his chin toward the dog. "Adolph's doin all tha work. Ah ain't got nuthin ta do but watch."

Bob introduced himself, and the demon said his name was Bubba.

"Come on," Bob said. "No demons are named Bubba."

"Yeah, well, yer right bout that," the demon said. "Ma real name is Tablat, but Ah'd perfer ya call me Bubba. Goes with tha territory, you might say, an besides, Ah'm a methid acter. Gotta keep in charicter, ya know."

"Okay, Bubba. Look, I've been walking around for a week or so, ever since I got out of the lake of boiling shit...."

"Howja manage that?"

"Trade secret," Bob said. "If I tell you, then you'll tell someone else, and pretty soon all the inmates are running around loose."

"Ah get yer drift," Bubba said. "But that might not be inny worse'n thangs is now."

"I was going to ask about that. How are things going in Hell?"

"Look round fer yerself," Bubba waved. "This place is gittin downright crowded. There ain't hardly no place decint ta torment yer charge nomore. An that ain't ta mention tha overtime."

"Overtime?"

"Yeah. Over tha last hunerd years er so, we keep gittin more n more folks here, but ya know there ain't but a limited number a demons. We're elemental, ya know. Created. We ain't indiscriminate breeders like people. Tha more people breed, tha more we git comin here, but thays only so many uv us demons ta go round. Hell, Ah already wuz pullin double shifts til bout 1900, but then, fer bout fifty years, humans started killin each other in real quantities. We had us a mighty big influx there fer a while, then fer a decade er so, thangs slacked off a mite. But thay started ta pick up agin in tha mid-'60s. This bastard," he indicated the man Adolph was masticating, "cum in bout that time. Since then, Ah bin pullin triple shifts. But Ah guess Ah'm lucky. Summa ma buddies have ta deal with soldiers who committed war atrocities, an you kin imagine how noisy an exhaustin that might be when ya gotta do it twenty-four/seven/three-sixty-five."

"Don't you have any time off?"

"Right now, a coupla hours a day. Barely enough time ta get ma rocks off an grab a bite ta eat. But who kin say whut tomorrow'll bring? You humans cain't seem ta stop fuckin each other over in escalatin amounts an ever more ingenious ways."

"It is pitiful," Bob agreed. "But at least you have a job."

"Like Ah really need one," Bubba said. "Look, don't ya thank all this gits tiresum after a while? Ah mean, Ah sit here fer hours a day watchin Adolph chew up Charlie's arms, then his legs, then his arms, then his legs. It's pretty fuckin repetitive. An that's not tha worst uv it. All uv a suddin, tha Boss'll show up—he makes reglar rounds, ya know. Visits ever few months er so. But all he ever does is criticize an then try ta tell ya how ta do yer work. Micromanagin, like he knows whut tha fuck goes on in tha trenches. Who's here day in an day out with Charlie, here? Tha Boss? Fuck no. It's me!" Bubba thumped his chest. "But tha Boss cums in an says, why doncha do this, er do that, er do it faster, er do it harder, er do it differnt? It's worsn ma fuckin ol lady. Hell, it's easy fer him ta talk, but all he really does is throws kinks inta pracedures an disrupts schedules an genrally mucks thangs up. He'd see it wuz true if he wuz down here doin this stuff day after day instead uv flyin round all high an mighty like he does."

"Sounds to me like you need a vacation or something."

"You thank fuckin managemint gives a shit bout us grunts?" Bubba snorted. "Thay don't give a rat's ass bout innythang but thay's fuckin quotas. It really chaps ma ass." In confirmation, a puff of noxious smoke rose from behind him.

"Isn't there anything you can do?"

"Ah don't know," Bubba said. "Maybe. Me an ma buddies bin sayin there needs ta be a change round here. Sumthin a little less stringint than tha reglar way thangs is run."

"Why don't you organize?" Bob suggested.

"Whut you mean organize?"

"Like a union. You know, get together to demand fair hours and decent working conditions."

190

"That's an idear," Bubba said. "Hell, Ah thank we got us sum corrupt union organizers here sumwheres. We could get us sum perfeshunul advice."

"I'm sure you can," Bob said. "Listen, what I wanted to ask you is, have you noticed anything unusual going on around here the last few months?"

"Unusual?" Bubba guffawed. "Ah tell ya, Bob, ever since this here Angel bitch showed up, thangs round here's bin goin all ta hell in a handbaskit."

"You mean there's an angel over here?"

"She ain't really no angel," Bubba said. "Thay jist calls her that cuza tha way she looks. She's sum chick in a white robe who's bin hangin round with tha Boss. She even lives in tha palace. Rumor has it she got him by tha short-uns, if ya know whut Ah mean."

"But she's not an inmate or a demon?"

"Naw. Ah seed her onct, an it's obvious she don't belong here. An frum whut Ah hear, if she ain't screwin tha Boss, she's jist screwin thangs up."

"How so?"

"Makin tha Boss go soft," Bubba said. "He even sent out fer mouthwash an deodrant an such cuz she complained bout his BO. Haw! Kin you imagine! She prolly got him usin talcum powder betwixt his cloven hooves by now."

"What's she look like?"

"Long blond hair, real purty face. A genuwine honey. Cain't say as Ah blame him, but it jist ain't right lettin her suck up ta him an distractin him whilst tha volcano cools off, tha glacier melts, an tha power plant shuts down."

"What?"

Bubba explained to Bob about the three major utility outages that were plaguing Hell at the moment.

Bubba leaned close and whispered confidentially in Bob's ear, "Sum folks thanks it's all her fault cuz all tha shit started right after she showed up."

"Really? And when was that?"

"Exactly three months, one week, two days, six hours, forty-seven minutes, an four seconds ago."

Exactly as long as I've been here, Bob mused to himself, though he knew he'd been alone with both Cerberus and Remoron.

"Well," he said, "Looks like you've got problems."

"Yeah," Bubba said. "An now we got us a inmate on tha loose." He chuckled. "Hell, Ah might as well join in tha fun. Hey, Adolph!" Bubba jerked on the leash, pulling the demon dog off Charlie. "Back off, boy. Hey, Charlie, wanna go get a brew with me an ma buddies? Maybe watch sum football?"

"Sure," Charlie said. "Gimme a few minutes ta let ma arm heal, will ya? Cain't hold a frosty cold'n when ya ain't got no hand."

"Sure thang." Bubba turned to Bob. "Wanna cum along?"

"Thanks, but I've got something else to do. What's the shortest way to the Devil's palace from here?"

"Jist go that way." Bubba pointed. "Be seein ya," he called after Bob. "An thanks fer tha union idear. Me an Charlie's gonna talk ta ma buddies bout it."

Bob barely heard him, thoughts elsewhere—namely on an outrageous but very intriguing possibility. His lawyerly mind went to work—not like a shark voraciously ripping and tearing its prey, but like an octopus patiently prying open an oyster shell one ligament at a time. And Bob knew that inside an oyster lay not only meat but, possibly, a pearl. And this pearl was mind-boggling. Bob was in Hell because of the curse he'd laid on the unknown person who'd thwarted his plans back on Earth. Could that unknown person have been...?

Bob shook his head. No, that couldn't be. It was crazy.

But crazy or not, maybe his curse *had* worked in some oblique manner. The evidence was circumstantial, but it pointed in a single direction. First, there was the interesting coincidence of this Angel person's inexplicable appearance at the exact moment that Bob had entered Hell. Next, there was the seeming congruence of their appearances with all the failing utilities and the growing dissension in the demonic ranks. And apparently, Angel couldn't be destroyed, even by the Devil, while Bob not only had gotten out of his punishment but couldn't be harmed, even by Beelzebub acting under the Devil's direct orders.

Those last two inescapable facts cemented the bizarre truth. Inadvertently, Bob had cursed the Devil, and all hell had broken loose!

ჿ 30 ჾ

"I'M AFRAID HE WON'T GO."

"Won't go?" The Devil was nonplussed. He wasn't used to being denied, and Beelzebub could see dark coals smoldering in the depths of his eyes.

"Back to the lake of boiling shit," Beelzebub amplified. "I did everything I could. Nobody could touch him."

"Like Angel," the Devil mused.

"Yes. They've got to be linked."

"But which came first?"

"Bob, I think. We have a complete dossier on him but nothing at all on Angel." Beelzebub set a thick folder on the Devil's desk. The Devil picked it up and sped-read through it, pausing here and there to chuckle or nod approvingly. Until he got to the end.

"What the hell is this?" he demanded. Beelzebub didn't have to look to know what his boss meant.

"It's a curse," Beelzebub replied. "Bob was a pretty marginal fellow, but he would have wound up back in Purgatory except for that. It's what actually landed him here."

"Who did he curse?"

"We haven't gotten that far, yet," Beelzebub said. "Apparently, he cursed somebody at his company who screwed up his chance at the big time—a chance, I might add, that would have put him here for sure, curse or no curse. Then he croaked with the curse on his lips. I thought you'd want to see the dossier before we wasted precious demon-hours tracking down some smarmy company exec with a more deft touch than Bob. We'll be seeing him, or her, soon enough."

"That could take another thirty years," the Devil snorted, tossing the dossier onto his desk. "I don't think we can wait that long. Look how much things have deteriorated in just a few months." He got up, stepped to the window, and stared at the volcano's sputtering crown. "All this can't be happening because of one measly little curse," he muttered. "There's got to be more." He turned back to Beelzebub. "This jackanapes is causing problems well beyond his capacity. I want you to find out who he cursed, and you better be damn quick about it."

"I'll get right on it," Beelzebub promised.

"Where is Bob right now?"

"Last time I saw him, he was passing by those cretins we assigned to eviscerate Dr. Applewhite—you know, one of our quack surgeons. He's probably not there now, but he won't be hard to find. He's leaving a distinct trail behind him."

"Like the slime trail left by a slug?"

If the Devil expected Beelzebub to smile at the vague lawyer joke, he was disappointed. The Archon merely wrinkled his mouth and shook his head, dislodging a horde of flies that began buzzing around, partially obscuring his features.

"Order," he said. "He's leaving a trail of order."

"Order?"

"Grass, flowers, sweet smells, happiness."

"Shit!"

"It's worse."

"What could be worse?" The Devil was trying to visualize grass and flowers in Hell, and that was almost as hard as visualizing order.

"Camaraderie," Beelzebub said. "Between the jailers and the inmates. You wouldn't believe it, but I saw General Means playing poker with the enemy."

"No! That guy is positively xenophobic."

"Not since Bob talked to him."

"What did he say?"

"I don't think he had to *say* anything. He's got this aura about him. It's not goodness, but it is something that encourages organization. He even started quoting *The Rule Book* to me."

"This is outrageous. He's got to be stopped."

"I agree, but I'm not the one who can do it. He said he'd only talk to you. He said you'd have to come to him, but I don't think he's waiting. In fact, he seems to be working his way toward the palace."

"Is that right?" The Devil nodded, his eyes narrowing. "Smart fellow to go right to the top. Maybe I'll go see him."

"Excuse me, sir, but I don't think that's wise."

"He's fucking everything up. I've got to do something."

"Going to him will be a sign of weakness on your part."

"Quite right. You say he's on his way here? Well, let him come. When he arrives, I'll have Behemoth make him wait a suitable length of time before admitting him into my perfectly demonic presence."

"Sounds like a good plan, sir."

"How long until he gets here?"

"A few more days. What will you do until then?"

"I'm not going to sit around stewing in my own juices, that's for sure. I think I'll go to the volcano. That's our biggest problem, and if I have to be there personally to whip the technicians into shape, so be it."

"Very good, sir. I'll call you when Bob arrives. By then, I should know more about this curse."

"Curse?" came an all-too-feminine voice from the doorway to the Devil's office. "What curse?"

It was Angel, of course, and not a hair was out of place, not a smudge marred her clothes, and not a drop of sweat disturbed her pearly brow. It really pissed the Devil off. He calculated he'd made her walk maybe two hundred miles this last time—far enough, anyway, that his wing muscles ached—and she was still as fresh as driven snow, as pure as....

Stop it! he ordered himself. Aloud he said, "Excuse me, my dear, but I have to fly off immediately. My presence is required elsewhere. I don't think you should try to follow me because I'll be back by dinner, and if you do, you won't."

He didn't try edging by her through the doorway—he knew her cloying touch would entice him to linger indefinitely with promises of sweet surrender—the sweet syrup of the trap and a surrender that would never come. Instead, he simply turned without another word or glance, strode onto the balcony, and flung himself from the parapet.

As his ebon form sped away from the palace, Beelzebub turned to Angel, who was staring forlornly after her paramour.

"The poor dear," she said. "He's been so busy, he hasn't had time for me all week. I'll just have to *make* him slow down before he hurts himself." Then she looked at Beelzebub. "What's this about a curse?"

Beelzebub wanted to lie, but he'd already learned that he couldn't lie to her. Apparently no one could, except maybe the Boss, and Beelzebub sometimes wondered about *him*. But Beelzebub *could* prevaricate, but even this talent was weakened in her presence.

"Oh, nothing much."

"But it must be if you two are talking about it. Tell me."

He had to tell her. Something.

"It's just one of the humans. He died with a curse on his lips."

"But surely there are lots of such people down here. What makes this one so special?"

"It seems that, somehow, he has escaped his punishment, and he's running around loose, disrupting things. We're not sure if the curse is involved or not."

"My goodness!"

She actually seemed upset, the first time Beelzebub had seen her that way. Maybe she's beginning to turn, he thought, then immediately rejected the notion. More likely, in her goodness, she understood the necessity for punishment, and it distressed her to know that someone had escaped her beloved's clutches. Or maybe she vaguely realized that Bob might have something to do with the way everything was breaking down. Of course, all she'd really care about was that the extra work was keeping her beloved away from her.

"What does that mean?" she went on. "Surely Nicky can do something about it, can't he. After all, he's the boss."

"I'm afraid it's not that simple," Beelzebub said. "You understand that all of this," he waved around, "is merely a physical representation of universal constants."

"Yes," she said. "I know. The yin and yang. And my dear Nick is the perfect embodiment of the yin in all its contrariness."

"That's right. But universal constants are held in place by universal laws, and nobody—not even the Boss or the Big Cheese—can alter those one whit."

"You mean that curses are a universal law?"

"Not exactly. Deathbed curses are...how can I put it? They're like clauses that invoke certain universal laws that normally lie dormant. Once they're invoked, no one quite knows what's going to happen, but you can be sure it'll be bad."

"But can't Nicky stop it?"

"If a star goes nova, there's nothing anybody can do. It will burn up everything in its range without regard to whether it's incinerating the good or the evil."

"Then there's nothing he can do?" She sounded so forlorn that Beelzebub had to reassure her.

"Perhaps."

"That sounds like there *might* be something."

"We're still looking into it," Beelzebub waved offhandedly. "It's probably not even worth mentioning."

"Please. I need to know there is some hope Nicky can restore order."

I wouldn't call it a hope, Beelzebub though. Or order.

"All right," he said. "Look. The nature of a curse is that if the one who laid the curse apologizes to the one who was cursed, then the curse is negated and the one who laid it is absolved of the sin, since sin is directly linked to action—or inaction—and its consequences. So, if this man tells the person he cursed that he's sorry for cursing him, we can send him to Purgatory and stop him from further disrupting the workings of Hell."

"That's wonderful," Angel clapped, her eyes lighting up. "Then all we have to do is find out who he cursed, get him to apologize to him, and everything will be all right again."

Or all wrong, Beelzebub thought, but he didn't say it aloud. Angel just wouldn't understand.

"That's just what I'm going to do right now," he told her. "If you will excuse me...." He left the room quickly before he was forced to mouth any more disgusting syllables. Or be forced to reveal to Angel that, apparently, she was a major manifestation of the curse.

He didn't want to hurt her feelings like that.

❧ 31 ❧

THE DEVIL FLEW AS FAST as he could away from the palace, but after a few minutes, he realized with a shock that he wasn't even heading toward Mount Etna. Instead, he was simply fleeing from Angel. He stopped and hovered for a few moments, gathering his wits and staring out over his crumbling domain. Even the fiery sky was losing its luster.

"Fuck it," he said, after thinking about the volcano. "I want to get a gander at this Bob fellow." He'd do it surreptitiously, so Bob wouldn't even realize he was there.

So off the Devil flew, toward the last place Beelzebub had seen Bob. He arrived there an hour or so later and settled near the surgical table. Much to his surprise, the table was empty, and the surgeons were nowhere to be seen.

He found them a few minutes later, sitting on some small boulders they'd rolled into a circle around a larger one. Highball glasses sat on the larger boulder, and there were four bimbos in nurse's caps, white stockings, and black spike heels sitting with them. A short distance away, a jazz band was playing an upbeat rendition of "I Put a Spell on You."

"Aren't you supposed to be torturing this man?" the Devil asked as he came over to the boulder, gesturing to Dr. Applewhite. Applewhite was still opened up from sternum to pubis, but all his insides were holding nicely in place, mostly because he was leaning back a little. A taller boulder was positioned behind him to help prop him up.

"Hi, Boss," said the first surgeon, lifting his glass in a salute. "We were, but then it was break time."

"Break time? What's that supposed to mean? Hell's punishment is constant and eternal. There are no breaks."

"We used to think that, too," the second surgeon said. "But it seems that there are other factors involved."

"What other factors?"

"Well, Dr. Applewhite butchered forty-seven patients, each averaging thirty years of ruined life, for a total of 1,410 years, right?"

"Yes, yes. Get on with it."

"But he's going to be here for eternity."

"And?"

"Well, if each inmate is to be punished in a manner equitable with his or her crime, and the good doc here only destroyed 1,410 years' worth of life, then he should only be punished for an equal number of years. As soon as we reached that conclusion, we realized we could space out his punishment and have a bit of fun here and there in between. Break the monotony, you know."

Perturbed, the Devil looked from one surgeon to the next, his eyes finally settling on Dr. Applewhite, who smiled jovially and raised his glass.

"Care to have a drink with us?" Applewhite asked.

The Devil looked at the first surgeon again and said, "Get him back on that table right now."

"But what about the rules?"

"Has he completed the 1,410 years that you so cleverly assume is his equitable punishment?"

"No, sir," the surgeon said. "Only a little more than seventeen."

"Then he has 1,393 to go, right?"

"Right."

"Get him back on the table. He is to serve his full sentence immediately and without a break."

"Can we finish our drinks, Boss?" asked the third surgeon, who appeared to be in his cups already.

In answer, the alcohol burst into flames, shattering the glass and spilling the burning liquid all over the third surgeon's paw.

"There," the Devil said. "You're finished."

The demon surgeon yelped and tried to shake out the flames, but that only fanned them more.

"I want to know who gave you the idea that you could make decisions about punishment on your own," the Devil demanded, ignoring the third surgeon's antics.

"Nobody, sir," the first surgeon replied, carefully but quickly setting his own drink on the boulder table. "We just sort of realized it on our own."

"Right after a fellow named Bob came by," the second surgeon put in. "Real nice fellow."

"He didn't suggest altering the punishment?"

"Not exactly, sir," the first surgeon said. "He did say something to Beelzebub about Rule #14,342 and punishments being meted out equitably for crimes committed on Earth."

"Would you get to the point?" the Devil snapped.

"I am, Boss," the first surgeon said nervously. "Bob said maybe he'd gotten out of his punishment because his crime on Earth had been brief, so his punishment had been equally short. Well," the surgeon shrugged, "he was out, wasn't he? So he must have had a valid point, which set us to thinking, after he left, about Dr. Applewhite's tenure on the table, and that, according to Rule #14,342, he really has only 1,410 years total punishment."

"Your thinking is as confused as your syntax," the Devil sneered. "Which way did Bob go?"

By now, the third surgeon's flaming paw had burned itself out, and he was just standing there, staring disconsolately at the seared flesh and melted talons. Anxious to redeem himself by being as helpful as possible, he lifted the still-smoking ruin and pointed with it to a path lined with grass and wildflowers.

"That way, Boss," he said.

"Get Applewhite back on the table, now," the Devil snarled, and he took off without waiting to see if the surgeons complied.

As soon as he lofted high enough to spot the direction Bob's trail led, however, Mount Etna belched a huge pall of black smoke, and the glow from the crater dimmed noticeably. Bob would have to wait, the Devil realized. Right now, other matters were more pressing. Besides, Bob would work his own way to the palace before long.

Abandoning his search for the renegade inmate, the Devil winged his way toward the volcano.

When he arrived, he immediately regretted his side trip to spy on Bob, which only had pissed him off, anyway. As he flew over the crater, it was giving off a mere feeble sputter and a few sparks, and he could see that the lava dome inside had retreated a couple of hundred feet more than the last time he'd viewed it. Even the vents on the slopes no longer emitted steady rivers of magma—some were reduced to puny trickles, and a couple had ceased to flow altogether.

He swooped low over one of these and saw that the lava gleaners in it were now held immobile by the solidifying magma. Since the lava was now rock hard and it was impossible for them to pick half-melted chunks from it, they seemed to be doing nothing but chatting amicably among themselves. Not surprising, he thought. The hardened lava was probably several thousand degrees cooler than the molten version, which meant they no longer were in terrible pain. Some of the women were even fixing themselves up, using shards of obsidian as mirrors and ash as mascara, and a group of men tossed a rounded piece of pumice among themselves like a ball.

The Devil landed on the surface and went over to the demon in charge, who was lounging back on his boulder, smoking a cigar and reading *Seduction of the Minotaur* by Anais Nin.

"What the hell's going on here?" the Devil bellowed, and the demon, who had been so engrossed in his book that he hadn't seen the Devil approach, jumped, dropping the book and scattering cigar ash all over his stiff, leathery prong.

"Shit!" the demon spat. "You scared the bejeezus out of me."

"I asked you what the hell's going on here?"

"What does it look like?" the demon asked.

The Devil didn't appreciate the demon's snottily seditious tone any better than he did the noncommittal reply. With a flick of a talon, both the cigar and the Anais Nin vanished in puffs of smoke.

"If you don't want that to happen to you," he warned, "you'd better straighten up."

"Yes, sir," the demon said, straightening up but not even attempting to mask the supercilious insubordination in his eyes.

"Now tell me what is going on here. These people are supposed to be in torment, and it's your job to see that their work gets done."

"As you can see, sir, the lava's stopped flowing, hence there's no torment or work to be done. What can I do about it? Keeping the lava flowing isn't my job."

"You could improvise," the Devil said with annoyance.

"You know we demons don't know how to improvise," the demon said. "We're sticklers for the rules."

"Well," the Devil said with more than a trace of sarcasm. "Let me improvise for you. Get the hell off your ass and go out there and kick some butt."

"But their butts are all buried in solid rock."

"Well kick their heads!"

"You know I can't do that," the demon said, looking a little shocked. "Rule #14,342 says prisoners are to be punished in a manner equitable...."

"Don't you dare quote the fucking rules to me you two-bit...."

"There's no need to get abusive with me," the demon snapped, puffing himself up a little. "It's bad enough you personally demoted me to this rock from my cushy delivery job, and now you're trying to blame me for problems I have nothing to do with. It's not my fault that the public utility services around here are worthless. If management did its job properly, we wouldn't have these problems."

"I don't think I like your attitude," the Devil snarled, holding his composure with effort. "I'm assigning you to this rock around the clock."

"I don't think so," the demon said. "CRUDE says I don't have to work more than one shift a day."

"The crude what!?" The Devil was so mad that his tail whipped back and forth, snapping little bolts of lightning off its spearhead tip.

"The Consolidated Roster of United Demonic Employees," the demon told him. "The union. I've been elected corresponding secretary."

"And what brilliant mind thought that up?" the Devil demanded scornfully.

"One of my buddies, Bubba, mentioned it while we were watching football. He said some fellow named Bob suggested it. The organizational structure here in Hell is just too flat. Leaves no room for advancement since nobody ever retires or vacates the higher positions. We're gonna change all that."

"You don't seriously think I'm going to stand for your fucking union, do you?" the Devil asked, but his voice lost its edge as he suddenly registered the name Bob.

"What are you going to do? Bring in a bunch of scabs to run things if we go on strike?"

"You demons *are* the scabs," the Devil said.

"That's it," the demon said, huffing himself up. "It's bad enough that you keep those who do the real work under your thumb, but now you resort to racial stereotyping to further your imperialistic aims. I'm reporting you as soon as my shift is over."

"Reporting me to whom?"

"We have a list," the demon warned. "We'll be watching you."

"We'll see about that," the Devil said coldly as he launched himself into the balmy, not-so-smoky air.

"Fair wages!" the demon shouted after him. "Fair hours and decent working conditions!"

His voice faded, thankfully, as the Devil flapped angrily toward the volcano's control room.

❧ 32 ☙

XAPHAN, THE CHIEF VOLCANOLOGIST, WASN'T lounging around reading salacious novels, the Devil noted as he entered Etna's control room. And for good reason, he chuckled. He'd made the volcano staff hot-natured, and with the ambient air temperatures cooling off to a balmy 180 degrees, Xaphan and his two assistants, Tagnon and Buriol, were shivering and blue-lipped despite the heavy fur coats they wore.

"Is there any news?" the Devil demanded.

"I'm afraid nothing concrete, sir," Xaphan chattered. "The flow simply has stopped, and we don't know if it's because the magma is being re-channeled or simply has begun to diminish due to Etna's age. It's a pretty old volcano, as you know, sir."

The Devil knew. It had been his first creation after he'd separated from his brother—the result of his first orgasm. And since that was the case, he didn't appreciate the implication that it was drying up.

But he didn't smite Xaphan because he knew the chief volcanologist hadn't meant to impugn his virility. Besides, he needed Xaphan's expertise to get the damn thing flowing again.

"We're doing everything we can," Xaphan finished lamely.

"Well, you'd damn well better hurry up," the Devil said. "You know that the three of you will freeze solid at one hundred degrees."

"I have teams boring test holes all over the mountain," Xaphan said, fear taking away the chatter of his fangs. "We're sending fire sprites down for a look. We'll find the problem."

The Devil noticed that Xaphan hadn't said anything about fixing the problem once he found it. Had the union gotten to him, too? For a moment, he wondered if he should ask, then he realized that now was not the time for circumspection. Things were bad, and he had to know where the cards lay.

"Have you been approached by anyone from this so-called union? CRUDE"

Xaphan dropped his eyes, and Tagnon and Buriol hung their heads and shuffled like dogs expecting to be kicked.

"Yes, sir," Xaphan admitted. "The day before yesterday. A group of their representatives came and talked to us about joining."

"What did they want?"

Xaphan hesitated.

"Speak!" the Devil commanded.

"They said if we curtailed production sufficiently, together we'd be able to gain considerable strategic political advantage."

"Is that so? Just who were the members of this committee?"

"I don't know, sir. I never saw them before, and they didn't identify themselves."

"What did you tell them, Xaphan?"

"What *could* I tell them, sir? I'm half frozen now. If I curtail production any more, I'll be solid before you know it. What kind of political advantage is *that*?"

Both Tagnon and Buriol nodded as vigorously as they could, their necks creaking with cold.

"I'd better not find out that you're lying to me and you're really in bed with the union," the Devil warned. "I'll plant all of you in the middle of the glacier." Assuming, he thought with a touch of unease, that it wasn't completely melted by then.

"I would never lie, sir," Xaphan said. "At least, not to you."

"All right," the Devil said. "Get back to work."

"Yes, sir," the three volcanologists chorused, and the Devil strode out of the control room and took to the air. On a whim, he wheeled around the lava field a couple of times, then landed on the rock in its middle, where the insolent demon had resurrected the Nin book and was engrossed in it.

"You again," the demon said, looking up. "What now?"

"This," the Devil hissed, and his tail lashed out. At least that was working properly. Its razor-sharp, spade-shaped tip sliced neatly through the demon's neck, and the demon's head toppled into its own lap. There was no blood, of course, and both the head and the body remained alive, though the body became inert after losing what little intelligence it once had.

The Devil picked up the head by the tuft of hair on its crown and watched it mouth silent obscenities for a moment before he laughed in its face.

"Tell it to your CRUDE friends," he said, then he lobbed the head to the nearest of the men who'd been tossing around the chunk of pumice. "Here," he called. "This'll be more fun to play ball with. Be careful, though—it might bite."

With that, the Devil again lofted and headed toward the palace. But after a few moments, he changed direction. Cutting off that insolent demon's head had lightened his mood and made him realize how seriously he'd neglected his rounds lately. He thought he'd fly around a bit, have a little fun, and at the same time, scope out the effect that the union was having on his domain.

For the rest of the day, he landed here and there, adding a little heat, a little more weight, or some other embellishment to each punishment he attended. All the minor demons seemed deferential enough, though he caught several of them looking sideways at him when they thought he wouldn't notice.

He had a particularly good time with a prominent American televangelist who'd used his pulpit to preach hatred of various sorts while privately engaging in just about every one of the mortal sins. The fact that he'd been about one inch from being insane hadn't prevented him from winding up here, continually doomed to seek Biblical justification for his evermore-bizarre pronouncements and behavior. The Devil brought in a woman who'd sold her children to pay for cosmetic surgery and silicone implants. When she came up, rolling her humongous breasts before her in a large wheelbarrow, the televangelist practically foamed at the mouth with lust while his hands quickly flipped through the Bible for some passage that he could twist to his advantage.

"God hates gays, and this proves I'm not gay," he babbled as he tried to dive head first into the half a ton of smotheringly salacious flesh quivering before him. But the Devil had chained his ankle to a rock using links forged from the coins that cripples had donated to the televangelist in hopes of being miraculously cured, and the man's slavering lips were brought up one inch short of the woman's platter-sized nipples.

For her part, the woman tried to back up in horror, but the Devil fused the tire of her wheelbarrow to the ground, and she couldn't get away.

The Devil's next stop was even more satisfying, at least at first. It was a ruined town of stone and mud brick houses. In a constant confusion of motion on both sides of the street, men carrying bombs strapped around their bodies emerged from houses, kissed their families goodbye, and rushed to the other side of the street where they detonated the bombs, only to see, in the final instant, that their families had been transported to the exploding buildings. After the last of the rubble rained down, the house, the bomber, and the family would be resurrected, only to reenact the scenario time and again. The families weren't the bombers' actual families, only simulacrums, but the bombers didn't know that—only that their acts of terrorism had horribly destroyed their own loved ones.

Picking out a few of the more heinous, the Devil swapped machine guns and rocket propelled grenades for their bombs, but he grew impatient with the results. Then he tried nerve gas and deadly viruses and watched the terrorists' anguish as their wives and children died hideous deaths. The accelerated Ebola was pretty neat, but after an hour or so, he found he was getting bored. And antsy, as well. Hell was going to hell, and he was just sitting around playing compensatory games when there was real work to be done.

He wasn't, he realized, trying to avoid the work. He was avoiding returning to the palace. And Angel. All that awaited him there was another cloying meal and another dull evening watching some insipid movie on TV. Or worse, one of the reality shows Angel had grown fond of lately. No—worse was the fact that he wouldn't be able to stop himself from going along.

He'd sit there, uncomplaining, as he ate food that turned his stomach and watched entertainment that was even more boring than watching the terrorists replay their final acts of familial destruction ad nauseam.

But what choice did he have? He couldn't perpetually fly around Hell or go find a corner to cower in. He had to go home sometime.

Steeling himself, he flapped off toward the palace.

By the time he reached it, he was bushed. He tried to sneak in through the sliding glass doors to his office, but as usual, Angel had some sixth sense about his location, and she entered moments later.

"You look tired, dear," she said. "How about a nice hot bubble bath to relax you, then we'll eat. I've cooked up a nice mutton roast."

She bustled out to fix his bath, leaving the Devil to ponder how much he hated lamb. Almost as much as bubble baths.

Later, after dinner, they watched an episode of a crime-buster show. As usual, the detectives solved the case and the perpetrator went to jail. Why couldn't TV be like real life, he wondered, where the really bad guys often got away with it? Then they watched some so-called reality show about a corporate executive who was choosing a new apprentice from among a group of people who thought they had the stuff to be really mean, arrogant bastards.

It was nonsense, of course, but it, combined with the crime show, did give the Devil an idea. How about a show featuring corrupt corporate executives who had gotten away with their crimes and were living in luxury in exotic locales on the proceeds of their ill-gotten gains? Now, that would be reality TV! And it would involve almost all the mortal sins simultaneously, making them look not only like suitable means but desirable ends in themselves.

Then he had another idea. That same host could be made president of the U.S. and destroy it from within. He'd put a team on it first thing in the morning. If he had the time. Or a team.

In another ten minutes, he was fast asleep on the couch, his pointed ears subliminally twitching at the sound of canned laughter coming from a dull sitcom.

ᖱ 33 ᖰ

BOB WAS FEELING PRETTY DAMN good. The mountain holding the Devil's castle was only a short distance away, which meant that his long trek across Hell was nearing its end. And boy, was he glad. He'd had just about all he could stomach of pain and madness and heat and stench and choking fumes and revolting nastiness and every other disgusting and abominable thing in this wretched domain. Wasn't there any place here where a guy could feel normal? One public park in this wasteland of torment? One amusing note in this cacophonous maelstrom?

What really pissed him off the more he thought about it was that he'd been incarcerated here along with the most repulsive scum the Earth had ever seen for one measly little curse that he probably would have forgotten about by the next day—if he'd had a next day. But no. Thanks to a freak accident, here he was, senses overloaded, legs aching, and head swimming with all 17,653 rules. Even if he had organized them all, they were a lot to contemplate.

For the last couple of days, he'd avoided everyone as assiduously as he could, human and demon alike. He was sick of the sick bastards, one and all. He almost longed to return to the lake of boiling shit— not because he'd liked the pain or the odor but because he had fond memories of the low-level sinners incarcerated there. They were good folks who'd just made minor mistakes, as he had, and had been treated just as shabbily.

But with the Devil's castle looming almost overhead, he wasn't about to turn back now. Especially since he'd figured out that he was the cause of all the Devil's problems. For once in his life—or, rather, existence—he had a chance to become a real player. It made his aborted tenure at ENDRUN look like practice. Well, the Devil might have thwarted him that time, but it wouldn't happen again. Bob held a strong hand, and even better, he was infused with a sort of supernatural confidence. After all, look what had happened the last time the Devil—the Devil!—had tried to fuck with him. Bob had gone down, but not out, and done what no other human ever had done in the history of Hell by escaping. And even if the trek across Hell had finally worn thin as well as worn him out, he'd done that, too, which he doubted that few could say.

He was ready for anything, he thought jauntily. Even taking on the Devil.

Just then, he strode around a huge boulder and stopped dead in his tracks.

"Hell," he sighed, staring at the river that blocked his way. The sluggish flow looked like it was composed of pus and blood and other equally nasty components, and it's awful reek was nearly palpable and highly redolent of slaughterhouse.

So *this* is where they dump all their wastes, Bob thought. Maybe all the hospitals, too. Not that he cared. He only wanted to get across. He *had* to get across. It was what he'd come all this way and endured everything for. Just on the other side rose the crag on top of which sat the Devil's black castle, and directly opposite him, he could see the path he was on continue in steep switchbacks up the precipitous, jagged slope. But there was no bridge between this side and that.

He'd just been thinking that he was ready for anything, but was he ready to immerse himself in that loathsome liquid and swim to the other side? He'd sooner dunk himself in the lake of boiling shit. Hell, he *had* dunked himself in the lake of boiling shit.

He looked upstream and down, seeing neither bridge nor boat in either direction. But he did see a rather hideous, eight-foot, roach-shaped demon not thirty feet down the bank, supervising a group of inmates who were performing synchronized swimming movements in the gangrenous river. A megaphone dangled from one of her serrated upper limbs. He knew the demon was female, not because he could tell the sex of one roach from another, no matter how huge, but because this one had large, perfectly formed human female breasts jutting from her thorax. As he approached, he saw, disconcertingly, that in place of nipples were eyes that swiveled to watch him as he came closer.

"Are you staring at my tits?" the demon demanded when Bob stopped in front of her. Her voice was a sort of wispy hiss.

"Kinda hard not to when they stare back," Bob said.

"Gotta keep an eye out around here," the demon said. "Lot's of pervs and gropers."

"Are your charges performing water ballet?" Bob asked.

"Pretty good, aren't they?" the demon said proudly. "Trained them myself. I call them the Plisonanauts."

"Is Plisona the name of the river?"

"No," the roach hissed, the eyes in her breasts blinking demurely. "I'm Plisona. The river is the Acheron."

"I thought it might be the Styx."

"No, that's over on the eastern edge of Hell."

"Kind of thick and nasty for water ballet, isn't it?"

"Maybe, but it's very buoyant. They aren't going to drown any time soon." Plisona gave a wheezing laugh. "And at least they only serve one master. See that guy?" She pointed to an aged Japanese man about ten feet away. Though he was standing stock still, he seemed like he was struggling mightily with something. "He serves four: Darek, Isigi, Rigios, and Apormenos. They're all servants of Ashtaroth. Each of them has given him contradictory commands, and so he can't do anything but stand there until one of them relents. That's not likely, at least for a while, since they all are constantly vying with one another and trying to show each other up."

"That doesn't seem so bad," Bob said.

"Oh, yeah?" the female demon asked. "Look closer."

Bob did and saw that the man's feet were rooted in a large mound of dirt.

"Is that what I think it is?" Bob asked.

"Check it out," Plisona answered, tossing a pebble onto the mound.

Instantly, it began to boil with thousands of fire ants.

"What the hell did you do that for?" the man demanded as the ants swarmed up his legs, leaving masses of swelling red welts in their wake. "I just got them settled down."

"Those things are all over the place where I live," Bob said. "Or, lived," he amended. "They don't call 'em fire ants for nothing."

"Well, you can thank Haures for them," the demon said. "One of his specialties is destroying and burning."

"No shit!" cried the man, now covered with the tiny red demons whose bite felt like a pinch of Hell.

"I heard they came from South America," Bob said.

"Maybe," Plisona replied. "But you don't think some Amazon headhunter conjured them up in the first place, do you?"

"He's not going to pop, is he?" Bob asked, gesturing to the man, and taking a few steps back. By now, the man had swollen nearly to the bursting point with toxin, making him resemble an over-inflated balloon with fat appendages and sausage fingers.

"Don't worry," the demon assured Bob. "He used to explode quite nicely in the past, but over the years, he's grown pretty elastic."

"What did he do?"

"He was a shogun," the demon replied, as if that was all the explanation necessary." She stopped for a second, the eyes in her breasts staring intently at him. "Say, you must be Bob."

"Why, yes. How'd you know?"

"Word gets around here pretty fast," she said. "Especially when it's about someone as unusual as you."

"Well, I did escape my punishment," Bob said.

"And stood up to Beelzebub, from what I've heard."

"It was nothing, really."

"What are you doing around these parts?"

"Actually, I was looking for a way across the Acheron."

"You want over *there*?" Plisona asked, pointing with a ragged leg toward the craggy mountain. Amazement was in her voice. "Why?"

"I'm going to see the Boss."

214

"Don't that beat all," she said, shaking her tiny head, twitching her long antennae, and rolling her eyes up in her breasts.

"Are there any bridges or boats?"

"Not any that I know of," she replied.

"Crap. I'm not looking forward to swimming across that." He waved at the Acheron's dreggy flow.

"Can't say I blame you," she said, then her eyes lit, perking up her breasts slightly. "But I might just have an idea."

Lifting her megaphone, she hissed loudly, "All right, troupe, get in a straight line across the river. Space out evenly."

It took the troupe a minute or two to get into position, but when they did, their heads formed a nice stepping stone bridge to the other side.

"Think you can make it across that, Bob?"

"I can make it," Bob assured her.

"Don't mention it. You're the first excitement to come along since this place started, and I want to be able to look back on it and say I did my part to liven things up."

"I won't forget it," Bob assured her. "Thanks, Plisona."

He took a running start and bounded from head to head until he reached the opposite shore.

Once there, he waved back at the giant roach before beginning his arduous climb to the top of the mountain.

❧ 34 ❧

"THE ARCHONS ARE HERE, SIRE," Behemoth told the Devil. "They're in the board room. All except Belphegor."

"Where the hell is he?"

"I don't know, sire."

"Probably holed up somewhere having a snooze," the Devil said, shaking his head. "What about the rest of them? How do they seem?"

"Nervous, sire. Edgy and a bit anxious."

"Excellent," the Devil chuckled. "Maybe I should keep them waiting for a few more minutes."

But, no, he thought. Too much was happening to waste time like that, no matter how entertaining it might be.

"Where's Angel?" he asked.

"She's in the sitting room with some of her female demon friends," the butler answered. "It's their weekly coffee klatch. I believe they're reading poetry and quilting."

What a relief, the Devil thought. Though he couldn't say he approved of what she was doing, at least she was preoccupied, which would give him a chance to have a full meeting without her barging in and disrupting things.

"Tell me the instant her friends leave," the Devil commanded.

"Yes, sire."

Turning, the Devil entered the board room. Indeed, all the Archons were present, even Mammon.

"It's about time you showed up," the Devil said to the demon of greed as he strode to the table and took his place at its head.

"Sorry, Boss," Mammon apologized. "It took me a while to catch up with Adramelech."

"I trust you brought him back with you."

"Of course, Boss. He's in chains in the dungeon. You want the chefs to prepare him for your evening meal?"

"Oh, forget it," the Devil said with a huff. "Let the bastard go. I have more important things to think about now."

What he really was thinking was how repulsed Angel would be if he asked her to butcher and cook the renegade demon. Not that he wouldn't like to see her repulsed, but he just couldn't bring himself to do it.

"All right," he said. "I want to hear the latest on the utility outages. Go ahead, Asmodeus. What's going on at Mount Etna?"

"I'm afraid there's nothing new to report, Boss. The lava dome is still receding, and everything is cooling off. They've drilled a lot of bore holes—so many, in fact, that Xaphan expressed concern about geological instability—but so far, they haven't discovered what's causing the problem."

Shaking his head, the Devil gestured for Leviathan to go ahead.

"Same here, Boss. There's not much new to say, except that the glacier is still melting."

"Don't give me that crap!" the Devil snapped. "How can the glacier be melting if the volcano is cooling and the temperatures in Hell have dropped off? It doesn't make any sense."

"I asked the refrigeration engineers the same question," the whale-like demon said. "The only thing they've come up with is that the cavern where the glacier enters is the main draft hole for Hell. Normally, all the convection currents set up by Mount Etna cause a terrific suction through the cavern, drawing in frigid air from the surface that reacts with the heated damp air inside that region of Hell, causing the dampness to condense and freeze around the cavern. Kind of like frost build-up in a freezer."

"So," the Devil said. "Without Etna's eruptions, no convection currents, and without convection currents, no downdraft."

"That's about the size of it." Leviathan shrugged, causing brine from her tub to slosh onto the floor. In the past, it would have sizzled into steam in an instant, but now, it just lay around the tub in tepid pools.

"What about the power plant?" the Devil asked, then he realized he'd foolishly assigned Belphegor to investigate that, and Belphegor wasn't here. "No matter," the Devil muttered in a resigned voice. "I'll check on it myself. But now to the real problem at hand. Bob. As you all know, Bob seems to be the real cause of all the trouble down here, including Angel. Beelzebub, tell them what you've learned."

Beelzebub gave them a recounting of how he'd discovered that Bob had entered Hell alone and at the exact same time that Angel had appeared, how he'd escaped his punishment, how he was walking around Hell and leaving a trail of order—not to mention grass and flowers—behind him, and how he was, at that very moment, climbing the path among the lower crags of the palace's mountain, apparently intent on paying the Devil a personal visit.

"The evidence is circumstantial that he's the cause of the easedis that's plaguing Hell," Beelzebub finished. "But we know he must be. His trail of order, alone, is a sufficient enough indicator."

"What we're looking for," the Devil said, "is the smoking gun. Something that definitely ties Bob to the disruptions in Hell. Now, we know it has something to do with this deathbed curse he laid, but until we find out exactly who he cursed...."

"Ahem," came a subdued voice.

"What!" the Devil demanded. His temper was on a pretty short leash, and he wasn't used to being interrupted.

"Ah, sir," Mammon said cautiously. "Ah, I think I can tell you that."

"Tell me what?"

"Who he cursed."

"You can? Well, would you please be so good as to inform us so we can get on with resolving the matter?"

"I believe that he must have cursed you, Boss."

"Me! That's ridiculous." The Devil gave a hearty laugh, and the other Archons joined in. Except Mammon.

"Is it, sir?" the demon of greed pressed. "Remember that scheme with ENDRUN a several months ago? The one concerning the phony broadband deal?"

"What of it?"

"I believe you engineered its takeover."

"And a pretty piece of work it was, if I do say so myself."

"Yes, sir, and if I remember correctly, Bob was the one you took it over from."

The Devil sat there for several seconds, his face frozen, thoughts turned inward. Then he looked at Beelzebub.

"Do you have a transcript of Bob's curse?"

Beelzebub reluctantly produced his PDA and keyed in Bob's name.

"'God damn it!'" the demon quoted. "'I'll get whoever is responsible for this if it's the last thing I do! Curse 'em! Curse 'em 'til the day they die!'"

"That'll be an awful long time, Boss," Asmodeus said.

"It would explain a lot of things," Leviathan said. "It looks like the smoking...."

"Me!?" the Devil bellowed. "It's a curse against me!? Who the hell does that bastard think he is?" He snatched Beelzebub's PDA and looked at the screen.

"I don't think he ever pondered that," Beelzebub said, wincing as he healed the gouges the Devil's talons had left on his hand.

"Don't be so damn literal!" the Devil snapped.

"He's loose," Lucifer shrugged his little blue arms. "And apparently untouchable. It all fits."

"Where was he incarcerated, again?" the Devil asked.

"The lake of boiling shit," Beelzebub answered. "He was up to his thighs."

"Up to his thighs!" the Devil blazed. "He cursed *me*, and all he had to suffer was being thigh deep in the lake of boiling shit?" At the very least, the Devil thought, he should have gotten chin deep—or worse—working the scythe fields or serving as one of the innocent bystanders in a wild gunfight. Now that not only was painful but completely nerve wracking. It was quite amusing to watch the inmates cringe behind pitifully flimsy objects—or even one another—and scream and moan in their fear. Especially when one of the other bystanders got hold of one of the weapons and decided to join in the fray. Usually, the tyro would rack up more of his fellow bystanders than did the original combatants. Family and friends, even. Ah, the looks on their faces!

The thought cooled the Devil's ire somewhat and reintroduced his innate sense of foul play.

"This is pretty good," he said grudgingly, nodding as he reread the curse. "The little shit's got me by the balls."

Suddenly, all the Archons started speaking at once, vying for the Devil's attention and empowerment. They wanted to waste Bob in his tracks, and each had his or her own idea of how to obliterate the offending human.

"He'll go for this," Leviathan said, rising in her tub and putting on the guise of a beautiful, lusty woman. "He'll never be able to resist, and when he tries to embrace me, I'll turn back into a whale and crush him to a pulp."

None of the other Archons bothered to tell her that her naked rump sported a vestigial fluke. Plus, she'd overdone her hair—going for a seductive red, she'd wound up with a color probably invented by American ketchup bottlers.

"You ever think he might prefer boys," Lucifer piped, cocking his slender hips.

Asmodeus offered his personal harem of perpetual virgins to entice then smother Bob, and Mammon wanted to try to buy him off. Everybody wanted to go after Bob, it seemed, except Belphegor, who wasn't present, and Beelzebub, who'd already tried and failed.

Looking at the Archons making fools of themselves in their haste to please him, the Devil had the disgruntled realization that he shouldn't have given them the small modicum of inventiveness that he had. But it was, he knew, unavoidable. He needed them to be able to operate without him having to constantly pull their strings. After all, while a lot of evil is perpetrated in a rote manner, the fact that humans have free will required that those who would subvert that will be allowed a certain, if limited, amount of creative license.

"Shut the fuck up," he ordered, and the pandemonium in the room ceased instantly. "Beelzebub can tell you that you can't accomplish a damn thing with this Bob fellow. I'll just have to deal with him personally. Go on back to your duties and try to keep the effects Bob and Angel are having to a minimum until I figure out what to do. Until then, Lucifer, I want you to find out where Belphegor is and bring his fat ass here. I'm going to need all my powers for this."

"Yes, Boss."

"Now get out!"

Nodding, the Archons filed out, leaving the Devil to ponder the future and Bob.

☙ 35 ❧

"THERE'S SOMEONE HERE TO SEE you, sire. A human." Behemoth's tone managed to convey equal portions of distaste and bemused amazement.

"Are you being insolent with me, cretin?" the Devil demanded harshly.

"I wouldn't think of it, sire," Behemoth replied in a way that said he'd thought about it plenty lately.

"I assume it's Bob," the Devil said, trying to ignore his butler's rudeness. It was the day after the board meeting, and he knew the renegade human was due anytime.

"That is the name he gave me."

"Well, send him in. And let me know as soon as Angel arrives at the palace."

"Very good, sire."

"Don't use that word around here," the Devil snapped.

"Good, sire? Very well." The servant exited, leaving the Devil to unclench his fists and sigh. But he didn't let himself get too relaxed. Beelzebub had told him that Bob wasn't much to look at—just an average sort of guy—and that made the Devil all the more wary. He knew from practical experience that the average human was much like the average attack dog: apt to turn on its master in an instant.

A few moments later, Behemoth ushered Bob into the office and hurriedly shut the door. As he did, the Devil drew himself up to his full height, let some sparks dance around the tips of his spines, raised his tail so the spearhead tip swayed like a cobra above his head, and raked his talons across the obsidian desktop, leaving ragged, smoking gouges in their wake.

"How dare you defy me!" he thundered. "I'll have you torn apart, cell by cell, and put back together at random. I'll have you subjected to torments more vile, degrading, and painful than humanly conceivable!"

The Devil was pretty impressive, Bob thought. He was pitch black, except for red veins snaking across his body, his fiery eyes, and tastefully green talons. He was enveloped in what Bob at first took to be a well-fitting cloak, but the cloak, he quickly realized, was a pair of leathery wings that unfolded to a magnificent, light-blotting span. The Devil actually was equipped to fly. Sharp points —equally weapon and protection—protruding from every joint and all down his ribcage, and they were dripping with some sort of purplish liquid that Bob figured was probably toxic and maybe even acidic. You sure couldn't grab this fellow by the shoulders to hustle him away—or embrace him.

Not that you'd want to embrace him. He was repellent, but not in the way the demons were. All the demons he'd met so far were ugly, smelly, and crude, but the Devil was different, exuding an aura more subtle but more powerful and pervasive. There was no stench of brimstone, no slime, no heat—if you discounted the obvious red-hot anger flashing in his eyes. It was more like a projection of evil intense enough to be called a force field, and it made Bob feel really creepy and a little light-headed. He figured he couldn't get closer than about ten feet. At least not on his own or without strong provocation. Or, perhaps, permission.

But even if Bob felt pretty insignificant standing there facing the Devil's fury—a fury that would have even the Archons crapping themselves—he didn't let himself flinch visibly.

"I may be a skunk," Bob said, "but I'm a low-level skunk, and there's not much you can do about that." He hoisted *The Rule Book*. "According to your own rules, the worst you can do is put me back in the boiling shit, but even that might be difficult, now."

"I can do whatever the hell I please," the Devil thundered.

He was right, of course, Bob reflected. Rule #13,013 essentially made all the other demons as subservient to the rules as the inmate were, but it gave the Devil carte blanche.

But there *was* the curse, so maybe even Rule #13,013 was moot.

"Doesn't the fact that I could get out and walk half-way across Hell to talk to you like this interest you?"

The Devil had to admit to himself that it did, but he wasn't about to show weakness to this mere puny mortal.

"All right, Bob. I'll listen to what you have to say." He sat regally in his chair and, in an unostentatious show of power, passed a casual palm across the scarred desktop. The obsidian glowed briefly, and when he lifted his hand, the surface gleamed like new. He didn't invite Bob to sit, but there wasn't another chair in the room anyway. The Devil never let anyone get too comfortable, at least not in his own office. "What's this all about?" He said it in a bored voice, but really he was genuinely curious. "You want out?"

"Is that possible? Everyone tells me we're here for eternity."

"Generally speaking."

"Well, I'm sure you know by now that I'm here because I laid a deathbed curse."

"So I've heard." The Devil's eyes smoldered. "It seems you cursed *me*."

"I guess so, though I assure you, I didn't know it was you at the time."

"That makes it worse, doesn't it?" the Devil asked. "Cursing someone you don't even know. Spewing a curse, so to speak, into the wind to let it land on a complete stranger?"

"I was upset," Bob temporized. "I'd been working on this sweet deal that would have set me up for life, and someone comes along and screws it up. How was I to know it was you?"

"You're obviously a clever fellow, Bob. You should have figured that I'm behind all top-level corporate shenanigans."

"I guess so. But it is funny, isn't it? Cursing the Devil himself and winding up in Hell for it."

"Yes," the Devil said, obviously unamused. "Very ironic."

They both laughed insincerely. Neither planned on mentioning Angel, at least not yet—the Devil because he didn't know if Bob knew about her, Bob because he didn't know if the Devil realized she was part of his curse, and both because they wanted an ace in the hole.

"You know what's really ironic?" Bob asked. "Now that I've gotten to walk around a bit, I kinda like the place. I think there might be a lot of use here for a fellow like me."

"You want a job?" The Devil sounded amazed.

"Not just any job," Bob said. "I'm tired of working in the trenches and coming up short, while someone above me rips me off. I want something more. I want to be appreciated and rewarded for my talents. I mean, look at you. Look at this place. You got a nice setup here. It's a palace."

"Of course it's a palace," the Devil snapped. "I am the Lord of Hell."

"I just want a piece of the action," Bob said.

"You want to be Lord of Hell?" The Devil laughed so thunderously—and horribly—that Bob, grimacing, was forced back several steps.

"Look," Bob said, holding up his hands. "I'm not trying to take *your* job. From what I've seen, this place is an administrative headache, and that's the last thing I want to deal with."

"What is it you want?" the Devil asked.

"Let's look at this place like a corporation," Bob said. "You're chair of the board and CEO. Beelzebub is president, and the other high-ranking demons—your Archons—are VPs. That's what I want—a vice presidency."

"Vice president of what, exactly?"

"Oh, I don't know," Bob said. "How about public relations?"

"Public relations?" The Devil couldn't help but smile, though it did have a fiendish twist to it. "That's not a mortal sin. Yet. Though I'm sure we can easily work up to it. In any case, you realized that the last thing I want to do is spread information about this place."

"Not information," Bob said. "Disinformation. If it works for corporations, politicians, and the military, it'll work for you, too."

"I already have most of the first, half the second, and the upper echelons of the third in my pocket," the Devil said. "What makes you think I need you?"

"Not for Earth," Bob said. "I figured you already have that covered. I meant for here. Hell."

"Disinformation in my own domain?" The Devil barked a laugh. "You must be insane."

"I'd have to be crazy not to see how things are falling apart around here," Bob said. "I understand you're having trouble with the volcano and the glacier, and the power plant's on the fritz. And I hear your demons have organized a union."

"No thanks to you," the Devil snapped.

"It was a landslide waiting to happen. I was just the random pebble that sent it all rolling." Bob gave a supercilious smile. "But no matter how it all started, the way I see it, you need me."

"Is that right?"

"That's right. Haven't you put two and two together yet?"

"You mean, of course, that all this is the result of your curse?"

"Isn't it obvious?"

"Do you have any idea how long all this has been down here?" the Devil asked. "A long damn time. What's so surprising about it needing a little maintenance now and then or the workers occasionally getting restless?"

"Nothing, I suppose. But you're forgetting one more little thing." "And what's that?"

Bob tossed in his ace.

"Angel."

"Oh," the Devil said, and for just an instant, Bob thought he saw him blanch to a charcoal gray. "You know about her?"

"Come on," Bob chuckled. "*Everybody* knows about her. She's been bugging you and making you look weak in front of your demons, and there isn't a damn thing you can do about it."

"So what? It doesn't have anything to do with you."

"Doesn't it? How long has she been hanging around?"

"I'm not sure…."

"I am. Exactly three months, one week, six days, eighteen hours, twenty-two minutes, and thirty-seven seconds. Oddly enough, that's exactly how long I've been here. And you know what? I didn't see her in Cerberus's pit when I came in because I was by myself. Word is, she just appeared out of thin air. You know what I think? I think *she's* the principal manifestation of my curse."

"Nonsense."

"You know I'm right."

"Let's say you are," the Devil conceded. "What are you going to do about it if I give you this vice presidency? Remove her?"

"I'll work on it," Bob said. "But not right away. I'll want to see how things go, first."

"You don't trust me?"

Bob laughed.

"I'll tell you what I *will* do. I'll work on discrediting her. That should help restore some confidence in you and strengthen your position without weakening mine. We'll talk about completely eliminating her later, when you've seen how indispensable I am."

"I can see it's not a bad idea," the Devil said musingly. "I know you're a lawyer, but what kind of PR experience do you have?"

"None," Bob admitted. "But I manipulated the rules enough to get out of my appointed place in Hell and make my way here. Let's call that a demonstration of my basic expertise."

"Indeed." The Devil tented his fingers and stared at Bob over the talon tips. "All right. If I agree, what do you want?"

"What any sane man wants," Bob said. "Cushy digs, good food and drink, compliant women, a loyal staff."

"You want your own little corner of Hell, is that it?"

"Yeah," Bob nodded. "That's a good way to put it. But I'd prefer something away from the more noxious odor-producing torments."

"Naturally. I know just the spot. All my demons live in a cluster of resort hotels. The staffs consist of world leaders who used their positions of power to gain personal wealth at the expense of others, along with a scattering of hotel magnates thrown in for good measure. They really hate making beds, cleaning toilets, and begging for tips." The Devil chuckled. "I can easily have another one built."

"That sounds fine," Bob said. "Could you have mine staffed with corporate execs? It would give me a chance for a little payback."

"No problem."

"Now, about my personal staff...."

"I can supply that as well," the Devil said. "We have plenty of PR people down here."

"Maybe," Bob said, "But I'd prefer to pick my own people."

"Who'd you have in mind?"

"I thought I'd start with my fellow inmates from the lake of boiling shit."

"All of them?"

"Why not? I'm sure you can fill it up again."

"There's likely a waiting list," the Devil chuckled. "But why them?"

"I know them, for one thing."

"And they're your friends."

"Possibly. But that's not what makes them good candidates. They were all pretty good at their corruptions—all of which will be useful to me—but they weren't so bad that they'll be a threat."

"Good thinking," the Devil said, looking at Bob with new respect. "All right. I'm sure we can make arrangements. They'd still have to suffer some sort of torment, but we can adjust it so they'll have time to work for you."

"How long until the hotel is ready?"

"Shouldn't be long—a week or so. We have plenty of workers down here, and they all work around the clock. Until then, you're welcome to stay here." He punched the button on his intercom. "Behemoth, have an apartment prepared for Bob. He'll be spending a week or two with us. And send for Belial right away." He let up on the intercom button. "Belial is my chief of all the demons —sort of my foreman. He'll act as general contractor."

"Will I get to look at the architectural drawings?"

"Of course. You'll have a say in every phase of planning right up until the final construction. In the meantime, I'll have Behemoth assign you someone to help you arrange for your staff."

"Sounds good," Bob said. "Say, listen, what do I call you?"

"You can call me Boss, like everyone else," the Devil replied.

"That's all? I thought you'd prefer something more regal, more imposing, like...."

"Not that." The Devil held up his hands, interrupting Bob. "That name has a nice ring to it, but I'm afraid it isn't mine. Not really. Oh, that's what some people call me, all right, but that particular nom de guerre was given to me by one of the hack monks working to transcribe the old documents. The officious, drunken, little fool couldn't spell, and besides, he was masturbating at the time, and he transposed some of the letters. It was supposed to be Santa. Luck of the draw." The Devil shrugged, the sharp points jutting from his shoulders jabbing upward and squirting little jets of purple toxin. "In any case, it's a human fabrication, anyway, not the name I was formed with. But I let it stand, on Earth, at least, because it serves my purpose."

At that moment, the door opened, and Behemoth poked his head inside.

"Um, sire, you asked me to inform you as soon as...you know."

"Oh, yes," the Devil said with forced casualness. "Listen, Bob, I've got to fly over to the power plant right now. I'm sure you know what trouble we're having there." He began to move toward the doors leading to the balcony.

"Before you go, there's one small favor I'd like to ask," Bob said.

"Make it quick," the Devil said, trying to keep from eyeing the doorway to the rest of the palace.

"These," Bob said, raising his copy of *The Rule Book*. "We have so much to do, and we've memorized all the rules anyway. I'd like for my people not to have to lug these around anymore."

"Fine," the Devil said hastily. "You've already proved how flawed the rules are, anyway. You and your people can dispense with them, but don't spread it around."

"Right. Thanks."

"Behemoth will take care of you until I get back," the Devil said. With a wave of dismissal, he hurried through the sliding glass doorway to the balcony and threw himself into the air.

As Bob watched him flap off, he heard a sweetly musical voice behind him calling, "Nicky? Nicky?"

ᕱ 36 ᕱ

BOB TURNED TO SEE A beautiful young woman in a white gown enter the room. She stopped when she saw Bob, then she smiled glowingly. Bob wished he could ogle her, but her shift prevented it.

"You're a person," she said, looking surprised.

"Is there something wrong with that?"

"Not at all," she said. "It's just that you're the first human being I've seen in the palace except for the chefs. I thought everyone else here was a demon."

"Yep," Bob said. "I'm all too human."

"I was just looking for Nick."

"He's gone," Bob said, pointing out the window to the still-visible form of the Devil flapping over the hellscape.

"Oh, dear," she said, looking distressed. "I did so want to see him. Did he say where he was going?"

"I'm afraid not," Bob lied. "But he said he'd be back shortly."

"He so busy," she said. "I just can't seem to keep up with him."

"I'm Bob," Bob said. "I'll be staying here for a couple of weeks. You must be Angel."

"Yes," she said.

"Nick told me so much about you," Bob said. "It's a pleasure to make your acquaintance."

"If you'll excuse me," Behemoth said, "I'll go see to your quarters."

"Sure," Bob said, not even looking at the demon. "I'll wait right here until you come back."

"Why aren't you in torment like everybody else?" Angel asked after Behemoth left.

"I'm on holiday," he replied with a grin.

"You're joking with me. There's no such thing as a holiday in Hell."

"I suppose you're right."

"I know who you are," Angel said, her eyes lighting. "You're the one who cursed somebody and is now free of your punishment."

"That's right," Bob said, wondering just how much she knew.

"Why did you come to the palace?"

"I guess you could say I'm here for a job interview," he told her, realizing she probably didn't know much if she asked that. "It looks like I'm going to be working directly for the Boss."

"Really?" Sudden suspicion lit her eyes. "What are you going to be doing? Not torturing your fellow humans, I hope."

"Nothing like that," Bob said. "I'm going to be vice president in charge of internal public relations."

"I wouldn't have thought that Nicky needed anyone to help him with that. After all, this *is* his domain." There was a touch of pride in her voice.

"You'd be surprised," Bob said. "Operations are going a bit roughly right now, and he's tapped me to help him smooth things over."

"The poor dear *has* been terribly overworked lately. He keeps flying here and there. It's simply exhausting him. First it's the volcano, then the glacier, then the power plant. And the next thing you know, he's off to the volcano again. Sometimes, I think he cares more about that stupid mountain than he does me."

"It *is* pretty important," Bob pointed out. "From what I've heard, we'd be in freezing pitch darkness without it."

"I suppose you're right," she said, but she didn't sound convinced. "But that doesn't make it any easier for me. He can fly to the volcano in an hour or two, but it takes me just days and days to walk."

"I know what you mean," Bob commiserated. "It's no picnic walking around Hell. Something that looks close can really be miles away, and everywhere you turn, there's some kind of blockade or other impediment. Ever since I got out, it's been one damn thing after another trying to get up here. But here I am."

"Where is it that you got out of?"

"The lake of boiling shit."

"I haven't been there yet," she said. "Is it painful?"

"Not too much, really," he admitted. "I was only in thigh-deep."

"That doesn't sound too bad," she said. "I've seen a lot worse here."

"Yeah, ain't it the truth. Some of the people I met along the way were really horrible and frightening individuals who made my skin crawl. It didn't bother me a bit to see them in terrible pain for their sins. What about you?" he asked. "You don't look like you belong here."

"I wouldn't have thought so, either, but here I am."

"What sin did you commit?"

"None," she said. "I'm pure as the driven snow."

"Then why are you here? I thought only sinners came here."

"Strange as it sounds," she said, "I'm here because of love."

"Love? I don't get it."

"I'm not sure I do, either."

"How long have you been here?"

"Three months, one week, six days, eighteen hours, thirty-three minutes, and eight seconds," she told him.

Wow, he thought. Some of the rules work on her, too.

"That's exactly how long I've been here," he said, "but I didn't see you in Cerberus's pit."

"Who?"

"Cerberus. The three-headed hound guarding the gates of Hell."

"I don't remember any dog. All I remember was telling Tommy Mason to keep his hands off my...you know. When he left, I cried and prayed to be rid of all those groping boys and to find my own true love. And poof! Here I was."

"You mean the Devil is your own true love?"

"Sounds nuts, doesn't it?" She shook her head. "Mama always told me that love works in mysterious ways. You know, everyone tells me he's the demon of wrath, but I don't know why. He as sweet as anything to me."

"I only just met him," Bob said, "but he seems like a pretty straightforward guy."

"Oh, he is. And generous, too. He lets me do anything I want."

Like he can help it, Bob thought with sarcastic self-satisfaction. He smiled benignly at her.

"Well," Angel said. "You'll have to excuse me. I've got to be going. Nicky's flown off somewhere, and I have to go find him."

"He'll probably be back soon," Bob said.

"I'm afraid I can't help myself," she said. "I simply cannot abide not being constantly near him. Some days, it's positively frightening."

"How will you find him?" Bob asked. "He didn't say where he was going."

"Oh, someone will tell me. They always do. Will you be all right?" she asked with proper concern for a guest.

"Sure," Bob said. "Behemoth is fixing up a guest room until my own place is ready."

"How nice. We'll have to invite you for dinner while you're here."

"I'd like that," Bob said. "I haven't eaten since I came to Hell." But she already was turning away and heading out of the office.

"Behemoth," she called out. "Do you know where Nicky went?" The butler met her at the door, more obsequious than he'd been with either the Devil or Bob.

"I believe he's on his way to the power plant, miss," the demon said courteously. "If you hurry, you should be able to catch him."

"Thank you," she said, and she traipsed off down the hallway, her white chemise billowing in her wake.

"I was under the impression that the Boss didn't want her around," Bob said. "Why did you tell her where he went?"

"I couldn't help it," Behemoth answered. "I simply can't lie to her. Nobody can."

"Is that so?" Bob mused, thinking of how he'd lied to her a couple of times already—or at least concealed the truth. Aloud, he said, "Why doesn't the Boss just ravish her or throw her in the volcano or something and be done with it?"

"He can't touch her. Not in violence, at least."

"So I've heard," Bob said. "But damn, imagine a good-looking woman like that in love with you, and you can't even rough her up a little."

"It's a shame, isn't it?" Behemoth shook his head. Then he squinted at Bob. "Is it really true that you walked all the way up here from the lake of boiling shit?"

"Yep," Bob nodded. "And it was one hell of a hike, I'll tell you."

"You've probably seen more of Hell, then, than any human in history. Except maybe Angel. What do you think of it?"

"To tell the truth," Bob said, "I never gave it much thought before I died. Now that I've seen a lot of it, I have to agree that most of the inmates deserve to be here."

"Most? But not all?"

"Yeah. Take that Slough of Despond, for example, where all the suicides are."

"I'd rather not," Behemoth said. "Too depressing."

"That's the point," Bob said. "As a lawyer, I have to say that something's wrong with the sentencing phase, at least in those cases."

"How do you mean?"

"Well, Earth can be a pretty nasty place—no thanks to the Boss, I might add. And living there are some people who are unjustifiably slammed around by life or unbalanced or simply too sensitive to be able to stand living any more, and they're forced to take the only possible way out. But suicide is a sin that automatically sends you to Hell. Wow!" Bob shook his head. "Earth was too awful to take, but in punishment for not being able to take it, you're forced to endure an eternity of deeper depression in a far worse place. It just doesn't seem fair."

"It's the exception that makes the rule," Behemoth said.

"I never bought that argument."

"Yet, here you are," Behemoth pointed out. "The exception in the flesh, so to speak."

"If that's so," Bob chuckled, "Maybe I'll be making the rules."

"Maybe," Behemoth smiled. "But in the meantime, let me escort you to your suite, then I'll show you where the board room is. Belial should be here about two o'clock, and he'll go over the plans for your new accommodations."

"Great," Bob said. "Is there any place I can freshen up?"

"Are you kidding?" Behemoth looked at Bob like he was crazy, but then he brightened and nodded. "Actually, we do have a whole batch of personal care products that the Boss ordered but hasn't used. Soap, shampoo, toothpaste, mouthwash—stuff like that. I don't think he'll mind if I give them to you."

"Great," Bob said. "Lead on."

❧ 37 ❧

PEDRO WAS THE FIRST INMATE of the lake of boiling shit to see the demon flapping toward the lake carrying Bob.

"They're bringing him back!" he yelled loudly.

He didn't have to explain who "he" was—it could only be Bob. Ahmed sloshed over to Pedro—or at least as close as he could get since his torment was to be a couple of inches deeper than Pedro.

"I knew it wouldn't last," Ahmed said, staring at the huge, crimson-scaled bat with Bob dangling like a white worm from its arms.

"I wonder if it'll put him in deeper," Margaretha said, joining the two.

"He'll be lucky if they gave him a snorkel," Ahmed chuckled. He was referring obliquely to Sokah, who, for a lieutenancy from Pol Pot, had not only sold out his own clan to the Khmer Rouge but tortured and executed them himself. Sokah was in over his head, and the only way he could breathe was to hop upward every thirty or forty seconds until his head cleared the surface long enough for him to gasp in a fetid breath before sinking again. When he rose, he often had to endure the jibes of his fellow inmates, like "Long time no see, Sokah." or "Where you been hiding?" or "I didn't expect you to pop up like this."

One of the inmates, Tim, had grown up in America in the 1960s, and he'd sing the *Flipper* theme song, exchanging Sokah's name for Flipper.

But at the moment, nobody was paying any attention to Sokah as his head broke the surface with sputtering regularity, because word had spread like a methane flash fire over a swamp: Bob was being brought back.

Everybody was extremely surprised, of course, when the demon gently alighted on the bank next to Sapason instead of unceremoniously dumping his charge headfirst into the lake. Sapason looked as astonished as the rest of them as the demon carrying Bob deferentially set Bob on his feet then sat back as Bob ambled down the slope to the edge of the lake. Sapason wasn't so dumbfounded that he didn't notice that Bob was careful not to let even his smallest toe touch the surface.

"Hey, Ahmed!" Bob called. "How you doing?"

"Same old shit, Bob. You're looking pretty good, though. When we saw them bringing you, we all thought you were done for."

The other inmates murmured assent, and Margaretha asked, "What's going on, Bob? How are you staying out of the shit?"

"Same way I got out of it to begin with," Bob replied.

"But you're not going to tell us?" Pedro said in a disgruntled tone. "Shit, man. We're your compadres."

"That's right," Bob said. "You're my compadres. We were in the shit together, and even if I got out, I'm not forgetting it. I want you all to know that things are gonna change around here."

"How's that?" Tim asked. "They puttin' you in charge of the thermostat?"

Everybody laughed, including Bob, and when the laughter died down, Bob held up his hands.

"Even better than that," he said. "I've been promoted."

"Promoted?" Ahmed said. "I never heard of an inmate being promoted."

"Well, you've heard of it now," Bob assured him. "You are looking at Hell's new vice president for internal public relations."

"You've got to be kidding," Margaretha said.

"The Boss himself gave me the word," Bob said. "If you don't believe me, ask him." He jerked his head toward the demon who'd brought him, and it nodded.

"He's giving you the straight poop," the demon said.

"I don't know how you did it," Ahmed said, "but it sure is a wondrous thing."

"It gets better," Bob said. "A VP can't go around without a staff, can he? The Boss told me I can choose whoever I want, so guess what?"

"You don't mean you're taking us with you?" Ahmed said.

"You're a sharp fellow, Ahmed. That's why I'm appointing you my chief of staff."

"No shit!"

"Don't worry," Bob said, holding up his hands to quiet the rising murmur from the rest of the gathered crowd. "I'm not leaving any of you behind. There'll be plenty of room at the Ritz for all of you."

"The Ritz?" Pedro asked.

"Our new headquarters," Bob amplified. "Get this: It's a luxury hotel with all the amenities. Even a pool."

"It's not full of shit, is it?" Tim asked.

The rising murmur broke in a combination of laughter and excited babble.

"No more shit," Bob said. "But don't forget that this is Hell. I can't promise anything beyond that."

"That's enough," Margaretha said.

"When's all this happening?" Ahmed asked, already calculating the perks his own position likely would bring.

"Why wait?" Bob said. "You can head toward the Ritz as soon as we're done here. The construction isn't quite finished, but I'm afraid you'll have to walk, which'll take about a week, and it'll be ready when you get there."

"What about you?" Ahmed asked.

"I have a few more details to look into. This fellow has been assigned to take me wherever I need to go."

"How will we find the Ritz?" Pedro asked.

"You ever see the *Wizard of Oz*?"

Pedro shook his head.

"Must have been after my time."

"I read the book," Margaretha said.

"Well, instead of a yellow-brick road," he told her, "here's it's a green grassy path with flowers all along the edges. Just follow that, and it'll take you right to the Ritz. Come on, now, everybody. Up here with me!"

One by one, the inmates, amazed expressions on their faces, waded out of the lake and up onto the bank. Some of them shed tears, some were laughing, but all of them praised Bob as they filed past him, and that made him feel pretty special. It was a whole lot better than being scorned for being just one more little turd among many.

"There's the path." Bob pointed. "Off with you, now, and I'll see you in about a week. Oh, and one more thing." He waved his copy of *The Rule Book*. "You can get rid of this."

To demonstrate, he tossed his copy to the shit-spattered ground.

As the inmates hurried off down the path, laughing and talking excitedly and leaving the trail littered with discarded copies of *The Rule Book*, Bob gestured for Ahmed to hang back.

"There are a few people I met along the way that I'd like you to pick up and bring with you," he said, handing Ahmed a typed list.

"Sure, Bob," Ahmed said, taking the list. "Anything else?"

"Not for now. If anything comes up, I'll give you a call."

"A call? How?"

"With this, of course," Bob said, smiling. He handed Ahmed a cell phone. "My number's already programmed in."

Ahmed took the phone, looking choked up.

"I don't know what to say, Bob. I thought I was in there for eternity." He gestured toward the now-empty lake.

"Eternity's a long damn time, Ahmed. Let's just see what we can make of it."

At that moment, a spot in the middle of the lake bubbled, and a head popped above the surface for a second, sputtered, then went down again. It was Sokah, who was too preoccupied with breathing to understand what had happened.

"What about him?" Ahmed said.

"Ah, fuck him," Bob said, looking out across the lake. "He's just an ignorant peasant who sold out his family and friends. I could never trust him. Anyway," he turned back to Ahmed, "I need people like you with organizational skills and some sophistication. That's all for now. I'll see you in a week."

"Okay," Ahmed said, and he hurried off along the path after the rest of the former inmates of the lake of boiling shit.

"What about me?" Sapason asked glumly. "You can't just leave me here. There's nobody left to guard except Sokah, and even I can't piss that far."

"Listen," Bob said. "I could use a liaison to CRUDE. You want the position?"

"The union? You're not asking me to undermine their efforts, are you?"

"You've got scruples?"

"Well, no, but they *are* my peeps."

"Don't worry," Bob said in a comforting voice. "I won't ask you to do more than spy on them and report their activities to me."

"And what will I get in return?"

"Away from here, for one thing," Bob said. "I'll even give you a position at the hotel. Maybe make you manager of the night club."

"Night club?" Sapason's eyes lit. "With liquor and floor shows and everything?"

"The works."

"All right," Sapason agreed.

"In the meantime," Bob said, "Why don't you act as my personal supervisor at the hotel worksite? Fly on over there and make sure things are ready when my staff arrives."

"Sure thing."

Sapason launched himself into the air and headed out across the hellscape. His stubby wings looked ridiculous as they struggled furiously to propel the demon's bulky body, but he made pretty good time, anyway.

"Jeeves," Bob said, turning to his demon carrier. "Let's be off to the volcano. I want to find out what's going on there."

"To Etna, sir," the demon said. He picked up Bob and flew off toward the mountain, whose barely smoking crown could be seen in the murky distance.

Jeeves, whose real name was Corodon, reached Etna in about two hours. Bob didn't complain about the time. He was too busy scoping out Hell as it reeled out beneath him. He was amazed that he actually could detect some sort of organic order to the place since it had seemed quite confusing and chaotic when he'd been traversing it on foot. It was a little like a huge, albeit grotesque, amusement park, with the rides and other features carefully placed along artfully wrought lanes and byways, all making the most of the ergonomics of the terrain.

About half way through the trip, Bob noticed a small white figure picking its way across the blasted landscape below. Its whiteness was almost blindingly sharp in contrast to the muted and dark colors—certainly shocking in the context of what lay all around it.

"Go down there," Bob ordered. "But not too close."

Corodon complied, and in a moment, Bob confirmed what he'd suspected. It was Angel, plugging along like a real trooper, seemingly oblivious to the horrors she passed through. And to Bob being carried along above her. Bob wanted to keep it that way.

"Okay, Jeeves. Back to maximum altitude."

The demon's wings stroked the air more firmly, and inside a minute, Angel was just another speck on the floor of Hell.

At last they reached Etna, and Corodon circled it for a few minutes. It was Bob's first visit to a live volcano, but he'd seen plenty of great eruption footage on TV, and he recognized the sickly thing below as definitely subpar.

"It wasn't always like this," Corodon said. "It used to be quite impressive. All those frozen magma flows there and there and there were running like glorious rivers of fire, and the sparks and flames and flares from the caldera lit up the whole countryside. A real nice place to picnic with the missus. Ah. There's the control room." The demon pointed to what looked like a cave opening about halfway up mountain's slope.

Corodon spiraled down, and in a few minutes, Bob was inside the control room, meeting Xaphan and his assistants. The heat in the rock-walled control room was blistering, but the demon operators wore bulky, fur-lined snowsuits that would have done justice to polar explorers.

"Oh, yes," Xaphan said. "The Boss was just here, and he mentioned you. Some new kind of vice president, aren't you?"

"That's right," Bob said, puffing himself up a bit.

"He said of what," Xaphan continued, pulling off his glove and massaging the bridge of his nose, "but I don't remember. There simply are too many of them."

"Internal public relations," Bob supplied, deflating a little.

"Yes, yes. I remember now. The Boss said you might be by for a briefing."

"Have you found out what's wrong?" Bob asked.

"Not yet, but we're working on it even while time is running out." Xaphan looked so desperate that Bob realized that some real deadline was involved, and the answers to a few well-chosen questions told him why. Xaphan and the other volcanologists were literally freezing alive.

When Bob learned that Xaphan and his crew would freeze solid if the temperatures fell too low, he recognized it as a clever way for the Devil to exert constant control over the demons who maintained the volcano. After all, Xaphan and his crew might freeze, but the freezing wouldn't kill them, just immobilize them, and they'd be facing an eternity of immobile consciousness. But Bob also understood that the threat to Xaphan also was, essentially, a mechanism to ensure that this vital public utility would continue operating, for without the volcano, all of Hell would plunge into frigid darkness. Bob immediately vowed to use his office to help keep the volcano online because, while frigid darkness probably wouldn't negatively impact the Devil, it certainly would put a damper on Bob's plans.

And Bob was fast developing plans. He'd gotten free of the lake of boiling shit, and that was good but not good enough, because he still wasn't free of Hell. He'd learned that adherence to the rules is the demon's realm and that humans have to go beyond the rules into the realm of self-control to attain spiritual oneness with the deity. But therein lay Bob's problem. Lawyers, by their nature and training and occupation, are driven by external rules, and Bob didn't think he'd ever be able to break out of that mold. Memorizing the rules might have been an approximation, but it wasn't actually internalizing them. He knew that probably would never happen and he was stuck here in Hell, but it didn't mean he had to take it lying down.

If his wanderings around Hell and subsequent visit to the Devil's palace had taught him anything, it was that the average existence on Earth was a lot better than the average in Hell, but the best in Hell was a whole lot better than what the vast majority of people ever had on Earth. If you accepted in yourself somewhat crude tastes, that is.

But Bob suspected that most humans—himself included—had pretty crude tastes, and he knew that he could be satisfied with an eternity among the upper echelons of Hell.

But if Bob really admitted the truth, it was that, ultimately, the whole thing was like a duel fomented by the frustration of his thwarted deal back on Earth. The Devil had humiliated Bob and hadn't even given it a second thought, and that really pissed Bob off—even more than having his sweet broadband deal snatched from his clutches. And in this duel, Bob was determined to win. He might even have a chance. After all, his curse not only had been heartfelt but his aim had been true and the results all that could be hoped for, leaving his enemy in disarray and prepared to retreat.

In short, Bob had meant the curse when he uttered it, and he meant it even more now. And he was determined to see it through to a satisfying conclusion.

❧ 38 ❧

"Relax, dear. Everything will be all right," Angel soothed.

"Yeah, sure," the Devil groused. He was slumped in his favorite chair in the living room—wrought iron with no cushions.

Angel got up from her sofa, came around behind him, and began rubbing his shoulders. The Devil had to admit it felt good and helped relieve his tension, though he hated the way his venomous spines turned flaccid under her touch, reminding him that too many other things in his domain were flaccid or off kilter.

But he didn't stop her. Instead, he closed his eyes and visualized her and Bob cast together into Mount Etna's caldera and burning to cinders as they tried to swim for shore. That made him feel a little better until she finished rubbing. He opened his eyes and saw her return to the adjacent sofa to flip through a copy of *Woman's Day*, and the spines on his shoulder sprang erect again, dripping purple venom.

If only the bitch would let me fuck her, he thought, I'd be in control again. But, no! The prissy little twit remained as pure as the driven snow, as unsullied as the morning dew. Not that he'd want to screw her in that awful bedroom of hers. She'd decorated it right out of the pages of those cheesy magazines she read, with bright pastels, colonial-style dressers and side tables, and a four-poster bed complete with a lace canopy, an embroidered counterpane, and lots of fluffy pillows with floral slipcases. It looked like a bouquet had exploded in there, and it made him sick just to walk by the open door. Worse, she was making it her mission to redecorate other rooms, and her chintzy style was gradually creeping into every corner of the palace like a nasty fungus from the epicenter of disinfection that was her bedroom.

He picked up the remote and tried to turn on the wide-screen TV, but it wouldn't come on.

Must be another power outage, he thought, more depressed than angry. He tossed the remote aside, and at the movement, Angel looked up from her magazine.

"Bored, dear? How about a nice game of rummy?"

"No," he said simply as he got up and walked to the wide windows that opened onto a southern exposure over his domain. From this side of the palace, the volcano wasn't visible, which was just as well. The thing barely gave a belch of indifferent steam now and then, and the lava lake in the caldera was nearly cool enough for a human to walk on without discomfort. It wasn't a sight he wanted to see, but the plains stretching to the south weren't any more comforting to look at.

In that direction lay most of the lakes of formerly burning and boiling substances, the fields of never-ending combat, the various mazes inhabited by scientists and religious dogmatists, and other torments suited to flatter terrain. But even without resorting to his telescopic vision, he could tell that nothing was as it should be. Once, he'd have seen the whole realm boiling with activity, the tiny figures of demons and humans running this way and that like ants on a heated ant bed. Now, it all looked practically pastoral. Hell, even the perpetual forest fire and burning building where murderous arsonists were incarcerated now looked more like cheap Hollywood special effects than real infernos.

The worst thing was that the pastoralness of the scene was enhanced by the green serpent of the trail that had followed Bob as he'd wound his way toward the palace from the lake of boiling shit. The Devil might have liked the way it snaked across the landscape, but he knew only too well that the green color was from grass, and that made the shape an ironic slap in the face.

It's that damn volcano, he thought. It was like he was impotent. If only he could get Mount Etna working again, that would be a step in the right direction. The volcano would get the power plant going, heat up all the boiling pools, rekindle the smoldering areas that should be blazing merrily, and give the air that smoky, blast-furnace feel he liked so much. Man, he thought, that sure would do a lot for my sense of ill-being.

And it would show all those slackers out there who was the real boss.

"Where are you going?" Angel asked as he headed toward the sliding glass doors that opened onto the balcony.

"Business," he growled. "I have to visit the volcano."

"Again?" she complained. "Every time I turn around, you're running off to play with that old volcano. Why don't you just sit here with me and enjoy the day? We could cuddle. Or if you're feeling restless, we could go for a walk. I just discovered there's a nice path outside all covered with grass and bordered with flowers. It's quite lovely now that the air outside is brighter and cleaner."

The Devil felt a great rage boil up within him, but since he couldn't turn it on her and he didn't want to turn it on himself, he simply disintegrated the sliding glass doors instead of opening them before he stalked out onto the balcony.

"Wait, dear!" Angel called out a bit plaintively behind him. "I'll come with you." He could hear the rustle of her immaculate gown as she got up from the sofa.

Like hell, he thought as he reached the parapet and flung himself from it.

Angel frowned as she watched him flap away across the hellscape. It wasn't the first time the old grump had abandoned her like this, she thought testily. Well, if he thought she was going to charge after him *this* time, he had another think coming. She'd just stay right here and have a good time all by herself.

She settled again to her magazine, clipping out some likely looking recipes, but she soon grew restless. She switched on the TV, which came on instantly, but somehow, watching it didn't feel right without Nicky there. She wanted to ignore her emotions, but it was just so darn hard not feeling his presence, not knowing where he was. She knew she could stand it, at least for short periods of time, but that didn't mean she *wanted* to.

She thought about calling up some of the lady demons she'd made friends with and invite them over for tea, but it was such short notice, and she knew that everybody was busy, not just Nicky, what with so many things breaking down all at once.

Instead, she rang the bell for Behemoth. She didn't really need the bell. She could just call his name—or even whisper it—and he'd hear her summons, no matter where he was in the palace, and come at once. But the bell was a pleasant affectation, and she liked pushing the button and knowing that someone somewhere was jumping.

True to form, Behemoth was at the door, giving a discreet knock. "You rang, madam?"

"Do we have any more of that Chablis?"

"I believe we have some left," Behemoth said politely. Actually, there was an endless supply of Chablis in the wine cellar, just as there was an endless supply of anything either Angel or the Boss requested with any regularity. And that included white wine, which Angel now ordered with barely a blink from the supply demons.

"Bring up a bottle, please."

"Right away, madam."

Behemoth disappeared, but he was back almost instantly, carrying a silver tray bearing a chilled bottle and an exquisite wine glass. He set the tray on a table, opened the wine, and poured the glass half full.

"Madam," he said, handing her the glass.

"Thanks, Behemoth." She glanced up at him. "Wouldn't you like to share a glass with me?"

"That would be nice, madam."

Another glass magically appeared on the tray, and as Behemoth poured wine into it, the Chablis turned dusky red.

"My apologies, madam," he said, glancing ruefully at her "White wine doesn't sit well on my palate."

"I understand," she said as he gulped his glass and poured another. "It's handy that you can do that."

"You mean change the kind of wine that comes out of the bottle? I wouldn't be much of a butler if I couldn't do something as simple as that."

"I just don't understand," she said, shoulders slumping.

"Understand what, madam?" Behemoth suddenly felt uncomfortable. What if she started crying and wanted him to comfort her? He didn't know the first thing about comforting. He slung back his second glass of wine, ready to bolt.

"If you can do that, why can't Nicky just wave his hand and make everything that's going wrong around here right again?"

"You mean the volcano and the power plant and the glacier?" Behemoth relaxed and poured another glass of wine.

"He's so distracted lately. I mean, it's his realm isn't it? He's the lord and master. It's all an expression of his being. All of it. Even you." She raised a hand to her mouth, her lips forming a dainty little circle. "Oh, no. I didn't mean that, Behemoth."

"No offense taken, madam," the servant said, downing his third glass. "You are, of course, absolutely right, except for one point."

She gave him a quizzical look.

"You, madam. You are not an expression of his being. You are the only other real thing here besides him."

"How poetic of you, Behemoth."

"Thank you, madam. May I pour another?"

"Certainly. I know you demons have insatiable appetites. Don't let my sipping hold you back."

"Thank you, madam." The fourth glass disappeared down his gullet, followed by a fifth.

"But it doesn't matter if I'm real or not, does it?" she lamented. "It doesn't help solve the problems. I just wish there was something I could do to help, but I'm afraid I just don't have a head for technical matters."

"Oh, it's not a technical matter," Behemoth said as he drank up his sixth glass of wine. Insatiable appetite or not, he found the elixir of grape going to his head and loosening his tongue. "It's the curse."

"Curse? Beelzebub mentioned a curse. What does this curse have to do with Nicky?"

"Oh, damn," Behemoth snorted, tossing back a seventh glass. "I knew I shouldn't have started drinking this stuff."

"Don't change the subject," she ordered. "Tell me what you mean about a curse."

"All this that's been happening," Behemoth said. "The problems with the volcano, the power plant, and the glacier. It's all because of the curse. Even CRUDE."

"The crude what?"

"Not a what, madam. A union. The Consolidated Roster of United Demonic Employees."

"There's a union here? I wouldn't have imagined."

"Nor I, madam. It's made up of rebellious demons of the second and third orders—kings and dukes and princes and such —who banded together to complain. There isn't enough room for advancement, they say. The pay is lousy, the work hours are too long, working conditions are too hot or cold or noisome or whatever. The list of their demands is endless."

"Can a curse do all that?

"Apparently so if the Boss is the object of the curse."

"You mean somebody cursed *Nicky*?"

"Rather ironic, don't you think, madam?"

"But who would do such a thing? Who could conceive of such a thing?" Suddenly, her eyes went wide. "Bob!" she exclaimed. "The Bob who is staying with us laid the curse!"

"That's right, madam," Behemoth said reluctantly. "But as I understand it, he didn't know exactly who it was he was cursing."

"Why that no good little...," Angel sputtered. "I'm going right down there and give him a piece of my mind."

"I don't think you should do that, madam," Behemoth said, sobering suddenly.

"And why not?"

"It might not be in your best interest," Behemoth hedged, knowing full well that she was a principal ingredient of the curse but not wanting to say so to her.

"And how couldn't it be?" she demanded. "He's preoccupied my Nicky to distraction and is making him lose face among his subjects."

"There are forces at work here beyond anyone's control," Behemoth warned. "Interfering will only make matters worse."

"But I want to *do* something." She wrung her hands. "Beelzebub said that if Bob will apologize to the one he cursed —Nicky—then everything will be all right again. Yes! That's it!" She sat up perkily. "I'll just get Bob to take back the curse."

"I don't think that will work," Behemoth said.

"And why not?"

"As you pointed out, Bob is a guest here in the palace. How do you think he rates staying here instead of standing thigh-deep in the lake of boiling shit?"

Her face fell.

"The curse."

"That's right. He's not about to remove the curse now that he knows it's his ticket to the good life. In fact, if you confront him, he may just attempt to make things worse."

"But isn't there anther way?" she persisted. "There must be."

"Well, madam," the demon said. "There is a second, lesser-known method: The one who has been cursed can forgive the one who cursed him, which also negates the curse."

"There you have it," she said. "As soon as Nicky comes back, I'll ask him to forgive Bob, and that will remove the curse."

"I wouldn't bank on that, madam."

"Why not?"

"The Boss might be tempted to forgive Bob, but while temptation is part of the Devil's nature, forgiveness isn't. I'm afraid the curse is going to stand."

↬ 39 ↫

WORK ON THE RITZ WAS completed by the time Bob's staff arrived. It was a pretty swanky joint: ten floors wrapped around an Olympic-size pool. The entire first floor was devoted to the restaurant, nightclub, spa, and health club. Out back were a gaggle of rude lean-tos where the inmate service staff—all corporate execs, as Bob requested—dwelled.

Bob welcomed the former denizens of the lake of boiling shit with a brief but grandiloquent speech, and they cheered him soundly before he sent them off to pick out rooms, have a meal and a drink in the restaurant and club, or frolic in the swimming pool. For an hour or so, he visited here and there. Then he drew his closest associates—Ahmed, Pedro, Margaretha, Mwendi, and Yung-tzu—into the conference room, located with the rest of the executive offices, on the ground floor of one of the wings.

"Don't worry about your rooms," he told them when they'd assembled. "I've reserved the best suites on the next floor down from the penthouse for you."

"Listen, Bob," Ahmed said. "We all want to thank you for getting us out of that shit back there. I didn't know how good it would feel not to be parboiled all the time."

"Forget it," Bob said. "You all treated me right when I came, but I'll be frank: Friendship has never counted much with me, so don't think that's why I rescued you. I brought you here, instead, because each of you has talents I think will be useful for my organization."

"Public relations?" Margaretha asked. "I'm not sure any of us know much about that."

"Yeah," Mwendi agreed. "I pretty much ignored it since there usually were simpler solutions, like murder. Why bother trying to convince people to see it your way when you can just eliminate them and all that expense and aggravation?"

"We might have trouble waging genocidal war on the demon hordes," Bob pointed out. "Even the angels couldn't win that one. Besides, the PR bit is just a ruse to let the Boss save face." Bob paused and looked around the table, giving each of them a momentary but steady stare. "Before I go on, I want you all to swear an oath of loyalty to me."

"We're inmates in Hell," Yung-tzu reminded him. "What makes you think our word is worth a plugged nickel?"

"Call it a verbal contract," Bob said. "My version of *The Rule Book*. I plan on going places around here, but I don't want to have to watch my back all the time. You swear loyalty to me, and you'll go wherever I go."

"I assume that if we don't," Ahmed ventured cautiously, "you'll send us back to the lake of boiling shit."

"No," Bob said. "If you don't want in on my organization, fine. You can walk, and I won't say anything to the Boss. He might put you back in the shit, or he might not notice you're no longer working for me. I don't know. You might even be able to stay free for a long time. But I can promise you this: If you swear loyalty to me and break that trust, you'll be back in the shit for sure."

"Just asking," Ahmed said.

"That's why I want you for my chief of staff," Bob said. "You think of the angles."

"I'm with you," Ahmed said.

"How about the rest of you?"

"You got us this far," Margaretha said. "You smell like a winner, and I don't smell like shit. You have my oath."

"Count me in," Yung-tzu said.

"Me, too," Pedro said.

"Yeah, me, too," Mwendi agreed. "What do we do?"

"You, Mwendi, are going to be head of security. In this room, we'll call you my chief enforcer. Yung-tzu is in charge of finance and administration. Pedro, I want you to lead business operations, and Margaretha, you're going to run my intelligence-gathering operation. Call yourselves my executive directors. Your offices are in this wing, next to mine. Before you go play in them, though, I want to let you in on a little secret."

"Is it how you got out of the lake of boiling shit?" Pedro asked.

"I'm keeping that to myself, for now," Bob said. "No, this has to do with why I'm now VP of PR."

"It wasn't because you got out of the lake of boiling shit?" Pedro asked.

"No. The two may be linked or they may be coincidental. I'm not really sure. But the reason the Boss gave me this job is because Hell is going to hell."

"Sapason's mentioned something about it while you were gone," Ahmed said. "He told us the utilities were breaking down and the demons are organizing a union of some sort."

"It's true," Bob said. "And it looks like *I'm* the cause."

"How's that?" Yung-tzu asked.

"It all goes back to why I'm in Hell in the first place."

"I thought it was because you were a shitty corporate climber who didn't care who he stepped on in his rise to power," Margaretha said.

"Nope," Ahmed said. "It's the curse, isn't it?"

Bob nodded, a quirky smile playing on his lips.

"What curse?" Mwendi asked.

"Go on and tell them," Bob urged Ahmed.

"Bob's here because he laid a curse with his dying breath," Ahmed told them.

"Yeah," Margaretha said. "That'll do it."

"I don't get it," Yung-tzu said. "A deathbed curse will get you sent down here, but how did it make you VP of PR?"

"It was the Devil I cursed," Bob said.

"You're kidding," Mwendi gaped.

"Man," Pedro chimed in. "That took some real cojones."

"Don't give me too much credit," Bob said. "It was inadvertent. I didn't know it was him when I laid the curse. But accident or not, I intend to play it for all it's worth."

"You've made a good start," Ahmed said. "What we need now is some real ammunition."

"Maybe we already have it," Bob grinned. "You know that Angel woman everybody's keeps talking about?" The others nodded. "Well, it seems that she's a direct result of my curse."

"Ah, ha," Ahmed said. "Certainly a source of power."

"More a source of disruption," Bob said. "And *that's* why the Devil agreed to let me have this position. I let him think I'll consider getting rid of Angel, but all I really promised him was I'd work internally to help correct matters and restore Hell to it's former glory."

"But what happens if you relent on the curse?" Yung-tzu asked.

"I'm not sure," Bob said. "I presume that Angel would vanish."

"Be careful, then," Ahmed warned. "Once she's gone, you'll be right back there in the shit."

"You're right," Bob agreed. "I'll have to play it smart. We'll need to put up a good front in a number of areas—especially the union."

"You don't want us to deal with the utilities crisis?" Ahmed asked.

"The power plant and glacier can wait," Bob said, "But we need to think about the volcano immediately. I was up there a couple of days ago, talking to Xaphan, who's the chief volcanologist, and I learned that if the magma chamber cools below a hundred degrees, all the volcano workers—fire sprites included—will freeze solid. That'll leave the volcano untended, and it might even go permanently dormant."

"That'd be all right with me," Pedro said. "Cool things off, at least."

"Very cool," Ahmed put in a trifle sarcastically. "Like frozen and pitch black."

"That's why Ahmed is chief of staff," Bob said. "The volcano is the key. Without it, we've got nothing. Ahmed, I want you to make sure that the union toes the line where the volcano is concerned. You can use Sapason as our liaison to the union."

"I saw him when we arrived," the Arab said. "I thought you hired him to manage the club."

"That's just to keep him busy. And it gives him the perfect excuse to hobnob with the union officials and open a line of communications. Margaretha, I want you to scope out this Angel. I met her up at the palace, and she's a real puzzler. She'll probably appreciate some human female company. All she ever socializes with are the female demons. Ask around and find out what you can about her, and while you're at it, set up a network of spies."

"I'd suggest keeping tabs on our own staff as well as the demons," she said.

"Good thinking. Maybe you should get some moles in among the working inmates too."

"That's not going to be easy," she said. "Nobody's going to want to go back to torment just to gather a little information."

"You can always recruit from among the current inmate population. Promise them early release or perks of some kind if they do a good job."

"Do we make good on the promise?"

"Sure. The way I see it, we're going to need a lot more humans helping run things around here, and it'll be a good way to screen candidates. Mwendi, it'll be your job to establish our security force. I'm sure you know the type we're looking for."

"A piece of cake," Mwendi said. "There are plenty of us down here."

"Pedro, your task will be to maintain operations here at the Ritz, but I'll need even more from you. I want to make our night club the talk of Hell. I want it to be *the* place to be. Spare no expense in decorating, staffing, and advertising. And I want the best entertainment Hell has to offer."

"Do we have gambling?"

"Of course."

"How about a brothel?"

"Keep it discreet," Bob said. "Classy."

"But what will clients pay with?" Yung-tzu asked. "There's no money down here."

"Maybe we'll have to reinvent it," Bob said. "Until then, money isn't the only currency. There are favors, information, maybe even loyalty. First, I need you to set up our accounts receivable bookkeeping."

"What about accounts payable?"

"I don't plan on any of those," Bob said, and they all laughed.

"Now I get the internal PR angle," Ahmed said. "Where do we start?"

"We start by upping the ante." At the puzzled expressions on the faces of the others, Bob amplified. "I want to make sure we're in a strong position, and the best way to do that is to make the position of the enemy weaker. In short, I'm going to try a few things to see if I can hike up the Devil's suffering another notch."

"Sounds like fun," Margaretha said.

"I just want to know one thing," Mwendi said hopefully. "Are you going for the top spot?"

"Patience," Bob said. "First things, first."

❧ 40 ☙

THAT NIGHT, BOB THREW A lavish party in the hotel's night-club, whose name, The Inferno, was proclaimed in dancing red and yellow flames over the door.

He invited not only his staff but a lot of demons, many high-ranking, though the demon contingent tended to remain in two separate camps: those who sided with CRUDE and those who remained loyal to the Devil.

There was booze, music, dancing, and general frolic among the staff. Ahmed had procured women for those who wanted women and men for those who preferred men. Yung-tzu pro-fessed amazement when Ahmed brought a hunky, well-hung model-type over to Margaretha.

"I thought you were a dyke," he said.

"Just because I couldn't ogle," she responded tartly, "doesn't mean I didn't want to."

But thanks to Bob, they all could ogle now, and there was much to ogle at—naked show girls doing a high-kick number on stage, the staff in a jolly and boisterous mood, and even the club itself, with its décor that resided just on the ostentatious side of elegant.

Bob had a brace of beauties with him in the back of the large circular booth reserved for him and his executive staff, but he wasn't ogling them. Not yet, at least. There'd be plenty of time for that later. He suffered their attentions, but his mind remained on business amid the din of merriment.

Occasionally some drunken reveler would stagger over to the booth and profusely thank Bob and vow his or her undying loyalty.

"Of course it's undying," Margaretha snapped at the first one who said it. "This is eternal Hell."

But Bob simply thanked the man, and when he'd staggered off, Bob said, "Let 'em be, Margaretha. They're just appreciative."

"Yeah, but do they have to be stupid, too?"

"Don't worry," Bob said. "They'll be useful, and if they fuck up, there are plenty of places we can send them where they'll regret it."

That made everyone at the table laugh, and the sound caught the attention of Sapason, who took his role as nightclub manager so seriously that he was dressed in tux. At first, Pedro had been a little ticked off that he hadn't been able to choose his own manager, but Bob pointed out two things: First, he wanted Sapason around so he could use him, and second, didn't it make Pedro happy to be giving orders to the demon who'd so recently been pissing on his head?

Pedro saw the justice in that, and was content.

"Is everything all right, sir?" Sapason asked.

"Fine," Bob said, then he looked around at his executive staff. "Anybody need anything?"

"I'd like some ice for my drink," Mwendi said, holding up his glass of Scotch.

"I'm sorry, sir," the demon said, and he looked it, too. "There isn't any."

"No ice?" Mwendi snorted. "What the hell kind of night-club is this?"

"Ever since the glacier melted," Sapason said, "we've had trouble keeping it on hand. We tried shipping some in through the hole left by the glacier, but it melted before we could get it here. Then we looked for a supplier, but we can't seem to find anyone who'll deliver here."

"No matter," Bob said, waving it off. "We can drink Scotch warm for a while. And we'll get the glacier back on line soon enough."

"And the volcano, too, sir?" Sapason asked.

"That, too," Bob promised. "And the power plant. Then we can bring in some refrigerators and have all the ice we need."

"I see you have a lot of ideas," Sapason said.

"All this place needs is a man like Bob," Ahmed said. "Someone with vision. Someone who can get things done."

"Begging your pardon, sir, but the Boss has been taking care of business for a long time now."

"And look what a shambles the place has turned into," the Arab retorted. "You'd better look around and wake up, Sapason. Hell is been going to hell, but Bob will set things right."

"You should be careful, sir," the demon said, looking around nervously. "You don't want the Boss to catch wind of words like that."

"Do you really think I'm afraid of the Devil?" Bob asked.

"I don't know, sir, but I sure am."

"Maybe that's why you were just a lowly guard watching over a lake of boiling shit," Yung-tzu said sarcastically.

"Okay, okay," Bob said. "Hell's state of affairs isn't Sapason's fault. But I do want you to take a good look around this place." This last was directed at the demon.

"It's a very nice place, sir," Sapason said.

"Do you think I got it by being afraid?"

"I suppose not, sir."

"You saw me get right out of the shit," Bob said. "And you couldn't touch me. I walked halfway across Hell, and even Beelzebub couldn't stop me. And when I waltzed right into the Devil's palace, even he had to dicker."

"That's true, sir."

"Doesn't that tell you something?"

"I'm not sure."

"Well, it should. It should tell you that if the Devil really is the big shot he pretends to be, why didn't he just crush me to a pulp in an instant instead of making concessions to me?"

Sapason seemed at a loss for words.

"Pedro. Tell him why," Bob said.

"It's really very simple," Pedro said. "Bob has the Devil by the cojones." He held out his hand, palm up, and flexed his fingers demonstratively.

"By the cojones?"

"That's right," Bob said. "And you'd best remember that. There are going to be some changes around here, and if you want to keep on top of things, you'd better be sure you're playing on the right team."

"I'll keep that in mind, sir."

"Good. Say, look." Bob raised his glass in a salute to some CRUDE officials who were looking their way from a table across the room. The rest of Bob's executive staff also raised their glasses. "Looks to me like they need a refill," Bob said to Sapason. "See to it. On the house."

"Yes, sir." The demon turned to go, but Bob stopped him.

"By the way, don't forget to keep your ears open while you're over there."

"Your wish is my command," Sapason said, and he hurried off.

"Not yet," Bob said, "but very soon." He raised his glass in a toast to his own companions, and they joined in with relish.

By now, the dance routine was over, and a popular comedian took center stage. Within moments, he had the whole crowd—demon and human alike—laughing so loudly at his off-color jokes that often featured the Devil and Angel that the whole place practically shook.

Bob tossed off the rest of his drink and said, "I'm going to make the rounds. You all can stay here, if you want, and enjoy the show." To the two bimbos at his sides, he said, "Why don't you ladies come with me?"

They scooted out of the booth and made their way across the room, all eyes following—even the comedian's—as Bob stopped here for some glad-handing and there to pat some demon on the shoulder and buy him, her, or it a drink on the house. Everyone was effusive, and no one more so than Bob.

After a few minutes, Bob and his escorts went into the casino to check on things. One of the first people he spotted was General Means, ensconced in the middle of a U-shaped blackjack table. It looked a little like his old foxhole, and he even wore his helmet and had his huge machine gun, though the weapon was hung on pegs on the wall behind him.

The old soldier stopped dealing the cards when he saw Bob approach, and his face lit in a huge grin.

"Well, if it ain't the fellow with the congressional budget committee. Good to see you, son!"

"Good to see you, too, General."

"I hear you're the one responsible for all this." The general waved around.

"That's right. What do you think?"

"Hell, boy, when you ran off saying you were going for reinforcements, I thought you were a goner. I had no idea you'd break through the enemy lines and bring back victory."

"Tastes pretty sweet, eh, General?"

"That it does. And to get me a cushy retirement like this...." The general seemed at a loss for words. "Why, I feel right at home."

"You don't miss all that fighting?"

"Look around you, son, and tell me what you see."

"Lots of folks having fun?"

"You're a good, all-American boy, son, looking for the best in people. But let me tell you what I see. I see a bunch of suckers itching to try and take what's mine." The general gestured to the table surrounding him. It was heaped with piles of bullets—the General was still using ammo for chips. "But you know what?"

"I think they've got a mighty big surprise on their hands if they try to take you on," Bob said.

"Ain't *that* right, son!" The general guffawed, and Bob joined in. "I like your spirit, General. How about a promotion?"

"I don't know, son. Not if you want to put me out to pasture. I kind of like here in the trenches."

"How does pit boss sound?"

"Sounds like commander of one mighty big foxhole."

"That it is. Interested?"

"Where do I enlist?"

"You just have. See Pedro after hours, and he'll set you up."

"Thanks, son. I'll do you proud."

"I know you will, General," Bob said, then he moved on, stopping here and there as he had in the nightclub, until he and his brace of beauties made it to the cocktail lounge for a nightcap.

"How would you ladies like to see the penthouse?" Bob asked as they finished their drinks.

They would, and they did.

∿ 41 ∾

A JAZZ–ROCK FUSION PIECE was playing on the stereo as the Devil came into the living room. Despite the upbeat tempo, he kind of liked it.

"What's that?" he asked.

"'Big Nick'," she said, looking up from the magazine she was reading. "By Lifetime." She looked as lovely as ever, but the pastel plaid fabric covering the sofa on which she sat made his eyes swim.

"I hope you don't have it programmed to play 'Sympathy for the Devil'," he said a trifle sharply.

"I'm sure it's in the mix," she replied blandly. "But I think 'The Devil Came from Kansas' is next. By the way, how was work today?"

"The same old stuff," the Devil said. "Encouraging people to turn wicked and punishing them for it when they do." He chuckled, but there was a sad note to it, and he shook his head. "It's really not all that hard. People are so fragile and gullible and filled with fear at the immensity of the universe and unknowns of the future that they're willing to adhere to any false belief that they think justifies their warped and puny views of reality. Kind of gives you pause."

"Well, not me," Angel declared. "If you're so all-fired ready to commiserate, maybe it's high time you stopped creating misery."

"You know that's impossible. Besides, I don't really cause people to be corrupt. They do it to themselves. They have free will, and there are plenty of examples to follow of people who don't let their baser instincts gain control of their lives."

She just sat there and stared at him with a look that said she'd heard it all before and was bored.

Maybe she was just too dim to understand the finer points of ethics. He liked to think so, but he didn't have a chance because she brought up something far less pleasant than human damnation.

"When are you going to take me on that picnic you promised?"

"You know I've been busy...."

"Well, you'll just have to get un-busy. Beelzebub and the other Archons can handle things for one day. It's important that we have some quality time together."

Quality time, the Devil groused to himself. I'd like to take some quality and stick it....

"And one more thing," she went on in that tone she used when she wouldn't take no for an answer. "I'm tired of walking all over the place every time we go anywhere together."

Every time you follow me around, the Devil thought.

"It's high time that you started to carry me when we go out. It's only the right thing to do. After all, people notice us. We have to set standards."

"Of course they notice us," he said. "I'm the lord of every-one and everything here."

Almost instantly he shrank a bit inside, realizing that that wasn't strictly true these days. He glanced at her, and a twinkle lit her eyes. She knew it wasn't true, too.

And by now, so did everyone else.

It was enough to make him sick, but he was too damn tired to feel sick.

Instead, he said, "I've got to wind up a few last-minute mat-ters. I'll be in my office."

She barely looked up from her magazine as he left the room and went to his office. Not the big, spacious one with the great eastward view and huge balcony where he could lean on the parapet and relax as he took in the hellish profusion of his domain. He'd had to move his daily operations from there to this new space. Already there was talk from Angel of refurbishing the old office into a mini ballroom that would enable them to get some good use out of the balcony and view.

"I don't know why you'd care," she'd said. "All you ever do out there is brood like some Romantic poet. Let me have the room, and we'll liven it up and have some parties."

The Devil wasn't enthusiastic. In the first place, that was his true office, and he felt uncomfortable being away from it for long. He took sustenance from its dimensions—exactly laid out to his specifications, of course—and also from his desk, which was rooted in the depths of the obsidian bedrock of Hell.

But he'd had to move. The new office, with a good but narrow view due west, was closer to Angel's suite. He'd found that if he was within a certain radius of her, she would feel that he was in her easy range and would occasionally ease up and let him have some private time. The daily operations of Hell bored her, anyway, though she recognized the necessity of conducting business in a proper businesslike manner—a holdover, she said, from something taught to her by her father, who was a relatively successful insurance salesman in the Kansas town where she'd grown up.

The Devil hated the man wholeheartedly, even without having met him, and secretly hoped that the old fart would end up over here so he could rip the guy a new one. There was an excellent chance of that happening, too, considering his occupation. Plus, it would allow the Devil to gloat at Angel in a way that would shame even her. He reminded himself to get one of the Archons to work on the old bastard. Mammon should be able to do the trick, especially if he had a little help from Leviathan's seductive powers.

But there was an even better reason not to turn the office into a ballroom and throw parties: He didn't know a single soul in Hell worth socializing with, and that included the demons, from the Archons on down, and they didn't even have souls. Who in their right mind would want to go to a party with a bunch of humans who were evil wrongdoers and an equally large number of ugly, smelly demons? He couldn't understand how Angel would want that when the Devil himself couldn't stand the thought, even if all those nasty, smelly demons were simply tangible manifestations of his personal identity.

And if a lot of the evil in the human souls had been encouraged by his own machinations, so what? It was a record to be proud of, he thought. And he was, but that didn't mean he wanted to be around the results constantly.

At that moment, his intercom buzzer razzed.

"What is it?" he said, meaning it to sound harsh, but the words only came out tiredly.

"Bob is here to see you, sire," Behemoth's voice replied over the speaker.

What does that little creep want now? the Devil wondered. Crap. Only one way to find out.

"Send him in."

A moment later, the door opened, and Bob came into the office.

"Is this a social call or business?" the Devil asked.

"Does it matter?"

"I guess not. I'm too tired for business, nor am I feeling very sociable. But you're here, anyway. What do you want?"

"Just a little chat," Bob said. "And there's nobody else here worth talking to."

"My sentiments, entirely." The Devil hoped that Bob would take the hint, but if Bob caught the slap, he ignored it.

"I wanted to talk to you about Belphegor."

"What about him?"

"You'll recall that, as part of my internal PR effort, I've asked all the Archons for their resumes, and everyone's responded except for Belphegor. He told me he'd do it by the next day, and that's the last I saw of him."

The Devil laughed.

"What's the joke?" Bob asked, looking a little hurt.

"What would you expect from the epitome of sloth?"

"Yeah, I guess you're right."

"For your information, even I don't know where that lazy bum is. He's been gone since about the time you showed up at the palace. Lucifer's out looking for him."

"Then what am I going to do?" Bob asked. "It's really important that I have all the information I need when I start my big PR push."

"I can help you, Bob, but I'll want something in return."

"Anything specific in mind?"

"Yes. Tell me how you got out of the lake of boiling shit," the Devil said.

"Order," Bob admitted after a moment's consideration.

"Order?"

"Yeah. While I was memorizing the rules and later studied them, I noticed that their sequence made no senses—in fact, made them practically impossible to remember much less follow. So I put them in order."

"Ah, the pencil you borrowed from Sapason."

"Yep. Mighty powerful instrument. Anyway, it got me out because Hell is the realm of extremes and thus the obvious place for punishment of extreme behavior, and order is a leveling of extremes—an averaging out, so to speak."

"Well, that makes me feel a little better. I thought you might be fomenting some kind of religious rebellion."

"Religion!" Bob laughed. "I never much believed in religion, and even less now that I'm here in Hell. What does Hell—or Heaven, for that matter—have to do with religion anyway if they're really just the archetypal abodes of the two primal forces of good and evil? All religion does is make a hell of Earth. You don't have to wait for this." He waved around. "Religious leaders can commit any atrocity with impunity because they are operating with a personal mandate from whatever god they claim is in charge. The way I see it, religion is really just a means to keep the little people in check, energies sublimated by enthralling but completely inconsequential belief systems that have nothing to do with reality or the genuine issues surrounding life and death."

"I can see you've been doing a lot of thinking lately, Bob," the Devil said.

"Wandering around Hell has given me a perspective I didn't have before," Bob said. "Now, the tit for the tat. What about Belphegor's resume? Will you get it from him?"

"No need." The Devil snapped his fingers, sending out a little flower of sparks, and a manila folder appeared on his desk. "There it is."

"Thanks," Bob said, though he left the folder lying where it was.

"Something else?" The Devil asked.

"I thought you might want to talk about Angel."

"What about her?" There was a dangerous edge to the Devil's voice.

"I don't know," Bob shrugged. "I thought you just might want to unload. She's got to be trying at times."

"Trying," the Devil said, mulling over the word like a promisingly sour wine.

"You must have the patience of Job," Bob said. "I'd be ripping her apart."

"Don't bother dissembling, Bob. I'm sure you're aware that I can't."

"But you don't try...."

"What makes you think I want my subjects to watch me ineffectually beat my head against a wall? I am the demon of wrath, after all. Nobody would give me respect if they saw that."

"But they should see you do *something*," Bob insisted.

"Don't think for a second that I give a damn about any of them." The Devil's scornful, backhanded wave took in all of Hell, and perhaps Heaven and, in its implications, the rest of creation, too. "But I am doing something. For myself, not them. I'm going to have that bitch if it's the last thing I do. It'll take a different technique than rage, though."

"Guile?"

"That's right," the Devil nodded. "I'm past master of that, too."

Past master is right, Bob thought. Aloud, he said, "Sounds good. I like sneaking up on people, too."

꩜ 42 ꩜

THE INFERNO WAS *THE* PLACE to be, and anybody who was anybody made sure to put in frequent appearances. And that was often since the sign outside proclaimed, "Eternally Open." Bob's human staff mingled easily with the demons, and everyone had a good time drinking, dancing, and watching the shows. But everyone knew that there really was only one show, and that was Bob. Guests vied to be present when Bob made his entrance, invariably accompanied by several of his executive staff.

"Look, there's Bob and his crew," they'd point and whisper. "Hey, Bob," they'd call and wave. "He's waving back," they'd breathe, feeling self-satisfied yet oddly timorous at the same time. "What a great guy!"

And Bob and his crew would sit in Bob's big circular booth, sip drinks, smile at everyone, and occasionally entertain VIP guests who were allowed to slip into the booth with them. CRUDE officials were regulars, as were the demons who supervised the various utilities, except for Xaphan and his assistants, who no longer could venture outside Mount Etna's main vents. Bob would take a few moments to listen to their reports, make a few suggestions, and then supply them with free drinks.

Yes, The Inferno was quite the spot, and it wasn't long before the nightly crowds had grown so large that there simply wasn't enough room to serve everyone. There was a perpetual waiting line at the doors, and demon bouncers constantly were vigilant for gate crashers and rowdy drunks. There were plenty of both in Hell.

"We're turning away ghouls, miasma wraiths, and troglodytes as well as a good number of lesser demons," Bob pointed out to his executive staff one afternoon. They were gathered in the conference room adjacent to Bob's office. "That's lost opportunity. I don't want anyone to go away unhappy, especially when they came for a good time. We'll simply have to expand. There's no other way. Ahmed, bring up the plans."

Ahmed switched on the giant-screen monitor that was on the wall behind Bob, and everyone watched as Bob stood and, wielding a laser pointer, outlined the plans for his new super entertainment complex. It was quite a spread, with multiple hotels, bars, and clubs, lots of fancy suites, several pools, a real casino, and even an amusement park complete with rickety rides, a midway rife with cheating hucksters, and a freak show.

"I'm calling it Alcazar on the Acheron," Bob said proudly.

"What's an alcazar?" Yung-tzu asked.

"It's like a Spanish castle," Pedro supplied. "But what's an Acheron?"

"It's the river that runs around below the castle," Bob said.

"Wow!" Margaretha exclaimed. "Who designed all this?"

"The architects from Caligari City," Bob explained. "Their crazy constructions are perfect for an amusement park. There's something for everyone no matter what their taste and income level."

"It's like all of Las Vegas, Broadway, Disney World, and Hollywood rolled into one mega entertainment complex," Ahmed said.

"I didn't think we had enough room around here for something that size," Pedro said.

"I'm not planning on building it here," Bob said. "We're stuck off in a corner of Hell, and we need something more centrally located."

"You're not thinking what I think you're thinking," Yung-tzu said.

"I think I probably am," Bob said with a grin. "The Devil's palace will make the fitting centerpiece for the complex. Sort of like Sleeping Beauty's Castle at Disneyland. Of course, the palace is too valuable a real estate to let just anyone wander in. We'll reserve it for living quarters for our executive staff."

"But what about the Devil?" Mwendi asked. "He's not going to let us waltz right in and set up house."

"You afraid Bob's going to have you try to strong-arm the Devil?" Pedro asked, and everybody laughed, including Mwendi, though a slightly paranoid look lurked in the corners of his eyes.

"Don't worry, Mwendi," Bob soothed. "I'll deal with the Devil. He'll realize that it had to come to this. Hell is overpopulated enough as it is, and right now there's just him and Angel living in that huge pile. That's a waste of valuable real estate. We can put him and Angel in a nice suite here—hell, we'll give them my penthouse—and we can fill up the rest of the hotel with other demons. That'll allow us to tear down a couple of the older demon hotels near the palace and replace them with new torment theme parks. That should make the Devil happy."

"We wouldn't even have to tear them down," Pedro said. "We could just tear them up real bad and move in a bunch of tenement slumlords. We could have a lot of gangbangers hang around to beat them up and terrorize them and spray-paint graffiti and vandalize and stuff."

"Great idea," Bob said. "No running water, overflowing toilets, leaky roofs, air conditioning in the winter, and central heat in the summer. I can just see it now."

"The Devil will understand the logic," Margaretha nodded. "I heard he filled up the lake of boiling shit within half an hour after we left. He knows space is at a premium, and he's been living entirely too extravagantly. It only makes sense for him to downsize, especially now that Bob is in charge."

"Whoa," Bob said, holding up his hands. "I'm not in charge. Yet. Not outside of this room, at least. But if we play our cards right, who knows?"

"Do we have the funding to build the complex?" Pedro asked.

"Not exactly," Bob said, "but I've been working some deals with the union bosses. Tell them, Ahmed."

"The trick is, Bob has gotten the union to agree to divert some of the labor. When you look around Hell, you see a lot of effort going completely to waste. People doing this task or that task and then having to do it all over again without result."

"Yeah," Mwendi said. "Like that Sisyphus guy rolling that boulder up the mountain."

"Exactly," Ahmed said. "Only instead of having the boulder just roll down again, we have some other guys up there to stop it. Then Sisyphus goes back down, finds another boulder, and rolls it up. So, he's still having to roll the boulder, but we've turned his effort into our advantage. Sisyphus and others like him gather our basic building materials, and other inmates do their normal work, too. Like those stone masons who have to keep refashioning building blocks only to have them transform back into boulders. We have a crew standing by to take the blocks away just before the blocks are finished and turn back into boulders and carry them to the work site. There are plenty of laborers here who's task is to carry heavy weights."

"What a brilliant idea," Pedro said. "Everyone still gets punished, but we get free labor and our complex, too."

"Well," Bob said, "The labor isn't quite free. The union bosses want a cut."

"How much?" Yung-tzu asked.

"I'm sure we'll figure out a way to make it as little as possible," Bob said, and everybody laughed. "Hell, when the job's done, maybe we'll just take over the union. In the meantime, I'll promise them what I have to within reason."

He looked around at his crew for a moment then said, "We've got a lot of work coming up, but right now, I suggest we go down to The Inferno and do a little celebrating."

Things already were heating up in The Inferno, even though it was only four in the afternoon. But it was Friday, and what with the new five-day work week, a lot of demons and their inmates had cut out early to get a jump on the weekend.

Two mid-level demons—Aim and Botis—were relaxing over drinks. Aim had the body of a man, but three heads sprouted from his shoulders. The one in the middle was human with two stars emblazoned in its forehead, and the other two were a serpent and a cat. Botis also had a human body, but he sported only a single head—this with huge teeth and two horns.

He also could appear as an ugly viper, but it's a little hard for a snake with no hands to sit at a table and drink a martini.

"Have you heard?" Botis asked Aim.

"Heard what?" Aim asked absently, using his human head to speak. He didn't really give a crap. He was busy watching the showgirls do their high-kicks. This was, after all, still Hell, and everybody was naked, so it was quite a sight.

"About Bob," Botis said.

"What about him?"

Aim pulled his attention away from the showgirls and focused somewhat blearily on his companion. He'd already had one too many, but he intended to have a couple more, at least. The serpent head was lolling, apparently passed out, but the cat's head was purring contentedly. There'd never been a joint like this in Hell in all the long millennia he'd been here, and he intended to take advantage. Besides, union members at drank half-price.

"That fucker's got the Boss by the cojones."

"By the what?" Aim took another slug of his scotch.

"The cojones. You know," Botis grabbed his crotch and shook himself.

"Oh, yeah. Sure."

"No, really. It's true."

"Bullshit. Nobody's got the Devil by the cojones. Not even the Big Cheese."

"Then you'd better call Bob nobody, 'cause he's done it. Hell, just look around at this place." Botis waved around at the interior of the nightclub. "You ever seen anything like this here?"

That hit Aim a little too close to what he'd just been thinking himself.

"No," he admitted. "But this place doesn't prove anything."

"No? Then you tell me why the Boss let this happen."

"I heard it was all some sort of PR stunt."

"Hah! You don't know anything."

"And you do?"

"I know Sapason. We used to play canasta after work on Friday nights before he became manager of this place. He was Bob's jailer."

"Wasn't Bob in the lake of boiling shit or something like that?"

"Yeah, and according to Sapason, one day he just up and walked out."

"Bullshit."

"No, really. And there wasn't nothing Sapason could do about it. His whip couldn't even touch Bob. And then Bob just walked straight across Hell and right into the palace and up to the Boss's office and told the Boss there wasn't nothing the Boss could do about it, either."

"Sounds like a fairytale."

"Maybe, but this fairytale is true. I talked to some other demons who met Bob along the way, and they said he was invulnerable. It seems he's found some quirk in the rules, and now he's on top."

"I don't know...."

"Well, I do," Botis said, then he quickly touched his companion's leathery forearm. "Look, there he is, now, coming out of his private elevator."

A group of six people had just entered the nightclub across the room. They were all naked humans, and all humans looked pretty much the same to Aim, but it wasn't hard to tell which one of the five was Bob because the rest obviously deferred to him.

"That's his executive staff with him," Botis hissed. "The guy on Bob's right, the one with the long dark hair and goatee? That's Ahmed, Bob's chief of staff. You ever see such a thing in Hell?"

Aim had to admit he hadn't. A five-day work week, humans on the loose all around, having fun instead of being in torment, and Bob and his bunch waltzing across the room like they owned the joint. Come to think of it, they did.

"Maybe you're right," he had to concede to Botis. "It doesn't seem natural that the Boss would let all this happen if Bob didn't know some loophole in the rules."

"Rumor has it it's more than that," Botis confided.

"Yeah? Tell me."

"Well, you didn't hear this from me, but there's talk that Bob and Angel are in cahoots."

"Angel?" Aim whistled. "Well, we know *she's* got the Boss by the cojones, that's for sure."

"No shit."

"Not for Bob, anyway," Botis said, and they both laughed and took sips of their drinks.

Across the room, Bob and his bunch had settled into their reserved booth, and several of the best-looking waitresses were fawning over them.

"Who told you that about Angel and Bob?" Aim asked.

"I'm not saying, but I'll tell you this much: He's one of the union officers, and you know they've got the inside scoop on everything. Bob's even given them a special suite up on the sixth floor where they hold their meetings."

"And who knows what else?" Aim said, and they both laughed again.

"Yeah," Botis said. "In fact, I've been thinking of running for a position, myself."

"You?" Aim shook his head. "It'll be tough breaking in. I mean, those CRUDE guys are going to hold on to their positions for eternity. It's not like you can make any of 'em vanish like we did Jimmy Hoffa."

"I know, but the organization is still young and expanding. They say they're opening up a bunch of locals."

"You mean like all the pit workers in one local and all the butchers in another?"

"That's right. I'm going to run for head of the water-workers local."

"You think you can get enough votes?"

"Votes, hell. Who needs votes when you've got friends. Like I told you, my buddy's one of the officers. I'm a shoe-in. Say, look! There's Beelzebub."

Sure enough, Beelzebub had come into the nightclub and was going over to Bob's booth.

"Look," Aim said. "They're not even offering him a seat."

"What'd I tell you," Botis said. "The cojones." He grabbed his crotch again.

"Maybe you're right."

The two demons watched while Beelzebub spoke with Bob for a few moments. Then the human named Ahmed got up, and he and Beelzebub left.

"Did ya see that?" Aim asked. "Bob sent his number one man to dicker with the Boss's number one demon. I wonder what it's all about."

"I don't know," Botis said, "But it should be obvious now, even to you, that Bob is moving up."

"You really going to head up the local?"

"Yep."

"Need a campaign manager?"

❧ 43 ❧

"OOOH!" ANGEL CRIED. "IT'S JUST like Margot Kidder and Chris Reeve in *Superman!*"

She was in the Devil's arms, and they were flying at a great height over the far western reaches of Hell.

The Devil glanced at her face. She looked absolutely ecstatic as she stared out over the hellscape. And lovely, with the breeze from their flight blowing her long blond hair. Her body felt nice and warm—and firm and shapely, too—beneath her chemise. It was the first time she'd let him so completely embrace her, though the embrace remained all too chaste for his liking.

He wished he could drop her.

They were on their way to the picnic she'd badgered him into. He'd suggested Mount Etna, but she would have none of it.

"You can forget that," she'd declared. "You spend too much time there as it is, and I don't want you to think you can mix business with pleasure. Remember, this is your day off, and even the Big Cheese had one of those."

Yeah, the Devil thought. But he doesn't have my problems. "Where is it you *would* like to go?" he'd asked.

"Leviathan told me there's a lovely beach along the coast of the sea where she lives. I want to go there. I grew up in Kansas, you know, and I've never seen a real beach."

"I'm afraid Leviathan's sea is constantly disturbed by storms and filled with hideous sea serpents and wrecked ships manned by doomed and haunted sailors."

"No problem," she replied brightly. "Leviathan said that, since the volcano's gone dormant, the temperature inversions that caused all the storms have vanished, so the water's as placid as a lake."

"Kind of defeats the purpose of going to the beach," he said. "What with no surf and all."

"Oh, stop being such a grump. We'll have a wonderful time. Leviathan promised she'd have the crew of one of the ghost ships hitch some of the sea serpents to the boat and pull us around. Won't that be fun?"

"Sure," he said. "Jolly good fun."

"Well," she said definitively. "*I* think it'll be fun. We're going, and that's that."

And it was, and here he was, carrying her along. And that wasn't all that bad except for the picnic basket clutched in her lap. The bright red-and-white-checked tablecloth neatly folded across the top of the wicker basket was a complete embarrassment. He just hoped that nobody else would fly close enough to see it.

Despite Angel's insistence that he forget work for the day and just enjoy himself, he couldn't. He loved work more than leisure, and flying across western Hell made him realize that he hadn't inspected this area since Angel and Bob had appeared and screwed up his life. He kept finding himself wanting to stop and get back into the swing of things. But he knew he didn't dare, so he simply flapped along, sometimes descending to lower altitudes to get a better look, hoping all the while that the mere sight of him would help keep the ground-level demons in line. But he sure as hell missed lending his hand in the torments. He was, after all, much better at it than anyone else, and he often could come up with interesting twists that elicited the most torment possible from the inmates and constantly refreshed his demons' appreciation of his power and ingenuity.

It looked like those days might be over, though, he sighed. At least until he found a reliable way to elude Angel. He'd better, or this whole place would fall into ruin.

But then they lofted over a region that gave him a sense of renewed confidence. Below was a mind-boggling profusion of dark, rocky, gorges that separated isolated, slender, bitter peaks. Each of the peaks was inhabited by preachers, priests, and holy men representing all of the world's faiths, past as well as present. These men—and women—had abused their positions as keepers of their particular faiths in order to reap personal financial and fleshly rewards and power and so were doomed to play the simplest and most secluded of religious roles: the hermit who hones his devotion to the higher power on the strop of self-denial.

Of course, those incarcerated on the peaks spent little time in self denial, instead screaming their demands for recognition and fealty across the gulfs between the mountain tops. It did little good. Even if their closest neighbors could have heard them, they were too busy screaming their own demands to listen.

The sinners who toiled down in the rocky chasms between the peaks were the followers of those on the peaks who had done terrible, often unthinkable, deeds to their fellow humans in the name of those who resided so far above them. Not all of the followers were clustered around the base of the peak that held their respective leaders. Many mobbed the bases of the peaks of rivals from other faiths. There they fought, quite literally, tooth and nail with their enemies, inflicting vicious wounds on each other that quickly healed only to be reopened in the next savage encounter. A few of the braver souls attempted to climb the cruel cliffs to the top of the pinnacles in an effort to cast down the rivals of their paragons, but the spires were eminently unclimbable, and the climbers invariably slipped and fell, to be broken on the jagged rocks below and finally crash onto the heads of their milling, battling fellows.

The area was one of the Devil's special favorites, particularly since it had posed such an ergonomic dilemma. Egocentric false prophets and their rash, insensitive, and willfully ignorant followers have been such frequent and overwhelming facets of human existence through the ages that this was the single-largest category of sinners in Hell. The population explosions of the nineteenth, twentieth, and now twenty-first centuries had added dramatically to their numbers, as leaders of sects, cults, and splinter groups manipulated their followers into enforcing their private perversions on the public at large.

The influx had grown so great that, for a time, it looked like it might inundate all of Hell. But the Devil had come up with an ingenious way to apply fractal geometry to the mountain range so that it could be contained within a bounded area of Hell while at the same time becoming, as it were, infinitely deep. Each convolution of each peak contained its own convolutions populated with tinier and tinier clusters of human fanatics milling around tinier and tinier peaks where their leaders shouted to the emptiness that constantly closed in on them.

The really brilliant touch, if he did say so himself, was that the larger fanatics were constantly stepping on and crushing the ant-like milling mobs of those smaller than themselves, compounding everything with random, deus ex machina cataclysms that only fueled the fanatics' paranoid furor.

The Devil chuckled. Humans could produce fanatics ad infinitum, and he'd still have enough room to hold them all. In fact, the idea was so successful, he considered applying fractal geometry throughout Hell to accommodate the constant influx of people who came but never left. Best of all, no demon jailers were necessary to maintain or enforce the disorder. What the fanatics didn't accomplish at their own level was taken care of by the crushing weight of those above.

It was the ultimate in automation.

Let those fucking CRUDE bastards get around *that!*

"It hurts my eyes to look down there," Angel said as she stared into the seething, constantly shifting perspectives of the fractal mountains.

"Then you mustn't look, my dear," the Devil said blandly as he flapped on, hating the way the words "my dear" totally lacked sardonic conviction. But he couldn't help himself. Just as he couldn't harm Angel, he found that, in some mysterious way, he was compelled to treat her as if he adored her. That meant his words and tone came out of him in an endearing way, no matter how much he seethed and fumed inside.

At that moment, he saw Beelzebub flapping rapidly toward them.

The Devil knew something was wrong because Beelzebub rarely flew so fast that his squadrons of flies couldn't keep up. Stopping, he hovered until the Archon caught up.

"Boss," Beelzebub said breathlessly. He'd been flying at top speed, which he wasn't used to doing. "I think you'd better get back to the palace."

"Why? What the hell's going on, now?"

"It's Bob. He's moving in."

"Moving into the palace?" The Devil almost laughed, but then reconsidered. Beelzebub never joked about anything, so he certainly wouldn't joke about something like this.

"And he has a work crew moving all your stuff to the Ritz."

The sudden fury that flashed through the Devil's mind almost caused him to drop Angel.

"Damn it!" he said.

"What, dear," Angel asked. "Bob?"

"Yes," he agreed, though really he'd cursed because he'd caught himself before he forgot himself long enough to actually drop her. They were still over the fractal mountains, and even if she wasn't immediately dashed to death on the rocks or impaled on one of the pinnacles, she'd have been lost forever in that squirming infinity. Maybe the fanatics would tear her up. Or at least overwhelm her with their numbers. "I'm afraid we'll have to return to the palace immediately."

"Oh, dear," she said in a resigned voice. "And I was so enjoying our little ride."

Yeah, the Devil thought as he turned and headed for home. You may be riding, but I'm doing all the carrying. And you're quite a burden.

Aloud, all he could say was, "So was I, my dear."

❧ 44 ☙

"WHAT THE HELL IS GOING on here?" the Devil boomed as soon as he landed and set Angel lightly on the balcony floor. It seemed like he'd been saying that a lot lately.

The sliding glass doors to his office were open, and four demon movers inside were attempting to lift his massive desk, which was the only thing left in the room. They weren't having much success, though, since it, like the rest of the castle, was rooted in the living heart of Hell's obsidian bedrock. The Devil raised his hand to smite them as much for their careless stupidity as for their temerity, when Bob came in, all phony smiles. He was holding a long roll of paper.

"I hired you to smooth out my public relations problems," the Devil snarled. "Not move me out of house and home."

"I heard you were back," Bob said with false joviality. "Kinda surprised to see all this, I bet. I tried to get hold of you to let you know what was going on, but Behemoth told me you were off gallivanting around the countryside with your lady. Probably good to get a day off now and then."

"Tell me what you are doing in my palace. Now."

"Hey, you guys, why don't you take a break." Bob waved at the workmen with the long roll of paper he carried. "And shut the door on the way out."

The workmen hurried out, leaving Bob alone with the Devil and Angel. The Devil looked at Angel, but she showed no sign of following after the workmen. Bob perched on the edge of the Devil's adamant desk, set the long roll of paper on the surface behind him, and started to explain.

"Look," he said, "Public relations is all perception, right?" The Devil didn't respond, so Bob went on. "Well, it *is* perception. Truth doesn't matter one bit. I mean, look at this place. It's like living in a barn—drafty, dark, harsh, completely without the amenities that lend comfort and make life worth living. So you and Angel live here even though it isn't all that great a place, while all your underlings live in luxury in those five-star hotels you built for them. But is that how the demons see it?" Bob shook his head emphatically. "Not at all. And do you know why? Perception. This heap is the palace, and that conjures up images of splendor and luxury far beyond what the hoi polloi enjoys. They think you live way out of their range, even if your quarters really are far more austere than theirs. So that gives them ideas. Ideas about advancing themselves and having a little of the luxury they believe you have. But they could only do that at your expense. By assuming your prerogatives. You're the Boss, right? I mean, who else are they going to try to take things from?"

"So to prevent them from *taking* my palace, you're *giving* it to them?" the Devil asked, a sardonic ring in his voice.

"Not me," Bob said. "*You're* giving it to them. None of them will ever live here, of course. This place is too valuable for that. Instead, you'll be living among them, bringing yourself down to their level. And what a magnanimous gesture on your part! Realizing the inequity that exists among your people, you are making the ultimate sacrifice to help erase that inequity and bring peace and prosperity to your domain."

"Yeah, right."

"Well, of course not," Bob said with a shrug. "But like I said, it's all perception. That's how your demons will see the situation once I explain it to them."

I'm sure they will, the Devil thought, remembering how the demon workers had been trying to lift the desk even though it was part of the palace's foundation. Anybody that stupid probably would believe anything Bob told them.

"What about *us*?" Angel asked. Her tone wasn't exactly plaintive, but her curiosity held the slightest trembling.

"The Ritz, of course," Bob said, smiling and lifting his hands like a ringmaster presenting the next act. "Nothing but the best for the Boss and his lady, and I assure you that the Ritz *is* the best place to live in Hell. Far better, really, than this drafty old castle. The demons will think you're giving up something and giving it to them, but it's you who'll be moving into the lap of luxury. In fact, I've had all your stuff moved into my own penthouse, which has its own private elevator not only to The Inferno, but to the executive office suite. I'm sure you'll be taking your Archons with you, right? There are excellent suites for them located on the floor just below the penthouse."

"They already have quarters," the Devil said.

"Sure they do, but you'll need them close for meetings and such. Since my own executive staff is sacrificing themselves to move in here with me, their apartments will be vacant, so your staff might as well move in with you."

"You and your staff are moving in here?" the Devil asked.

"Well, I *have* to," Bob said, shrugging. "I mean, it wouldn't look right to just leave the place vacant. It is a national treasure, and somebody has to be the caretaker. I have to move here, even if it means giving up the Ritz." He looked from the Devil to Angel and back again. "What do you think?"

"I think there's something going on here that you haven't told me," the Devil said.

"I knew it," Bob said, shaking his head. "I knew I couldn't pull the wool over your eyes. Okay, I confess. I do have plans. I wanted to surprise you, but...."

"I don't like surprises."

"Of course not," Bob said hurriedly. "But before you say no, hear me out."

"I'm listening."

"What I said about this place being a national treasure was the truth. I think it's far too valuable an asset not to leverage it to everyone's mutual benefit." He hopped off the desk, spread out the roll of paper, and beckoned the Devil over. Angel followed.

"Look this over, Nick. It's the thing that's going to make Hell the best place to be. I call it Alcazar on the Acheron."

"What is it?" Angel asked.

"It looks like an architectural rendering for an amusement park," the Devil said, bending over the desk.

"Not just *any* amusement park," Bob said. "*The* amusement park to end all amusement parks. Think of all those people who go to Disney World and Six Flags and such each year. They'll want the same sort of stuff after they die. Talk about temptation! Hell, they'll practically kill to get in here. Whole families will be coming in droves."

"You don't seriously believe this cockamamie scheme will work, do you?" the Devil snorted.

"Look, Nick," Bob said. "You gotta keep up with the times. What you got going on here is right out of Breughel and Bosch. It's positively medieval, man! The last time you went to Earth, how many people did you see listening to classical music? About this many." He held up one finger. "Everybody's into rock and hip-hop and modern country. You think all those people are going to be attracted to cultural icons that are half a millennium out of date? Not likely. You have to keep up with the times, even down here."

"Oooh," Angel breathed. While Bob had been talking, she'd been staring at the plans, apparently oblivious to the exchange between Bob and her paramour. "How exciting. I always wanted to go to Disney World, but Daddy was always too busy."

"See?" Bob said to the Devil, as if Angel had answered all the Devil's objections.

"All right," the Devil conceded. "I see you've put some thought into this."

"Not just thought," Bob said. "You've got all the best integrated market researchers here, and I put them to good use. Alcazar on the Acheron is guaranteed to boost admissions, not to mention productivity after all the new arrivals get here." He smiled a big smile. "What do you say?"

"I notice that the palace is the centerpiece of your plan," the Devil said.

"How could it be otherwise?" Bob asked demurely.

"Hmm," the Devil pondered, his tail twitching absently as he again perused the plans. "It's an intriguing idea. Logical. Well designed. But I'm not sure about moving." He turned to Angel. "This affects you as much as me. What do you think?"

"Living at the Ritz does sound a bit intoxicating," she said with a hopeful smile. "All that glamour. And Bob's right. This place is drafty and old-fashioned. And no matter how brightly I paint the walls, they always turn back to black in a few days."

"You can do what you like with the penthouse," Bob said. "Paint, redecorate, whatever. It's all yours. And it's completely up-to-date with modern conveniences. Even," he winked at the Devil, "a hot tub."

"As long as I'm with you, Nicky, I don't care where we live," Angel said, ignoring Bob's innuendo and snuggling up beneath the Devil's left wing. "But I would like to give it a try."

"I suppose we *will* be more comfortable," the Devil admitted uncomfortably. "I'll miss this old pile, but you're right—I can't be perceived as lording it over everything, and Alcazar on the Acheron is a well-conceived notion. All right. It will be a bit of a commute, but I guess that'll be okay."

"That's the spirit!" Bob crooned, nodding. "Shall I have someone show you over to the Ritz?"

"I think we can find our way," the Devil said. "Are you ready, my dear?"

Angel nodded, and he swept her into his arms, strode through the sliding glass doors, and flapped away from the palace toward the Ritz.

As soon as he left, Bob went to the door and called the worker demons back in, and they resumed their impossible task of lifting the Devil's desk.

ᕫ 45 ᕬ

THE RITZ WAS ENTIRELY TOO plush and chintzy for the Devil, but Angel seemed to love it.

"It reminds me of the hotel we stayed in when my parents took me to Kansas City," she exclaimed as they entered the lobby. She wanted to see everything downstairs, but the Devil managed to steer her to the private elevator.

"Plenty of time for that later," he said, and the car whooshed them up to the penthouse.

"Ooh," this, and "Ahh," that, she said as she pranced from room to room. The Devil tried to ignore the huge circular bed with its fluffy satin comforter that dominated the bedroom. "Won't have much need for that," he muttered, thinking of both Angel's celibacy and his own distaste for anything soft or comforting.

The hot tub was on a glassed-in balcony adjoining the bedroom. The Devil bent over the control panel and saw that the temperature was set at one hundred and five degrees. He dipped his finger into the swirling water, and a little steam hissed up around it before he pulled it back. Too damn cold, he thought, wondering how hot the heater could make it. He envisioned himself sitting in a nice warm bath of, say, three hundred degrees, and inviting Angel in to join him. He could have at her while she boiled to death. But he knew it was just a fantasy since there was no way she'd get into the hot tub with him no matter what the temperature was. Not without marriage, he thought, snorting. In Kansas.

Now that Angel was distracted by the penthouse, he left her to continue her inarticulate if emphatic monologue and went down to the office suite. The first demon he encountered was his trusty servant.

"There you are, sire," Behemoth said. "I hope everything is satisfactory."

"It is not," the Devil pronounced.

"I was afraid of that, sire. It's all so...." Behemoth waved around helplessly for a moment before he found the right term. "Unbearably flocculent." He shook his head sadly, and his trunk waggled like a limp python.

"Where's my office?" the Devil asked, turning away. He didn't want to see pendulous things that waggled limply.

"Right this way." Behemoth led the Devil to the office. After the huge basalt desk in the palace, the mahogany one here looked flimsy as hell, even if it was nearly as massive. The Devil just shrugged to himself. It would have to do for the moment. At least the office had a balcony from which he could fly when necessary. He sat down in the cushioned chair behind it, which bounced a little, swiveled, and tilted.

"Where are the Archons?" he asked.

"Their offices are down the hall. There is a conference room, if you'd care to meet them in there."

"I do not confer," the Devil snapped.

"Yes, sire. Of course not. Do you want them to come in here?"

"Immediately," the Devil said. "And after you've called them, bring me a bottle of whiskey. Then go find me a different chair. Something hard and straight-backed. Preferably stainless steel."

"I believe your old office chair is somewhere around here," Behemoth said. "I'll see if I can find it."

He hurried out, and a few moments later, Beelzebub and Lucifer came in.

"I hope your offices and quarters are as disgustingly luxurious as mine," the Devil said, wrinkling his lips.

"I'm afraid they are, Boss," Beelzebub said.

"Where are the others?" the Devil demanded impatiently.

"Just the two of us at the moment," Beelzebub answered.

"Is that so? And just where are the others?"

"Leviathan is in her sea," Lucifer said.

"And what's so important that she couldn't be here?"

"She told me she was lonely," Lucifer said. "She imported this huge sperm whale, and the two of them are just swimming around, having a good time and, well, you know."

"What about the others?"

"I think Mammon is in Los Angeles," Beelzebub supplied. "He told me he wanted to produce movies. And the last I heard, Asmodeus was in the Middle East."

"Helping foment more international terrorism, I hope."

"I don't think so, Boss. He told me he was looking for his roots. You know he was known in ancient Persia as Aeshma-deva...."

"I know perfectly well what he was called. I named him. And if he's looking for his roots, he ought to be right here in Hell with the rest of the demons."

Behemoth chose that moment to enter with the bottle of whiskey the Devil had requested and a glass.

"Just leave it there," the Devil ordered, pointing to the desk in front of him.

Behemoth complied and hurried out. He just couldn't understand why the master had had him stock up on this cheap rotgut when he could have had the best scotch in the world. Even if it wasn't the Devil's private stock, and hence inviolable, nobody would dare touch the stuff—it was just too nasty. The one supply demon who had tried it claimed he'd rather drink gasoline.

"And Belphegor?" the Devil asked, pouring himself a stiff one and downing it in one gulp. "Holed up in some dark corner, I suppose, taking a snooze?" He refilled his glass.

"Actually, sir," Lucifer said, "he's in Ft. Lauderdale."

"Florida?"

"Yes, sir."

"And just what is the attraction of Ft. Lauderdale?"

"Water skiing, mostly, but he did go to Daytona for that big car race."

The Devil almost choked on his whiskey.

"You mean to tell me that lazy fat ass has taken up water skiing?"

"That's right, sir. He told me it suits his conical form quite nicely. He's disguised himself as a beefy but athletic man, but anyone with a discerning eye could pierce that ruse in a second. When he's not out on the water, he's on the beach. He says that volleyball continues to elude him, but that he surfs tolerably well once he's managed to get up on the board."

"Damn it!" the Devil shouted. "I need those jerks here, not off gallivanting around having fun." He looked at his two chief Archons. "At least you're still here." He poured himself

"How can we be other than with you?" Lucifer asked. "We sprouted from your right and left arms."

"What do you want us to do?" Beelzebub asked.

"I want you to smash Bob to oblivion," the Devil said. He turned to Lucifer. "And I want you to fry Angel to a crisp." Then he sighed and shrugged. "But I know neither is possible, at least not the way things stand. Just give me your reports."

Beelzebub had little new to report regarding CRUDE.

"They've got it locked up tighter than a witch's ass," Beelzebub said. "Nobody's talking, but I did manage to learn that they're as concerned as the rest of us about the utility outages."

"Maybe," Lucifer put in, "but that doesn't mean they're not exacerbating the problems."

"How do you mean?" asked the Devil.

"Well, the union isn't actually curtailing the output from the power plant, but they are diverting it."

"Where?"

"Bob's new entertainment complex."

"Figures," the Devil said, and Beelzebub concurred by farting out a dense cloud of flies.

"Do you want me to do something about it?" Lucifer asked.

"What?" The Devil finished his second drink and poured himself a third. "Send Belphegor to bore them into ennui? Oh, that's right. I can't send Belphegor to do anything because he's out water skiing."

The two Archons wisely remained silent, and even Beelzebub's flies settled sedately into his fur and perched on his large, pointy ears.

"I'm just too tired to think," the Devil complained. "You two might as well take the rest of the night off. I'm going upstairs to try to relax. No telling what kind of mess we'll have to deal with tomorrow."

The Devil rose, picked up the bottle, and left the office. A few moments later, he reentered the penthouse. He was hoping that Angel wouldn't hear the door, and he moved as stealthily toward the living room as his tired legs could carry him. If he could make it to the couch and settle in before she discovered him, he might feign sleep long enough for her to leave him alone and retire to her own suite.

He'd made it about half way to the sofa when a sudden shrill yapping came from down the hall. The Devil turned just in time to see an energetic bundle of yellow fur slide around the corner from the kitchen, regain its gangly legs, and come galloping toward the living room. In seconds, it was bounding around his hooves and stretching it's neck toward his hand, pink tongue lapping.

"What in hell!" he exclaimed, pulling back and holding the bottle of whiskey out of its reach.

It was a puppy. A big puppy.

"Isn't he cute?" Angel asked, following from the kitchen. "His name is Benji. He's a golden lab."

Benji proved his lineage by slobbering lovingly all over the Devil's hoof and revealed his age by leaving a yellow puddle on the floor. Then he was off toward the sofa, where he grabbed a throw pillow and promptly began to shake it between sharp teeth and rip it to shreds.

"Why is there a puppy in our penthouse?" the Devil asked.

"Isn't it a little early to be drinking?" Angel asked, turning a jaundiced eye on the bottle of whiskey.

"No."

"Well, *I* think it is." She snapped her fingers at the dog. "Come here, Benji. This is your daddy."

"I am *not* its daddy," the Devil snapped in turn.

"Oh, stop it. You're going to scare him."

Indeed, at the Devil's harsh tone, the puppy had slinked behind Angel and was peeking around her gown at him.

"Come on," Angel told it. "Let's go back to the kitchen and fix you something to eat."

The two of them went off down the hall, Angel at her usual prim pace, the puppy running circles around her.

"What next," the Devil muttered. How much longer was he going to have to put up with this crap?

He plopped tiredly onto the sofa, resisted a sudden urge to reach for the TV remote, and simply leaned back and closed his eyes.

"Take a few minutes," he ordered himself. "Just a few minutes of peace and quiet."

For the first time in his long, long life, he understood how his many victims felt as their seemingly bright lives turned dark and began to close in around them. He'd always appreciated being on the giving end, but receiving was another story entirely. He knew it caused anguish and suffering and all that, but the thing that surprised him the most was the confusion, with rampant thoughts rushing madly and colliding and stumbling against one another and falling into squirming heaps on the floor of his consciousness. Falling, falling....

He must have fallen asleep because the next thing he knew, he was having a dream, which was peculiar since he wasn't fashioned to dream but to cause nightmares in others. In the dream, somebody was washing his face with a furry washcloth.

The Devil opened his eyes to find himself staring straight into a pair of large, loving, liquid brown eyes.

"Get away, you mangy mutt," the Devil said, pushing the puppy away. But it was back almost instantly, nuzzling it's head beneath his hand, and almost against his will, he found himself rubbing it's minuscule brainpan and scratching behind its ears. It was hard to hate something so stupid that it would beg the Devil's attention.

In a few moments, Benji was fast asleep, head pillowed on the Devil's lap. Too tired to argue, the Devil fell asleep, too.

⟊ 46 ⟊

HELL FOR BOB HADN'T EXACTLY turned into Paradise, but it had become a crude sort of Club Med, with wild parties every night and long, lazy days lounging beside the pool he had installed in the palace courtyard—or, as he'd taken to calling it, the atrium.

Even better, he was living with nothing but humans, now. There had been demon staff back at the Ritz, such as Sapason, but he'd left them behind. With human labor in the palace supplied by the union, he had no need for demons, who were all repulsive and stank, anyway. Why have something like that around if you didn't have to? Besides, the demons usually brought up bad memories for the humans, especially those who had been tormented by the beasts for centuries or more.

Best of all, though, work on Alcazar on the Acheron was nearly complete and well ahead of schedule, thanks to the fact that labor in Hell was inexhaustible as well as perpetual. And there was no inclement weather to hinder construction. Gangs of workers toiled around the clock, making the entertainment complex surrounding the palace look like a huge ant bed of activity, and the growth of the buildings and other features actually was visible, like a time-lapse movie. Everything was scheduled to be complete by the end of next week, and Bob was thankful. One of the structures was the New Ritz, a hotel even more sumptuous than the old Ritz, and Bob was only too anxious to move into it and get out of the palace.

Bob no longer operated the old Ritz, but the nightclub was still open. The Devil was running it, he'd heard, though The Inferno's clientele was almost exclusively demons now, since most of the humans preferred to party in the palace with their own kind. Occasionally, some would go back to the Ritz—slumming, so to speak—and Bob made it a habit to pay regular visits with his crew. He had to keep up his contacts with the union officials and a few other demons. Sapason was still the manager, and he kept Bob's old booth reserved, partly because Bob was still an attraction and partly out of gratitude. And he still fed Bob all sorts of information on the union leaders. After all, hadn't Bob released him from a form of torment as much as he had his personal staff? Managing The Inferno was far more preferable than standing around all day overseeing inmates in a reeking lake of boiling shit.

Bob and his crew would sit there in the booth and drink for free and watch the demons cavort to the most god-awful music you ever heard. It was positively sickening. They never saw the Devil there, though occasionally one or more of the Archons would join them for a drink and a bit of glad-handing. Then, after meeting with whatever CRUDE officials happened to be present, Bob and his cronies would go back to the palace, commenting sarcastically about the demons' lifestyle and how much better things were at the palace.

But Bob had to admit that things weren't quite as right as everyone pretended, which was why he couldn't wait to move to the New Ritz. Even if no one else noticed—or, at least, failed to note aloud—something was wrong with everything in the palace. Some of it was the nature of the gloomy, cold, old pile. They couldn't even paint the walls. Or rather, they *could* paint, but within a few days, the paint was gone, faded from—or maybe absorbed into—the obsidian. And the Gothic-arched ceilings made the place prone to drafts and impossible to heat, which was a definite concern now that the volcano's sputterings barely kept the ambient temperature above 100 degrees.

Really, the worst of it was the labor CRUDE provided, and that extended to the entertainment complex as well as to any renovations Bob had attempted at the palace. No matter what the union-supplied workers did, none of it was right. The method, say, of taking away a stone block from a mason just before he'd finished it so it would stay a carved block instead of reverting to a lump of stone, meant that nothing was ever quite complete, finished, or polished. And that meant that everything had multiple defects.

Take that damn desk in the Devil's former office. Former office, because Bob couldn't see that great view outside the windows going to waste on an office where he planned to spend as little time as possible. He wanted to have the room remodeled into a luxurious bedroom complete with hot tub, and with the windows just a few feet away, the place where the desk stood was the perfect spot for the hot tub.

The problem was, the damn desk proved to be part of the rock from which the entire palace seemed to be carved. The movers, of course, had discovered that they were unable to lift it, so Bob had some laborers brought in to jackhammer it out. that went well enough, aside from the fact that the stone was hard as hell and ruined several jackhammers—and jackhammer-ers—before what was left of it could be carted off. The workers continued to jackhammer until they'd carved out a shallow de-pression where the roots of the desk had been to serve as the tub, but they were unable to completely finish their task or the entire desk would have simply popped back into existence for them to jackhammer out all over again. Thus, the bottom of the bowl was rough and jagged instead of smooth, making it an uncomfortable surface on which to recline, and an impossible one on which to relax, negating the entire principle of the tub.

And the plumbing going to it was even more problematic. The tub was dozens of feet from the nearest wall, and the rock was simply too hard to drill through to install piping to the tub. Besides, no hole could be completed or it would automatically fill in again. Bob thought of hiring a succession of drillers, each of whom would be assigned to drill the hole a little deeper, but it always came down to that last driller. As soon as he'd break through into the tub, the part of the hole he'd just finished would fill in, and there still wouldn't be a completed hole.

So, Bob had the plumbing installed across the floor, but not only did it look like hell—all that ugly white PVC, with purple smears at the joints, stretching across the obsidian floor—it also leaked, which made the glassy surface dangerously slippery. Again, the plumbers couldn't quite finish their tasks because, if they did, they'd suddenly be facing a jumbled pile of pipes to be put together again.

The same held true throughout the palace. Bob had the best damn chefs in Hell, but they invariably overcooked or under-cooked every dish they served. They were instructed to have the finest ingredients brought from Earth, but somehow, the sup-plies just weren't the same when they arrived after their journey. Grains were weevily, cheese was moldy, meat was ripe, and fruit and vegetables overripe. The chefs said they could only work with what they had, which was the same damn excuse every-body around here gave for doing a shoddy job.

But Bob knew it didn't have to be that way. Even if no one else seemed to remember, things hadn't been like that at the Ritz. The building had been, if not exactly aesthetically pleasing, at least sound. The plumbing wasn't visible and it didn't leak. And the food had been good. In fact, he knew from his recent visits to the nightclub that it still was good. Something wasn't right.

It took him some pondering before he realized what the problem was. The Ritz had been demon built, operated, and stocked, but everything in the palace was done by human labor supplied by CRUDE. Well, Bob knew the way around that. He'd simply get the union bosses together and have them arrange for demon labor to construct the penthouse at the New Ritz and the suites to be occupied by his executive staff. He'd probably have to have the hotel staffed by demons, too, just to make sure things went smoothly and the food was decent. Some of the humans might not like it at first since the demons dredged up bad memories, but they were here for an eternity, and they'd eventually get used to it.

But there was something that worried Bob even more than the problematic accommodations in Hell, and it had to do with the eternity he'd just been thinking of. His new-found position was all well and good, but was it good enough to satisfy him forever?

He wasn't sure about that, but what else was there? Conquer Heaven? Somehow, he didn't think that was going to happen. But what about Earth? If he could, like the demons, occasionally travel back to his old home world, he'd be a lot happier all around. He'd have to put his legal team on the question of visitation rights.

Right now, though, he was tired and a bit hung over from the night before. He wanted to get in the hot tub with a couple of horny honeys, but he knew that the rough bottom of the tub not only would distract him but piss him off. Instead, he went down to the spa to have a nice, hot mudpack. That, at least, could be had without complication, even if the mud did smell foul.

On his way down in the elevator, Bob took heart. The complex's grand opening was within sight, and he planned to host the biggest bash Hell had ever seen. Everybody in Hell had been invited, except for the religious fanatics, who would be party poopers, and the terrorists and wanton killers and such, who would spend the entire time trying to blow things up or shoot or knife people. He even planned to send a special invitation to the Devil and Angel, though frankly, he had some second thoughts about it since he'd heard from the union officials that the Devil had turned into a lush.

But Bob couldn't very well snub the Devil. Not yet, at least. Besides, he wanted the Devil there, soused or not, to witness not only the party but Bob's success as he basked in an atmosphere of total devotion, where everyone loved him and he'd never again have to fear public humiliation because he would control the public.

ᘏ 47 ᘐ

IT DIDN'T TAKE ANGEL LONG to adapt to the penthouse at the Ritz. For about a day and a half, all she did was wander around, goggle-eyed, looking at this and examining that. But by the end of that time, she had a complete make-over in mind, and by the end of the week, crews were already doing the demolition work necessary to clear the way for her newest designer madness.

"I made so many decorating mistakes at the palace, I wouldn't have known where to begin in undoing them and setting things right," she said brightly. "But the penthouse is a blank canvas and will let me really exercise my new and expanded palette."

Wow, the Devil thought. I can't wait to see it.

"Well, my dear, I'll leave you to it," he said, making as if to leave, but her hand on his arm stopped him in mid turn.

"Stay for a few minutes," she said. "I really want your input. After all, you live here, too." She smiled at him, but as usual, something in the back of her eyes seemed a little vacant.

"Fine," he said, unable to put the slightest bit of resignation into his voice.

The few minutes dragged on to a couple of hours, of course, even though he did his best to agree with everything she proposed just to hurry things along. He knew it wouldn't have mattered if he objected since she'd have her way in the end, anyway.

At last, she let him go, and he slinked through the door that led to the elevator and went down to the executive office suite. Benji followed him, but the Devil didn't mind. Benji, who'd grown amazingly fast from a gangly little puppy into a lanky big puppy, was one of the few beings in Hell who seemed unshaken in his loyalty to the Devil. And much as the Devil hated to admit it, the mangy mutt had taken a hold on, well, not his heart, since he didn't have one, but on something within his breast.

In his office, the Devil sat down behind the mahogany desk, while Benji curled up near his cloven hooves. Already, the desk's knee-hole was showing signs of singeing, making him long for the obsidian slab in the office back in the palace. He wondered what had happened to it but caught himself and put all thoughts of the palace out of his mind. Plenty of time to think about that later. Right now, he had more important things to consider.

Like what the hell he was going to do about Bob.

He poured himself a large whiskey and leaned back in his chair—at least Behemoth had managed to locate his old chair, and the stainless steel was a real comfort as he gazed out the wide windows.

The view wasn't nearly as spectacular as it had been from the palace, and Mount Etna was completely hidden behind a banked row of industrial smokestacks intervening in the near distance. They barely were producing a faint waft of gray ash where before they had furiously belched great billows of dense black smoke. But production at the factories they towered over —where men and women who had committed sins against their loved ones labored incessantly and futilely to burn the memories of their failings and cruelties—had seriously been curtailed of late. The Devil heard it had something to do with a union-led strike, leaving empty rooms, discarded shovels, and cool furnace doors hanging wide open.

He would have been able to hear their shrieks from here, he thought wistfully.

Ah, for the bad old days.

A knock on the door drew him from his reverie. In the past, Behemoth would have been there to announce any visitors, but these days, Angel kept the butler almost completely occupied with her redecorating efforts.

"Come in," the Devil called, turning to face the door. It was Lucifer.

"Any news from the power plant?" the Devil asked.

"Nothing," Lucifer said. "But that's not why I'm here."

"What, then?"

"I just wanted to give you notice."

"Notice? What the hell's that supposed to mean?"

"I'm leaving, Boss."

"And just where do you think you're going?"

"I'm taking a cue from Belphegor," Lucifer said. "And that's saying a lot. I never thought that lazy bum would ever wake up long enough to have a good idea."

"You're going to Ft. Lauderdale, too?"

"California. I'm going to put on twelve or fifteen years, lose the blue-arm thing, and trade my culottes for jams."

"I take it you're going to surf."

"Surfing, jet-skiing, parasailing, sky diving, the works. When they say extreme sports, I want them to think of me as the ultimate X."

"Has possibilities," the Devil conceded. "Adrenaline-pounding rushes and all that. If you had any adrenaline."

"Don't forget the chicks, Boss. I'm tired of everybody referring to me as that 'immature little fucker.' I want some real action."

"Well, you'll definitely have an advantage over your human competitors."

"Maybe push them to real extremes?" Lucifer chuckled. "I might even send a few this way."

"More power to you, then," the Devil said, hoisting his glass and nearly draining it. "You're just about the last, anyway."

A knock sounded on the door.

"*There's* the last," the Devil said, pouring himself another drink. "All right." He waved at Lucifer. "Go on, get the hell outta here."

Lucifer did, neatly sidestepping Beelzebub as the flyblown demon entered.

"I don't suppose you're going to tell me that they've solved the problem at the volcano," the Devil said.

"They haven't solved it," Beelzebub said. "but Xaphan thinks they've found what's causing it." The Archon hesitated, then went on. "It's a rather severe obstruction of the bowel, so to speak."

"You mean my volcano is constipated?" the Devil demanded, though not without a slight touch of amusement.

"That's an apt description, sir," Beelzebub replied, but the Devil was only half listening. He was thinking that he hadn't had a healthy shit since he'd started eating Angel's cooking. There simply wasn't enough raw human flesh in his diet these days.

"You remember that earthquake in Pacific Ocean a while back?" Beelzebub went on. "That eight-point-nine?"

The Devil nodded. "The one that inexplicably failed to cause any damage despite its size?"

"That's the one. Well, apparently it did have consequences. It seems that all the force of the quake was sent through the space–time continuum, and the shock wave dislodged a huge mass of granite feedstock that promptly sluiced into Etna's main vent and clogged it. Oddly enough, it lodged right under the glacier, and the heat from the backed-up magma is what caused the melting."

"Took them long enough to find it," the Devil said with a snort.

"We had to automate all those areas in the last century because of a deficit in stone masons," Beelzebub said a bit defensively. "All we get down here anymore are guys who know how to rivet steel and pour cement."

"Nobody around here had anything to do with it, I trust."

"We didn't, Boss. I assure you. Xaphan says his fire sprites would love to tinker in the subduction zones, but they know you have strict orders."

"Correct. Natural disasters must remain natural, though we can take advantage of them after the fact."

Suddenly, the Devil halted, a frown creasing his brow. "Tell me," he said in a suspicious tone. "Just when was this quake?"

Beelzebub consulted his PDA then looked up at the Devil.

"It was exactly eight months, three weeks, six days, fourteen hours, six minutes, and thirty-seven seconds ago."

The storm brewing on the Devil's face dissipated into disgusted resignation.

"That little shit," he spat.

"Sir?"

"Bob. He entered Hell just a few seconds after the quake."

"It seems likely he was killed by it, then," Beelzebub ventured.

"I think his death—his curse—*caused* it. But to hell with that. I don't give a damn what caused it, I just want it fixed."

"Xaphan has an emergency crew on its way down there right now. They'll try to break up the obstruction with jackhammers, but it's pretty big. And things have cooled off so much, the fire sprites can't operate."

"Well, get the stone masons down there. Call in drilling crews."

"I'm afraid we can't."

"And why not?" the Devil demanded.

"They're all working on Bob's entertainment complex."

"You're telling me that Mount Etna might go permanently dormant, and we haven't got anybody who can do anything about it?"

"I'm afraid so," Beelzebub said.

The Devil poured himself another stiff drink, downed it in a single gulp, then poured another.

"Dammit to hell!" he said, staring into the amber liquid.

"I have to confess something, Boss," Beelzebub said in a tentative voice. "I'm resigning from the board. I've been offered a lucrative position I just can't pass up."

"Do tell," the Devil said sarcastically. "What better position could you want than second in command under me? Not *my* job, surely?"

"Never that," Beelzebub assured him. "Too many administrative headaches."

Where had the Devil heard that before?

"Then exactly what position could be better?"

"I'm going to become the publisher of the only newspaper in Hell," Beelzebub answered.

"What newspaper?"

"*The Daily Flame.*"

"Brought to you by spin-doctor Bob, I suppose."

"Yes, sir. That's true."

"I better not learn that you're in cahoots with CRUDE," the Devil warned, his ears cringing. He'd meant the words to be harsh and threatening, but they sounded more like a petulant whine than a powerful reminder of who was boss.

"I don't think that'll happen, sir," Beelzebub assured him. "Bob doesn't like them any more than you do." He glanced at his Rolex. "Well, I'd better get going. I'm interviewing reporters this afternoon. Can't operate a newspaper without reporters. Be seeing you, Boss."

And then the Devil was alone for several minutes, during which he longed intensely for his old office and the wonderful balcony outside where he could brood at length and feel damn good about it instead of pitiful.

His depressed reverie was broken by a knock on the door.

"Come in," he said, resigned to whoever—or whatever—might come through the door.

It was Behemoth.

"What is it?" the Devil asked impatiently.

"This, sire." Behemoth handed over a cream-colored envelope with gilt edges and the words, "To the Devil and Angel, a Special Invitation," etched calligraphically on the front.

The Devil was about to slit open the envelope with a twitch of his forefinger, when he saw that it already had been opened.

"I suppose you showed this to Angel first."

"Of course, sire. She says she's very excited."

Excited about what? the Devil wondered, as he removed the card inside. The invitation read, "Bob Cordially Invites You to Attend the Grand Opening Ceremonies for Hell's Newest and Greatest Entertainment Complex, Alcazar on the Acheron. The Festivities Begin at 7 PM."

The Devil tossed the invitation onto his desk and turned to Behemoth.

"I suppose she expects me to show up at this event."

"I believe she does, sire."

"Oh, all right then. Tell her I'll meet her there."

"Very good, sire." The butler turned to go, but turned back. "There is one more thing, sire."

"Don't tell me you want to quit, too."

"Me, sire?" Behemoth sounded surprised. "No, sire. I assure you I shall remain completely devoted to milady. But I did just remember that milady asked that you wear that nice suit you had made right after she first arrived."

"All right. Find the suit. But first, bring me another bottle."

⊱ 48 ⊰

THE GRAND OPENING CEREMONIES FOR Alcazar on the Acheron were held in the entertainment complex's grand ballroom. And it was quite grand: about the size of Reliant Stadium back in Bob's hometown and completely decked out for the occasion. Food tables lining the north and south walls featured catering by the palace chefs, open bars were on the east and west walls, and right in the middle was an above-ground swimming pool made from glass and filled with the Acheron's gangrenous water. Inside, Plisona's synchronized swimmers were performing a gorgeous, intricate, and lengthy water ballet based on *Faust*.

Bob and his executive staff watched from a balcony high up in the west wing as the ballroom filled.

"I have to hand it to you, Bob," Ahmed said with a suave bow. "You've really set Hell on its end."

"Thanks, Ahmed," Bob said. "But I couldn't have done it without all you guys." He raised his drink and saluted his crew. "And I just want you to know that the best is yet to come."

They all laughed and clinked glasses and drank.

"When do you want to make your grand entrance?" Margaretha asked.

"Let's let the place fill up some," Mwendi suggested. "Then you can come in just as things start to get rowdy. The excite-

309

ment level will be high, but your presence will give them a little focus and cause them to settle down."

"Good thinking," Bob said.

"What about the Devil?" Yung-tzu asked. "You think he'll show?"

"He'll show, all right," Bob said. "The only question is, what condition will he be in?"

"Let's hope he doesn't start having DTs during the party," Pedro quipped.

They all laughed again, having heard stories of the Devil's newfound but profound fondness for alcohol.

"Just make sure I know when he gets here," Bob said.

"Say, look," Mwendi said. He'd been sweeping the crowd with a pair of binoculars. "Isn't that Angel?"

He handed the binoculars to Bob, who looked where Mwendi pointed, though the single patch of white amid all the naked bodies wasn't hard to spot. Bob scanned the area around her but didn't see the Devil.

"If she's here, he'll be along shortly," Bob said. "Go on down there, Margaretha. Take her over to my booth, and make her feel welcome. I'll join you in a few minutes."

Bob's booth here resembled his old circular booth at the Ritz, but on a grander scale.

"My round table," he'd joked when he first sat it with his personal crew. That was the night before—their very own grand opening.

Down on the floor, Angel was feeling a little lonely, but it wasn't because of a lack of people and demons to talk to. She just missed her paramour terribly, and she could tell he hadn't yet arrived. But he'd promised to be here, so she kept her feelings in check and tried to have a pleasant time. Everyone was deferential enough, but even so, she could tell that something was different in their behavior toward her, and once she caught a snide comment being made about her one true love. But before she could respond, Margaretha came over and steered her to a huge circular booth.

"Bob's table," Margaretha explained. "You're his personal guest tonight."

Angel could see why Bob chose this location for his booth. It had a clear view of the water ballet to one side and, to the other, the main stage, where performers sang and danced and told jokes.

All the Archons were there, except for Belphegor, who hadn't managed to tear himself away from his water skiing adventures. They gave Angel a friendly greeting, and Asmodeus slid over to make room for her.

"It's all so dazzling," Angel told Margaretha as she settled in.

"Bob's really done wonders," Margaretha said.

"He has," Angel said. "I hope he'll have a place for Nicky in his organization."

"Don't you worry, dear," Margaretha replied. "Bob'll take care of everybody."

"After all," Leviathan chimed in, "we really must keep our coffee klatch going."

"Oh, yes," Angel said. "The girls would be so disappointed if we had to call it quits."

The Devil chose that moment to appear. As Angel requested, he was wearing his suit fashioned from the cloth of nightmares, but its frightful nattiness belied the actions of its wearer, who was weaving a little. It wasn't clear if the waiter who brought him over to the table was escorting him or bracing him.

"I see the gang's all here," the Devil said. "Hi, gang." He lifted his glass in a salute to the Archons, and some of the liquor sloshed out, but he didn't seem to notice. "Here's to the gang and a fine old time!"

He kicked back a good-sized gulp.

"Hi, Boss," the Archons chorused, moving over to give the Devil room next to Angel. He slopped some more of the drink as he sat, then spilled even more while attempting to clean up the first puddle with a napkin.

"Let me help you, sir," the waiter said, disdain hardening his features.

"You do that," the Devil said. "And bring me another."

"What is that you're drinking, sir?"

"Jack Black, straight up, no ice. Make it a double."

"Yes, sir. Madam? A drink?"

"Please," Angel said. "A virgin bloody Mary."

The waiter vanished with the alcoholic napkin, and a second later, Margaretha stood.

"Well, it's been nice chatting with you folks," she said. "But I really must run along. So many things to look after, you know."

She headed straight for Bob to tell him the Devil had arrived.

"Are you drunk?" Angel demanded as soon as Margaretha had gone.

The Archons pretended to watch either the floor show or the synchronized swimmers.

"Of course not," the Devil said. "I never get drunk."

"You look drunk."

"It's a party. Isn't that how we're supposed to look?"

"Well, you don't have to play the part so thoroughly."

"I'm sorry, my dear. Would you like to dance?"

"Why, Nicky," she said, a smile brightening her face. "That's the first time you've ever asked me to dance."

They left the table and went out on the dance floor for a slow number. The Devil tried to step on her feet, but it didn't work. Before long, the other guests had edged back to give them room and watch and gossip about how drunk the Devil was and how small he seemed now that he'd fallen from power.

"Aw, let him suffer," someone said. "He's done it to the rest of us often enough."

The couple, enrapt in their union, was oblivious to those around them, or so it seemed.

When the dance was done, the crowd reoccupied the dance floor as the Devil and Angel returned to the booth. There, they found their fresh drinks, and while Angel sipped on hers, the Devil slugged his back in one gulp and called for another.

"How's the newspaper business going, Beelzie?"

"Fine, Boss. We're all staffed up and ready to print."

At that moment, a man holding a camera approached.

"One of our photographers," Beelzebub explained. "Mind if he snaps a few for the society pages?"

"Snap away," the Devil proclaimed, shining a big grin at the camera and hoisting his glass.

The camera flash dazzled the air for a second, then the shutterbug left.

"I see you're arms are still blue," the Devil said, turning to Lucifer. "I thought you'd be in California by now."

"I leave tomorrow," Lucifer said. "I didn't want to miss Bob's big bash." He didn't address the comment about his arms, mostly because he was still trying to figure out how to change their color.

"Didn't bring your new boyfriend?" the Devil asked Leviathan.

"He's not much for social occasions," the whale-like demon said. "As long as he's good in private, what does it matter?"

The Devil laughed. He drained his drink and called for another.

"And you, Asmodeus. Did you find your roots?"

"Still looking, Boss."

"Well, keep it up. A demon needs something to keep him occupied." The Devil attacked his new drink then peered blearily at Mammon. "How's Hollywood? Made any good films lately?"

"We're not about making good films," Mammon said. "We're about making money. But we've managed to cut expenses considerably by filming nothing but remakes, sequels, prequels, and rip-offs of old ideas, thereby cutting creative costs. Our goal is to make nothing but remakes, and it won't be much longer."

None of the Archons commented that it didn't seem like it would be much longer before his listener collapsed entirely. The Devil's wings were rumpled, his spines wilted, and his formerly obsidian-like flesh had taken on a sickly, chalky pallor. The red veins embedded in it looked more tepid orange than fiery scarlet. By now, he was lurching in his seat and knocking over water glasses, attracting contemptuous looks from guests at nearby tables, uncomfortable aversion from the Archons, and a baleful stare from Angel.

"If you don't stop that," she said, "I'm going to leave. You're embarrassing me."

"Jush a coupla more, baby," the Devil slurred. "Ish a party, ya know."

"Okay, Nicky," she said. "You have your couple of more, but I'm going to mingle."

She got up and was soon swallowed by the crowd. But it wasn't long before her seat was occupied, this time by Bob.

"Hey, everybody," Bob said. "Nick. Mind if I join you?"

"Well, if it isn't Bob," the Devil said effusively. "Sure, sit on down and have one with your old pal."

Damn, but he looks bad, Bob thought as the Devil gestured to the waiter, who came over, took their orders, and left.

"Ish a hell of a party," the Devil said, pounding the table with his fist. "And a hell of a fabulous place you've built. What a great idea using the palace as your centerpiece. I wish I'd thought of it."

"No fault of your own," Bob said. "When you started the ball rolling, it was just you, and you had to invent the organization from the ground up. I guess you were so busy building that you never saw the potentials in what you built. I, on the other hand, honed my chops in organizations, so it was easy to envision the next steps that needed to be taken. It's just the natural progression of things to grow more complex and to leave the old and simple behind."

"Yeah," the Devil said. "The nashural progression of things. I gotta hand it to ya." He lifted his glass in a toast. "Ya certainly have it organized 'round here."

"Thanks," Bob said, raising his own glass. "But you know, it really wasn't so hard. And now look at how nice and neat and orderly Hell has become."

"The next thing you know, there'll be suburbs and malls and car dealerships." The Devil took another slug from his glass then stared moodily into the amber liquid. "No place for an old devil like me, jush for young devils like you." He looked up at Bob, a pleading look in his hazy eyes. "You'll still let me and Angel stay in the penthouse at the Ritz, won't you?"

"Don't you worry," Bob said, trying to cheer up his obviously depressed guest. "You're a celebrity, no matter what. Hell, you're an icon. We'll even give you some kind of ceremonial position commiserate with your status."

"Something fun, I hope. And not too taxing. After all, I'll be in retirement."

"Of course. I never understood why someone of your caliber would want to head up Hell, anyway. All the administrative stuff couldn't have been much fun, and there were all those rules to consider."

"They are a pain in the ass," the Devil admitted. "Over there in Heaven," he jerked his thumb toward the right, "you can do anything you want. The problem ish, they're nothin' but a buncha deadbeats over there. Ish a hell of a lot more entertaining over here. Take a look at your place, for example—pretty jazzy, lots a nice looking women, music, and everything. Do ya think thish sort a place could survive in Heaven? Hell, no. It'd be empty. You'd be lucky to get a second-rate heavenly choir to sit in for that band you have on stage."

The Devil tossed off the rest of his drink and waved for another, even though it was obvious to Bob that the old fart could barely sit upright. He didn't want the Devil passing out right in the middle of the ballroom. Maybe he should have some of Mwendi's security men escort him to the door before they had to carry him out and cause a scene. He signaled to the waiter, who hurried over.

"Go find Angel," he whispered in the man's ear. "Then tell Mwendi to report to me. Have him bring a couple of bouncers."

"What about *him*?" The waiter gave an imperceptible tilt of his head toward the Devil.

"Bring him one more. I'll watch him until reinforcements arrive."

"Yes, sir."

"Did ya tell him to bring me another drink?" the Devil asked as the waiter hurried off.

"I did. You look like you could use one more."

"I can always use one more," the Devil said, his head wobbling on his neck as he raised a shaky hand with the forefinger held up. He stared at his own wavering finger, eyes practically crossing. "Ish the price ya gotta pay," he slurred, pointing the shaky finger at Bob. Then he turned the finger on himself, sitting back and blinking. "Me, too," he proclaimed confidently. "We all gotta pay." He slumped back in his chair, head lolling.

At least he isn't a belligerent drunk, Bob thought, but he did wonder if the Devil might actually throw up.

Where were Angel and Mwendi?

"I think I oughta go home soon," the Devil said, lowering his head and dropping his hand heavily to the table. "Do ya think ya can find Angel for me?"

"There she is right now," Bob pointed thankfully. The waiter was leading her toward them, and there was a look of consternation in her eyes.

Bob turned back to the Devil, thinking, lo, how the mighty have fallen. He found himself actually feeling pity for the Devil and wondering what he could do to lighten the washed-up old bastard's spirits.

"Listen," he said. "Before Angel gets here, I just want to say one thing." Bob put his hand on the Devil's arm. "I want to say thanks. If you hadn't done what you did to me back on Earth, none of this would have happened."

The Devil raised his head, and Bob saw that his eyes were brimming with tears.

"Ya really mean that, Bob?"

"I do," Bob said sincerely. "I owe all this to you."

"But I treated you so badly," the Devil said. "I ruined your career and probably was responsible for your untimely death, and then I threw you into the lake of boiling shit."

"All that's water under the bridge," Bob said just as Angel sat down. "None of it matters, now. I forgive you."

"Well, it's about time you two boys made up," Angel said in that superior tone the Devil hated so much. "Don't you have anything to say, honey?"

"I do," the Devil said, wiping away his tears.

"You're not going to try to kiss me, are you?" Bob asked, half joking, half worried, because suddenly the Devil looked half off his rocker. And not at all drunk.

"No, Bob," the Devil said. "No kisses. I just want to say that I knew you'd never last."

❧ 49 ☙

THE TABLE JOGGLED, AND THE liquor in the glasses sloshed. The table jumped again, and one of the glasses fell over and broke, spilling its contents onto the tablecloth. In fact, all the tables were dancing.

"It's an earthquake!" somebody nearby yelled.

As if in reply, a dull boom vibrated from the area beneath the glacier. A moment later, a cracking sound and a larger, sharper boom split and shook the air from the direction of Mount Etna. The air became visibly redder.

Panic grabbed Bob's guests, who began milling around, trapped by the surge and sway of their own herd instinct as they sought an exit.

"Oh, shit!" Bob said, suddenly realizing what he'd done.

He wanted to run, but at that moment, the Devil stood and unfolded his wings. They seemed larger than Bob remembered. And the Devil seemed taller, bulkier. And even as Bob watched, the Devil's suit cut from the cloth of nightmares rent in flapping shreds that scattered among the cloud like frightful bats, instilling terror in everyone they touched.

Bob, sick to his core, sat petrified in his seat, unable to move. In fact, the whole panicked mob, demon and human alike, suddenly grew so still and quiet that everyone in the huge ballroom could clearly hear Angel's almost plaintive voice.

"Nicky? What's happening, Nicky?"

The Devil ignored her because he'd just noticed that he had an erection, and quite an impressive one at that. He turned to laugh fiendishly at Bob, and in that instant, Mount Etna blew its top!

The ground shook, the air grew smoky, and magma, boulders and rocks, and burning hot ash rained down everywhere in Hell. But that was just the prelude. Hurricane-force winds carrying dangerous debris whipped across the land, and acid rained from the sky.

Then the lights in the ballroom went out, all the windows shattered, and titanic, searing gusts whipped through the building. Angel, gripped in the fierce fist of a whirlwind, was sucked, wild-eyed and backwards, into the seething maelstrom, where she vanished.

"You fools!" the Devil bellowed in a most imperious and horrendous voice so overwhelming that it not only shook the tattered walls but beat back the searing winds. "You think you can supplant me, but none of you has what it takes! That's because it takes this!"

The Devil's eyes began to glow, and his stance seemed rooted in the very obsidian bedrock of Hell.

"Not again!" Beelzebub said, turning to Lucifer. The blue-armed boy demon stared back, eyes a-goggle.

"I hate this!" Leviathan wailed.

The other Archons would have agreed, but they didn't have a chance because the dense blackness of the Devil's body had begun to stir and roil as if heated from within. He began to glow, red at first, then hotter and hotter until he was so glaringly white that everyone in the ballroom was transfixed in the searing incandescence.

His veins, no longer varicose but deep blood red, still ran though his flesh, but now, they were pulsing, as if to a primordial rhythm that grew so strong that it hammered like the gong of eternity against the eardrums of everyone in Hell.

And then the veins began to darken, perversely sucking all warmth, love, and goodness from everything.

It was all quite hellish in its blistering intensity.

"Hot damn!" screamed one of the demons.

That's the last coherent thing any of them remembered, though they all remembered subsequent events quite well. It's just that none of it remained coherent as the energy radiating from the Devil went atomic then off any scale known since the Big Bang. Heat beyond white enveloped and permeated everything, searing from the inside out—from a small core of weakness that pierced each soul in Hell like an infection of the spirit. Like a leak.

The atmosphere, the buildings, the earth and rocks turned into wraiths of their former selves and were blasted through and through at the subatomic level. Everyone and everything took on an unreal appearance as if semi-transparent. Yet horribly, the souls of all the humans lived, suspended in the midst of the primordial fume. Nor were the demons exempt. Though they had no souls, their intellects hung equally seared.

Worst of all—beyond worst—was the ghastly and monstrously grim presence of pure Evil as the Devil, wracked with fiendish delight and orgasmic release at his victims' suffering, revealed his powerful cruelty and perfectly dark majesty. And all —souls and intellects alike— were in pain and torment so awful that it transcended all suffering, anguish, and misery in the world put together.

In that long, blessed interval, the Devil knew not only complete release but complete peace.

But all things must end eventually, even the bad, and so, finally, the Devil let it go, let things return to normal. He'd kept it up for exactly twenty-four hours.

Bob's large booth, minus its round table, was the only thing that remained recognizable in the rubble—all of Hell now resembled the battlefield where General Means waged his private war. Wreckage, most in very small pieces, lay everywhere, and apparently, nothing had survived intact. Nothing, that is, except Mount Etna, the Devil's palace, and the booth.

Gradually, around them, the people and demons began to reform just as they were before, purged by pain and torment far more pure than their normal state of Hell, leaving them drained of all thought and emotion. First to reform were the Archons, who reappeared in Bob's booth. They sat there holding perfectly still, trying their best to seem utterly insignificant.

"All right!" the Devil exclaimed, all smiles. Smoke and settling debris still clouded the air, reducing visibility to less than forty feet and making everyone, even the demons, choke incessantly. It was a nice effect, the Devil realized, and he considered leaving it that way indefinitely. But no, it would be more trouble than it was worth keeping all those particles constantly suspended, so he let the dust begin to settle and looked around. What he saw was complete carnage and destruction, and it pleased him.

He also was scanning for that bitch, Angel, but there was no sign of her, and he remembered with true delight the way she'd been sucked backwards into the maelstrom and right out of his life.

"Good riddance," he muttered, then he looked to his left and said, "Where's my damn dog? Benzene!"

A fearsome dog materialized out of the rubble and settling dust. Benji may once have been a golden lab, but that chrysalis had broken open, revealing an adult hound of hell. A pair of knobby horns protruded from his skull, and even better, the Devil noted, his fangs were stainless steel and nearly twice as large as before.

"Heel, Benzene," the Devil commanded, and the hell hound fell in behind him as he rubbed his hands and said, "Okay, now back to work!"

He turned on the Archons. They all were sitting demurely in the booth, looking pretty damn ridiculous and pitiful without that great big round table to protect them.

"Go to the boardroom," the Devil ordered. "Wait for me there."

The Archons vanished, and the Devil said to Benzene, "Let's go see Bob."

Bob was standing in the lake of boiling shit—back at his old depth. But he was too scared to feel the pain. Or scream. At any moment, the Devil was going to show up and single him out for extra-heinous punishment. He cringed at the thought, but he should have been cringing at something else.

A huge wad of boiling shit slapped up against the side of his head. He didn't have time to react before a second hit him squarely in the face, choking off any reply to the first.

Everyone around him was showering him with shit, cursing him, and yelling insults. His personal posse was particularly vehement, maybe because some of the others lobbed a few handfuls their way since they'd been Bob's closest supporters and advisors. Now they vied to show everybody that they wanted to put some distance between themselves and their former leader.

During a lull when those closest to him had quit throwing shit because their hands burned too much, Bob saw that, for him, there would never be any respite—everyone on the lake was sloshing his way, really pissed-off expressions on their faces.

Suddenly, the whole mob floundered to a halt, and Bob felt hot liquid running all over him.

Sapason was hosing him off. Bob's hopeful appreciation immediately soured as, sputtering, he beheld the Devil standing on the bank beside Sapason, who was visibly cowering away from his master. Next to the Devil was a really scary dog.

Realizing that he was naked and friendless before the majesty of the Devil's overwhelming and fiendish delight—not to mention his anger and huge erection—Bob cowered also.

"How was that, Bob?" the Devil asked.

"Horrible," Bob answered. "I hope I never have to experience anything like that for as long as I continue to exist."

"Now you know why I'm the Devil and you're not," the Devil said.

Bob could simply hang his head in shame and fear.

"Where did I go wrong?" he asked.

"Your first mistake was believing that being the Devil is a position, not a personage. But being only a person without the age, you could never *be* the Devil, only pretend to emulate him. In the Devil's realm, you were bound to lose."

"And my second mistake?"

"You broke the rules of Hell," the Devil told Bob. "Now you're going to have to pay."

The Devil drew himself up to his full, dark, and majestic height and took a step toward Bob, who seriously thought about trying to swim away across the lake of boiling shit. But he knew he'd never get far.

"Curse you," he tried in a weak voice. It was a long shot, but he had to try. "Curse you until the day you die."

"Too late," the Devil said flatly, shaking his head. "That only works on your deathbed, and you're way past that."

"I suppose now it's going to be an eternity in the lake of boiling shit, for me," Bob said, nervous that the Devil might have something even worse in store, considering his many recent transgressions.

"Keep on dreaming, Bob," he said.

"Are you going to flay me alive?" Bob asked, hoping for the best he could expect to get.

"Wrong again, Bob. Just as you've been wrong all along. Just as you failed on Earth because you could not live up to the rules of ruthless, mean, and psychopathic behavior that govern a true corporate climber's life. Just as your wimpy organizational order here failed in competing with the True Nature of Things."

"That sounds like it's in capital letters," Bob said.

"It is," the Devil replied.

"If you're not going to keep me in the lake of boiling shit or have me flayed alive, what are you going to do?"

The Devil laughed, and to Bob's surprise, there was a trace of real mirth in it.

"Bob," the Devil said. "You are such a fuck up. But what can you expect from a lawyer?" He glanced around at all the reformed humans and demons. "Did you hear about the lawyer from Texas who was so big when he died that they couldn't find a coffin large enough? Then they gave him an enema and buried him in a shoebox."

The Devil waved his hand like an orchestra conductor striking up the band, and everybody within visible distance started laughing maniacally at Bob.

"A man died and was taken to his place of eternal torment by the Devil," the Devil said, silencing the laughter. "As he passed sulfurous pits and shrieking sinners, he saw a man he recognized as a lawyer snuggling up to a beautiful woman. 'That's unfair,' he complained to the Devil. 'I have to roast for eternity, and that lawyer gets to spend it with a beautiful woman.' 'Shut the fuck up,' the Devil barked, jabbing him with a pitchfork. 'Who are you to question that woman's punishment?'"

The Devil waved again, and abruptly, every mouth in Hell was laughing at Bob all at once. And the longer they laughed, the more their millions upon millions of voices merged into one huge, raucous pounding bellow that shivered the fiery, smoky sky and thundered across the hellscape only to jolt back from the distant mountains ringing Hell in an echo made all the more hideous by the fact that Bob knew it was directed solely at him.

It was horribly humiliating, and all he could do was stand there and take it, knowing he didn't even have the shit that had just been covering him to hide behind.

The laughter continued for a very long time, though short by the standards of eternity, before the Devil chopped his hand down, and the sound cut off. In the dead silence that followed, all Bob could hear was his own panicked breathing. If this was to be his punishment, he knew he wouldn't be able to take it. He'd have to commit suicide.

But he didn't think that would work here. And anyway, if it did, he'd just end up in the Slough of Despond. Everybody would still be laughing at him, and he be worse off than ever.

Bob peered sideways from his cower and saw in the Devil's eyes a look of calm bemusement that cut deeper than all the laughter thundering its hellish din. Bob could only drop his eyes, ashamed.

But I had such potential, he whined to himself. What a waste.

"Don't worry, Bob," the Devil said, as if reading his mind. "I can't afford to waste such a terrible asset as you. No, my boy, I'm sending you over to the other side."

"You mean I'm going to Heaven?"

"Precisely."

"But I'm a sinner. How can I go to Heaven."

"The curse was the only thing that brought you here and the only thing that kept you. You've forgiven me, so the curse is lifted."

"But I tried to disrupt Hell."

"You tried to bring order to chaos, didn't you?"

"I guess I did."

"And during the past few months, you've brought hope of a sort to your fellow inmates and eased their suffering."

"Yes, but it was pretty temporary."

"Surcease always is," the Devil said. "But it's the thought that counts."

"But I did it for myself, not for them."

"Yes, well, that's what will make you such an ideal agent of infection."

"What about my people?" Bob asked. "Are you going to hurt them worse for following me?"

"They'll remain right here," the Devil assured him. "It's their rightful punishment, after all. Any more questions?"

"If I'm still bad, how can Heaven accept me?"

"That's their problem. You and I know you still deserve punishment, but I think you enjoy Hell a bit too much. Heaven should prove to be pure hell for you. But I'm sure you'll do well there. My brother can always use another clever lawyer to help eliminate complainants when natural disasters kill thousands, when wars in his name claim even more, and when innocents are murdered for pleasure and sport."

"I don't think I'm going to like this," Bob said.

"I'm sure you won't," the Devil said, smiling. "Off you go, now. Poof!"

The Devil snapped his fingers, and off Bob went in a chuff of foul-smelling smoke and a little snap of thunder. The Devil leaned into the smoke and boomed out in a voice that seemed to get swallowed up a long well.

"Give 'em hell, boy!"

⊶ 50 ⊷

STRAIGHTENING, THE DEVIL INHALED THE lingering smoke swirling in Bob's wake, gave an oily smirk, and instantly transported himself to the palace, where his Archons waited in the board room, meek and silent. Benzene was right on his heels.

"Now, what do you have to say to that?" the Devil demanded, the smirk's unction trailing off to a sharp edge. Benzene snarled at the board members and displayed his stainless steel fangs.

Nobody said anything. Nobody, in fact, moved.

All of the Archons were there except Belphegor, who was still Ft. Lauderdale. Because he'd been on Earth, he'd missed the Big Fry, as everybody began calling the Devil's most recent day of wrath. But then he'd also missed all the shenanigans, so technically, he hadn't participated and thus couldn't be punished. Rules, after all, were rules, and sloth, apparently, sometimes has its virtues.

The Archons were pretty scared. None of them actually was shaking—demons don't shake unless designed to—but they expressed their fear in different ways. Leviathan, for example, attempted to drown herself in her tub, while Lucifer tried to revert his age all the way to babyhood in the hopes that the Devil might be less inclined to harm an infant than a brat-sized boy. But he couldn't. He'd never been an infant, just a brat-sized boy.

Only Beelzebub seemed calm, but Asmodeus, who was counting his sins as fast as his fingers could manipulate the abacus he was holding, noticed that the Lord of the Flies was totally without his support squadrons. Asmodeus had been using the abacus ever since the power went out, having to resort to tried and true methods now that all the digital networks in Hell were down.

"Beelzebub, what about you?" the Devil demanded.

"Well, sir, um, I say you're the Boss."

"That's right," Lucifer chimed in, using his best honest, studious, schoolboy tone. "You're the Boss."

"Yes, I'm the Boss," the Devil said. "And I want to make one thing perfectly clear. We're getting rid of *The Rule Book*."

"No more rules?" Beelzebub asked.

"I didn't say that," the Devil pointed out. "As of now, there is only one rule, and that's my rule. Now, get the fuck out of here, and don't come back until you have produced stupendously evil results."

They got out, which is what the Devil really wanted. No. What he really wanted was to engage in some rotten fun. He'd been out of the game far too long. He flew off to tour his domain and add a little improvisation here and there.

On his jaunt, he noted that not only was the landscape gradually returning to the status quo, so were the torments. Sisyphus, for instance, already had worn a path through the rubble littering the slope of his hill, and at the university, all the ruins of the Academic Quadrangle strewn across the ground simply provided more pedestals, and thus the opportunity to increase the size of the faculty.

The crowding added a bit of an interesting quirk, the Devil noted. No sooner were the professors close enough to hear what their neighbors were saying than intellectual turf wars broke out, complete with charges of plagiarism—and worse.

Nor was he blind to the irony when he stopped to assist in the torment of a bitter woman with the gift of gab, who'd terrified a small college town with a serious series of poison-pen letters. He was, himself, returning to normal.

The Devil prepared to scald the woman with her victims' tears by loading them into a red plastic quirt gun that looked like a penis-shaped rocket ship. He was just aiming the gun at her when an unexpected clatter sounded from behind him.

Something was stirring in the rubble.

He was a little miffed since he hadn't ordered an expected clatter at that moment, and he turned to see what or who had caused it.

A twisted piece of metal clanged aside, and Angel emerged from a jumble left by the maelstrom. She brushed herself off, leaving her chemise as sparkling white as ever.

In that instant, a black blur with gleaming highlights streaked past the Devil. It was Benzene, and he was lunging right at Angel with his fangs bared.

"Yes!" the Devil cried. "Kill!" He was pretty disconcerted at the sight of Angel, but the promise of her torn flesh littering the ground in front of him—which was exactly what was going to happen when Benzene got his fangs on her—warmed him up.

Only instead of ripping her to shreds, the hellhound was trying to slobber her into submission with his big pink tongue, which, unfortunately, hadn't changed in keeping with his exterior and demeanor.

"Benji!" she cried, and she scratched him behind the ear. Then she stood up and looked at the Devil.

"Oh, Nicky, there you are! I've been looking all over. This part of your domain is really quite forlorn, isn't it?"

She traipsed over to him as she said this, and her words were punctuated by a quick peck on his cheek.

The Devil was too amazed, shocked, and dismayed to pull back. Everything in his domain had been blasted to Hell and back, but she still looked as unsullied as the morning dew.

"I thought you burned up," he said.

"I suppose the flames couldn't touch me," she replied without guile or pride. "After all, I am innocent as the driven snow...."

"I know, I know. Don't remind me."

"Oh, you old grouch. Did you have a bad day?" She snuggled under his wing. "To tell the truth, everything went completely blank for a moment. I didn't know where I was, or where you were, either. I looked all over for you, and I was afraid I might not find you again." She smiled brightly up at him. "But, I did! We're back together, now, and that's all that matters."

At that moment, she noticed the hapless but nasty old spinster crouched naked before them, awaiting her bath of tears. Angel's eyes went from the woman to the priapic red rocket clutched in the Devil's hand, then back to the woman. Angel pursed her lips slightly.

"What is that you're doing, dear? It doesn't look very pleasant."

He wanted to clutch and rend her, but he couldn't even muster a decent visualization. The Devil stared at the honey-haired beauty for a moment, then his eyes turned toward the fiery sky, a touch of torment lurking in their smoky depths.

"Oh, hell!" he said.

The Clay Guthrie Mysteries
from Phosphene Publishing Co.

THE DEAD DETECTIVE

Teetering on the edge of the gutter, ex-cop Clay Guthrie is offered a way out of his bitter isolation. All he has to do is locate a stolen sculpture. The task seems simple enough until Guthrie finds himself enmeshed in a series of surreal events that push him to the breaking point. His disturbingly dangerous employers threaten him with pain and death if he fails, and the mysterious old man who is their antagonist forces Guthrie to act on his behalf, warning that worse horrors will greet his success. The only way Guthrie can survive is to find the sculpture and help the old man destroy the terrible power that lives within it. But first, he must endure a series of trials that test his endurance and drive him into the core of his own corruption.

LANDSCAPE WITH BEAST

"Who better to send into a grave situation to find out what lies buried there than one who has known death? Such as you." With those words, mysterious old Tereba sends Guthrie on the trail of a missing artist. Having to deal with a witch from an ancient lineage and the ultimate hunter seeking the ultimate prey didn't bother him, but the doorway to another world was a different matter. Out there an unknowable predator waited, and it wanted nothing more than to lay waste to everything in its path. But Guthrie couldn't refuse. He knew that anythingTereba directed his way would be as interesting and important as it might be dangerous, and those were lures he couldn't resist. Besides, when he set a trap for his nemesis, the bait wasn't the only thing that disappeared into the unknown along with the artist. Now Guthrie's client had vanished, too.

THE TEXAS TROLL UNLIMITED

When a frightened railroad employee tells Clay Guthrie that a monster in a boxcar ate his co-worker, Guthrie finds himself drawn into a web of corrupt and warped ambition and wanton violence. Traveling to far West Texas in search of the monster, Guthrie and the trainman encounter an organization whose goal is the total destruction of social order and whose weapon is an abomination from the past. Waging a guerrilla war against their enemies beneath the harsh Texas sun, they quickly discover that the nights hold a mortal danger more terrible than their human enemies. With the fate of civilization in the balance, they must eliminate the humans who stand in their way before they can root out and confront a canny and clever inhuman foe.

DARKNESS INSATIABLE

Clay Guthrie is sent by his mysterious employer to track down a missing man, but finding the objet of his search in an unnatural place and in an impossible condition provides no easy answers. Far worse, he encounters a town the grip of an unknown, unseeable, and malevolent force that thrives on turmoil and destruction and has left the utter annihilation of three other towns in its wake. What will it take to learn the cause and remedy it before it's too late? And who—or what—will get in the way?

Phosphene Publishing Company
publishes books and DVDs relating to literature,
history, the paranormal, film, spirituality, and the
martial arts.

For other great titles, visit
phosphenepublishing.com